FOR LISA NORRIS

Praise for *Sabbath Night in the Church of the Piranha*

"For too long, Ed Falco has been a 'writer's writer.' With this collection, more readers can know the profound pleasures of his work. At once gritty and visionary, Falco's stories combine the nerve and edge of classic noir fiction with a transcendent lyricism. This synthesis—of the sinister and immanent, evil and sublime—give his work its indelible emotional depth and uncanny resonance. The sensibility is somewhat akin to that of Chandler or Carver, yet Falco's fiction is as distinctive as it is mesmerizing. No one has written anything quite like these deeply engrossing, lovely-harrowing stories. *Sabbath Night in the Church of the Piranha* is not a work so much as a *world* of novelistic integrity, a cosmos populated with criminals twisted by their crimes, with hapless parents and their mindblowing offspring: a young "mule" who smuggles drugs, a streetsmart child who falls into the hands of a molestor. Innocents struggle through the erotic wilds, encountering sexualities both disturbing and delicate, weirdly fascinating or frightening. These amazingly powerful stories encounter the deranged and disturbing, psychopaths and monsters, but they also show the strangeness of the ordinary: the oddities of the suburban soul, human suffering, impermanence, and love. Falco writes of such things—and other wondrous things—with singular compassion and psychological subtlety. He is, quite simply, a great artist of the story. His work lives among the masterpieces of American fiction." —Alice Fulton

"In this present time, Edward Falco's edgy, intense stories—ever conscious of the dark and violent forces at work in the world—are not only stunningly relevant but profoundly important. Artistically, too, Falco needs to be heard—he is an all-too-rare master of both character and plot. *Sabbath Night in the Church of the Piranha* is a truly outstanding collection." —Robert Olen Butler

Praise for previous work by Edward Falco

"Well crafted and engaging, these stories offer both high drama and deep emotion . . . Falco writes hard-edged, uncompromising fiction. His is a name to remember." —*Booklist*

"There is in Mr Falco's fiction a little of Raymond Carver's sesitivity to the menace of the everyday, and a lot of Andre Dubus's sturdy empathy with his characters' failings and regrets." —*New York Times* Book Review

"Falco creates nearly perfect short stories filled with interesting characters and wonderfully dramatic situations. The characterizations are so crisp that it's impossible not to care about these people. Falco proves himself to be a sterling practitioner of the short story form." —*Publisher's Weekly*

"Falco writes tense, gritty fiction that portrays ordinary people caught between the claims of normal life and the lure of the forbidden and untasted . . . stylistically akin to the plays of David Mamet or Sam Shepard. Falco's voice, though, is his own, and his work keeps getting better and better." —*Kirkus Review*

"Falco handles powerful, uncomfortable emotions with an understated grace. He is unafraid to make his characters show anger or pain, and he does so very believably. The language of his characters' thoughts is beautiful and poetic in the midst of their struggles."

—Laude Parker, *Book Page*

"Consistently well-crafted in a quiet, confident style . . . Falco does not back down from taking narrative risks . . . There is nothing tricky or flashy about the stories . . . They subtly yet surely lodge themselves in tihe reader's consciousness—and hold there."

—Peter Donahue, *Studies in Short Fiction*

"Falco is a serious writer who cuts events into glittering diamonds and then examines the diamonds. The entire craftsmanship is superb and the stories resonate in the heart."   —*The Book Reader*

"Distinction is a hallmark of these fine stories . . . writers like Edward Falco lend me faith, though not always a comforting one."   —Fred Chappell

"These are stories you don't confuse with one another and don't soon forget . . . There is a certain inevitability in all Falco's stories—which is a far cry from predictability . . . one marvels at the strong storylines; after that the craft of the story rises to the surface like good cream."

—Joan Schroeder, *The Roanoke Times and World News*

"Falco is at his best when he is walking a tightrope between satire and empathy, and the ways he maintains his balance are very pleasurable to behold."   —*Studies in Short Fiction*

"Falco sees how people are dangerous, both to themselves and to others. He is clearly a writer to be reckoned with."   —*The Hudson Review*

"Falco writes a sure-handed, unflinching prose that uncovers the day-to-day edginess and emotional uncertainty so pervasive in contemporary America. Like another of our best realist writers, Andre Dubus, Falco writes about people, who are all too painfully real and recognizable—and shows us that their lives matter."   —*Cimarron Review*

Sabbath Night in the Church of the Piranha

NEW AND SELECTED STORIES

Edward Falco

UNBRIDLED BOOKS

This is a work of fiction. The names, characters, places and incidents are either the product of the author's imagination or are used fictitiously, and any resemblance to actual persons liviing or dead, business establishments, events, or locales is entirely coincidental.

UNBRIDLED BOOKS
Denver, Colorado

Library of Congress Cataloging-in-Publication Data

Falco, Edward.
Sabbath night in the church of the piranha : new and selected stories / Edward Falco.
p. cm.
ISBN 1-932961-05-4 (alk. paper)
I. Title.

PS3556.A367S23 2005
813'.54—dc22

2005000014

1   3   5   7   9   10   8   6   4   2

Book Design by SH • CV

First Printing

CONTENTS

The Instruments of Peace

THE KID DROVE UP IN A CHARTREUSE SPORTS CAR. Convertible. He arrived with the top down, his dark hair windblown, a small, gold ring in his right ear. When he stepped out of that car in my driveway wearing blue jeans and a red T-shirt, my sixteen-year-old daughter went ghost pale and leaned back against the wall by the living-room window. He was tall—six-one, maybe six-two—broad-chested and muscular. I was in the kitchen making breakfast, scrambling eggs in a pink bowl with a wire whisk. I could see my daughter's back, and beyond her, through the window, Chad Barnnett, the youngest son of a well-known criminal. I had agreed to give him a job for the summer. We lived in the boondocks on a small farm where we stabled standardbreds from the racetrack in town. It was just me and my daughter. Her mother had left before she turned three.

"Oh my God," Amy said when she could finally speak. "Is that him?"

"Seems likely." I put the eggs down on the stove and joined her at the window. Chad appeared to have decided he was at the right place. He pulled a lightweight jacket out from behind the front seat, slipped it on, and started up the walk to the front door.

Amy bolted for her room. It was a little after nine and she'd been out of bed for an hour, though she hadn't showered and cleaned up yet. She stopped and pointed to me. "Do not tell him I'm up," she stage-whispered.

"Tell him I was out late last night and I'm sleeping in." She charged up the stairs two at a time, like a little kid, her pale-blue, wrinkled sleep shirt billowing out behind her.

I went out to meet him, and whatever anxieties I had about housing the son of a gangster dissipated quickly. He had a sweet smile and the kind of good looks that charmed even an old guy like me, who had essentially been ordered to give him summer work, as well as a place to stay. Not that I was actually given an order. Ollie Lunsford had asked me to do him a favor. Ollie, beside being the trainer who accounted for virtually all of my farm's business, was my only real friend. Every Friday night I played poker with him and a bunch of characters from the track. Between me stopping by his stables and him stopping by the farm, I saw him just about every day. When he asked me to hire Chad, I didn't think twice. I hired someone every summer anyway. Still, there was something in the tone of his voice that suggested an urgency to the request that couldn't really be refused. "I need you to do me a favor," he had said—and the word "need" had carried a ton of weight.

Chad offered me his hand. "Mr. Deegan?"

I nodded, we shook hands, and I invited him in for coffee. In the kitchen, he sat at the table and commented on my huge hardcover copy of Shakespeare's collected plays, which I was rereading for the umpeenth time. I had it propped up and opened on the counter next to the stove, so that I could read while I was cooking. He asked me if I was reading Shakespeare. I told him I was, and he told me he had read him for the first time in his English classes. He was twenty-two and had just finished his first year of college after working odd jobs out of high school. He liked sports, especially basketball and football, both of which he played on intramural teams. By the time I called up the stairs for Amy to join us—after explaining that she had been out late the night before and was sleeping in—I wasn't worried any more about this kid being the son of Jimmy Smoke, which is what the papers called his dad.

"Amy," I yelled from the foot of the stairs, holding the skillet in my hand and scrambling her eggs. "Come on down here and meet our guest."

A moment later, Amy came into the kitchen wearing apple-green, velvet-trimmed, cotton-knit pajamas that looked more like elegant evening attire than something you might actually sleep in. Her shoulders were bare and her breasts were prominently outlined under a flimsy cami before she covered herself, to my relief, by buttoning a matching jacket. Her hair was brushed and arranged, and she had makeup on.

Chad stood when she entered the room, and they shook hands politely. "Pleasure to meet you, Amy," he said, his tone of voice downright avuncular, which pleased me.

"Uh, oh," Amy gestured toward the scrambled eggs, toast, and orange juice in front of Chad. "I see my father's started taking care of you already." She sat next to him at the table. "You've got to watch out," she whispered, as if I couldn't hear her. "If you let him, he'll be tucking you into bed at night."

"Amy thinks I'm overprotective." I put her eggs and toast on the table in front of her, and buttered her toast and dipped it in egg yolk before she figured out the joke and slapped my hand away.

Chad laughed. He said, "You guys are pretty funny."

"We're a team," I said. "Me and Amy."

"Oh, please." Amy rolled her eyes. "I *can't wait* to get out of here and go to college. This is like hell, living in the middle of Nowhere, USA. You know how far you have to drive to get to a decent music store? Two hours. You know—"

"Amy," I said, "I'm sure Chad wants to hear about how miserable your life is." I picked up Chad's empty plate—he had inhaled his breakfast as much as ate it—and gestured for him to join me. "Time to see the farm."

Outside, the early summer weather had turned the land into an expanse of mud and grass. Everything that wasn't green was brown and muddy—and a lot of what was green was muddy, too. Things would remain that way until sometime in July, when the heat finally baked the ground dry. In the anteroom between the front door and the living room, two pairs of galoshes stood upright and waiting. I picked up my pair and directed Chad to a closet where dozens of old galoshes and boots were piled in a corner. "I hope you don't mind mud," I said. "You'll be living with it for the next month." On the brick walk, I looked up and drew in a deep breath of fresh air and let the sun warm my face. When he came up beside me, I said, "You have a girlfriend?"

"Several," he answered, and grinned in a way that was supposed to be a between-men thing, as if he expected me to pat him on the back for being a hotshot.

I said, "I'll show you the barns first."

Chad followed along quietly while I gave him a tour. He seemed troubled by the mud, which he sank into up to his calves at one point, muddying his clean denims. There were several fractious racehorses on the farm, and I pointed them out to him first. At the stud barn, we stopped in front of His Majesty's stall. HM was the worst of the lot. "This one," I said, pointing to HM, who had come to the front of the stall to check out Chad, "stay away from. I'd put him down if it were up to me, but Ollie insists on keeping him."

Chad moved closer to the stall. "He doesn't look any different from the others," he said.

"Take my word for it." I moved him along.

Just out of the barn, he stopped suddenly and looked around, as if he were actually seeing the place for the first time. He looked up toward the mountain ridges, which were already lush and green, and his eyes followed the satiny folds of hollows and rises down to the green pastures of the farm, which were divided and enclosed by white fences. Inside the farm's corrals, horses grazed lazily, some standing still, some ambling as if taking a leisurely stroll.

"Not a bad place to spend your summer," I said. "As long as you don't mind working some."

"I don't mind," he said.

At his cabin, he leaned against the door frame and pulled off his boots.

I opened the door for him. "It's hardly luxury, but it's cozy enough."

He looked behind him, through the doorway, at the single bed with its brass headboard; at the oval, cord rug in the center of the wood floor; and the red-and-white checked curtains over the windows on the back and side walls. "It's nice," he said. "It looks good."

I opened the doors to an old, ball-foot armoire I had dragged over from the storage barn and cleaned up a few days earlier. "This is your closet," I said, and then I pointed to the bathroom, which was directly across from the bed. "I thought about putting a door on the bathroom for you, but then I figured, it's only you in here, so . . ."

"Be fine."

"Okay, then. I'll send Amy to get you for lunch." I started for the door.

"Mr. Deegan," he said, stopping me. "I didn't mean, before, when I said about having girlfriends—I didn't mean to sound like some sort of lover boy or something. It's not like that."

"That's good, because—" I was standing in the doorway and I moved back inside the cabin and closed the door— "because Amy's at that age now where she's still a kid but she doesn't want to be anymore. It's a dangerous age for a young girl."

"I understand," Chad said. "You don't have anything to worry about from me." He brushed his hand through his hair. "I'll tell her I have a serious girl-friend."

"Good. Don't tell her I told you this, but—" I hesitated a moment, not certain I should continue. Then I figured I had already started, so I said, "She hasn't even had a first boyfriend yet. She'd be mortified if she knew I told you that—but it's something you should know. It's because we live out here, as Amy says, in Nowhereville. Still, she thinks she knows things, but she doesn't know anything yet."

"Like I said," Chad touched his heart, as if swearing an oath. "You have nothing to worry about from me."

I put my hand on his arm, as if to say thanks, and then turned to leave.

"Mr. Deegan," he said. "Long as were talking. You know about my family, right?"

"I know what I read about your father in the newspapers."

Chad closed his eyes for an instant, as if gathering the resolve to explain and pushing down frustration, like a celebrity who's just been asked the same dumb question for the millionth time. "He's not my father," he said. "He's my mother's husband. We have a simple relationship. I hate him and he hates me."

I looked at him in a way that I thought might prompt him to explain but his eyes had gone steely, as if he had just said all he had to say on the subject. I pushed a little. "Doesn't that worry you?" I asked. "Having someone like that hate you?"

"My mother'd never let him do anything. I'm not worried."

"Well," I said, meaning to dismiss the subject, "maybe time will make you closer."

"I doubt it," he said. "He had my father killed."

"He—" I started to echo him, the amazement in my voice momentarily turning me into the boy.

"You can see why I hate him."

"I guess so," I said. I had no idea how to continue.

"I have nothing to do with Jimmy and he has nothing to do with me. So you don't have anything to worry about on that score either. I just want to be a college student with a summer job, you know what I mean?"

"Yes," I said. "I do," and I touched his arm again. "I'll send Amy for you after lunch." I hoped my tone let him know that the subject of his family was done with as far as I was concerned.

On the way back to the house, I went over a few things in my mind. I was curious about why his stepfather would have had his father killed—but I wasn't about to ask. In a way, knowing that the kid had this kind of thing in his past made me feel closer to him—and protective. Amy never understood that about me, my protectiveness. Linda, her mother, hadn't either. If I am too protective, there's reason for it. I was raised poor, in a bad part of Brooklyn, New York. My father was a mean drunk, my sister was raped when she was sixteen, and, when I wasn't a lot older than that, I was robbed and beaten half to death by two guys wearing sweat shirts with drawstring hoods pulled to tiny openings over their eyes. They beat me with boards—not two-by-fours that would fit in a man's hand like a regular weapon, but boards so flat and wide they had to hold them with two hands. They beat me because they wanted to.

After the attack I spent months in the hospital, my heart full of murder. Nights I'd have dreams in which beatings my father delivered merged with the street beating. Days I'd fall into long, bloody reveries of violence so awful it frightened me—half daydreams, half trances in which I'd inflict every manner of nightmare on the men who beat me. I'd cut off their dicks and watch them bleed to death. I'd rape their wives and children while they watched. Nothing was too ghastly for those dreams. Nothing too cruel. For a while I thought I was losing my mind. I came back slowly. In the end, I didn't lose my mind and I didn't withdraw from the world. I just moved to a different, more secluded part of it, and I became careful, protective. My father's boss owned a horse farm up in the mountains, and I went to work for him as soon as I got out of the hospital. I started reading a great deal. A few years later I met Linda. I've worked around horses and on farms ever since.

Amy didn't understand the way I was and couldn't appreciate it, but I thought maybe Chad could, having obviously been through some things—and after working with him only a few weeks, it was clear that I was right. He rapidly turned into a combination ally and mediator in my frequent, though usually minor, conflicts with Amy. Whatever he told Amy, she seemed to hear more clearly. I suspected his working without his shirt on, sweat glistening over the muscles of his chest and stomach, had something to do with the explanations always being so convincing.

In any event, things ran a lot more smoothly with Chad on the farm. Amy seemed happier with him around, even if he did—as he had told her—have a serious girlfriend. She took to going to bed early most nights and sleeping late in the mornings. In general, she appeared to be more relaxed and comfortable than she had been in years. She was looking forward to the fall, when she'd start her senior year in high school. Chad turned out to be excellent help, working all day on jobs I'd give him, and then often going on to do other things that needed doing, which he'd find on his own initiative. Evenings he spent alone in his cabin, hardly ever going into town. The only problem I had with him involved the phone bill, which was exorbitant. Turned out he was spending some of his evenings on the phone all over the country. When I brought him the bill, he explained he was calling a girlfriend, and buddies from home and college. He agreed to pay the extra charges. When I pointed out that if he didn't cut back on the calls, he'd wind up sending a good portion of his summer earnings to Ma Bell, he nodded and seemed to understand and not be resentful of my pointing it out to him, the way Amy would have been. By midsummer, I was already worrying about him leaving and thinking of ways I might entice him back next year.

Ollie seemed to stop by the farm more frequently with Chad working for me, which I also considered a benefit. He was only about ten years older than me, but he had always treated me in a fatherly way. He was a stocky, blond-haired, blue-eyed Swede with a stout, churchgoing wife, and a fondness for poker. I knew he had connections to bad elements at the track—I had heard it implied by other trainers and farmers—but I never heard a word about it from him, and I never saw him do anything in the least bit unseemly. Asking me to hire Jimmy Smoke's son for a summer job was the only thing he had ever done in twelve years that gave me cause for worry—and most of the way through that summer, things were going fine. Then, on a morning in the first week of August, when I was at his stables picking up hay, he invited me and Amy to his house for dinner.

I had backed my truck into the stable and lowered the tailgate, while he opened the stall door and dragged out four bales of high-grade hay he had been holding for me. He tossed a bale onto the truck. "Hey, Paul," he said.

"The wife's making something special tonight. Why don't you and Amy come out and join us for dinner?"

I didn't answer right away. I pulled a bale of hay from the stack, threw it onto the truck, and went back for another, which I slid onto the tailgate. Ollie had never invited me to dinner before. Ollie never invited anyone to dinner. I said, as if he didn't know it, "We've never been to your house for dinner before. Actually, we've never been to your house at all."

"This will be the first time then, won't it?" He tossed a bale of hay at me, playfully.

I was knocked back a couple of steps before regaining my balance. "Okay," I said. I didn't see how I could refuse. "What should we wear?"

"Dress nice," he said. "My wife'll bring out the good china. We'll do the whole deal for you." He winked at me and closed the stall door. "Be there by seven. Don't be late." He turned and hurried to the other end of the stable, where he had an office.

At my truck, I pulled a ball of twine out from under the front seat and took my time tying down the hay, which didn't need to be tied down at all. The pit of my stomach stirred the way it does when something doesn't seem right. I was tempted to follow Ollie into his office and ask him what was going on, why all of a sudden the invitation to dinner? By the time the hay was tied down, though, I had decided to let things play out as they would. I got back into the cab of the truck and instead of heading out the front entrance, I did a three-point turn and started down the dirt road that crossed the stables and went through the farm and wound around to a back entrance, which was closer to town, where I planned on stopping at the supermarket. In the rearview mirror I saw Ollie come out of his office. He watched me drive away, with his hands on his hips, looking annoyed. I usually asked him if it was all right to drive across the farm but he had walked away abruptly, and I couldn't imagine why it wouldn't be okay. I couldn't imagine—until I passed the bunkhouse where he sometimes put up extra help.

At the back of the house, taking overnight bags out of the trunk of a deep blue Lincoln Continental, were two guys who might as well have had the word "gangster" emblazoned in neon on their backs. They wore dark suits with dark shirts and matching dark ties. Their hair was slicked back. At the sound of my truck approaching, one of them turned around quickly, and I saw the leather straps of a shoulder holster before he could adjust and button his jacket. Then the other turned around and our eyes met as I drove past. They didn't look happy. In my rearview, I saw one of them slam the trunk shut, and then they both disappeared into the bunkhouse. I drove a little farther up the road before pulling onto the grass and spinning back around toward the stables.

Ollie was still standing outside with his hands on his hips, and I pulled the truck right up to his toes before cutting the engine and jumping out and slamming the door. "Ollie," I said. "Guess who I just saw?"

Ollie set his jaw and crossed his arms over his chest.

"Two guys Jimmy Smoke sent. Right? That is why we're having dinner together tonight, isn't it? So it's just the kid on the farm when they get there?"

Ollie looked at me with disgust and shook his head slowly. He went back into his office and stood by the open door, waiting for me to join him.

I hesitated a moment, then went into the office and took a seat at the side of his desk, as if I were about to be interviewed for a job.

Ollie closed the door. "You saw two guests of mine, staying at the bunkhouse."

"No," I said, slowly, as if I had considered what he said and then rejected it. "I saw two killers. Sent to do something to a boy I've been working with all summer. A kid I like."

"Really," Ollie said. "You like him?" He walked around me and took his seat behind the desk.

"Yes," I said. "I like him."

He leaned forward. "Why would you think—"

"Will you stop it?" I said. "I know about the kid's relationship to his stepfather. I know who his stepfather is. I know they hate each other. Now all of a sudden out of nowhere you arrange for me and Amy to be off the farm and two thugs show up wearing guns under their thug uniforms. Have I led you to believe I'm stupid?"

"Never thought it."

"Then stop bullshitting me."

Ollie folded his hands in his lap and looked at me patiently. "You know those phone calls you mentioned, the ones the kid was making all over the country? What if they weren't to his college buddies and his girlfriend? What if the little asshole was trying to have Jimmy killed? What if the little clown had it stuck in his head that Jimmy killed his father and nothing but revenge

would do? What about that, Paul? Would that make things a little more un-
derstandable to you?"

I hesitated before answering. Half of me was ready to argue with Ollie. The
other half was in shock to hear him tacitly confirm what I thought I already
knew. I said, "The details of this are supposed to make a difference to me? Not
that I'm sure I believe them. But what is it you think—that if I understand
why, then it'll be okay? I'm not going to have any problem with two killers
coming out to my farm and murdering this kid who's working for me?"

Ollie put his elbows on the desk and covered his face with his hands. He
spoke into his palms. "All I said is what if."

"Well, what if nothing. It makes no difference."

"None at all?"

"None," I said.

He crossed his arms on the desk and leaned closer to me. "What if I happened to know for a fact that Jimmy's raised this kid like his own son? That
he did everything a father could do, but the kid's been screwing up since pu-
berty, between girls and drugs and money? What if Jimmy's spent a small fortune between abortions and lawyers and rehab with this kid, and now the
little asshole is hell-bent to do away with him, hell-bent to pull together
every old enemy Jimmy's got? What if, Paul? What if it's either, one way or
the other, Jimmy or Chad—and this is all Chad's doing? This is the way Chad
wants it? Then what? Still make no difference?"

"I don't believe it about this kid," I said. "He's—"

"He's slick, is what he is," Ollie said, raising his voice a little.

"I don't think so," I said. "That's not the way he comes across to me."

"I thought you were smarter than this," he said. "I thought you knew more
about the way things were than this."

"How's that? What have I ever done to make you think you could arrange
something like this on my farm and I'd look the other way?"

"What I just said," he answered. "I thought you knew the way things
were."

I got up from my chair. "I'm going back to the farm," I said. "I'm warning
Chad."

Ollie stood up behind the desk. "What good will that do, Paul? Except to
complicate your life."

"Is that a threat? *To complicate my life?*"

"Not from me," Ollie said. "But I can't tell you what Jimmy's going to do."

I stared hard a him for a long moment, my eyes locked on his eyes. I said, "I thought you were my friend."

"I am your friend," he said. "Come to my house for dinner tonight. What's going on between Jimmy and Chad— You can't do anything about it. Only a fool would get in the way of a thing like this. It's an act of God. The only thing you should be looking for is how to keep you and yours safe. *That*," he said, "is what I thought you'd understand."

"As I said"—I started for the door—"I'm going back to the farm. I'm finding the kid."

"Think about what you're doing," Ollie said. When I was already out the door, he called after me: "I'll be expecting you for dinner!"

I didn't answer. I got in my truck and went out the front gate and started for the farm. My foot fell heavier than usual on the gas as I sped along the two-lane roads, worrying over Ollie's threat. I didn't believe he'd do anything to harm me or Amy. I didn't think it was possible I had so misjudged the man. Nor did I think he'd let Jimmy Smoke do anything to us—as long as it was in his power to prevent it. That, of course, was the problem. What if he couldn't keep Jimmy Smoke from, say, burning down the farm, which is where his name came from, as I understood it—his connection to mysterious fires. While I was worrying about all this, I recalled Ollie stopping by the farm a few days earlier to check on His Majesty—he had looked the horse over, gone through his stall, even asked me if he was as mean as always—and I realized with absolute certainty that he kept HM for Jimmy Smoke. I was sure of it. When the time came that Jimmy needed a believable accidental death, HM would be there waiting. Sometimes I'm good at reading things, and I read this with certainty: Chad was going to wind up in the stall with HM, stomped and kicked to death. Jimmy would get Chad out of the way in an accident no one would question—an accident on a farm where the kid was working a summer job hundreds of miles away from Jimmy and his associates. Jimmy got rid of his kid, and he kept his wife. When I realized these things, I started worrying that maybe I *had* misjudged Ollie all these years. Maybe I *would* be in trouble once I warned Chad.

None of this had any bearing on what I was about to do. I wouldn't let it. When I considered Ollie's arguments, though, they began to gather weight. What if this was, really, a skirmish in a war between killers? I had to remind myself that Chad was a kid, a boy, and that to go eat a pleasant dinner while he was getting beaten to death would make me a murderer—and that pushed me hard, that thought. On the farm, dust flew up in clouds behind the truck as I drove the dirt road out to Chad's cabin. The horses looked up from their grazing to watch the truck speed past. Otherwise the farm was so quiet, you'd think no one worked it. Amy was around someplace, in the house probably, enjoying the air-conditioning. Chad was either working or eating lunch. I pulled up to the cabin and hit the brakes, and when I skidded into the concrete foundation, the rubberized front of my bumper thumping into the cabin wall, I realized how fast I must have been going.

I got out of the truck carefully, not wanting to look panicked. At the cabin, I knocked twice, and when Chad didn't answer, I opened the door and stepped inside. I was shocked for a moment by the mess I found. The bed was unmade and the sheets were rumpled and soiled. The floor was littered with garbage: grocery store bags, pizza boxes, clothes, even farm tools. I noticed, sticking out from under the bed, the wooden handle of a twitch I had been looking for just that morning. I knelt to retrieve the twitch and then jumped back at the sight of someone moving in the bathroom—which it took me only an instant to realize was my own reflection in the mirror. When I straightened up, my heart was pounding. The mess in the cabin made me angry. It seemed like a small matter compared to the larger situation at hand, but it angered me. I couldn't help it. Even the walls, which I had painted at the beginning of the summer, appeared soiled. At the top of the bed, a large discolored area darkened the white paint. I couldn't imagine what had made the stain. Sweat? Did he stand on his bed and lean against the wall naked and sweaty? The stain had roughly the proportions of someone's back.

I muttered a curse at the condition of the cabin, and looked around one more time for damage. In the bathroom I noticed a grapefruit-sized hole in the plasterboard by the sink, and my mouth fell open. When I examined it, it looked like he might have simply put his fist through the wall. "Son of a bitch," I said aloud, and I touched my hand to my forehead and looked down, gathering my thoughts. At my feet, the bathroom's waste basket overflowed. Under a crumpled, stained sheet of toilet paper, something glittery caught the light, and when I moved the paper away with my toe, I saw it was an empty condom wrapper. I kicked the basket over and scores of wrappers spilled onto the floor, along with a good number of used condoms, some of them still soggy, others stiff and brittle. I leaned back against the sink and I heard myself moan as if I had just been told someone I loved had died.

In the bedroom, a brief search turned up Amy's pajamas, the apple-green ones she had worn on his first day at the farm. They were folded neatly in one of the armoire's drawers, along with several other items of her clothing—and something about how her few things were neatly folded and stacked, surrounded by the squalor of his things, made it all more painful. I picked up the pajamas and held them to my chest, and when I turned around, Chad was standing in the doorway.

At first he looked like the same Chad, with the same boyish, sweet expression. Then he saw that I was holding Amy's pajamas, and he noticed the overturned waste basket, and the pleasant expression on his face melted away. It was as if a mask came off revealing someone I didn't know, someone different: cold where Chad was warm, impenetrable where Chad was vulnerable. He stood in the doorway, his legs spread as if for solid balance, his arms crossed on his chest. He said, "She wasn't going to stay a virgin forever, Deegan. She's nearly seventeen."

I dropped her pajamas back into the dresser drawer. I wanted to ask him when it had happened. I wanted to ask how long it had been going on. I knew, though, that it had to be at night, after I was asleep. Probably every night. The whole damn summer. That was why she had taken to going to bed early and sleeping late. It explained her mood, too—which I realized now was happiness. Hard to believe, how I didn't see it all summer. She was in love with him. That was clear.

Chad remained in the doorway, solid as a statue. I wanted to get past him, outside into the sunlight and out of the squalor of his room. I looked at him and he met my eyes easily, his stare hard and powerful, as if he were the stronger man and he knew it. I said, "Just get out of my way."

He didn't move. "Deegan," he said, "you can't protect her from the world. I'm telling you as a favor. She hates you for trying. She's not dumb. She sees the way you've kept boys away from her, the way you've kept her hidden out here."

"You're giving me a lesson on raising kids, Chad? After taking advantage of my sixteen-year-old daughter. After—"

"I didn't take advantage of her, Deegan. I'm the best thing that ever happened to her. Those are her words. Ask her. She'll tell you."

"I'm sure," I said. "I'm sure she will." I looked down at the floor a moment and then back up at Chad. I took a step toward him. "Get out of my way, Chad."

He moved aside. "It's insulting," he said. "Trying to keep her from growing up. Not letting her make her own choices, whatever the consequences."

I stepped past him. From outside, I said, "You make a good argument, Chad. You make your point well." I closed the door on him and walked away.

At the house, I found Amy sitting on the porch rocker, writing in her journal. She was wearing a white summer dress with bright red flowers, and she had her legs crossed under her, the light cotton fabric draped over her knees and the chair. She appeared sullen and barely looked up at me until I spoke to her, telling her we were going to the Lundsford's for dinner. She argued awhile, not wanting to go, but gave in without a serious struggle. She went up to her room. A minute later, I heard her music come on. In the living room, I sat on the couch and held my head in my hands. I wasn't thinking much about anything. Somewhere outside a colt whinnied, and the sound of it slid through the house, high, along the ceiling and out the windows, while the low pulse of bass notes came out of Amy's room and traveled through the floorboards

I spent the rest of the afternoon in a strange, spacey state of mind. It seemed impossible to me that I would just go to Ollie's and have myself a nice dinner while I knew Chad was being beaten to death and thrown to HM. I knew I would tell him. I knew I had to. Yet the afternoon went by with Amy in her room, and I never left the house. At six I went up to my bedroom and showered and dressed for dinner. When I was finished I knocked on Amy's door. I told her we would be leaving soon and asked if she would be ready. She didn't answer right away, but opened the door instead and offered me a bright smile and a kiss on the cheek. She said she'd be ready in half an hour. I said fine and then went down to the kitchen, thinking that gave me plenty of time to go tell Chad—but I never left the kitchen. I stood by the sink looking out the window, until I heard Amy coming down the stairs. I was looking out the window at the mountains, at the thick, velvety coat of trees in the evening light, at the patterns of sun and shadow and the effect that created, turning the lush green woods into a garment fit for a king, thick and luxurious, draped over the body of the mountains.

"Well?" Amy said.

I turned away from the window and found her dressed neatly in a long, dark, drawstring skirt and a modest white blouse. "You look lovely," I said.

She smiled and did a pretend curtsy.

In our car, in the driveway, with Amy in the passenger's seat alongside me, I took the keys from the glove compartment and put them in the ignition, but hesitated then, as if I were trying to remember something.

Amy said, "Is anything wrong?"

I turned to look at her, but didn't respond.

"You're sweating," she said, and handed me some napkins from the glove compartment.

I mopped the sweat from my forehead, and I understood in that moment, for the first time, that I was planning to go to dinner and leave Chad to his fate; that someplace, on some level, I had decided that Ollie was right, that Chad was the reckless character bent on revenge he had described; that what was going on between Chad and Jimmy was one act in an endless bloody drama; and that my responsibility was to Amy, to keep her safe, to take care of my family. I also understood in that moment before I started the car that I couldn't do it. That I didn't want to be made a killer, too. That I didn't want to be a murderer. I said, "Would you mind waiting one minute, Amy. I need to tell Chad something before we leave."

"What?" she asked, obviously annoyed.

"It won't take a minute," I said, and I hurried from the car to the pickup, which was parked alongside us in the drive. I winked at Amy as I drove away. She looked back at me as if I had grown another head.

At the cabin, I flung the door open without knocking and found Chad standing by the armoire. "Chad," I said, approaching him, "you're a heartless little bastard and you probably do deserve to die." I hit him hard across the chest with a forearm and knocked him down on the bed.

For a moment, he looked like he was going to jump at me. His eyes were fiery. Then he seemed to change his mind. He said, "What the fuck are you talking about, Deegan?" He pulled himself along the mattress and sat up with his back against the headboard.

"I saw two guys at Ollie's farm," I said. "They were driving a blue Lincoln Continental and wearing shoulder holsters. I saw them right after Amy and I were invited to dinner by a guy associated with your stepfather, a guy who's never invited anybody to dinner before in his life."

Chad didn't say anything, but his face started to go pale at the mention of the blue Lincoln.

I said, "Turns out your stepfather owns HM, Chad. Why do think he'd own a horse like that? That's a dangerous animal. Especially around someone not experienced with horses."

Chad seemed to think a moment. "Sure," he said, talking more to himself than me. "Of course."

"Be gone when I get back, Chad. You can leave Amy some sort of sweet note—but don't see her again. Is that fair?"

He didn't answer. He was still pale and looking away from me, at the far wall, as if he were looking through it to the mountains beyond.

I closed the door firmly and drove back to Amy, who was waiting for me with a puzzled, exasperated expression. "All done," I said, and I started for Ollie's.

It didn't take long to figure out why Ollie never invited anyone to his home. We weren't in the house two minutes before Margaret asked us if we were saved. In the years since I'd last seen her, she'd gone from stout to massive, and the glittering intensity in her eyes struck me as half mad. When we told her no, we hadn't been saved, she brought out the Bibles, three of them, one for Amy, one for me, and her own. Ollie watched all this with a sad, impotent expression, letting us know he was sorry for her behavior and unable to do anything about it. Until dinner was ready, Amy and I sat trapped on two uncomfortable, straight-back chairs, answering questions posed by Margaret about our interior, spiritual lives. She asked questions; we answered politely, and then she lectured us, beginning every little lecture the same way: "When you know Jesus," she'd begin, and then she'd tell us how much fuller our lives would be once we were saved.

Ollie and I never got a chance to talk. I think he assumed that because I was there I must have seen the error of my ways, and was leaving Chad to His Majesty. I figured he'd see his mistake soon enough and I didn't feel the need to say anything. Regardless, with Margaret hovering over all of us, there was no way we were going to get off alone to discuss it. From time to time, while Margaret went on and on, I worried over the consequences of what I had done. I imagined a blue Lincoln Continental arriving at our door and delivering a pair of thugs who'd execute us, gangland style, a bullet apiece in the back of the head. At one point, I had a vision of the farm in flames, while a dark-suited young man held a gun to the back of Amy's head, and the image was so disturbing I think I must have made a noise of some kind, grunted or moaned, because Ollie and Amy both turned to look at me simultaneously, though Margaret went on, deaf to anything but her own words.

Eventually, we were saved by dinner, which was a dried-up, barely edible meat loaf. Margaret did indeed bring out the good china for us, but she apparently neglected to wash it before setting the table. The plates and glasses, and even the pewter candle holder at a center of a wrinkled, white table cloth, were coated with a thin, greasy substance, the kind of grime that might accumulate after years of disuse on a pantry shelf. It was a strange experience, that meal. It began with a standing grace, during which we all held hands while Margaret intoned St. Francis's prayer, the one that begins "Lord, make us the instruments of thy peace." It ended with no one having eaten more than a bite or two of meat loaf, which Margaret seemed not to notice. By the time we were finally back in our car, heading for the farm, Amy had gone from discomfort, to distress, to amusement. "She's crazy," she laughed, grasping her seat belt with both hands, as if she needed to steady herself. "The woman's out of her mind!" She leaned close and gave me a deadpan look. "Did you see that meat loaf?" She screamed in horror.

I laughed along with Amy, but my thoughts were racing ahead to the farm, I worried that she would notice Chad's car was missing. There was a stretch of driveway right before we reached the garage, from which Chad's cabin was visible, and the spot where he parked his car. It was late and dark, but the moon was almost full and she'd be able to see the area clearly if she were looking—and I suspected she would be looking. I started up the drive speedily, hurrying to the garage, but almost hit the brake when I saw the cabin. Chad's car was still there, as was Chad. The lights were on in the cabin, the car was parked by the front door, and Chad was dropping a suitcase in the trunk. Through the front window and the open door, you could see that the cabin was empty, that he had packed up his stuff and was preparing to leave. Amy said, "What the hell?" and got out of the car as if I weren't there. She marched to the cabin through the dark, while I lagged behind, trying to sort out what was happening. In front of me, Amy's small figure faded to a dark shadow before emerging into the tongues of light that reached out from the cabin's window and door. I stopped a moment in the dark once she reached Chad. He had just closed the trunk, and he stood with his arms folded over his chest, his legs spread slightly, the way he had stood in the doorway when I argued with him earlier. Amy talked, a high, urgent quality in her words, but I couldn't make out what she was saying. Chad answered in monosyllables that sounded like a dog's bark. She'd go on for several seconds, and he'd answer her with a handful of syllables. After a couple of minutes, her voice reached that high-pitched place where it goes right before she cries. I went to her, coming out of the shadows, unable to help myself, though I knew I should hang back. She saw me as I approached the car and turned toward me, startled. When she turned back to Chad, he said, "Good-bye, Amy," and he said it forcefully, like a command. Amy covered her face with her hands, and ran away like a child. In the moment before she covered her face, I saw the look in her eyes, and it was full of confusion and fear and a kind of pain I had never seen in her before.

Chad was dressed neatly, his hair still damp from a shower. "Took you a long time to get packed up," I said. "I thought you'd have been in more of a hurry. What happened? Did you make a phone call to your mom?"

He got into his car and started the engine. "I made it clear with Amy," he said, looking up at the moonlight on the mountains. "She won't be expecting to hear from me." He put the car in gear and then, as if reluctantly, turned to face me. "Thank you for the warning," he said. "I'm sorry about Amy. I'm sorry about the problems I've left you with." Without waiting for a response, he hit the gas and sped away.

I watched his car wind along the drive and out to the road. When it disappeared around the bend, I went into the cabin and turned off the lights and sat on the front steps, letting the darkness and quiet of the night settle around me. I figured he must have called his mother and bought himself a reprieve. For a time, I just sat there, with my arms crossed over my knees, looking at the farmhouse and gazing around at the barns and the horses in the fields. I wasn't ready to go back to the house. I didn't want to see Amy. I didn't know what I would say. I took a few steps away from the cabin, and then turned toward the stud barn when I heard a horse whinny. I walked toward the barn, only curious at first. Then, with my heart pounding. I understood, somehow, that it was HM that had whinnied. And then I heard Chad's voice in my mind as if he were standing alongside me. He said, *I'm sorry about the problems I've left you with.* When I reached the barn, I was running, and when I saw the light on in HM's stall, I knew what I was going to find. I was running when I reached the barn, but I stopped before I got to the stall. HM stood looking out, facing me. When he first saw me, he threw his head back and snorted, cocky and full of himself. Then, at the far end of the barn, through the open doors, I saw the long, dark hood of the Lincoln. I hadn't looked into the stall yet. I knew what I was going to find and I didn't want to see it. When I did finally step up to the stall door and take hold of the bars and look in, there they were, like a nightmare made real, both of them, with their dark suits and dark ties, their heads bashed in, their faces bloody and slack over the crushed bones of their skulls. I backed away from the sight of them and walked out of the barn, dazed.

I made my way toward the house, through the open gates of an empty corral, in the moonlight. I was stunned and dizzy. I wasn't really thinking at all. I was listening—to the small sounds coming from the grass at my feet, to horses moving in pastures, like there was a peaceful song being composed around me in the dark somewhere and I had to strain to hear it. I was looking—at the mountains, which seemed to undulate in moonlight, powerfully, like ocean swells. I made my way toward my house, as if moving to a place of safety, a place where I could rest and figure things out. I touched my face and felt that both my hands were slick with still-wet blood—and for a moment then I must have lost my mind because I stood there in that field thinking I had murdered them, those two kids in HM's stall, those boys who were only Chad's age, if not even younger. It lasted a second or two, that belief, that *knowledge* that I was the murderer, before I solved the equation and understood that the bars of the stall must have been bloody and I got blood on my hands when I gripped them. But it lingered, that sense that I was the murderer. I was shaken. I struggled across the pasture toward the house, surrounded by the peace of dark mountains and fields, knowing only that I needed to get cleaned up before Amy saw me. I didn't want to frighten her. I didn't want her to see me with blood all over my face and hands. I didn't want her to wonder who I was.

Gifts

———

for Raoul Vezina and Jay Walter

STORM-BLUE CLOUDS, A CIRCLE OF SLATE-BLUE MOUN-
tains, a ridge I could barely make out between the mountains and the
clouds—that's what it looked like from the bedroom window. The storm
winds had entered my dreams as wolves and a woman screaming, and I was
relieved when I woke and heard the wind slapping against the cabin walls.
For a long time I lay in bed looking at the slow-moving clouds and the leaves
rushing through the little alley of cleared land between my window and a
hillside that fell off into a long, wide, thickly wooded ravine. I smelled coffee
brewing in the kitchen and the smell was enticing, but the bed was warm and
the room cold, and I huddled down under the covers and pressed my head
into the pillow.

A week before, our house had burned. Ellie and I lost most of what we
owned, but we were thankful for our lives, and so I worked things out with
the court and my clients and my partners, and took two weeks off from being a lawyer so I could take this vacation at Howard's cabin. Actually, it's our
cabin: Howard willed it to us when he died. Howard was our son. He was
twenty-six when he died six years ago, and since then we've only been to the
cabin twice, both times in the last year. It's situated on a little peninsula of
land that juts out into the ravine, and it's not a very valuable piece of property because it won't be around much longer: the land it rests on is slowly

eroding. In another ten years the cabin will sit on the edge of the ravine, and in another twenty it'll be gone. But the view—the view is magnificent. More so now than when Howard was alive.

The first time we saw the place was 1969. Those were hard years. The world was changing before my eyes, and I didn't like what I was seeing. Howard did, and we were always at odds. In college he let his hair grow long, and he came home for holidays with hair like a girl's reaching down to his shoulders. I tried not to look at him. I tried to tell myself it was a fad. He always had a delicately handsome face, and then with that long hair he looked so feminine, he looked so much like a girl that I wanted to smack him and make him get his hair cut. I can still hear myself yelling at him, telling him to act like a man. He was full of ideals—and all I could see was long hair, and a face that seemed too pretty.

But 1969. That spring he had graduated from college and with money he had borrowed for grad school he bought this cabin. We found out not from Howard—we had given up trying to keep track of him—but from his girlfriend's father. His girlfriend's name was T.J., and though he had been seeing her for a couple of years, we had never met her. One night that summer her father called and threatened to shoot Howard if he didn't send T.J. home. After I got him calmed down he told me about the cabin, and I promised I'd go up there and talk to Howard. By the end of the phone call, though I don't think my voice showed it, I was angrier than T.J.'s father, and not about Howard and T.J., but about the way Howard had spent his grad school money—money he had gotten from a loan I cosigned.

I had wanted to go see him alone, but Ellie insisted on coming.

"We really should let him know," she said.

I glared at the rutted dirt road. This was not the kind of driving my Buick had been designed for, and every time a rock clunked against the frame I cursed the mountains and grew angrier at Howard. "How?" I said, trying to sound even-tempered. "How do we let him know we're coming?"

Ellie didn't answer. She turned and looked out the window at trees that crowded the road.

"No phone," I said. "No mail delivery. How am I supposed to let them know?"

Ellie touched her fingertips to her forehead, just above her eyebrows—which is something she always does right before she cries.

"Don't cry, Ellie," I said. But the tears were already falling. Ellie is a frail woman with delicate features. I knew we were only a short way from the cabin, and I didn't want Ellie crying when she saw Howard—so I tried my best to calm her. By the time we got there she was feeling better. I had agreed to walk the half-mile trail to the cabin first, and then bring Howard back to the car. This, Ellie reasoned, would give T.J. time to straighten out her house before we all arrived. I didn't argue. It still makes me smile to think of how concerned Ellie was that T.J. have enough time to straighten out her house for guests.

I was glad for the half-mile walk. It gave me time to compose myself and rehearse what I wanted to say. The sweet smell of the woods was calming, though I was constantly annoyed at the overhanging branches and the uneven path. I was going to tell Howard about how much Ellie and I had sacrificed for him, and what he owed us: first of all, to live someplace civilized, and then to contribute something to society, to give something back in return for what had been given to him. I remember rehearsing that speech when the path opened onto a clearing and I saw the cabin. It's a big log cabin with a slate roof, and there's one large bay window in the front that brings the morning light into the living room, and there's a little three-step stoop that leads up to the front door. The way I was standing at the edge of that clearing, with my legs and arms so stiff, I must have looked like just another tree, because no one noticed me. The cabin door was open, and I could see in through the living room to the kitchen. Howard was sitting at the kitchen table smoking a pipe, and a much older man—he looked to be in his late forties to early fifties—was sitting across from him. T.J. was sitting on the table between them with her legs crossed and folded under her. Her eyes were closed and her hands were resting palms up on her knees. All three were naked. I stood there a long time taking in this sight: T.J., with her boyish chest and skinny body, with her long straight hair that reached down to the table top; the older man, whose face was lost somewhere under a disheveled mop of curling mouse-brown hair and a beard that grew wildly over his face; and my son . . . my son Howard, who, if not for the evidence of his sex, could have been mistaken for a pretty, flat-chested girl with silky, dark hair falling over her shoulders. I had just about decided to turn around and leave, and to tell Ellie no one was at the cabin, when a huge chow that had been lying on the cabin floor under the bay window saw me. He was a dopey looking dog with a full ruff of long, silver-gray hair. When he saw me, he jumped right into the window. I'm still surprised it didn't break.

All three naked bodies at the table turned at the same time. The older man stood up, and Howard and T.J. leaped for the chow, who had regained his bearings and was about to make it out the front door. Howard caught it by the collar and T.J. had it by the tail, and still the thing carried them halfway out the door before they managed to pull it back into the kitchen and tie it to a short leash. I could hear Howard explaining over the chow's barking, "It's okay! It's okay! He's my father!" and then T.J. closed the front door and ran through the living room to the bedroom. The older man—whom I later learned was an ex-lawyer, ex-stock broker, ex-corporate executive named Tom McGuinn—must have left through the back door because I didn't see him again. Then the front door opened and Howard, dressed in a white robe with a black silk rope for a belt, walked across the clearing and joined me.

"I'm sorry you didn't let me know you were coming," he said. He was looking me in the eyes—something I taught him to do when he was a boy. He said, "I'm sorry about how this must make you feel, Dad."

I nodded.

Howard looked away and we were both silent awhile. Then he started talking casually. "Lieberman loves T.J.," he said. "He's such a big, dumb puppy."

I guessed that Lieberman was the chow.

"A couple of weeks ago T.J.'s father came busting in the cabin and Lieberman bit him." Howard smiled.

I nodded again.

"He sent you up here, didn't he? T.J.'s father."

"He's threatened to kill you."

"He's told me in person. T.J. says he won't do it."

"That's nice to know. If she were my daughter, I don't think you'd be so lucky." As soon as I said that, I felt like a jerk.

Howard said, "I love T.J."

"So you let her sit naked in front of another man?"

Howard looked at me defiantly. "She sleeps with him too. In fact—"

I grabbed his robe and pulled him close. When he didn't resist, I pushed him away and turned and walked down the path, half expecting him to follow. He didn't, and I remember cursing him as I followed the trail. When I got back to the car I told Ellie no one was at the cabin. She looked at me and knew I was lying. "What happened?" she asked. I didn't answer. I started the car and we drove in silence until we found a motel where we could spend the night.

After I carried our suitcases into the room and stretched out on one of a pair of double beds, Ellie asked me again to tell her what had happened. I told her and she kept shaking her head through the whole story. When I finished she asked, "Are you sure about the other man?" I hadn't told her what Howard had said, or even that we had argued. I just told her I had been upset with them and had left. She wanted me to go back. "You have to go back," she said. "We can't leave things this way."

I agreed. Ellie had meant for me to go back in the morning, but I was too upset to wait. After the TV news was over, I left her alone in the motel room and drove back to the cabin.

By the time I arrived it was dark. There was no moon that night and as soon as I turned off the lights and stepped out of the car I couldn't see a thing. I held my fingers in front of my eyes and I still couldn't see them. I got the flashlight out of the glove compartment and let its thin beam of light guide my way. The woods were full of strange noises: at one point as I walked along the trail, I must have surprised an owl or some other large bird, because I heard a great, thick flapping of wings from a tree limb only a few feet in front of me. Then, after my heartbeat slowed somewhat, I began to hear an irregular clicking noise, like someone sending Morse code, and as I continued walking the clicking got louder, until, standing once again at the clearing in front of the cabin, I saw T.J. sitting at the kitchen table typing.

I remember how intent she looked at her work. She stared at that typewriter as if it could talk to her, as if she were waiting for a message to come whispered from its innards. Then suddenly, as if she heard what she was listening for, she'd type furiously for a minute or two, and then stop again to listen. I must have watched her there for ten or fifteen minutes. Occasionally she'd rub her nose with a bent forefinger, or pull a long strand of hair across her lips and bite at it—but always she'd return to her listening and typing. Lieberman was sleeping on his back in front of the bay window, and McGuinn was sitting on the couch reading a thick, dark book.

I walked around to the back of the cabin. There, through the bedroom window, I saw something that it took several minutes to make out. It appeared to me—standing alone in the darkness outside the cabin, looking in through the bedroom window—that Howard was floating naked through space, and it took me the longest time to take the pieces of that optical illusion apart. When I eventually did, it seemed somehow tremendously funny. Howard had painted the room black—floors, walls, ceiling, everything. He had covered his bed with a black blanket. And then, in the manner of Jackson Pollack, he had splashed the room—floors, walls, ceiling, bed, everything—with splotches of luminous white paint. Somewhere in the room he had hidden a black light, and with the darkness outside and the black light shining inside, and with him lying on the bed, he appeared to be floating naked among stars.

The way Howard had decorated his room reminded me of when he was nine or ten years old and a Boy Scout: when he camped out, he loved to fix up his tent. He liked it better than anything, and he was always stealing things from around our house to use as decorations. I associated that wildly painted room with his old Boy Scout tents, and it struck me as so amusing that I suddenly felt at ease. I approached the window and knocked at the glass as if I were standing at the front door. "Hey, Buck Rodgers!" I called, and this also struck me funny. I bent over and folded my hands across my stomach and laughed so hard my cheeks and jaw and sides started to hurt. When I finally looked up the light was on in the room, and Howard was tying a knot in his black belt. He was flanked by T.J. and McGuinn, and Lieberman was standing on the bed. They were all staring at the window.

I smiled.

Howard opened the window. "Dad," he said, "what are you doing?"

I shrugged and then we smiled at each other. Howard motioned for me to go around to the front of the cabin.

He and T.J. met me on the steps, and I heard McGuinn and Lieberman walking out the back door.

T.J. held out her hand. "I'm very sorry about this afternoon," she said. "I'm really terribly embarrassed."

Her voice was so sweet and her manner and tone so intelligent, that I liked her immensely as soon as I heard her speak a few words. It didn't hurt that she was apologizing—which, at the very least, was an effort at courtesy. I shook her hand. "There's no need to apologize," I said.

"Oh," she said. "I just wish our first meeting had been different." She was barefoot and wearing a pair of baggy jeans and a man's blue cotton work shirt. She clasped her hands together behind her back. "Let's go in," she said, and she stepped back through the door.

Howard started to follow.

"T.J.," I said. "I hope you won't mind, but I'd like to talk to Howard alone for a while. Out here. I'll feel more comfortable out here."

"I understand," she said. "Can I make you some coffee or tea?"

"Coffee," Howard said. "My dad's a big coffee drinker."

T.J. closed the door, and as Howard and I sat alongside each other on the cabin's steps and listened to her, she went about making a pot of coffee.

"She seems like a nice girl," I said.

Howard said, "I love her, Dad. If this were a different time we'd be married."

I looked away. I didn't want to get into serious matters so quickly. I had hoped we might at least start out talking about the past and sharing memories. I wanted to talk first about those things that joined us before getting to the matters that divided us. But there we were after our first few words and my son was indirectly attacking marriage and the family. I took a deep breath and let it out slowly. "Howard," I said. "I don't understand you, and I really want to. Where can we start?"

Howard shrugged and we were both quiet for a long time. T.J. brought me some coffee, and then we both listened as she went back to her typing. Finally, I asked him what T.J. was writing. She was working on a novel, he told me. That got us started talking, and once we were started we talked through the night while T.J.'s typewriter clattered behind us. Howard believed, he truly believed, that he could love everybody, that we are all beautiful, God-like creatures—and I couldn't make him see it wasn't true. I tried to tell him what poor, desperate animals we all are at heart, but he didn't know what I was talking about, and after a while I began to feel deranged and unhealthy for trying to make him see things as I saw them.

At dawn T.J. joined us and we walked around to the back of the cabin and watched the sunrise over the ring of mountains. It came up bright and red and it turned a thin line of clouds red all along the horizon. I could almost see Ellie at the motel stumbling out of the bed and shuffling groggily toward the bathroom. Ellie has gotten up at dawn every morning for as long as I've known her. I said, "I've got to go now."

"You're thinking of Mom, aren't you?" Howard said. "She's getting up now."

I laughed and Howard added, "I wish she were here so I could tell her I love her."

The sun had risen clear of the mountains. It was a big, red circle floating above us and casting a red glow over the trees. "I love her, too," I said. And we all three sat there quietly a little while longer before I shook Howard's hand and T.J. hugged me, and finally I left. On my way to the trail I passed McGuinn and Lieberman sitting on the front steps. McGuinn was wearing a bright green vest and he had dressed Lieberman in a blue flannel shirt, putting the chow's legs through the sleeves and buttoning it under his belly. Around the dog's neck he had tied a red bandanna. I waved and McGuinn waved back, but Lieberman just stared intensely. He's never been a very trusting dog.

I've dreamed of that sunrise a number of times since Howard's death, and I must have been dreaming of it again the night of the fire. I awoke to the high pitched, piercing sound of the smoke alarm, and I don't remember dreaming of anything, but I was groggy and a little dizzy and the living room was filled with a thin haze of smoke and an eerie red glow. For a second before I realized what was happening I thought I heard Howard's voice. I thought I was back at the cabin watching the sunrise. Then I came to my senses. It was a cold night, but the living room was so hot, sweat fell off my body. Ellie was more unconscious than she was asleep, and I had to pick her up and carry her out on my shoulder. When I opened the front door and stepped out into the cold night air, the house seemed to explode behind me. Within minutes there were flames hurrying behind every window, and several hours later the house had burned to rubble—and I watched it burn with Ellie, at first shivering in the cold, and then warm behind a neighbor's window. And all I could think of was Howard. Watching the house where we raised him burn down was like watching his cremation.

He had gotten sick in 1973 and died early in 1974. During those last days in the hospital, he had grown so frail and emaciated that it was hard to look at him. He was twenty-six and he looked like a little old man, his skin sunken around his skeleton, his eyes looking like they might pop out of his head. It took all the courage I had to sit beside him and talk in a normal tone. Ellie couldn't do it. She tried, but toward the end she couldn't look at him without burying her face in her hands and crying, and so she sat in the lounge and waited, trying to build up her strength.

The night before he died, Howard said something to me that I thought I understood, but didn't really until the night of the fire. It was late. I had stayed past visiting hours because Howard seemed more alert than usual. He was able to understand what I was saying, and if I bent down and put my ear near to his mouth, I was able to understand his occasional whispered replies. I was trying to tell him, amid the sickening hospital smells and the fluids dripping through tubes all around us, that his life was the greatest gift Ellie and I had ever been given. But each time I tried to speak all my emotions rose up and choked off the words. Finally I said, "Howard—your life —your life is like a gift—" and I couldn't go on.

Howard motioned with one finger for me to come closer, and he whispered in my ear, "Death is a gift, too." When I backed away and looked down at him he said, loud enough for me to hear, "From me to you," and he managed a weak smile.

I thought I knew what he meant then. I thought he meant death would be an end to his suffering, and to my having to watch him suffer. But now I don't think that's what he meant at all. The night of the fire, watching thick flames consume our home, seeing everything I owned drifting away as smoke, I was struck with a physical beauty so solid I could feel it. Death came to me suddenly as a fact, because I saw everything turning in time to dust and ashes—me and Ellie and our house . . . and Howard. I looked at the flames and felt all through me the uniqueness and the beauty of things in time—and often now I feel sure that's what Howard was talking about when he said death was a gift, too. It was a revelation when I thought my time of revelations was long gone.

Ellie called from the kitchen. "Joseph, get up!" she yelled. "You've got to see this."

I sat up in bed and looked out the window. The storm clouds were so thick it looked like night out there, but I knew it was midmorning. Still, I didn't feel like getting out of bed. Alongside my pillow, on the mahogany night table, was a copy of T.J.'s first novel. It had just been published by a small press and it wasn't getting much attention, but she was excited about its publication. I hadn't read it yet: it had come in the mail with a long letter the day after the fire. I remember meeting the postman on the street and how we both laughed as he delivered the mail to an acre plot of debris. T.J. said the book wasn't getting many reviews, but the reviews it was getting were good. McGuinn, she told me, had gone back to being a lawyer. He made lots of money these days and dressed very conservatively. She said I wouldn't believe it to see him, but I did. It was 1980 and the country was back to normal. It was like the '60s and '70s had never happened. I hoped McGuinn was happy.

"Joseph!" Ellie called, "come out here! You're going to miss this!"

I grumbled to myself. I still didn't feel like getting up, but I struggled out of the warm bed and put on my robe and walked out to the kitchen.

For a moment I was disoriented: sunlight poured into the cabin through the bay window and the front door. It was an exceptionally bright day. Then a violent gust of wind slammed the front door closed, and I turned and looked out the back window and the back door, and it was dark as night.

"Wow," I said. I had never seen anything like this and neither had Ellie. Even Lieberman, who had quietly watched our house burn from the distant seclusion of his doghouse and who seemed to want nothing more out of life than to lie somewhere and grow old in silence—even Lieberman was trotting back and forth between the front and back of the cabin and sniffing wildly at the doors.

"Isn't it magnificent?" Ellie said. "Isn't it glorious?"

I nodded. Through the back window I could see the darkness of the storm, and through the front window I could see the mountains rising up around us in bright sunlight. I could see the sky clear and blue beyond the mountains' ridge and I could see the crisp play of light and shadow between the hollows and rises.

"Yes," I answered. "Yes it is."

Sweet

—◁◖◗▷—

ON THE WAY TO WORK I MEDITATED ON THE SUNRISE, which I watch every morning through my bedroom window, and then when I got to work, the barn doors weren't completely closed, which meant some-one had arrived at the stables before me, which was unusual, so I was quiet as I approached the gap between the sliding doors and then I stepped back out of sight when I saw Sweet. She was in her stall, eating out of her colt's feed bucket with a white plastic spoon. The galvanized steel bucket looked huge next to her small body, looked as though she might as well swim in it as eat out of it. She had on work boots and faded jeans and a yellow halter top that caught slices of morning sunlight shooting through the bars of her stall's high window. Behind her, Bobby G watched as she leaned over his mix of oats and molasses. His head was lowered, as if he were thinking of using it as a battering ram, but he appeared more confused than angry at the sight of his groom eating his mash. I waited a minute and then made a big production out of opening the barn doors, and when I walked onto the floor of the sta-ble, G was at his feed and Sweet had her tack box open and a curry comb in her hand.

"Sweet!" I said, pretending to be startled. "What are you doing here so early?"

She answered, without looking up from her tack box, "Do I need your fucking permission, asshole? I'm here early. What do you care?" She went back into her stall and began brushing out the tangles in G's tail.

I ambled over to my stall and looked in on Miss Payday. She was lying peacefully in a bed of straw, head up and alert. When she saw me, she whinnied. "And good morning to you, too, Sister Payday," I said, loudly. I settled myself down on my tack box, using it as a bench, and slowly went about unwrapping a pair of chocolate croissants that I bought at the French bakery by my apartment. I like to eat my breakfast at the stables and say hello to the other grooms as they stumble in to work. Most grooms, they're a sorry lot: drunks, gamblers, illiterates, fools. Mostly drunks and gamblers. Myself, I guess I fit into the fool category, because I've always liked grooming horses, ever since I started doing it as a kid, more than thirty years ago, and I've never tried to make anything better of myself, though I know I could.

When I finished unwrapping the croissants, I arranged them attractively on a pewter plate from out of my tack box, and I poured myself a steaming cup of coffee from my thermos. Across the stable floor, Sweet was getting G ready to jog. She was such a tiny, frail girl, probably no taller than five-four, five-five at the most, maybe a hundred pounds. When she first showed up at the stables—during the season, about two years ago, at the Meadowlands in New Jersey—everyone knew she was a runaway. She couldn't have been older than fourteen. She had short blond hair and bright dark eyes and a fresh-scrubbed look, and she was wearing good clothes, khaki shorts and a nicely fitted blouse and high-quality sandals, like a child of some upscale, uptown couple. When she told Victor she was seventeen, he laughed, but he hired her anyway, which no one could figure out because she didn't know shit about horses. He arranged for her to work on his farm in Orlando for the rest of the meet, and then when we all came back to Florida for the winter, she was already here, at the stables, grooming. Some of us were thinking he had helped her out, that he might have had a spark of decency he had been keeping hidden—but then it turned out he was screwing her. We shouldn't have been surprised. We all know Victor. But she was so tiny then, it didn't hardly seem possible.

"Sweet," I called across the stable, "I've got some coffee and an extra croissant, if you're interested." She didn't answer, but I could see she had heard me. She was brushing G's mane.

I liked watching Sweet as she worked. I had lately discovered in myself a spiritual bent. A while back, I found a book by Kahlil Gibran in a new age bookstore in town. I was attracted to the store by crystals hanging in the window. Several large crystals were positioned to catch the late evening light and break it into rainbows. I wandered through the store, enjoying the thick scent of incense, checking out the books, and fingering small vials of brightly colored aroma therapies. I found the Gibran book next to a genuine crystal ball that cost several hundred dollars, and I bought the book after reading only a handful of pages and being impressed.

Though I never actually read the whole book cover to cover, Gibran's words affected a deep change in me. His observations awakened a place within me that had long been sleeping. Suddenly I began seeing all the ordinary things of the world in a new light. The sunrise is a good example: what used to be just part of every morning—watching the sunrise from my bed, through my bedroom window—became something spiritual, as if the light were like God's love, His love washing over the world. But also other simple, everyday things, like the way light reflected off stalks of straw in Miss Payday's stall, turning the straw gold and casting a golden tone throughout the stables; and the horses, the beauty of working muscles under sleek hides glistening with sweat; and Sweet, too, her beauty. Sometimes I used to just quit what I was doing and lean against the bars of my stall to watch Sweet as she put down a bed of straw or bathed her colt. I liked especially the lean muscles of her legs as she stood on her toes and stretched for something, and the way her breasts moved and shifted as she worked. Watching Sweet used to be about the favorite part of my day until Paul, who was going out with Sweet at the time, told me he'd put my fat ass in the hospital if he caught me staring at her again. And I knew he would. He told me that Sweet had asked him to tell me, but Sweet never said anything to me herself about it, and I'm sure she would have if I were really bothering her—which I'd never want to do.

Paul was the real beginning of Sweet's problems. She took up with him after Victor dumped her. Paul was the stable manager and second trainer, and it was him that got Sweet into crank. Now she was living with Robbie, another groom, and she made the stuff herself, getting the ingredients she needed, somehow, from Wal-Mart of all places.

I finished my first croissant, and had my hand on the second one. "Sweet," I called again. "Last chance. This extra delicious French chocolate croissant is tempting me sorely."

Sweet stopped working on her colt and turned around to give me a look.

"You'd be doing me a favor," I said, and I patted my gut, which extended way out over my belt and sort of rested on my thighs. I've always had a problem with weight.

"You bet your fat ass I'd be doing you a favor," she said. "You have a cup for me?"

"Hell, yes!" I shouted. "For you, Sweet, I'd run out and scramble up some eggs, just say the word!" I folded my hands over my belly and laughed.

Sweet mumbled, "Oh, for Christ's sake," and tossed her curry comb down into the dirt outside her stall.

I pulled a cup out of my tack box, and had her coffee and croissant waiting for her by the time she crossed the stable.

"Jesus," she said, holding the steaming cup of coffee to her face, "this smells fucking great."

"Should!" I said, my voice that high-pitched, fat man's whine that I hated and tried hard—with no success—to suppress. "It's only Colombian Supreme," I said. "Fresh ground last night, ten bucks a pound over at Starbucks!"

Sweet sipped the coffee and nodded appreciatively. "It's good," she said. "What kind of coffeemaker you got?"

"Brüne," I said. "What's Robbie got, Mr. Coffee?"

Sweet snorted, making a kind of half-amused, half-disgusted sound that came from way down deep in her chest. "The cocksucker," she said. "The asshole . . ."

I smiled but looked away, out through the stable doors to the training track, where a couple of grooms already had their horses out jogging. I didn't like to hear Sweet curse. She didn't used to curse at all. In fact, when she first started, she didn't used to say hardly anything at all. She was a sweet thing. That's what we started calling her, Sweet Thing—and then it just worked its way down to Sweet.

"What's the matter, Fats?" Sweet sat down next to me on the tack box. "My language offend you?" She held the croissant to her nose, inhaling its chocolate fragrance, and then took a small bite that she chewed with her eyes closed.

I said, friendly as could be, "Please don't call me Fats. I've asked everyone here not to call me that."

"I don't even know what your real name is." She looked me in the eyes, curious, as if I were about to reveal something of interest to her.

"It's Winston," I said. "I prefer to be called Win."

"Son of a bitch," she said. "I never heard anybody call you anything but Fats."

"That's because they're no-class fools around here. You know I tell the truth!"

"Got that right," Sweet said, looking back toward her stall and G, who was looking back at her.

"You mad at Robbie?" I asked. "I thought he was your old man?"

"Was," Sweet said, with her mouth full. "The prick threw me out last night. I had to sleep in the goddamn stall."

"Threw you out?" I said, my voice doing its high-pitched squeal again. "Just threw you out on the street? Just left you with no place to spend the night?"

"That's what I said," Sweet answered. She covered her face with her hands and rested her elbows on her knees and massaged her temples with her fingertips. "Jesus Christ," she whispered, almost as if she were talking to herself. Then she sounded angry. "I'm strung out on speed, I've got no place to stay, I don't have a fucking cent to my name. I'm such a fucking mess."

I surprised myself and put my arm around her shoulder and then kind of moved back a little when I realized what I'd done, expecting her to haul off and punch me. She didn't though. She just kind of stiffened a bit and swallowed hard.

"Sweet," I said "you're welcome to stay at my place till you get yourself straightened out."

"I can't stay at your place," she said, dismissing the idea as if it were totally absurd.

"Why not? I got an extra room with a fold-out bed. It's not like I'd expect anything from you. There's no strings attached or anything. Nothing at all."

"Right," Sweet said. She pulled away from me, out from under my arm, and went back to her stall without saying another word.

"Just remember," I called after her. "No strings!"

Back in her stall, G nipped Sweet's shoulder and she slapped him hard on the muzzle and cursed him out a blue streak, and then went about putting him in harness. I watched her awhile, until I heard another groom's car pull up to the stable, and then I got to work on Miss Payday. Rest of the day, I kept thinking back to when I put my arm around Sweet, a natural thing, wanting to console her, and how she didn't resist me at all, and I knew there was bound to be something between us. I felt it in my heart, and I thought she felt it too, and then that night when she showed up at my apartment lugging two big cardboard boxes full of her things, I felt my feelings were being confirmed.

"Sweet!" I said. "I'm overjoyed!" And I was. Honestly. It was a little after ten at night, and I had been thinking about her constantly since that morning.

"I'm sure you are," Sweet said. She crossed her arms under her breasts and gave me a hard look. She seemed tired, and she was bedraggled, as if she hadn't showered or cleaned up or slept well in a long time. Her eyes were red and puffy, from crying it was obvious. "Look," she said. "Before I come in, let's get it straight. You said no strings, right?"

"Of course," I said, my voice shooting up high. "Sweet," I said, sincerely, "you don't know me at all if you think I'm wanting anything other than to help you out when you need it."

"Right," Sweet said, and she shook her head and whispered "mother-fucker." She picked up her boxes and toted them into the apartment.

I closed and latched the door behind her, and when I turned around I saw her standing in the center of my living room, checking the place out. She had a ferocious look about her, like a cat ready to tear something up, and I had to remind myself what a kid she was, still only sixteen at the oldest, and that underneath that mean-looking exterior there was a scared girl who needed someone to help her get straightened out. "Put 'em down, put 'em down," I said. She was clutching her boxes, holding them to her chest, her arms wrapped around them. I pointed to the floor next to the Lazy Boy recliner that was against the wall.

Sweet wouldn't let loose the boxes. "Where's the extra room?" she said. "Where's the extra room you said you had?"

I folded my hands over my belly and leaned back against the door. "You're standing in it," I said. I opened my arms. "This is it."

Sweet looked around the room: at the Lazy Boy and the nineteen-inch TV positioned on a stand a dozen feet in front of it, and at the table and two chairs by the room's only window. "Fats," she said "this is your living room."

"You can have it," I said. "You can move right in here long as you need—"

"Fats—"

"Win. Please."

"Win. You said you had an extra room."

"Well, this is an extra room!" I said, my voice soaring.

"The living room isn't an extra room, Fats! It's the fucking living room!"

"Well, this is the room I meant, Sweet. My bedroom's over there." I pointed to the red bead curtain that separated my bedroom from the living room.

"Son of a bitch . . ." She dropped the boxes. "And you said you had a fold-out bed." She looked around. "All I see is a table and a recliner."

"That Lazy Boy's better than a bed! That's where I sleep most nights!"

Sweet covered her face with her hands. She rubbed her temples. After several long moments, she took her hands away from her face and looked at me. "I'm supposed to sleep in the recliner and make myself at home in your living room?"

"Sweet," I said. I was quiet awhile. I gave her a paternal, loving look, trying to communicate to her that I cared and was concerned and was just trying to do a good deed, to help her out.

She sighed. "Fats," she said. "Win . . . Win, do you have a shower?" She ran her fingers through her hair and rubbed at a spot on the back of her neck, looking away from me. "I need a damn shower," she said. "I smell like a fucking horse." Her voice trailed off, getting softer, almost inaudible. "I haven't had a fucking shower in days."

"Do I have a shower?" I yelled. I laughed loudly. "Of course, I have a shower!" I opened the door to the bathroom and flipped on the light. "Tell you what," I said. "You take a shower and I'll whip us up a late-night breakfast: eggs, bacon, toast, and juice. The works. What do think?"

She nodded and gave me the slightest smile, and I could see that her eyes were watery. She picked up her boxes and carried them into the bathroom, and after she closed the door, I heard her slide the lock closed and then it was quiet. I listened awhile, just looking at the door, and I couldn't help imagining her getting undressed, taking off her clothes only an arm's length away from me.

"Win!" Sweet's voice boomed from behind the door. "Are you just standing out there or what? I haven't heard you move."

I tiptoed quickly to the kitchen and then called back: "What was that, Sweet? I had my head in the refrigerator."

She didn't answer. A moment later I heard the shower going, and I started cooking up the bacon. By the time she turned off the water and pulled back the shower curtain, I had set two places at the table and dropped three slices of bacon on each plate. Next to each plate was a glass of orange juice, and in the center of the table a stack of toast rose up off a white, ceramic Lazy Susan that pictured a standardbred racehorse trotting across a finish line. When everything was ready but the eggs, which I planned on cooking up once Sweet was at the table, I hurried to my bedroom and brought out my leather-bound blank book, which I had been writing the best of my sayings in for the past year. I put it on the far end of the table, away from the plates, hoping it would look like I just happened to lay it there.

Sweet came out of the bathroom wearing lightweight, silklike pajamas that hung loosely from her body, but clung to all the right places. I almost fainted.

"Win," she said, "do you have a robe?" She gestured to her pajamas, showing she was aware of how sexy they were. "These are the only pj's I've got," she said, "and I don't want to sleep in my clothes again."

I shook my head.

"Great," she said. She looked at me a moment, and then added, "Well, at least you could quit fucking staring at me, all right?"

"Oh," I said, startled. "I didn't realize. I'm sorry." I looked away from her, toward the kitchen, and then I remembered what I was doing. "I'll whip up the eggs!" I yelled. "You sit down, Sweet! Make yourself comfortable!"

In the kitchen, I cracked two eggs into a bowl and dropped a fat slice of butter in my biggest cast-iron frying pan. "Scrambled okay?"

"Scrambled's fine," Sweet answered, softly, as if distracted.

When I glanced back at her and saw that she had my book opened and was reading in it, my heart did one of its flutter things that scares me sometimes.

"Did you write this stuff?" Sweet said.

"What stuff?" I said. I didn't turn around.

"This stuff," Sweet said. *"The heart is like a broken furnace. The heat of its love is squandered."*

"Oh, that," I said. I carried the frying pan to the table and portioned out the scrambled eggs. "That's just my notebook where I write down my thoughts."

Sweet put the book down alongsid

"Jesus," she said, "I'm starving. This is th

croissant."

"That's terrible, Sweet," I said. I bro

kitchen and by the time I sat down to my

She propped her head up on her hands

may have been the very first time she ever g;

obviously had a good effect on her mood. "

heart is like a broken furnace?"

"Well," I said, "that's hard to explain, Sweet   ..bout it."

She nodded and made a cute face, as if she   _ me entertaining, and

then she opened up the book again. "How about this one," she said, *"The life*

of a wounded soul is a Ferris wheel that spins wildly out of control. What's that

mean?"

"Well," I said, "there again, you know. Same thing. Got to think about it."

"Got to think about it," she echoed. Her appearance seemed to shift as she

watched me, as if she might be seeing me differently, as if it might be occur-

ring to her that I was a deeper person than I might look to be. She folded her

hands in front of her on the table. She said, "Are you sure *you* know what you

mean?"

"Well," I said. "Sweet, it's not that simple." I clasped my hands over my

stomach and leaned toward her slightly. "Sometime you have to let your

thoughts lead you into deeper waters, if you know what I mean. You have to

be willing to ponder things. A deep thought's always going to be a little mys-

terious, at least at first."

"Oh," she said. She nodded, her eyes fixed on me. "You mean, something

like this: 'The stupidity of the good is unfathomably wise.'"

"What?"

"'The stupidity of the good is unfathomably wise.' Friedrich Nietzsche."

"Who?"

"Nietzsche. German philosopher."

When I didn't say anything more, Sweet offered me another smile. "My

father read me Nietzsche at night. He was obsessed with Nietzsche. He'd

read to me from Nietzsche's books, and he'd give me sayings to memorize,

like that stupidity one. This is from the time I was five or six. My mother

thought he was reading me Winnie the Pooh." She laughed.

anything to say. Sweet fiddled with her plate and

I repeated the name, "Nietzsche," and the sound of it felt

remember any other sayings?"

she said. "You don't want to hear."

do," I said. "I've been reading Kahlil Gibran myself lately."

"Never heard of him," Sweet said.

"He's a philosopher, too," I said. "Eastern."

Sweet looked away, out my window, which overlooked a junk-strewn alley. "'Woman was God's second blunder.' That's one that stuck in mind."

"Nietzsche said that?"

"So sayeth my father."

"Lord," I said. "What kind of thing is that to say to a little girl? What was His first blunder?"

Sweet shrugged. "How about this: 'Morality is the herd-instinct in the individual.'"

"What?"

"Enough," Sweet said. She twisted around in her chair to look at the recliner, and then looked back at me. "Fats," she said, "let's work this out." She crossed her arms in front of her on the table, very businesslike. "I'm desperate for money and a place to stay, but I'm not going to fuck you, so you can just forget that."

"Sweet!" I said. I grasped the table with both hands. "I can't believe that you'd—"

"Oh, cut the shit, Fats. You've been jerking off over me for two years. Tell me it's not true."

I could feel my face turn bright red. "It's— It's not—"

"Oh, please . . ." She stared at me a moment, and then sighed dramatically. "Listen," she said. "How about this? I'll share your bed with you at night and walk around naked and stuff, and we can even cuddle some. You can even touch if you want," she said. "I don't mind being touched. But that's it," she said. "No penetration, no bodily fluids. Period. Nothing except nakedness and light touch." She smiled and winked at me. "It'll be fun," she said.

"Sweet," I said. I was shocked. I tried to make my face express my sadness and disbelief. "If you think for a moment that I was offering you a place to stay because—"

"Right," Sweet said.

"I was trying to—"

"Do a good deed," she said. "Right."

"Honestly, Sweet. I swear."

"I believe you," she said. "I know." She rubbed her temples, and then sat back in her chair with her eyes closed as if she were doing a meditation exercise meant to calm her. When she finally opened her eyes and spoke, her tone was friendlier, less businesslike. "Win," she said, "I'd appreciate it if you'd let me share your bed with you tonight, because I'd really rather sleep in a bed than a recliner."

"Well," I said. "I mean—it's a big bed. If you really want to . . ."

"I do. I'd appreciate it." She propped her head up on her hand, cutely, and smiled. "And listen, I know this is a big thing to ask, but if you could let me have some money, just, like, a hundred bucks maybe, to hold me over, I'd be in your debt. Can you do that?"

"You mean," I said, "like a loan?" When she didn't answer, I said, "Well, sure, Sweet. For you, I'd do that."

"Thanks," she said. "And if you could take me shopping tomorrow, after work, I'd appreciate that, too."

"That wouldn't be Wal-Mart where you want to go shopping, would it Sweet?"

"Yes. Wal-Mart," she said.

"I don't know about that, Sweet."

When I said that, her face hardened and she swiveled around in her seat, turning to look at the recliner.

"But," I said. "Okay. If you really feel you need to."

"I do," she said. "I need you to help me out there, Win."

I nodded. "Okay, then," I said. "I will. I'll help you out."

"Good." She slid her chair back and patted me on the knee. "Why don't we get to bed then, all right?"

"Okay," I said. I gestured toward the dishes. "I'll clean this up and you go ahead."

She winked at me and then got up and went to the bathroom, and when she closed the door behind her, I noted that she didn't bother to pull the latch. I cleared the table and scraped the dishes and when I turned on the water to wash the plates, I heard Sweet leave the bathroom and get into bed, and then this wonderful, intense moment happened. I had my hands under the running water, which was warm and soothing, and I was running a sponge over the surface of the plate, and I realized—it just sort of hit me—that Sweet was actually getting into my bed. Sweet. She was getting into my bed. We were going to sleep together, me and Sweet, and when that dawned on me, I was just, suddenly, like, miraculously happy. It was a transporting feeling. It was like God was placing this gift in my hands, putting Sweet into my care—delicate, beautiful Sweet. In my bed. I almost couldn't believe it. I almost thought it was all going to turn out to be a dream.

I finished up the dishes and turned off the lights, and when I got into bed, it wasn't a dream. Sweet was there, her back turned toward me, the covers pulled up to her neck, her head snuggled into the pillows. I pulled back the covers to get into bed and saw that she was naked, and my heart fluttered so wildly I was frightened for a second that I was going to die right there, before I ever had a chance to get into bed with her. I had to just stand there a long moment, holding up the covers, waiting for my heart to quit jumping, and it occurred to me then that she might already be asleep, since she didn't turn around to see what I was doing.

When I finally got into bed, I was careful not to touch her, I don't know why, but after a while I regretted it, because I was just dying to put my hands on her body, just to feel her skin. Then I did something that I had no idea I was going to do. I turned on my side and put my arm around her, touching her forearm first, letting the palm of my hand follow the length of her arm, and I touched her breasts and whispered my great secret to her, something I hadn't told a soul: that I had never been with a woman in my whole life. Not one. Not one single time, and I could feel the heavy tears splashing down onto my chest as I told her. She reached back to pat my thigh. "It's okay," she said. "But that's enough touching for now, all right? Let's go to sleep." She took my hand gently by the wrist and pulled it away from her. "Okay," I said, and I settled onto my back with my arms crossed over my chest. I was breathing hard, kind of choked up. It took a while for me to get calm again, and then I wasn't at all sleepy. After I lay there for several minutes, I realized that the blinds were pulled closed, and we wouldn't be able to see the sunrise in the morning. I got out of bed and went to the window to open the blinds.

Sweet said, "What are you doing, Fats?" Before I had a chance to explain, she added, "You are going to be a gentleman, aren't you Fats, and not tell anyone about this arrangement?"

"What arrangement?"

"My sharing your bed. Others don't have to know about that. You can just tell them you're doing me a favor, giving me a place to stay."

"Well, that's the truth," I said. "That is what I'm doing."

"Okay," Sweet said. "Good then." She was quiet a moment, and I thought she was going to say something else, but she just said, "Good night."

"Good night," I answered, and I got back into bed. For a long time I lay there quietly, listening to Sweet breathe, and thinking about what I might be able to do to help her. I'd buy her stuff for her tomorrow, because I didn't think I could stop her. But maybe over time I could help, maybe even get her into some kind of program. I lay there thinking about that for a long time before my thoughts shifted to the morning, and I fell asleep imagining the sight of the two of us in bed, imagining what we'd look like with morning sunlight coming through the window, with God's light washing over both of us, golden and brilliant and clear, the way His light is, always.

Smugglers

BY FOLDING HIS LEGS SO THAT HIS FEET TOUCHED his thighs, Matt was able to completely immerse himself in hot water—water he had paid for shilling by shilling, dropping small English coins into a rusted metal box one by one to keep the water flowing until the bathtub was full. The tiny washroom was freezing and filled with roiling white mist. Matt held his breath until his chest began to hurt and then he popped his head above the surface just long enough to grab some air before sliding back under. It was three o'clock in the morning.

A half hour ago he had been fucking Janice. She was wiped out and crazy on some lunatic assortment of pills and coke and grass, and she had literally jumped on him and torn off his shirt and bit his shoulder. Janice was fifteen. He hadn't wanted sex, but there no way to deny her. When he came, she was already asleep. He rolled off her and closed his eyes, and then—it seemed to happen instantly—he was dreaming. Uncle Mike, his father's brother, strode toward him in an open, empty place, no surroundings really, just his uncle taking a few steps toward him. He was dressed immaculately in white, like a movie version of a Southern plantation owner, a crisp, white suit tailored to his portly body. He wore a white, brimmed hat, and a white vest with a watch's gold chain dangling stylishly from a vest pocket. His hands were clasped in front of him and he said "Matt, you'll never make it." Then there was a noise and the dream dissolved and Matt woke up with the image of his uncle vivid in his mind, his uncle who in reality was a ragged-looking, thin man with tattoos, who always wore wrinkled clothes and who, his family guessed, had never run a comb through his long, greasy hair.

Someone had been knocking on the door: that was the noise that woke him. The clock on the nightstand said 2:46 A.M. He had rolled off Janice at 2:30. The knock came again, three times, a little louder, but still soft, as if the knocker had doubts about waking him so late at night. When he fully realized there was someone at the door, he sat up straight and his heart took off like a sprinter. His apartment consisted of a single room with a bed; a gas fireplace, which also worked by feeding coins into a meter; and a table and chair that served as a desk and an eating area. He turned on the nightstand light and checked the room. The cocaine was hidden, wrapped in aluminum foil inside his guitar case under the bed. A package of condoms sat in the middle of the table, beside a pair of airline tickets. He tossed the condoms and the tickets out of sight before answering the door. For a moment he had considered flushing the drugs down the toilet, but even half-asleep he realized the bobbies wouldn't be knocking so tentatively.

It turned out to be his landlady with a telegram from home. "It's urgent," she had said, her hair in curlers, her heavy body wrapped tightly in a wrinkled blue robe. "It's from the States." Matt thanked her and she walked away quickly, as if embarrassed. The telegram read: *Uncle Mike had heart attack. Died Tuesday morning. Wake Wednesday and Thursday. Funeral on Friday. Please come home for funeral. Please.* It was from his mother, and when he read it, sitting on the edge of his bed, he got suddenly light-headed. He was twenty-two and he hadn't been home in more than a year. The words his uncle had spoken in the dream came back to him as if through an amplifier: "Matt, you'll never make it." His legs and arms began to shake. In the morning, with Janice, he was supposed to smuggle cocaine into Paris. Janice had done it many times. They were to wrap the cocaine inside condoms and swallow them just before the flight. When they got to Paris, they'd take a laxative and the condoms would come out, the cocaine safe inside. He needed the money and he had flirted with Janice and cajoled her and insinuated himself into her favor, and then he had started sleeping with her, a crazy fifteen-year-old lost little rich girl—all so that she would let him in on her deal. And now he was sure he would never make it. His uncle had come back from the dead to tell him. The flight would take too long and the latex would break down in his stomach and the massive dose of cocaine would kill him.

Water clung to Matt's skin as he climbed out of the bathtub. When he saw himself in the full-length mirror on the back of the bathroom door, he was streaming clouds of mist. He dressed quickly, putting on heavy combat boots and jeans and a torn flannel shirt over a union suit that needed washing. Back in his room, the clothes that Janice had picked out for him, the cordovan loafers and khaki pants, the light-blue shirt with the button-down collar, and the London Fog overcoat—they lay neatly over the back of a chair, pressed and ready for the trip. Janice was sleeping on her side with her knees pulled up to her chest and her hands between her legs. Nights, out in the clubs, she looked like a teenage Shirley Temple gone bad, in torn blue jeans and a leather jacket, with a lingerie-model's body and a little girl's face, a bad little girl. Asleep she looked almost innocent, almost like a baby—but still wild, a wild innocence, even asleep, the way her wavy blond hair curled and tangled around plump cheeks and big eyes. In the morning she would scrub herself pink and pull her hair back into a ponytail before dressing up in a knee-length skirt and schoolgirl white shoes. That was her outfit for the Paris run.

Last time, Matt had helped her slide the condoms down her throat. She didn't need him to help, but there was something perversely erotic about it, pushing the cocaine-stuffed condoms down her throat while she sat on the floor by the bed, her head tilted all the way back and her eyes glittering with something that looked to Matt like craziness. Afterward they had sex. Without asking, she had knelt by the bed, with her stomach on the mattress, and Matt had pulled up the knee-length skirt and pulled down the white cotton panties, and when he looked at her he saw that she was laughing quietly to herself, as if amused by his predictability—as if she knew the whole scene would turn him on because he was a man and she was amused that she was right about him, that she had him pegged.

He pulled his guitar case out from under the bed and unlocked it with a small key he kept on a chain around his neck. He opened it carefully, holding each of the metal snaps as he pulled them up one by one. Inside the case, his guitar nestled snugly against a plush red lining. The polished blond wood of the soundboard reflected the red and blue flames from the gas fireplace, and the hand-carved hummingbird on the pick guard appeared to move in the wavering firelight. Matt lifted the guitar and removed his wallet from a small compartment under the neck. He had two five-pound notes folded neatly next to his long-expired visa. He put the wallet in the back pocket of his jeans, locked up the guitar case, and slid it back under the bed.

Once on the street, he started for Stevie's apartment. Stevie sang for the Flesh Puppets, a band Matt had played with up until a couple of months ago. Matt had quit because he wanted Stevie for himself, and she wanted to do what she wanted, which included sleeping with women. After a few months, he realized anyway that her relationship with him was mostly for show. Really, it was other women that she wanted, lots of other women. So he left. But now, when he needed someone to talk with, someone to tell what had happened, to tell about his dream, he couldn't imagine who else but Stevie. Who else on the planet? He was twenty-two and there had been three women in his life, excluding his mother. There was Cathy from home, from Wisconsin, whom he had started dating in ninth grade and gone out with at least once a week up until the time he shocked everyone and bought the ticket to London. But he had never really been able to talk to Cathy. He might tell her about his dream, and she would listen—but she would be uncomfortable. She would feel like he was turning the tables on her. Cathy was supposed to talk. He was supposed to listen. Then there was Janice, but her communication, with him anyway, was mostly physical. That left only Stevie, and so Matt was headed for her building, which was only a short walk from his. With Stevie, the time of night wouldn't be a problem.

When he arrived at her apartment, he found the door half open. A chokingly sweet haze of incense wafted into the hallway. Matt pushed the door open and found Richie and Dave sitting on the kitchen floor looking back at him with guitars in their laps.

"American Pie," Richie said, a clear note of relief in his voice.

"We been gettin' ripped off by the local scags," Dave said.

Richie opened a cabinet door under the sink and pulled out an ashtray with a couple of half-smoked joints. He placed the ashtray on the floor between him and Dave and took a long drag off a joint. "We heard you coming up the stairs," he said, his voice high.

Matt said, "I'm looking for Stevie."

"There's a surprise," Richie said.

Dave pointed down the hall toward Stevie's bedroom. "She ain't alone, mate."

Matt said, "Is she ever?"

Dave turned back to his guitar. "Not often," he said softly, and he played a few chords and then looked up to Richie, who began to play along with him.

Matt followed the dimly lit corridor to Stevie's room. He stopped in front of the hanging beads that served as a door. The room behind the beads was lit by a single red candle on a curtainless window ledge, and drippings from the castle-shaped candle spilled over the ledge and down the wall to the baseboards. There was no real furniture in the room, only a mattress on the floor and some cardboard boxes spread around to serve as dressers and drawers. In the candlelight, Matt could see Stevie sitting up on her mattress, a sheet held over her breasts, her back against the wall, smoking a cigarette and looking at him through the bead curtain. She was a small woman, graceful in her movements offstage; but when she sang onstage, she moved in jerks, as if some great electric current regularly jolted her: first she'd be singing motionless, limp as the dead, then she'd suddenly fly in spasms around the stage, her arms and legs everywhere, as if she had lost her mind and all control of her body and the music had possessed her, as if she'd suddenly gone crazy—and usually the audience went crazy with her. Matt hesitated on his side of the curtain. He could see another figure curled up beside Stevie on the mattress.

"My, my, hm, hmm, hmm," Stevie sang softly. "You just want to watch?"

"Watch what?" Matt parted the bead curtain and stepped into the room.

Stevie pulled back the covers on the girl sleeping next to her. She was young and smooth-skinned, her body sleek as an athlete's.

"Beautiful," Matt said.

She touched the sleeping girl's hair gently. "You want to join us?" she asked. "She'd be up for it. She's into good-looking men."

Matt sat on the floor beside Stevie. "Maybe," he said. He had tried that once before, sleeping with Stevie and one of her pickups. It had been strange in the beginning, in bed with two women, and even stranger at the end, when it was over, Stevie and her girl asleep cuddled into each other, and him on his side of the bed, alone. He felt like a sexual accessory. And he had been frightened, a kind of deep, unnamable anxiety shaking him up, keeping him from sleeping. In the morning, when he had told Stevie he wouldn't do it again, she had been disappointed. But now, with Stevie's offer, he could feel his blood moving. "I need to talk to you," he said. "Something incredible just happened."

"What?" She put out her cigarette and leaned toward him. Her interest was apparent in her eyes, which took on a vibrant, glittery quality when she was excited. "Really?"

Matt told her about his dream and the telegram.

"Was he sick?" Stevie asked. "Could you have known?"

"He wasn't old. He wasn't sick." Matt touched his forehead as if checking for a fever. "It's blowing me away."

Stevie grinned. She seemed pleased, as if something she already knew was now being revealed to Matt, something that would make them closer when they both knew. "You never saw him dressed like that? An old picture or something?"

"He was a slob. That's the last way . . ."

Stevie said, "Then you know it was real."

"But I need to know what it means."

Stevie slid down on the mattress and propped her head up on one hand. The sheet fell loosely over her breasts. "You want everything wrapped up," she said. "That's why we could never work."

Matt said, "What are you talking about?

"It happened. It's a mystery."

"It doesn't make you ask questions? Like, where's he going? How come he was dressed like that? What happens when you die?"

She touched Matt's knee. "I'm not into controlling things. I'm into the music of it."

Matt closed his eyes and let his chin drop to his chest. He wanted silence for a moment. He wanted to think. Stevie and Richie and Dave—they thought of him as an innocent, as a boy. They called him American Pie, or Apple Pie, even though he smoked dope with them, and played with them, and slept with Stevie: no matter what he did, it didn't seem to change their perception of him. Partly, it was the way he looked. He had a round, boyish face that made him look even younger than he was, young enough that no one ever questioned him hanging around with a fifteen-year-old girl. And he had the straight, white teeth and the healthy skin of a milk-fed, well-cared-for child. He looked like a six-foot, two-inch baseball player from Iowa—which is exactly what he had been in high school, except he was from Wisconsin. But he was twenty-two now, and he wanted something different. He wasn't sure what Stevie meant about "controlling things," or "the music of it," but he wasn't going to ask. "Me, too," he said. "I'm into the music of it, too, but—"

"What about what he said?" Stevie interrupted. "What do you think *that* means?"

"That's the scary part." The sheet over Stevie had drifted down, revealing most of her breasts and her back. Matt could feel his breath catching in his throat when he spoke. "Can I lie next to you?" he asked. "Would that be all right?"

Stevie lifted the sheet, inviting him to crawl in next to her. Matt looked at her for a long moment, taking in her body, the swellings and curves, the light and dark places. Then he lay down next to her, facing her, and she covered them both with the sheet. Behind Stevie, the other woman stirred and then sat up and looked, surprised, at Matt. "What's this?" she said, not bothering to cover herself up, an edge of anger in her voice.

"He's a friend," Stevie said, without turning around. "We're talking."

The woman seemed to think about this for a moment. Then she smiled and said, as if excusing her momentary anger, "I'm still asleep," and she cuddled up into Stevie, wrapping her arms around her chest and snuggling against her.

"What's the scary part?" Stevie said. "Just what exactly did he say?"

"What I told you. He said I'm not going to make it. He took like two steps toward me, and he had this concerned, like sad look on his face, and he goes 'Matt, you'll never make it.'"

"You think he meant as a musician, an artist? You'll never have any success, you'll never be any good? That way?"

Matt shook his head. "I'm supposed to smuggle some coke into Paris tomorrow with Janice. She's done it a couple of times to make money: you put the coke in a condom, you swallow—"

"You're not going to do it, right? Right?"

Matt didn't answer.

Stevie put her hand on Matt's neck, her thumb gentle against his cheek. "You know what can happen?" she said. "You know how long it'll take that much coke to kill you? About two seconds."

Matt laid his head on her shoulder. "I'm out of money," he said. "I've been out of money for weeks. If I don't do this, I've got to go home."

Stevie was quiet for a time. She stroked Matt's hair, running her fingers over the back of his head and his neck. "I see my father sometimes in dreams," she said. "He was killed in the Falklands war—which no one even remembers anymore."

Matt tried to look up, but she was holding his head pressed tightly to her.

"I know it's not just a dream when we're standing under a big orange moon, because that really happened when I was very little. He held me on his shoulder under a moon just like that and told me always to remember it and the moment would never disappear. When we're standing under an orange moon like that, then he's visiting me and it's not just a dream."

"Do you believe that, really?" Matt pulled away from Stevie. "That the dead come back and talk to you?"

"Absolutely," she said. "You shouldn't go tomorrow. No matter what."

Matt turned over on his stomach and pressed his head into the mattress. "I told Janice I'd go with her," he mumbled. "She's expecting me to go with her." He felt sick. His stomach was jittery, on the edge of being nauseous.

Stevie lay her head on Matt's back. "What are you doing with that girl?" she asked, her voice not much above a whisper. "Do you even know what you're doing?"

Matt thought about Janice, about how he could explain her to Stevie. On the surface she looked like a brat. Her father was an earl or a duke, or some such title, and her family was wealthy—extravagantly wealthy. But she hadn't taken a cent from her family since she turned twelve. She had run away and been brought back time and again, until they just gave up on her. She had been making her own way for the last year—mostly by smuggling drugs. She was fifteen. She had poems by Rimbaud committed to memory. She listened to Bartók and Frank Zappa. Matt had met her at a bar when he was still sleeping with Stevie and playing with the band. She had walked up to him and said, "A third of the world lives in poverty and my father has four homes." She was wrecked, of course. She was so high she probably had no idea what she was saying. Matt had laughed and then felt stupid when Janice appeared hurt by his laughter. She had stumbled away before he could think of anything else to say.

Matt closed his eyes and fell asleep without realizing it. When he woke up, it was light out and Stevie and the other woman were curled up together in a ball on the far side of the bed. The other woman was snoring lightly. He picked himself up slowly from the mattress, thinking he might have already made his decision, that Janice might already be in the air, on her way to Paris without him. He quietly left Stevie's room and entered the dark hallway. In the kitchen, he found Richie asleep on the floor, an ashtray near his head and a gallon jug of wine held tightly to his chest, as if he were a child and the jug were a teddy bear. He looked around the room for a clock, but the walls were bare. The only furniture was a kitchen table, and the only thing on the table was Richie's guitar.

Matt stood quietly in the kitchen. He thought about what it would be like to call Cathy. She would be happy to get his call. She might not act that way at first, but she would be happy. When he left the apartment and went out to the street, he saw a husky old man unlocking the doors to a newspaper stand, and behind the newspaper stand, a steady stream of people descending the stairs into the tube station. If he called Cathy, she'd book him a seat on a flight home. When he got off the plane, she'd be there at the airport, waiting. She'd tell his parents and they'd be there, too, as well as her parents. It would be a party, a reunion, a welcome home; he could see Cathy standing there, picture her face, round like his own, her shoulder-length brown hair falling toward her shoulders, the ends turned under in a satiny curl. She was not an especially attractive girl, though she certainly wasn't ugly. Matt thought of her as plain. He had known her since she was thirteen. At the airport, her mother would cry. His mother would cover her mouth with her hands. The men would hang back. Then would come the embraces, the hugs and tears, the pats on the back—and he'd be home.

Matt asked the time at the newspaper stand. It was a little after seven. He started for his apartment. The Paris flight left at nine-fifteen from Heathrow. First he walked and then he ran, and when he opened the door to his room, he found Janice standing by his bed, glaring at him. She pointed to his guitar case, which was in the middle of the floor. "I broke the lock," she said. "I thought you'd just split."

Matt closed the door by leaning against it. "I fell asleep," he said. "I woke up with a dream that—"

"There's a cab on the way," Janice said. "I'm all ready. If you want to do this thing with me . . ." She gestured toward the back of the chair where Matt's clothes were waiting.

In her navy-blue skirt and white blouse, with her hair pulled back in a pony tail and her face scrubbed clean of makeup, Janice looked like a child, like a little girl. For a moment, Matt didn't move. He stood there as though he were paralyzed. Janice stared at him, waiting, and the look in her eyes was a question: What's it going to be, Matt? What are you going to do? Matt's hand moved slowly toward the buttons of his flannel shirt. He imagined again the airport scene as he arrived home: his parents and Cathy's, Cathy walking toward him. Then he remembered a summer night when he was a senior in high school: both families had come to one of his baseball games to watch him play; he had his own cheering section in the bleachers. After the game, Cathy's two little brothers came running across the field to him, as if he were a hero. His parents went home and he went to Cathy's, where Cathy and her mother prepared dinner, while he drank a beer with her father and talked about the game. After dinner they all watched television, and after her parents went to bed, he made out with Cathy until they were both half-naked and supremely frustrated, and then he went home, where his mother had waited up for him and wanted to know how the night had gone. The memory of that night felt like a great weight, or like a pressure suit—something that enclosed him and pressed against him. He undid the top button of his shirt and looked again at Janice, who was looking back at him now with curiosity, like a scientist observing the behavior of an animal.

"Matt," Janice said, her voice not angry. "Just tell me. Are you coming with me or not?"

Matt nodded.

"You're coming?"

He nodded again.

Janice pushed his hands away and began undoing the buttons of his shirt. "You're scared," she said. "I was scared the first time, too. I was terrified." She leaned into him and peeled the shirt off his back.

Matt wanted to tell her about the dream, but the words weren't coming. When she unfastened his belt and pulled his jeans down around his thighs, he sat on the bed and lifted his legs. She knelt in front of him and let his feet rest in her lap while she untied his shoe laces and pulled off his boots. Matt was watching Janice undress him, but he was thinking about his uncle. Once, when he was a boy of eight or nine, he had bicycled to his uncle's farmhouse. He hadn't told his parents because this was a period of time when the talk about his uncle was all hushed and solemn. From hearing the grown-ups, he knew that his uncle Mike had been to war in Vietnam. He had heard bits and pieces of things about drugs and shootings. He had heard some things about women. His uncle kept leaving town and coming back, as if the town were a prison and he could never manage a successful escape, and every time he came back he looked stranger. He had a beard. No one else in the family had a beard. He had long hair. No one else in the whole town, that Matt knew anyway, had long hair.

This time when Matt bicycled to the farmhouse, it was one of the times when his uncle had just come back from being away, and everybody was whispering about him. Matt had bicycled the five miles out of town to the rundown farmhouse where his uncle lived, and he had found him asleep in his living room. He remembered that the house had been neat, but weirdly decorated: hubcaps were nailed to the wall in the kitchen and living room, and his uncle's sculptures that he made out of farm junk were displayed on tables and in nooks and crannies, places where anyone else in his family would have placed a lamp or a knick knack—and there was a closed up wooden crate in the kitchen, hanging by a chain from the ceiling, the kind of crate that's made of wire and thin wood. This one was closed, and a padlock was looped through the wire, so that you'd have to break the crate to open it. Inside the crate was a candle. It was round and it was big, the size of a carnival fish bowl. It was rust-red with a thick black wick that was lit and burning. Wax dripped down the sides of the candle and onto the crate and through the slats to the floor. Matt looked at the crate with the lit candle and he couldn't imagine why anyone would do such a thing: put a lit candle inside a locked wooden crate. He tiptoed into the living room, where his uncle was sleeping in a tilted back recliner with a bottle of whiskey on the floor beside him. He was wearing a crisp white T-shirt with *I* ♥ *Wisconsin* printed beneath an idyllic picture of a farmhouse surrounded by barns and silos and cows lazily chewing grass in a pasture. He was curled up in the chair, hugging his chest, his arms underneath the T-shirt, as if it were a straight jacket. Matt remembered being struck by the contrast between that clean white T-shirt and his uncle's haggard face and jaundiced-looking skin and long, stringy, unwashed hair. He had never told his uncle about the visit, his uncle or anyone else.

This was the uncle who had come to him in his dream. This was the uncle who had told him he'd never make it.

When Janice finished undressing him, Matt stood up and put on the cordovan penny loafers and the khaki slacks, the blue shirt with the button-down collar and the London Fog overcoat. Janice brushed his hair for him and kissed him on the cheek. "Don't be scared," she whispered. "We can do it," she said, and she took him by the arm, gently, and had him sit on the floor by the bed and tilt his head back, the way he had seen her do it, and open his mouth wide. First he closed his eyes; then he opened them and he watched her coat the outside of a condom with some kind of a gel before she lowered it into his mouth and began pushing it down his throat. He gagged the first time, and she told him to relax. Outside, the cabbie honked his horn. Janice opened the window and yelled that they'd be right down. Then she came to him again, and this time he closed his eyes and he imagined what they'd look like as they boarded the plane, like a brother and sister, like a couple of kids going off by themselves on a journey, and he relaxed and tried to ignore the pain as best he could, the feeling like he was being ripped open at the neck as she pushed the condom down his throat.

Tulsa Snow

SHE SAID, "YOU HAVE NO CHARACTER. I SEE RIGHT through you." She leaned across the table, closer to me, her eyes glittering a little, as if she had just told me I was cute.

I tried hard to appear amused. We were seated in a high-backed booth, in a Tulsa, Oklahoma, café. I hardly knew this woman. I had met her maybe an hour earlier in the airport coffee shop, where we were both killing time, drinking coffee, stranded by a snow storm—and beyond the café's big plate glass windows, snow continued falling thick and slow, floating to the ground in big flakes that seemed almost to rock like little boats as they descended. I looked around the café, embarrassed by the turn in the conversation. There were five other people in the place. Three old guys, with big guts and gray hair, in cowboy hats, were seated at one of the round tables in the center of the room. They were silent, looking down at their coffee cups. Behind the counter, a waitress in a black uniform with a white name tag pinned to her breast wiped a saucer with a dish rag. Behind her, the cook stood over the grill with his arms crossed, looking down at the metal surface as if something were cooking there, which nothing was. They were listening to us. They had been watching us and listening to us since we walked through the door. I said, "What do you mean I have no character? What kind of a thing is that to say?"

"The truth," she said. She pushed her hair back off her face. She had crimped blond hair that fell over her forehead and cheeks. She was young, maybe twenty-five, twenty-six. I figured about ten years younger than me.

"Why is it the truth?"

"Why is it the truth?"

"I mean," I said, "why do you think I have no character?"

"Just listen to yourself." She crossed her arms under her breasts and leaned back. She still had that bright look in her eyes that seemed to say she didn't really mean any harm: she was just noting something fascinating. "You're talking like me," she said. "You're picking up my inflections, my tone, even my mannerisms. You're a blank slate. It's as if you're turning into my image as I watch."

I laughed, but it was an obviously uncomfortable laugh. I thought about just getting up and walking out. Unfortunately, there was no place to go. We had taken a taxi from the airport, and I'd have to walk over to the phone, which was in plain view against the opposite wall, call a cab, and then wait. Meanwhile, the place was still as a closet. The cook was a big, heavy guy. You could hear him breathing. I said, "You're an interesting woman, Jessie. Here we were, talking amiably about things—and then suddenly: I have no character. Did I say something wrong?"

She looked at me a long moment, as if deciding how she should continue, as if measuring me and trying to determine what she could tell me and what she couldn't. At the airport, I had joined her at her table because she was pretty and seemed nice, an ordinary attractive blonde with crimped hair, wearing bright sneakers and blue jeans and a green suede shirt with the top two buttons open, looking dreamily out the window at falling snow. I knew myself to be a good-looking man. I had been told so all my life by women and by men. I was tall and muscular, with a squarish, rugged-looking face. I knew I could walk up to most unattached women and start up a conversation and my advances would be welcome. As a salesman, my looks were my chief asset, and for that reason, I kept myself in good shape, working out an hour every day with weights, jogging two miles every morning.

From a distance, Jesse had seemed nice—attractive and nice. And she had acted that way, too, sharing pleasant, friendly conversation with a stranger stuck in an airport during a snowstorm, though her eyes did seem to probe, and she had hesitated often before responding, as if feeling me out. Still, it had all been friendly and pleasant until the character remark. There was something about her that I liked, and I was hoping we might get back on that easy-going track. I sat quietly on my side of the table and watched her watching me. Finally, she said, "Didn't you ever meet someone and have the urge to tell the truth? I look at you and I see someone without any real identity beyond what can be absorbed from others. You're like a sponge, an absence waiting to be filled. You're—"

"Excuse me, Jessie," I said. "I'm not interested in this conversation." I picked up my coat from the bench and tried to take the bill off the table, but she pulled it away.

"On me," she said.

"No, thank you," I said. "I'll buy my own breakfast." I went to the counter and paid for my meal. I wanted to strike up a conversation with the waitress—but she wouldn't meet my eyes. Nor would anyone else in the room. The cook was looking at the back wall and the three cowboys were still staring at their coffee. I thought, *The hell with this*, and went to the wall phone and dialed the airport taxi, only to find the taxis weren't running. Too much snow. I asked, "How am I supposed to get back to the airport?" and the voice on the other end suggested I should worry about how to get to a motel, since I was certainly going to be in Tulsa at least another twenty-four hours. "Oh, great," I said, and hung up. I looked toward the waitress. "No taxis," I said. "You allow camping here?"

One of the cowboys looked up from his coffee and tipped his hat in my direction. He said, "I'll give you a ride, pardner. If you don't mind waiting till I finish my coffee."

My first thought was, given the rate at which he was drinking that coffee, waiting out the snowstorm might be the better bet. My second thought was that he really looked like an asshole in that cowboy hat. I said, "Thanks. That's very kind of you." And then, there I was, just as I had feared: standing next to the phone with my coat over my arm in a room that was like an empty stage—and I felt like I was onstage. I felt as though Jessie and I were actors in an impromptu theatrical production, and everyone was waiting for the climax. In a few seconds the silence grew overwhelming. I thought about joining the three cowboys, but that would have been like walking off the stage and taking a seat in the audience.

The quiet wasn't broken until Jessie shifted around in her booth. She turned to face me, and stretched her legs out across the bench. She spoke as if I were still sitting across the table from her. "Tell me if I'm wrong," she said. "You had a parent who overwhelmed you as a child. Someone who crushed the character out of you."

The cowboys, the waitress, and the cook all looked at Jessie for a moment and then turned and looked at me. It was beginning to occur to me that I had found myself a genuine crazy woman. I thought, *The bitch, the cunt. She's a lunatic.* I put my coat on, taking my time sliding my arms into the sleeves, and then crossed the room to Jessie, not really knowing what I was going to do until I did it. I walked to her table with my eyes on her eyes and I leaned into the booth and put my lips close to her ear. "Jessie," I whispered, "fuck you." Then I walked out of the café and into the snow.

Except for a single pick-up truck, the parking lot was empty. A couple of inches of snow had accumulated already, erasing the yellow lines that divided the blacktop surface into parking spaces. As I crossed the lot to the truck, flakes of snow stuck to my hair. I jammed my hands deep in the pockets of my overcoat and waited by the passenger door of the pick-up, where I had a clear view of the interior of the café. After only a minute or two, the cowboy said a few words to his buddies, and then picked up his coat and came out to give me a ride. Jessie had turned around in the booth again, and was sipping her coffee as she stared out the side window toward a snow-covered field. I yelled, "Thanks! I really appreciate this!" before the cowboy even reached the truck. He nodded and climbed into the driver's seat and I climbed in alongside him.

"Name's Bob," I said. "Bob Resttler."

He nodded, without looking at me. "Pleased to meet you, pardner."

I said, "Do you believe that woman? I never met her before in my life." I made a face that I hope suggested my amused disbelief at her behavior.

"Don't know her at all?"

"I don't know that woman from Adam. I met her an hour ago in the airport coffee shop."

He seemed to think about that a moment and then shook his head.

"Unbelievable, isn't it?"

"Well," he said. "Women . . ." And he shook his head again, as if sorry for the state of the world.

I thought he might say more, but that turned out to be it. For the whole ride. When I got out at the airport, I thanked him again. I said, "I really appreciate this, pardner. Thanks again." I slammed the door and walked away, and it wasn't until I was inside the airport and approaching the airline counter that I realized I had said "pardner" and that was why he had given me such a funny look right before I closed the door. He had sort of stopped midway in a nod and given me this strange look. I tried to laugh at myself—but someplace not very deep at all under the surface I was bothered. I said aloud, "Fuck him." Then added, "Fuck her, too."

Luckily, the airline people were friendly. They arranged a decent motel room for me and even found me a ride—and I know I should have been more appreciative, but I was in a seriously sour mood. I think I might have been able just to laugh off the whole thing if I hadn't called that cowboy "pardner," a word I had never in my whole life ever even considered using. By the time I got to my motel room, I was wondering about the things Jessie had said to me, how much truth there was to them. It was the case, I was willing to grant, that I had a tendency to pick up other people's speech patterns. Put me in Mississippi for a few days, and I'd be talking with a drawl. Put me in Vermont and I'd become taciturn. But so what? That didn't mean I didn't have any character. I was a salesman. I sold financial software to midsize businesses. I had probably just learned to pick up local speech characteristics as a way of relating to people. Why did it have to mean anything bigger than that?

Still, by the time I got settled into my motel room, my sour mood had only deepened. I made a quick phone call to my parents' house and left a message on their machine, telling them not to worry, I was stuck in Tulsa, I'd give them a call tomorrow. I didn't give them the motel number because I knew my mother would call as soon as she got the message, just wanting to be sure I hadn't really been in a plane crash and just wasn't telling her. Then my father would bitch at her for making a long-distance call for no good reason, and when I got back he'd bitch at me for not calling, for only leaving a message, knowing my mother would then have to call back. I'd tell him she didn't have to call, and we'd be off, at each other's throats, same as always. My life was nothing if not predictable. For a while, after I hung up the phone, I sat on the edge of the bed and debated calling back and leaving her my number so that she wouldn't worry—but eventually I decided against it. I had other plans, which didn't involve talking to my mother. I got up and pulled the curtains. I stopped up the bathtub drain and ran the water nice and hot, and then stripped out of my clothes and popped open my suitcase and pulled out a brand new, unopened bottle of Jack Daniel's. I unwrapped a tumbler from the bathroom sink, filled it halfway, and slid my body down into the hot water. There. I was feeling better already. The hell with Jessie I-Have-No-Character. I was in a nice warm motel room with a bottle of whiskey and cable TV—and nobody calling to check and make sure I wasn't drinking. Life was just fine.

I settled back in the tub and lifted the tumbler of whiskey to my lips, savoring the sharp aroma of the bourbon—and just as I was about to take my first sip, someone knocked at the door. I pulled myself up out of the tub, wrapped a motel towel around my waist, and went to the window, where I peeked out through the curtains. It was Jessie. She was standing in the snow without a jacket. I opened the door a crack. "You'll freeze," I said.

She moved closer to the door in order to get a better look. "Got more clothes on than you."

"That's because I was in the bathtub. Did you come to apologize?"

"No, not really," she said. "I came to take you up on your invitation."

"What invitation?"

"Right before you left the restaurant. Wasn't that an invitation you whispered in my ear?"

"I said 'Fuck you.'"

She nodded and smiled. "I've been looking forward to it ever since."

I opened the door and let her in. She came into the room and looked over the matching beds and then up at the fake oil paintings centered over each headboard. They were both seashore paintings, copies of some French painter, people in old-fashioned bathing suits carrying umbrellas, a crowded beach. I hadn't noticed them until I noticed her looking at them. "Well," she said. "Which bed?"

I said, "I've got a feeling I'll regret this."

Her eyes brightened. "You don't need to fear," she said. "I'm not crazy, I promise. I've never been your standard-issue human being, sure. But I'm not dangerous."

I said, "And I don't have any condoms."

She pulled out a crushed box of condoms from the pocket of her jeans. "I had the driver stop at a pharmacy on the way here. Haven't the airline people been really nice?"

"Amazingly so," I said. "Did they just direct you to my room?"

"Same guy drove me as drove you." She tossed the condoms onto the center night table, and then sat on the bed closest to the far wall. "This one okay?" she asked.

"Fine," I said.

"Good, then . . ." She unbuttoned her blouse and undid her belt buckle. "Do you like to watch?" She patted the edge of the second bed, across the small aisle from where she sat.

"You're very attractive," I said. I sat across from her.

She yanked the bottom of her shirt out of her jeans, undid the cuffs, and took it off. "I should be," she said. She took a strand of her hair between her thumb and forefinger. "The crimp is artificial, of course. So is the color. I'm naturally a dingy shade of blond, a sort of sandy blond. No luster at all. But, for a significant amount of money and with bimonthly treatments, we get this: pretty, bright blond hair."

"Very nice," I said. "It's worth it." She had me feeling good again, as she had when we first met. The stuff about my character was fading out of memory. I was beginning to concentrate on the fact that I had an attractive, entertaining woman in my motel room getting undressed for me.

She took off her bra. Her breasts were lovely. "You like them?" she asked.

"I adore them," I said. I reached across the space between us to touch them, letting the warm flesh rest in the palm of one hand while my thumb traced the circle of her nipple.

"Umm . . ." she said. "But they're not real unfortunately. Saline implants."

"No kidding?" I squished a breast in my hand. "Feels real to me."

"That's what counts," she said. She leaned forward and kissed me on the bridge of my nose. She pointed to her own nose: "This isn't the original model either: resized and reshaped." She pointed to her green eyes, which were one of the first things I had noticed about her, how strikingly the green of her eyes picked up the green of her suede shirt. "Contact lenses," she said. "They're really brown."

"Your eyes are brown?"

"Brown," she said. "Plain old. See? I should be attractive. Look at all the effort." She summed up for me: "Dyed hair, colored contacts, breast implants, redone nose." She stood up and kicked off her shoes and then shimmied half way out of her pants and underwear before falling back on the bed, onto her elbows, smiling wickedly and putting her feet in my lap. I pulled her pants off the rest of the way and then climbed onto the bed with her. She kissed my chest, hungrily. I kissed her breasts. They felt great. They felt like real breasts. She pulled back the blankets and slid under. I joined her. "One other thing," she said. "Before we commence."

"What?" I was worked up and breathing hard. I had only one thing on my mind.

"Nothing," she said. She smiled, revealing perfect teeth, white and straight—but she looked, somehow, worried suddenly. A little frightened. "Condom," she said. She handed me the box from the night table. "Can't forget."

There had been something in her look that worried me, though I couldn't place it. It felt as is she had started to tell me something and then changed her mind. I said, "I don't have any diseases. You don't, either, do you?"

"No," she said. "I'm healthy." She pointed to the condom, and her casual, playful look returned to her face. "But you still have to wear it."

"Sure," I said. I put on the condom and we made love. It took me maybe at most a minute and half and then I was finished. This had happened to me before, more than once. It was one of the reasons I wasn't really all that into sex. I pulled myself away from her. "I'm sorry," I said. "I . . . I just . . ."

"What is it?" she said. She touched my chest, her eyes again with that sparkle.

I looked around the dark room. The curtains were pulled and the lights were off. I was tempted to reach for the remote control, which was bolted to the night table, and see what was on the tube. I thought about my tumbler of bourbon on the rim of the bathtub. "Excuse me," I said, and I scurried out of the bed, the condom dangling from my dick like a misplaced elf's cap. I peeled it off in the bathroom, flushed it down the commode, and then fortified myself with a couple of solid swigs of bourbon before returning to the bed.

Jessie was sitting up, her back cushioned with pillows. Her knees were pulled up to her chest and her arms were wrapped around her legs. She said, "Want to see a picture of me?"

I pulled the covers to my neck and lay on my side, my head propped on my elbow. "Sure," I said.

She reached down between the beds and pulled a slim wallet out of the back pocket of her jeans. From the wallet, she carefully extracted a photograph and handed it to me.

"Who's this?" I said. I dropped the photo on the bed, as if I were worried about catching something from it.

"It's me," she said. Same smile. Same sparkle.

I picked up the photo again. The girl pictured in it was terribly ugly. She had the flat, dingy hair of the poor, and a hooked beak of a nose that, amazingly, wasn't her worst feature. The worst feature was her teeth, which were gnarled and twisted in what appeared to be double rows. She looked like she had two rows of teeth and they were all fighting with each other for some space to grow. A couple of the teeth stuck out almost horizontally, useless and freakish. Several of the teeth were discolored and appeared to be rotting. "This is you?" I said. "Was you?"

"It's still me," she said. "Only with the benefit of cosmetic science and a lot of money."

I looked at the photo again. I studied it. It made me feel weird to think that this might really be the same woman I had just had sex with. "I don't believe you," I said. I tossed the photo to her. "Who are you? You are crazy, aren't you?"

She didn't answer for a moment. She watched me with that searching-out look again.

I said, "I just hope you're not dangerous."

That made her laugh. "Why don't you believe it's me?"

"Because!" I said. "Look at this!" I snatched the photo up off the bed. "Look at this girl's teeth!"

"Ah," she said. "Teeth." She smiled brightly, showing off her perfect teeth—and then she blew up her cheeks and made an odd motion with her jaw and she pulled her teeth out of her mouth with her thumb and forefinger. She placed the teeth on the night table beside her.

I got out of the bed. I stepped back, away from her.

"Teeth," she said, sounding suddenly like an old woman.

"Put them back in," I said. "Please." I turned my back to her.

"They're back in," she said, her voice normal again. "Turn around. Look at me."

When I turned around, she was posing. A sultry look about her face, a corner of the sheet held sexily to her breasts, hiding just enough to emphasize her beauty.

I touched my fingers to my forehead. "I'm feeling a little dizzy," I said. I sat down on the edge of the bed and dropped my head between my knees.

She knelt behind me and rubbed my back. "The teeth," she said. "They're a shocker, no?"

"Slightly," I said.

She leaned over me, shaping her body to mine, holding me in her arms. She kissed the back of my neck. She said, "Do you not find me attractive now . . . because of the teeth? because you know how I used to look?"

"No," I said. "It's not that. But it is . . . It's disorienting."

"I can understand that," she said. She nuzzled against me. Her cheek was warm against the back of my neck.

We were both quiet for a while, me with my head between my legs and her with her body wrapped around me. I kept seeing in my mind that picture of her looking so ugly, and then I kept going over the pure weirdness of seeing a young, attractive woman reach into her mouth and pull out her teeth and place them on a night table. Her body felt good against my body, and I knew if I turned around I'd see a beautiful young woman—and one generous enough to not make a big deal out of my pathetic sexual performance—but I was having trouble getting past the picture and the teeth. It was as if, somehow, she wasn't really who she appeared to be. I saw an attractive young woman—but it felt as if that were a mask somehow, as if it somehow weren't real. I tried to think of something to say, but no words came. Then she pulled away from me, and when I sat up and turned around I saw her peek out the curtains and then pull them open, filling the room with daylight. When she turned around she appeared solemn. She said, "Do you want me to leave now?"

Beyond the window, the snow was falling thick as fog. A moment earlier, I think I would have asked her to leave. But seeing her standing there by the window, her body so lovely, her face so attractive, I didn't want her to leave. "Not if you don't want to," I said.

She said, "I don't want to," and came and got into bed with me again.

I leaned back against the headboard and put my arm around her shoulder, and she lay her head against my chest. I said, "How come you showed me that picture? I mean . . . Why?"

"Because," she whispered. "I don't know. I just wanted to tell you. I don't really know why."

"You don't know?"

"Not really."

"Not really?"

She looked up at me, amused. Then I heard myself say, "I'm an alcoholic." She said, "I'm not surprised. I figured something like that."

I didn't say anything right away. If she wasn't surprised, I was. I had never said those three words out loud.

Jessie turned her body toward mine and nuzzled up against me. "Do you mind if I go to sleep?" she said. "I'm deliciously tired."

I stroked her forehead. "But I'm curious about you," I said. "I want to know . . . how . . ."

"We'll talk about it later," she said. "We'll go into details. Both of us. I'll tell you all about my transformation." She turned away and snuggled up with a pillow, and I watched her face relax and her eyes begin to move around under her closed eyelids. I kissed her on the shoulder, and then I went to the window and stood in front of it and watched the snow fall for a long time. In my head, there were words floating: *transformation, Tulsa, snow* . . . I could see the parking lot and a sloping hill and then beyond that the highway and a long line of trees—and all of it, except for the trunks of the trees, was covered with snow. Then, when I turned around and looked at the room again, everything was different. The colors, the textures . . . everything. It was as if something inside the substances of the room had been altered and now all the surfaces looked different. It was very strange. I kept staring at everything: the soft brown wood of the headboards, the blue cotton fabric of the blankets, the white sheets—and the surfaces seemed almost to glow. The colors appeared to pulse and shimmer. It was beautiful, but it was also frightening. I had no idea what was going on with me. Not really. I went to the big mirror over the bathroom sink and looked at myself. At first nothing seemed different. It was still me. Just me. Same muscular, healthy body. Same rugged looks. I stared at my own eyes staring back at myself, and then I guess because I was staring so intensely, the room disappeared out of the background. I stared into the mirror and it was just my body, with a kind of light around me, as if I were floating. I closed my eyes. I extended my arms and tilted my head down, and then I felt as though I were plummeting. I felt as though I were flying. For a few moments it was as if I had no body at all. What I sensed, it was ominous. I felt as if I were a dark spirit, something dense and hard, rocklike, but soaring like a crow, gliding though a pitch-black place, looking for something . . . like hunting, like I was hunting.

When I opened my eyes again, everything was back to normal. I lay beside Jessie on the motel's mattress as if I were climbing into my own bed. I pressed against her. "Jessie?" I said, even though I knew she was sleeping. I looked at her face and tried to imagine under her attractive features the old face with the twisted teeth and a beak for a nose. I laid my head on her breasts and closed my eyes, and I settled toward sleep, thinking not about Jessie, not about how she had once looked so different, but about myself, about my life, what there was of it, and just before I fell asleep that sense of being a small, dark spirit returned, something hunting and angry. I lifted Jessie's arm from where it lay at her side and I draped it over my shoulder. I pressed closer to her, pushing my body into hers, anxious to join her in her sleep and inexplicably grateful to be lying next to her in bed, in a Tulsa motel, with snow falling beyond the window.

Radon

In the summer of 1988, when my older sister turned sixteen and started dating a thirty-four-year-old Amway salesman, my father discovered we had unacceptable levels of radon trapped in our house. That was ten years ago, though it doesn't feel like it. It was a presidential election summer, and in addition to Howard, Julie's new boyfriend, my mother was upset about George Bush's campaign tactics, which she called Nazi-like and un-American. My father was worried that Michael Dukakis might win the election and ruin the economy, and he was also upset because his favorite TV preachers were all in trouble—Oral Roberts said God was going to kill him unless he raised $4 million soon, Jim Bakker was being revealed as a bisexual, and Jimmy Swaggart had been caught with a prostitute—but most of all my father was going crazy about radon, which he was convinced would give us all cancer soon. And everyone was worried about AIDS, which I heard one newscaster describe as a plague that could eventually wipe out half the world's population.

Luckily, no one was worried about me. I was fifteen, an average student, on the baseball, football, and basketball teams, and my two best friends, whom I hung out with constantly, were Mary Dao and Allan Freizman. Mary—a year younger than us and a grade ahead of us—was the smartest girl in the district, and Allan was another all-around athlete, like me. One night that summer my parents were in the living room arguing. They had started out discussing politics and eventually got around, as usual, to radon and Julie's boyfriend. My father wanted to spend four thousand dollars to seal up and ventilate the basement, and my mother wanted him to do something about Howard. "Honey," my father said, "breathing the radon trapped in this house is the equivalent of smoking ten packs of cigarettes a day." "Honey," my mother answered, "your sixteen-year-old daughter is sleeping with an Amway salesman." Upstairs, in my room, I was searching my closet for a dark jacket. Mary, Allan, and I were meeting at McDonald's. We were casing a house we planned to rob.

I don't really know which one of us started the whole robbing thing, but that summer was the beginning and end of it. No one in the world would have ever suspected us. No one did. We must have robbed a dozen houses, all told. In the beginning it was a game. There's not a lot to do on Long Island, so we'd walk around, through the developments. Pretty much, we'd wind up in people's yards, where we'd sit and talk and drink beer and smoke grass when we could get it, and we'd keep an eye on the people through their windows. One night Allan brought binoculars, hoping to catch a peek of someone getting undressed. We didn't. It turned out to be an old lady's house where we wound up. We had a couple of joints with us and Allan wanted to go hunting for a better yard, but Mary just wanted to get stoned. So we compromised. We'd get stoned where we were, and then go looking for a better yard.

Mary's skin looked like it was always deeply tanned. She had big eyes and black hair slicked straight back (she claimed she'd rather die than wear bangs) and pulled into two little pony tails that made her look pixieish, along with being so frail. But God, was she smart. She spoke Vietnamese, French, and English, all fluently, and she always had a book in her pocket. Half the time, Allan and I didn't know what she was talking about, and she knew we didn't know and went on anyway. It impressed us and I think she liked impressing us. Allan and I admired the hell out of Mary, and we were both trying to get her to take off her clothes.

That night in the old lady's yard, Mary was explaining our philosophies to us. "Rick," she said, sitting cross-legged under a tree, slightly above me. She toked on a joint, held the grass in, and then spoke as she exhaled, her voice high and thin. "You're a materialist," she said, pointing at me, the joint between her fingers. "You don't care about what you can't see or feel—and maybe use. But if you can't see it or feel it, man—you don't give a shit about it."

"You mean," I said, "that's like because I'm always saying how I want a hot red Ferrari Testarossa and a big house on the ocean."

Allan took the joint from Mary. He said, "You been watching too much "Miami Vice," man."

I must have been stoned, because I remember rolling on the ground laughing at that.

"What about me," he asked Mary. "What am I?"

"You, man—you're a grade A, number one, no-holds-barred nihilist."

"A what-ist?"

"A nihilist. That means you don't believe in shit. Nothing. Nada." Mary picked up the binoculars and looked at the moon.

Allan thought for a moment, then said: "How do you say that again, what I am?"

"A nihilist."

"And what about you," I asked her. "What are you?"

"Me?" She handed Allan the binoculars and took back the joint. "I'm an existentialist."

We both stared at her.

"That's like a nihilist who's into self-delusion. Sort of."

Allan checked out the house with the binoculars. "Hey," he said. "Look at this."

And that's when it started. Allan had seen the old woman take some money out of a bowl and put it in her handbag. A few minutes later, a car pulled up the driveway and a man took her away. I don't remember who said what first, or if anybody even said anything—but we must have all been thinking the same thing, because a few minutes later we kicked in a basement window, climbed up a flight of stairs, and ran out the back door with the money. Later, Mary said it was the most exciting thing she had ever done. The money came to a little over eighty dollars, which we split evenly. That was a couple of months earlier.

The place we were casing—Allan spotted it driving home with his dad. Allan's father is an ex-cop who owns a topless bar on Jericho Turnpike. Or he did then, anyway. Now I hear he's retired in Florida. Allan always said he didn't hate his old man, because it would take too much energy. He said his father was a stupid drunk who didn't care about anything but screwing the dancers who worked for him. His mother he didn't know. She had left when he was a child. Allan told us that she had moved to Alaska and married a Husky. He said he couldn't blame her for wanting to move up in life.

The house he spotted was only a few blocks from his own. An ambulance had just driven away and a police car was parked at the curb. Allan's dad stopped to talk to the cop, the way he always did, and Allan overheard that the man who lived there was old and three-quarters dead, and kept a loaded gun in every room. At the mention of the guns, Allan said he slunk down in his seat and acted bored while trying to hear every word. The old man used to be important—something about something in World War II, but Allan didn't get the details. Now he refused to live in a home or with his children. The whole thing was too good to pass up. Guns were easy money in the city: we knew a pawn shop that bought them, no questions asked. All we had to do was sit in the old guy's yard and wait for him to leave the house.

I couldn't find the dark jacket I was looking for, so I settled for denim. In the living room, Julie had joined the argument. From the top of the stairs, I could see my father sitting back in his Lazy Boy like a reluctant judge, while my mother stood on one side of the chair and my sister on the other.

"I won't have this!" my mother said, slapping the arm of the chair. "I want you," she said to Julie, "to bring him here tonight. And I want you," she said to my father, "to tell him we'll have him put in jail if this doesn't stop right now." She looked at Julie. "I won't have this," she repeated.

Julie talked to Dad as if they were the only two people in the room. "This is nobody's business but mine," she said calmly. "I'm grown up now. I'll make my own decisions and I don't need any help from anyone."

My father had lain back and crossed his arms over his eyes, as if bracing himself for a crash.

"Dad," Julie said, "look at me."

He lowered his arms. Julie's hair was bright red and shaved at the temples, short over the top, and long in the back, where it was dyed blond. She wore a gigantic crucifix dangling from her right ear, and a 'Jesus Is My Friend' T-shirt that was too small on her: it left a few inches of her stomach bare and her nipples struggling for freedom. Her pants she had slashed with a razor from top to bottom, so from where I stood I could see she was wearing neon pink panties.

My father said, "I realize you're grown up now, Julie—"

My mother sighed.

"But," he continued, "your mother has a point—"

Julie groaned.

"Why don't we compromise," he said. "Bring him over, just so that we can meet him."

"I don't want to meet him!" my mother screamed. "I want you to shoot the son of a bitch!"

"See!" Julie yelled.

My father jumped up, excited. "You know!" he shouted, quieting them both. "We didn't always used to argue like this, did we?"

I thought to myself: this was extreme, granted, but, actually, yeah—they did always argue like that.

"Did we?" my father insisted.

"What?" Julie said.

"What? Radon—that's what!"

My mother covered her face and Julie turned her back to him. They both sighed.

"Go ahead!" he screamed. "Treat me like I'm mad! I'm telling you, this poison we're breathing is half our problem."

For a moment, everyone was frozen: my mother with her face covered; my sister looking at the wall; my father glaring at both of them. Then his shoulders drooped forward, and he left the room with tears brimming in his eyes. He went out into the yard.

My sister went to her room. As she passed me, she said: "What are you staring at, jerk off?"

My mother looked up. When she saw me, her face brightened. I've always had that effect on her, even now. She says I'm the best thing in her life. "Rick, honey," she said. "Come here."

"I'm meeting Mary," I said, on my way down the stairs. My mother loved Mary. When she came to visit, they'd often sit and talk for hours while I wandered in and out, pretending to be interested. My mother never questioned what I was doing, as long as I was doing it with Mary.

By the front door, she put her arm around my shoulder. "Five minutes for your mom," she said. "I need to talk to somebody sane around here."

We sat down on the front steps, under the dim yellow light. Behind us, the bug zapper was working overtime: I can still hear the pop and sizzle of bugs getting fried. "Really, Mom," I said. "I've got to go in a minute."

"Did you witness all that?" she asked. "The whole pathetic scene?"

With me, my mother was always dramatic like that—like I'm this pure thing besmirched by a dirty world. "Maybe Dad's got a point about the radon," I said. "Do you know what it is—radon?"

"Yes," she said. "It's wishful thinking."

I looked down at the steps. I always hated it when she said things that I guessed made some kind of sense if you were smart enough to figure them out—which I never was. I blamed it on the teacher in her. She was a high-school teacher.

"Your father," she said. "Your father's a fool. You know I don't love him anymore."

"I know," I said. "You've told me."

She looked at me. I guess she heard something in my voice. "I shouldn't do that," she said. "I know. Talk to you about your father like that—about me and your father." She was about to cry. Tears were building in her eyes. "It's just that— I need to—"

"It's okay, Mom." I put my hand on her arm.

"Poor Rick," she said. "You have so much to deal with. It must be hard, growing up now: the whole world literally falling apart, society degenerating the way it is."

"Yeah," I said. "It's tough."

"This Willie Horton commercial," she said, perking up. "Here's a man climbing into the White House on the shoulders of a rapist. Could anything be more cynical, more devoid of morality? What's happened to ethics in this country?"

I said, "Yeah." Which is what I always say when I don't know what the hell my mother's talking about.

"Reagan," she said, "coming on the television and lying to the American public like that, lying through his teeth—with *such* sincerity. Liar. Liar. Liar."

I was tempted for a moment to ask her what Reagan lied about. I liked him. I thought he was a good guy. But the temptation lasted only for a second. "Mom," I said. "I have—"

"Go ahead!" She gestured as if she were talking to someone standing in front of us. "Pollute the water, foul the air, destroy the planet! Who cares, as long as you make a buck? God Bless the almighty dollar in whom we trust!"

I tried again. "Mom," I said. "Mary's waiting. Okay?"

"Sure," she said. "You go have fun. Between this greenhouse thing, ozone holes, nuclear weapons everywhere, and, God help us, this new plague, this AIDS—" She stopped suddenly and took hold of my wrist. "Rick," she said. "You're not— You haven't started—"

"No," I said. "I haven't."

"Well, you know about condoms, though? Right?"

I stood up. "Yes," I said. "I'll see you later."

She hugged me. "I didn't embarrass you, did I?"

"Not a problem," I said.

As I was walking down the steps, she asked, "Have you read about the hospital waste washing up all over the East Coast? It's unbelievable what they've found: AIDS-contaminated hypodermic needles, vials full of AIDS-contaminated blood, a stomach lining, chopped off body parts, eye—"

"No, I missed that," I said, walking into the shadows. I called back, "See you later, Mom." Behind me, she stood there by the front door, under the yellow light, and looked out at our quiet suburban street, her face a mixture of disgust and fear, as if in the line of dark houses and neatly mown lawns she saw something repulsive.

I always liked walking on Long Island. There you are, surrounded by millions of people—but they're all locked up tight in their houses, and you could just as well be on the moon as you pass by the blue television light coming from their living rooms fifteen feet away. It's nice: private. I always liked it. A few weeks earlier, I had sneaked out of my house at three in the morning to go over to Mary's. It was dumb, really. We hadn't done anything: touched each other, seen each other, nothing. Then we just decided one night—I'm fifteen, she's fourteen—that we'd do it: have sex, sleep together. So I climbed out my window at three in the morning, and Long Island's something different at that hour. It's changed. The streets are dark and quiet, hardly any cars on the roads. You can hear natural things: the wind shuffling leaves and branches, a bird chirping, that kind of stuff. When I got to Mary's, she had left a ladder leaning against the house, and I climbed up to her bedroom where she was waiting, kneeling by the window in a white cotton gown that pictured Sylvester the

Cat looking over a picket fence at Tweety Bird. I should have known she wasn't serious.

Even if she were, I don't know that I could have done anything: I was so nervous about being in her house, her parents asleep a few door over. Mary's parents were tough. I'm sure her old man would have killed me had he found me there. He used to be a colonel in the South Vietnamese Army. Mary obeyed her parents, but she said she didn't respect them. Her brother, Robert, was gay. According to Mary, he had been all his life. She loved him, and she used to love having him around the house when he was a teenager, in high school, and his friends were over all the time. They practically lived there, especially between three and seven—after school and before their parents got home. Then, when Robert was sixteen and a junior, his parents found out and everything changed. They sent him away to school and forbade Mary to even mention his name. The parents paid his bills and pretended he was dead. And lost Mary's respect. She said her life had never been the same after Robert went away. She was never as happy as she used to be when Robert and his friends were always around the house. They paid attention to her, she said. They treated her like a princess.

In her room, Mary took me by the hand and led me to her bed, where we crawled under the sheets together. She had a flashlight there, and I had this feeling like I was seven years old again and playing "tent" on a sleepover. Mary was happy. I could see it. She smiled and held my hand and her eyes were mischievous and bright. I didn't know a lot about sex then, though I had seen enough of it on television to know I was going to have to get past Sylvester and Tweety before anything happened. Mary had started talking about the heat, which was unbearable that summer, in the nineties and one hundreds day after day; and everybody was talking about the greenhouse effect. Mary was getting into what was going to happen when the polar ice caps melted, flooding the poor, underdeveloped countries where the people were already suffering terribly. She said, "Thirty-five thousand children die every day from hunger. Right now. Imagine what will happen when their whole country turns into a giant lake."

I put my hand on her breast.

She smiled. "The industrialized nations," she said. "They'll have the technology to just pump—"

I tried to pull up her gown.

She pushed my hand away.

"Mary, I thought we said—"

"We did. But I'm worried about AIDS."

"Jesus," I said. "You sound like my mother."

"I like your mother."

"I know you do." She had been to the house a few days earlier and spent most of the evening talking to her. "Mary," I said, "we're both virgins."

Mary lay back on her pillow and let the sheet settle over her like a shroud.

"How can you be worried about AIDS if we're both virgins?"

She said, "You could have gone walking on the beach and stepped on a needle. It's possible."

"I'm going to kill my mother."

Mary grinned. "Mother-killing. I read about a primitive culture once . . ."

Mary went on, but I stopped listening. Every once in a while I'd reach over and touch her breasts and she'd let me, but if I tried anything more, she'd just say, "AIDS, you know," with this look like there was some kind of joke going on that I didn't get. I stuck around till daybreak anyway, and from then on I was always grabbing feels off Mary whenever I could get her alone, which I was constantly trying to do. Years later I found out from Allan that he had had about identical experiences with Mary, only she had never let him into her bedroom in the middle of the night—which I was unreasonably pleased about.

When I reached McDonald's, Mary and Allan were waiting in the fenced-in playground area, sitting under a ten-foot plastic statue of the Hamburglar.

Allan said, "How come you're always late, man? You'd be late to your own funeral."

Mary said, "So what's up with Julie and her new dad?"

Mary had this thing that Julie was seeing Howard because Dad was a nonentity and she needed a father she could love. "Same stuff," I said. We left McDonald's and started for the old man's house. "My father's still got radon on the brain."

"Didn't you tell him," Mary said, sounding exasperated, "that radon's not a problem in this part of the country?"

"He says the tests show radon."

Mary put her hand over her eyes. "I told you," she said. "You can't trust those tests. They're rip-offs."

"But he had some professional radon guys check it out."

"Oh, great." Mary laughed out loud. "What are they charging him to get rid of it?"

"Four or five thou."

Allan joined in. "What are you saying, Mary? They're ripping him off?"

"It's a possibility." Mary rolled her eyes.

Allan thought for a moment. "You think we could pull off something like that?"

"We're too young," Mary said. "You have to be an adult male to work that kind of rip-off."

"Oh," Allan said. "Too bad."

When we got to the old man's house, we found all the lights off. In the backyard, we sat by a mimosa tree. Thick clouds had sailed in, and we couldn't see much at all in the darkness.

"What do you think," Allan said. "You think he's out?"

"I don't know." We had been there once before when all the lights were out, and then just as we were about to break a basement window, the television went on. Loud. Very loud. We could hear it clear all the way out in the yard. "Don't forget last time," I said. "This guy never keeps the lights on. He's weird."

"I wish he had a car," Allan said. "Then we could just look in the driveway."

Mary said, "That's very helpful, Allan."

"I was just saying."

Mary touched my arm. "Go kick in the window. If he's home, we'll just take off. The hell with it."

"Oh, yeah," I said. "And I get shot in the back."

"That's not Wyatt Earp in there. The guy's a hundred and fifty years old."

"Shit." Allan walked casually to the house and kicked in the basement window. He just stood there.

I looked at Mary.

"He's showing us what balls he has."

After a minute or two when nothing happened, he slid through the narrow window and disappeared.

Mary ran to join him. I checked all the windows one last time, watching for any movement, and then joined them.

The basement smelled like no one had been in it for years, musty and damp. Allan was searching the place with his penlight, looking through cardboard boxes and inside closets. Mary and I took out our penlights and looked around. When Allan started up the stairs, we followed. At the top of the steps, a door opened on a dark corridor.

"Let's search the rooms together," Mary whispered.

"Over there." Allan pointed his light at an open doorway.

"This is the part I love," Mary said, almost to herself. "It's so exciting. You never know what you'll find."

Inside the room, I said, in a normal voice, "How come you're whispering when we're the only ones here?"

Mary shushed me. We were in a den, and Allan was searching through the drawers of a rolltop desk. "Bingo," he said, and dropped a Colt .45 on the desktop. "This guy's a regular cowboy." He spun the barrel. "Loaded."

From the other side of the room, I heard a loud click and then Mary: "Holy goddamn shit," she said. "It's open." I turned to see her kneeling in front of a safe. The thing was three feet high and must have weighed five hundred pounds.

Allan said, "Won't be anything in it," and went back to searching the desk.

Mary grabbed the handle and pulled the door open.

I knelt behind her. Inside the safe was a small open area full of papers, and then a bunch of compartments with little round keyholes. Mary tried one and found it locked. "Shit," she said. They didn't look like the kind of compartments you could break into without plastic explosives. I reached around her and pulled the papers out. They were mostly insurance policies and legal documents. One was an eight-by-ten picture of an old guy who I guessed was the guy that lived there. He was dressed in all that long black Jewish gear. "Shit," I said, and turned back to Allan. "I think this guy's a rabbi or something."

"So, man?" Allan sounded pissed. "I'm supposed to give a shit?"

Mary said, "He didn't mean anything."

"Hey!" Allan hurried around the desk. For a second I thought I had gotten him mad enough to fight me, but it turned out he had found a key inside an envelope. He crouched beside Mary and tried one of the compartments. The key turned and he pulled out the drawer. It was full of hundred-dollar bills. Mary whipped the drawer out and started counting, and Allan unlocked the other compartments. They were all stuffed with money—mostly hundreds, some fifties and twenties. "Oh my God," I kept saying. Mary said, "Jesus" every time Allan opened another drawer. By the time he pulled out the last compartment, Allan was laughing out loud, Mary was repeating "Jesus, Jesus, Jesus," and I was slapping them both on the back and whooping.

"Fifteen, twenty thousand," Mary whispered.

"Vacation in Vegas," Allan said. "Shit, we'll go to Monaco!"

"I'm putting mine in CDs," I said. "I'll be rich by the time I'm twenty."

Mary said, "You're such a—"

Behind us, there was a fourth voice. It was small and thin. "Eric?" it said. "Audrey? Is that you?"

We all turned around slowly, and all three of us looked at the gun on the desk top. It was strange. We didn't yell, or make a sound out of fright, or jump for the gun—we just turned around slowly and looked. Perhaps it was because the voice was so small none of us was sure at all that it was really there.

In the doorway, an old man was bent over behind a walker. "Is that you?" he repeated, sounding a little frightened this time, and then he reached up and switched on a light.

Allan and I leaped across the room simultaneously and hit him so hard we knocked him the length of the hallway. He slid back and banged into a closed door. I shut off the light and in another couple of seconds Allan had pulled two trash bags out of his jacket, thrown all the money into them, and handed one to Mary. We went out the back door and tore through a trail of yards until we neared Allan's house.

"Damn," Allan said when he caught his breath. He was smiling. "That guy flew like he had wings, man! He must have thought a truck hit him!" He laughed.

"Shit," I said. "I was scared to death. I thought sure the old son of a bitch would be carrying an assault rifle or something! I thought we were dead, man!"

"He couldn't have hit you with a bazooka," Mary said. "Here. How come I'm carrying this?" She swung the bag of money over to me.

Allan said, "How much you think we got?"

Mary didn't answer. Allan and I got quiet, because when Mary didn't answer, it meant she was mad.

By the time we reached Allan's house, it was drizzling. The light was on in his father's bedroom, so we crossed around to the side of the house, toward the entrance to his basement, which was finished like an apartment. When we passed the kitchen window, we saw a naked girl by the kitchen table, and we froze because she was only a few feet away from us. She was standing there taking the last bites of a sandwich as calmly as if she were fully dressed in the privacy of a locked-up room, and not stark naked directly in front of an uncurtained bay window. She had long, blond hair and a body that made me stare, even though Mary was right there. The girl didn't look a hell of a lot older than us, and the letters LDB were tattooed once in a diagonal line across her right breast, and once again where her pubic hair should have been but wasn't. The letters were tattooed so low there that if she ever let her hair grow back they'd be covered entirely. She finished the sandwich, wiped her mouth with the back of her hand, and left the kitchen.

"Ouch!" I looked at Mary. I was trying to make a joke, because I was a little embarrassed about the way I had stopped and looked. "You think that tattoo hurt?"

Mary was standing with her hands on her hips. "I don't know," she said. "I heard branded cattle don't really feel it."

Allan said, "Another dancer—my dad's latest. Come on." Inside the basement, we emptied the money onto a poker table, and Allan pulled down all the shades and locked the door to upstairs. Mary sat at the table and started counting. Allan stood across from her. "So what are you so pissed about?" he asked.

"You didn't have to hit him so hard," Mary said, without looking up from the money. "You probably killed him."

"Get out of here!" Allan said.

I said, "We didn't kill anybody." It turned out later that I was right, though we did break the old guy's hip.

"You didn't have to hit him so hard," Mary said, counting faster.

Allan leaned over the table. "What are you, feeling guilty?"

She didn't answer.

"Shit," Allan said. "What's an old guy like him need it for?"

"All he's going to do is leave it to his kids," I said. "And I don't see them doing anything for him."

Mary looked up from the money. "Twelve thousand, four hundred."

"Man," Allan said. "I thought it was more."

"Me too," I said.

Mary divided the money into three stacks. She took one, wrapped it in her bag, and stuffed the bag into her jeans. "This is the last time for me," she said, and started for the door. "I'm not doing it anymore."

I grabbed my money, bagged it, stuck the bag under my shirt, and hurried to catch up with her.

Allan threw himself across the table. "Hey, come on guys! Why don't you stick around awhile?" He gestured toward the ceiling, meaning he couldn't go upstairs because of his father.

Mary was halfway out the door. "Can't you just go up and go to sleep?"

"Too many funny noises." Allan grinned.

Mary hesitated, as if she might change her mind and stay—which I hoped she wouldn't because I was looking forward to being alone with her. Finally, she said, "Just go to sleep down here, Allan." And she walked out.

"I got to go," I said. "I told my parents—"

Allan waved me off. As I closed the door he was counting his money.

I walked Mary back to her house. The clouds had blown over and it had stopped raining. We hardly said a word to each other until we reached her block. I always knew she was more sensitive about things than she let on because of how she talked about Robert, and because of that night I spent at Mary's: once when she had fallen asleep for a while, I looked through a bunch of books she had lined up under her window, where she liked to lie and read, and they were all books on philosophy and religion, the kind of stuff I don't think anybody even writes anymore, and there was another book too, about the Vietnam War, something Mary never talked about, and when I opened it up, I found things underlined, including the number 13,500,000, which wasn't just underlined but circled, and it turned out to be the number of Vietnamese killed and wounded in the war—which surprised me, because I always thought it was such a small place that I wouldn't have guessed there were that many people in the whole country.

When we reached her house, all the lights were out. Mary said, "My parents must still be in the city. I thought they'd be home by now."

"Can I come in then?" I asked. "Come on—we can just forget about tonight."

"Why?" she said. "Why do you want to forget about some old blind guy we just beat up and robbed?"

"He wasn't blind and we didn't beat him up."

"Christ," Mary said. "He was mostly blind—that's why the lights were never on in the house. And he was mostly deaf—that's why the TV came on so loud. He's probably a little senile, too. I'll bet anything he thought we were his kids. I'll bet anything he's got children named Eric and Audrey. And I still won't be surprised if I read in the paper tomorrow that you guys killed him, you hit him so hard."

"We didn't kill him," I said. "All we did was knock him down the hallway so we'd have time to get out. You know," I said. "Nobody had to drag you into this. You liked the whole thing as much as we did."

"Because it was a game. We were stealing little shit. We weren't hurting anybody."

"Come on, Mary. Insurance'll cover the guy's losses, plus he's got kids who can take care of him. Plus he's so goddamn old what's he going to do with the money?"

Mary just looked at me. She said, "You don't believe in anything, Rick. Nothing at all."

I took a step back. Without thinking, I said, "What's there to believe in?" Then I added, quickly, "I know what I believe. I believe that you and I should make love, the way we said we would, because I don't know what the hell we're waiting for."

Mary nodded, as if agreeing with herself about something. She was quiet for a while, and we both stood there on her doorstep staring at each other. Finally, in response to my proposal, she smiled and said, "AIDS, you know."

"Stop that shit." I moved closer to her. "We're virgins. We can't have AIDS."

"I'm not a virgin," she said. "I had sex when I was twelve with one of Robert's friends, and now I found out he has AIDS. So does Robert. That's where my parents are tonight. Making arrangements for him to stay in a hospice in the city."

My knees got that feeling, like they'd turned to water, and I felt shaky and chilled. I was thinking about the times I made out with Mary, how we'd stuck our tongues in each other's mouths. I didn't say it, but Mary knew what I was thinking.

She said, "You can't catch AIDS from kissing," and went into her house and closed the door. That was the end of it. I never saw her again, except at school, and she never said another word to me or Allan.

I walked home telling myself you couldn't catch AIDS by kissing, and by the time I got home I had myself pretty well convinced, but I couldn't help feeling a little nervous about it anyway. On the porch, I checked to be sure the money was well hidden under my shirt, and I tried to look casual as I walked through the front door. No one was in the living room, but the door to the basement was open, and Julie and Dad and a guy I guessed was Howard were all crawling around on their hands and knees. They looked like they were grazing. They didn't notice me and I walked by the open door and found my mother alone in the kitchen with the lights off, sobbing. I didn't know what to say, or if I even wanted to say anything, but she had seen me, and I couldn't just ignore her. "What's wrong?" I asked.

She shook her head.

I pointed to the basement. "Is that Howard with them?"

She nodded.

"What are they doing down there?"

"Looking for cracks," she hissed. "Howard sold your father some gunk to seal up the cracks and keep the radon out. The three of them are down there like a little happy family sealing up the basement."

"Oh," I said. I had forgotten about Dad's radon problem.

"You know what he told your father?" she asked, still hissing. "That they were just friends. That they had a 'platonic' relationship. That's what he said." She spit out the word "platonic."

"Right," I said. Julie had been sleeping with the guys she dated since she was thirteen. At fifteen she had an abortion, and after that my mother put her on the pill.

"And he believes her," my mother said. She started crying again.

I left her there in the kitchen sobbing and went up to my room. I undressed and stuck the money under my pillow and got into bed, and for some reason that little time between getting into bed and falling asleep is what I remember best and sharpest about that night. It's a vivid memory—clear and troubling in a way I can't pin down. I think now that I was in love with Mary, and I remember that night because that was the end of it—but it's something more, too. Like it means something, but I don't know what. I've never stolen anything since, and neither, I'd guess, have Mary or Allan. They both went on to college, as I did, and now Allan does something with some corporation, and Mary's married and has a couple of kids—so she didn't have AIDS after all. I never heard what happened to her brother, but I'm sure he's dead by now. I'm an engineer with Toshiba. I'm still single, I screw around a lot, but someday I want to get married. I never spent my four thousand from the robbery. It's mixed in now with a few thousand more, all in CDs. I can't say I ever really felt guilty about the robbery—so that's not what bothers me in the memory. It's something else. I'm in that bedroom waiting to fall asleep, the money's under my pillow, Mom's crying downstairs, and Dad and Julie and this guy Howard are crawling around trying to seal up the basement— and it all feels like it means something that it's somehow beyond me to understand. It's like one of those dreams when you've lost something important, when something tremendously important is missing, and you don't even know what it is.

The Professor's Son

———⟁———

THAT WINTER I WAS FIFTEEN, AND HOW MY FATHER was related to me was still a mystery. He was a mathematics professor. I, his only son, could barely multiply. He wore khaki slacks and solid-colored shirts to university meetings, while I wore denims and holey Ts to the "alternative" high school, which was where they sent all the troublemakers at that time, in a whole separate building from the regular high school. He drove a forest green Ford Taurus. I had a chopped Harly in the garage, which I worked on constantly and hoped to have on the road within the year. He was mellow, calm-talking, even-tempered, no matter what the situation. I wore a thin leather jacket, had a natural snarl and a temper that regularly got me into trouble, and was the principal reason I wound up in the alternative school with all the hoods and druggies. To his credit, he never tried to force me to be like him. He seemed, genuinely, to accept me as I was, which I found al-ternatingly maddening and life-sustaining. In general, and to the surprise of everyone who knew us, we got along well. The only serious problem between us was my mother, and it was only for that winter, when she was living two blocks away with Vance Howell, a guy my father actually worked with at the college.

　　She had moved out the previous fall, just up and disappeared one morn-ing and then waited twenty-four hours before sending word of her whereabouts. I was hardly heartbroken over her departure. If we had ever gotten along, I had no memory of it. She drank too much, she was always on somebody's back about something, and she had a bad habit of hitting people, especially me. She was a small, thin woman. By the time I was thirteen and five-foot-ten, 150 pounds, I was a good six inches taller than her and forty pounds heavier—and I still flinched whenever she made a sudden movement in my direction. I had seen her hit my father on numerous occasions, though he was so much bigger than her that he could just turn his head, absorb the blows, and wait for her fury to pass. I never considered her leaving a terrible loss, but I did consider it an insult. It made me crazy that my father was so damn calm and understanding about it all.

One night that winter, I was awakened by the wind and came down into the living room to find him sitting by the window with all the lights off. He was in his stuffed chair, looking out at the backyard, at moonlight on a crust of icy snow. The weather was nasty. Wind blew a wild range of music, from low, agonized moans to high-pitched, hysterical howls, back and forth, up and down. In the dark, it was eerie. The house was messy and full of clutter, just as my mother always predicted it would be should she ever stop picking up after us. There were coats and scarves piled up on the couch, discarded newspapers and magazines everywhere, and shoes and boots and socks all over the place. I had recently had a cold, and my discarded, crumpled tissues, like little white pock-marks, were spread all over the house. I looked into the kitchen, where the digital clocks on the stove, microwave, refrigerator, and clock-radio said it was 12:00 A.M., 12:17 A.M., 12:03 A.M., and 5:30 P.M., respectively. I couldn't tell whether or not he knew I was there, standing at the foot of the stairway, looking at him across the dark house. Then he turned around. He didn't say anything. He just took hold of the back of his neck and started kneading the flesh as if he were searching for something under the skin.

I pulled an ottoman up to the window and sat alongside him. "Look, Dad," I said. "Why don't we do something about it?"

He sat back in his chair, gripped the armrests, and turned his gaze on me in full Abe-Lincoln pose. He's a tall man with a unruly beard, though, unlike the president of myth, he's burly and thick-chested. He said, "About what, Matt?"

I didn't bother to answer. We both knew what I was talking about.

"There isn't anything to do about it," he said, after several long moments of silence. "It's just the way it is." He turned back to the window.

"We could do something to him." I folded my legs under me and wrapped my arms around my chest, as if the chill from outside were making its way into the warmth of our house. "Not Mom," I said. "We don't have to do anything to Mom. Just him."

"Matthew—"

"Why not?" I jumped in as soon as he used my full name, which meant a patient explanation was coming. "I mean, why the hell not, Dad? I'm not saying kill him or anything. Just, like, beat the hell out of him. Put him in the hospital. Show Mom what's up, that's all."

He looked up to the moon at that point, as if there were another adult up there who shared his consternation at my suggestion. Then he turned his most pissed-off glare on me. "I don't know where to begin responding to that."

I snarled, "I didn't think you would."

"What does that mean?"

"It means, what the hell *do* you know, Dad?" I kicked over the ottoman. "She walked out on you for this prick! Don't you have any pride?"

"Oh, Matthew," he said immediately. "Please." His response was so rapid and dismissive, it blunted my outburst completely—which made me even more furious.

"Okay," I said. "Fine." I tried a small laugh, as if I weren't really bothered at all. "You don't have to do anything," I said. "I'll do it."

He leaned over and righted the ottoman. "And what is it that you think you're going to do, Matt?"

"I don't know," I said. In truth, I had been thinking about things I might do to Mr. Vance for months and had a whole slew of options from which to choose, most of them having something to do with his precious car. He drove a Porsche Boxster convertible so bright red it looked wet in any weather. He had the thing polished to a sheen that could blind in bright sunlight. Every time I saw him and Mom driving some place in that thing I wanted to take a sledge hammer to it. "How about I pour a pound of sugar down the gas tank of that car of his?" I said.

He laughed at that and blushed, as if he were embarrassed at his reaction. "The car is a little flashy, isn't it?" he said. "He told me he's adding a garage to his house in the spring. Just for the car."

"He told you." I put my hands on my hips.

"Yes. He told me. We talk, Matt. We're civilized human beings." He got up then and went into the kitchen, where he turned on the light and began rummaging through the cluttered cupboards. "Actually," he said, and then hesitated. "Actually," he repeated, "he says that he and your mom are thinking seriously about marriage."

"Oh, they are?" I walked out of the kitchen, into the living room, and then back into the kitchen again. I could hear a whine in my ears, as if my blood were moving so fast it was starting to whistle. "And you have no problem with that?"

"Matthew . . ." In the cupboard alongside the refrigerator, he located a jar of honey, which apparently had been the object of his search all along. It was glued to the bottom of the shelf by drippage and he tugged at it distractedly until it finally came away, pulling the whole sheet of shelving paper along with it, upsetting boxes, jars, and bottles in the process. The shelving paper was actually plastic of some kind and wouldn't tear loose. I noticed a scissors lying on the stove and handed it to him. "What am I supposed to do?" he said, while cutting a circle around the bottom of the jar. "Chain her down?" He pressed hard on the top of the honey jar, straining until it finally came loose. He held the jar in one hand and the top in the other. "This is a lesson you might as well learn, Matt. Some things, there's nothing you can do about it, no matter how much. It's just the way it is. Better to accept it, deal with it, live with it, than to run around blowing yourself up over it."

"Blowing yourself up over it?"

"You know what I mean." He put the jar down on the counter and went about heating up a small pan of milk. "You want some?" he asked. "Milk and honey. It's good to help you sleep."

"I'm not going to blow myself up." I crossed my arms over my chest. "I'm going to blow him up," I said. "I'm going to blow up his fucking car."

"Matthew," he said. But I had already marched out of the kitchen, and was halfway up the stairs.

In my bedroom, I changed quickly into full winter gear, including thermal undies, as if I knew exactly where I was going and what I was going to do—which I don't think I did. When I was dressed and ready, I turned out the lights and went downstairs to the hall closet for my winter coat and gloves.

My father was on the couch, across from the closet, sipping his milk and honey. He said, "Where are you going?"

I ignored him. When I was all buttoned and zipped up, I started for the door.

"You forgot your hat," he said.

I touched my head. "Thank you." I found my wool hat in the top of the closet, pulled it down over my ears, and left the house, closing the front door tightly behind me.

Outside, the wind was blowing hard. The street and the narrow sidewalks that ran around the development were clear of ice, but everywhere else the glazed surface of the snow glowed a luminous white under the pale circle of a full moon. I trudged around to the back of the house, ice cracking and breaking under my feet, until I reached our shed, which was a fairly elaborate structure compared to the everyday, suburban storage shed. Ours was as much a workroom as it was a storage area. It was heated and insulated, half as tall as the house, with a large loft space, reachable by ladder, and a worktable and sufficient tools hanging from Peg-Boards and stored in metal cabinets and on wood shelving to build just about anything. There was also a television hooked up to a cable jack, and a screaming yellow telephone that lit up like a firefly with each ring. The phone had its own separate line, with its own phone number, which always impressed me as a kid. Before my mother left, my father spent a good deal of time in the shed, including numerous nights on the cot in the loft.

By the time I closed the door behind me and turned on the lights, I had settled on a plan. I was going to blow up Vance's Porsche. I couldn't be sure that it would literally blow up, but I thought the chances of that were pretty good if I dumped five or so gallons of gasoline onto the luxurious leather and carpet of the interior and then tossed in a match. I was pondering the problem of how to toss in the match without killing myself in the process, when the phone rang. It startled me. My heart leaped so hard at that first ring, it was like I felt the whole organ move, and I was afraid I might have ripped or shifted something that wasn't supposed to rip or shift. I picked up after the third ring. "Sheffield residence."

"Very funny," my father said. "What the hell are you doing, Matt?"

"Looking for the five-gallon gas container we have out here somewhere. You know where it's at?"

"Behind the lawn mowers," he said. "What do you plan on doing with it?"

"Just what I said."

"Which was what again?"

"Blow up Vance's precious Porche."

"Matthew," he said, "you're not going to do that."

I said, "Yes, I am," and hung up.

In the back of the shed, behind the two identical red lawn mowers, one that worked and one we kept for parts, I found the five-gallon container. It was almost full, as I knew it would be because it was my job at the end of summer to empty the oil in the lawn mower, clean and store the spark plugs, and dispose of the leftover gasoline—and I knew I hadn't done any of that. On the work table, I found an oversized screw driver that would work perfectly for slashing the convertible top. I put it in my coat pocket and surveyed the shed again. I still had the problem of igniting the gas. I noticed a brand-new, shiny ax handle leaning against the wall next to the shed door, and the notion of using it as the stem for a torch that I could light and toss into the car from a distance popped into my head with the recognizable click of inevitable rightness. I had just finished wrapping the rags around the top of the handle when the phone rang again.

"Matt," my father said. "What the hell are you doing out there?" He sounded tired.

"Getting stuff together," I said. "I'm just about ready."

"To do what?"

"I told you what I'm doing."

"Matthew," he said. "Do you have any idea the number of years you're taking off my life?"

"Hey," I said. "You might be willing to let him get away with this shit, but I'm not. This is just the start. Who knows what I'm going to do next?"

"Certainly not me," he said.

"Damn right."

"Look, Matthew." He paused and made a pained noise, half-sigh, half-moan. "Look," he repeated. "Come back in the house. You're not blowing up anybody's car."

"Really? Why not?"

"Because," he said. "Civilized human beings don't go around setting fire to their neighbor's Porches."

"Civilized human beings don't go around stealing their neighbor's wives."

"Yes, they do," he said.

"Then they also blow up Porsches." I hung up on him again.

A moment later I was outside, making my way across the lawn toward Vance Howell's red Boxster. As I stepped into the street, I noticed, out of the corner of my eye, a movement in our lighted living room window, and I knew if I turned around I'd see my father standing there, probably with his hands on his hips, watching me walk away with a gas can in one hand and an ax handle in the other. His face would have that sad, stricken look. He'd be wondering what the hell I planned on doing with his new ax handle. I considered stopping while he could still see me and then lighting the torch. I liked the idea of the reaction it might produce in him. I imagined him stepping away from the window and rubbing the back of his neck violently, as if the things I did aggravated some nerve center back there. I also thought it would be really cool to light up the torch. I was looking forward to it. I decided to wait though, for obvious reasons. It wasn't all that late at night, and just one neighbor watching Letterman to the end who noticed a kid walking through his or her yard carrying a lighted torch could blow the whole plan.

I wondered, as I trudged over the crusty snow, what my father's life would have been like without me or my mother in the picture. I suspected that numbers and equations and woodworking projects were all he ever really needed to be happy. As a little kid, I used to watch him at work in his study, bent over his papers for hours on end. I'd look in on him in the morning, before going outside to play, and he'd be there at his books, oblivious to anything and everything around him. Because noises distracted him, he put in ear plugs and wore shooter's headphones/earmuff things to keep out the sounds of the everyday world. Because he chilled easily while working motionless for long periods, he wrapped himself in a thin tartan blanket, summer and winter. I grew up thinking it was normal to have a father who spent his days wrapped in a tartan, wearing earplugs and headphones, bent over scraps of paper utterly motionless, just staring at numbers and symbols indecipherable to me, or most anyone else for that matter. If it weren't for my mother and me, I really don't think he would have thought about anything else at all.

My father was in the back of my mind as I cut across those neatly maintained suburban yards. I was probably worried about him. Neither one of us had had a decent meal since my mother left. We'd been eating stuff out of boxes and cans for months, stuff that came in shrink-wrapped plastic, designed to be thrown into a microwave. I didn't mind for myself, but, as I said, I just found it all insulting and somehow dangerous for my father. A man like him shouldn't be left to his own devices. I felt like my mother shouldn't be allowed to get away with it. There was something outrageous about her leaving, and now actually thinking about marrying that asshole Vance Howell. What did it say about me and my father that she would leave us for a guy with a shiny red car? Nothing good, that was for sure. If she had to drink to deal with us, fine, let her drink, but to just walk out— That was too much. Someone had to do something about it.

When the Howell residence came into sight, my heartbeat started picking up noticeably. The place was one of those fake two-story Colonials, with fake white columns and a sloping lawn that slid down to the street and a wooded area that curved around the side and back of the house. The blacktop semi-circle drive was cleared entirely of snow, and the Boxster was parked by the front door. It looked as though it had been perfectly centered so that Howell could step out of his house and into his car with a minimum number of steps. It occurred to me that there might be, given the car's location, some danger of human injury when the thing blew—not to mention the possibility of catching the house on fire. It was not my intention to cause anyone any actual physical harm. I was intent only on doing serious property damage. Lights were on inside the house in upstairs and downstairs rooms, which surprised me since at home Mom was always asleep before ten o'clock, sometimes by nine. I decided that it was probably Howell awake inside the house, doing whatever the hell he did late at night, and that that was good. It meant he would notice the flames and call the fire department before the whole neighborhood went up in smoke. Hopefully, he would have enough brains to get him and Mom out of the way before the thing blew up. Myself, I planned on watching it all from behind his neighbor's house, across the street.

I checked the windows one more time to make sure no one was watching, glanced up and down the street, rested the ax handle on my shoulder like a rifle, took a deep breath and marched up the driveway. When I reached the car, Vance Howell opened the door and stepped out to greet me.

"For God's sake," he said. "You were actually going to go through with it, weren't you?" He was dressed in a long, navy-blue overcoat, one of those dumb-ass Russian hats that look like little boats or something, with boots and gloves. Between the bottom of the coat and the boots, though, I could see his flannel pajamas, and I figured out immediately that my father must have called and gotten him out of bed.

"Go through with what?" I said. I put down the gas container, gripped the ax handle in both hands like a baseball bat, and shifted it to my right shoulder in a position that I hoped looked threatening. Howell was younger than my father, closer to my mother's age, who was something like eight or nine years younger than my father. That still made Howell an old guy, though, probably in his forties, but he didn't look that old. He looked like he was in good shape, even with the coat and that stupid Russian hat.

"Your father said he thought you wouldn't actually do anything, but I don't think so," he said. "You know that? I think you were actually going to set fire to my car."

"What makes you think that?" I said. I looked down at the gas container and up at the torch. "Are you psychic?"

I hadn't quite gotten the word "psychic" out when he grabbed me by the coat collar and pulled me up against his chest. His nose was only a few inches from mine, and my arms were pinned between us. The ax handle stuck up out of our pressed-together bodies like some kind of flag pole. "You were," he said. "Weren't you? You were going to set fire to my car."

"Me? Set fire to your car? No," I said. "I just came over to see if I could borrow my mother back for a little while. Our place is a total wreck and I was hoping—"

"Shut up," he said, and pulled me up against him tighter, almost lifting me off the ground. "I'm not like your father. You mess with anything of mine and I'll rip your heart out, you little prick." He picked me up and threw me down on the ground, hard. I landed flat on my back and I think I bounced and turned over because I remember seeing the sky go all red-maroon for a second before I found myself lying on my stomach, my face on the blacktop, with blood coming out of my mouth, a front tooth wobbling under my tongue. The ax handle was still in my hand and I remember just sort of waiting there a moment, waiting to see what he'd do or say next. I half-expected him to kick me, like in the movies, a kick to the ribs followed by some smart-ass comment. I didn't know what I was going to do if that happened, but I do know that I was gripping that ax handle hard.

He didn't kick me, though, and he didn't say another word. When I looked up, in fact, he was gone. I pulled myself to my knees, wiped the blood from my face, and surveyed the house. I would have heard the door had he gone back inside, but I looked there anyway. The front door and the storm door in front of it were both sealed closed, just as they had been when I first arrived. I stood up and checked all the windows. It occurred to me that my mother might have appeared on the scene, and that was what kept him off me, but the windows were all curtained, with half-circles of ice like crooked smiles on the lower panes. I was beginning to think the guy might have had a heart attack and just keeled over somewhere out of sight, but when I walked out onto the grass, away from the porch light, I saw him floating backward at the bottom of the lawn. It looked like he had two heads: one turned up toward the sky, the other whispering into the first one's ear. And he was floating, not walking. His legs were actually off the ground.

When I took a few more steps in his direction, I saw that the second head belonged to my father, who was holding Howell's neck between both his arms, in a hold that looked like something you see the cops do on the news when they're restraining some maniac. He held him off the ground in his arms as he moved backward toward the woods. "Dad!" I yelled, and ran to him, where it was apparent that he was strangling Howell. My father's face was so deep red it seemed almost black. Howell's face was rapidly turning blue. "Dad," I said, standing right in front of him. "Dad," I repeated. He didn't seem to hear me. He just kept taking backward steps, whispering indecipherable stuff into Howell's ear. "Dad?" I jumped up and hit him on the shoulder, but even that failed to pull him out of whatever trance he had fallen into out there. At that point, Howell's eyes were bulging and his head was wobbling as if he were about to lose consciousness. We were well off the lawn and making our way into a maze of shrubs and bushes and trees. "Jesus Christ, Dad!" I screamed, loud as could. "All he did was knock me down!" He still looked as though he didn't even know I was there, and it suddenly became clear to me that if he didn't let Howell loose mighty soon he was going to kill him. I realized that at about the same time I realized I was still dragging my torch along with me. I put the two realizations together and smacked him across the head with the ax handle. Hard. The part with the rags wrapped around it, but still, hard. Like swinging a baseball bat.

That seemed to get his attention. He dropped Howell, who fell on his face into the ice-crusted ground, choking and grunting. At about the same moment, my mother's voice came from the house, calling for him. "Vance!" she called. "Vance? Are you out there?"

My father looked at me and then back toward the house, the redness draining from his face. He said, "I think we'd better get out of here." He rubbed the spot on his head where I'd hit him.

My mother couldn't see us where we were standing in the woods, but we could see her perfectly. She was on the porch, directly under the light, in slippers and a robe that she was holding pulled tight around her. She looked different. Better. Her face seemed less gaunt and pinched, as if she were recovering from a long illness and just regaining the fullness of her features. It pissed me off. "Yeah," I said softly. "Good idea."

My father took my arm and led me out to the road, on a long route back to our house that had the advantage of keeping us out of sight. When I looked behind me one last time, I saw Howell pulling himself to his feet, bent over and breathing hard, both hands pressed against his chest, as if he were busy giving himself CPR. Under the porch light, Mom stared at the gasoline can as if it were a puzzle piece and she was trying to figure out where it went.

After we had been walking awhile, with Howell and my mother a good way behind us, my father said, "Everyone in the department knows he's an asshole."

I said, "I thought you were going to kill him."

He shook his head. He said, "I can't believe I behaved like that." He sounded genuinely sorry and surprised. "Thank-you, Matt," he said. "Thank-you very much."

"For what?" I said. "Hitting you with an ax? Any time."

"For stopping me," he said, ignoring my attempt at lightening things up a bit. "It was as if— It was like I fell right back into the way I was as a kid. Like I dropped right back into it."

I said, "You used to strangle people as a kid?"

He made a little gesture with his head and shoulders that suggested that, in fact, there were some such occasions in his youth.

"You're kidding?" I said. "You got into fights when you were a kid? You?"

"It never seemed like the kind of thing I should tell you about," he said. "I didn't want to encourage you."

"That's—" I said. "This is—" I was amazed. At first it was just shock and surprise that my father could have ever been anything other than the calm, even-tempered man I'd always known, but then I started thinking about the implications that held for me. If my father was like me as a kid, would I be like him as an adult? The very possibility silenced me completely, and I walked along beside him through the icy cold in a reverie of contemplation. When we'd been walking awhile and I realized we were finally nearing our house, I stopped, found the matches in my coat pocket, and lit the torch. It rushed into flame with an audible pop.

My father looked at the flaming ax handle a moment, and then at me, and said, "Why did you do that?"

"I don't know." I shrugged. I held the torch up. "It's cool."

"You understand," he said, "you're going to have to pay for that ax handle. It was brand-new."

"Okay," I said. "How much was it?"

"Not much." He sounded disappointed. "Listen, Matt," he said, and started walking again. "What happened back there, with Howell. You know, there are going to be repercussions."

"Like what?"

"I don't know," he said. "We'll find out soon enough."

"Whatever," I said. "We'll deal with it."

He smiled at that and moved a little closer to me. I held the torch out high in front of us, as if our suburban neighborhood were a cave or a wilderness that I was exploring, and I went back to thinking about me and my father, and also about what the repercussions of almost strangling one of your colleagues to death might be. I was glad we were near the house at that point, because it was really vicious cold. Above our heads, black smudges of clouds rolled and tumbled. I put my other hand in my pocket and leaned in close to him, letting his body block the wind while I wondered over it all.

The Match

—⊲⫘⫘⊳—

MERETRICIOUS, FAKE-DIAMOND EARRINGS — GAUDY, two-inch pendants, dazzlingly glitzy—dangled from Mark Fletcher's ears. A handsome man in his late thirties, Mark was otherwise dressed casually in sneakers, jeans, and a knit shirt. He grinned, amused as he looked himself over in a full-length mirror on the back of his bedroom door. His reflection suggested an essentially ordinary, good-looking, well-educated, well-heeled guy—except for the earrings.

Below him, in the kitchen, his children were squabbling: Jeffrey was teasing Louise about the color of her hair, which she had dyed blue the previous night. Mark hadn't seen it yet. Jeffrey was ten, into Little League and Goosebumps, a popular series of horror-story books. His sister, Louise, was fourteen, in ninth grade, into Nine Inch Nails, body piercing, and hair dyed outrageously unnatural colors. Mark took off the earrings and dropped them into a canvas bookbag hanging from the doorknob. He checked the bag's contents, riffling through tubes of glue and make-up, a vinyl chess board, Staunton chess pieces, and a thin make-up instruction book that he didn't really need since the techniques were simple and he had pretty much memorized the book anyway.

Downstairs he found Penny, his wife, at the island counter in the center of the kitchen, sprinkling cinnamon into a pink ceramic bowl of eggs and milk, her small body turned away from him, toward a bay window that looked out over the green pastures of Ellett Valley. On the deck, beyond thrown-open doors, Jeffrey sat at the breakfast table, hunched over french toast and a new Goosebumps. A light breeze blew through the dining room and kitchen, carrying the bitter scent of manure and the low rumble of lawn mowers. Louise was on the other side of the kitchen island, watching her mother slice off thick slabs of crusty wheat bread and soak them in the eggs and milk before dropping them into a sizzling skillet. Mark stiffened at the sight of his daughter. Her hair wasn't just blue: it was Kool-Aid blue; electric, vibrating, clown-bright blue. Louise was a beautiful girl. She had her mother's intense-dark eyes and full, sensual lips, and she dressed in ripped-up, ragged jeans and awful T-shirts, and now this—clown hair. When she looked up at her father, she smiled sweetly, like the little girl she still was under the outrageous hair and the orange band T-shirt with big black letters that spelled out BUSH, which she swore was British slang for marijuana and not American slang for a woman's sex, as if the original intent of the band's name made a damn bit of difference.

Louise said, "Morning, Daddy."

Mark answered, "Morning, Bozo."

Louise flushed, her face turning red, her eyes instantly watery.

Penny snapped the spatula down on the counter. "I don't like the hair either," she said. "That's no reason to be cruel."

"It washes out," Louise said, quickly turning surly.

Mark opened the freezer portion of the refrigerator and knelt to retrieve a frozen bagel from a lower shelf. "Washing it out is a great idea."

Louise crossed her arms over her chest. "You said. You said I could as long as it washed out."

"That's right!" Mark flung the bagel into the microwave and stabbed at the flat black surface with a fingertip, setting off a series of beeps, followed by a loud hum. "I said as long as it washes out in case it looked ridiculous—and that's how it looks. You're a goddamn circus clown, for God's sake. Step right up!" He gestured toward Louise and mimicked an angry circus barker. "Right this way to see the freak!"

At the stove, Penny bit her lip and folded her hands in front of her, as if partaking in a moment of silent prayer to keep from throwing the frying pan at her husband.

Louise grew preternaturally calm, her lips twisting into a sneer of disdain.

She sauntered away from the kitchen island and leaned back against the sink. "You said I could—" She shook her head slightly as she spoke. "And I am."

Mark pulled his bagel from the microwave and went about slicing and buttering it. "Fine," he said. "You want to wear an orange T-shirt that says "bush" and have bright blue hair . . ." He shrugged.

Penny went back to work at the stove. She tossed fat chunks of french toast onto a waiting plate.

"Fine," Louise said, mocking her father's tone.

On his way out to the deck, carrying the bagel in one hand and a steaming cup of coffee in the other, Mark said, "But you're washing it out before school on Monday. You can wear it today and tomorrow, the weekend. That's it. And you can't come to church with us Sunday like that."

"Fine," Louise whispered.

On the deck, Mark sat across from his son at the breakfast table. Jeffrey didn't look up. He was studying the cover of *Egg Monsters from Mars*, the latest R. L. Stine. The cover pictured a mutant green egg rising above ordinary white eggs in a purple carton. The green egg was cracked open and some sort of horrifying slime with eyes oozed out over the white eggs. The illustration was captioned: "They're no yolk!" Mark wondered what Jeffrey could possibly see in the cover that so absorbed him. He waited, watching Jeffrey, hoping he'd look up. He wanted to talk to him about his plans for the tournament. Jeffrey already knew—the whole family knew—what he planned on doing. There was a guy name Bozeman in the chess club who was unquestionably the strongest player. No competition. Mark hated him profoundly. Bozeman was a strong master's-level competitor. Mark, an occasional expert-level, usually class A player, was the second strongest member of the club, good enough to beat everyone else most of the time. But never Bozeman. He had never even come close to beating Bozeman. Which wouldn't have been so bad if Bozeman didn't happen to be an arrogant, mean-spirited, belligerent ass. A short, fat, cigar-smoking dope with a goatee, who—God help his patients—was a rich psychiatrist in his non-chess life. Mark was a lifetime assistant professor of history at Blue Ridge Community College. He wasn't rich, but—mostly because of Penny's income as an illustrator of children's books—he was comfortable.

Mark had hit upon his plan after the last tournament, which he had sat out because he couldn't handle the thought of losing to Bozeman again.

Bozeman, of course, won the tournament—but not easily. In the final round, he played a college kid, a decent player but nowhere near as strong as Bozeman. The kid, like Louise, was into piercings and outrageous hair. Everyone assumed he would be beaten handily. Midway through the game, however, with the chess club standing around watching, he had an overwhelming positional advantage. Give Mark that kind of advantage and he'd beat Bozeman. No doubt. Then Bozeman made a scene. He threw his chair back, knocking it over, and snarled at the kid: "I'm not used to playing punks with earrings."

"Hey," the kid said. He was clearly shocked. He had been deeply immersed in the game and the insult must have come like a unexpected smack in the face. His voice quavered. "Who are you calling a punk?" For all his outrageous dress—multiple, brightly colored earrings in both pierced lobes, red-streaked hair that looked as if it had been cut with a machete—the kid seemed deeply shy.

"Isn't that what you call that—look?" Bozeman said, his hands resting on his substantial hips. "Punk?"

"Punk's long gone," the kid whispered, trying for a dismissive tone—but his bottom lip quivered slightly.

"*Long gone,*" Bozeman mocked. He righted his chair. "I'm taking a piss break." He slid the chair back in position. Before he left for the bathroom, he said to the kid, "Just don't think frippery will win you this game."

When Bozeman was out of the room the kid looked up at Mark. "What's frippery?"

Mark pointed to the earrings. "Don't let him shake you up," he said. "He's trying for a psychological edge."

After Bozeman returned, the kid's positional advantage disappeared within five moves. Ten moves after that, he resigned.

Mark was certain that Bozeman had been distracted by the earrings. That was the only way to explain his early poor play. Later that week, Mark called the U.S. Chess Federation headquarters in New York to check on current tournament regulations. "Can I wear whatever I want?" he asked the official on the other end of the line.

"Yes," the voice answered.

"I mean . . . Can I, like, wear a monster mask? Could I, like, have painted blood dripping from my eyes?"

The voice on the other end didn't miss a beat. "You can do whatever you want. We've had players dress up like Liza Minelli; we had one guy who played zipped up in a rubber bondage suit. Our policy is you can wear whatever you want. You can play stark naked, for that matter. If you're arrested, however, you may have to forfeit the game, at the discretion of the tournament director." The voice was perfunctory and absolutely serious.

Mark hung up the phone and went out to a department store in Roanoke, where he bought the earrings. Then he went to a specialty shop and bought the monster makeup kit when he had doubts about wearing them. He was afraid Bozeman might see—or just invent—some deep psychological underpinning for the wearing of earrings to a chess match. He didn't want to think about the reasons Bozeman might invent. He foresaw the possibility of having to spend the rest of his chess career talking football and basketball just to convince everyone he was an ordinary guy.

Mark thought there actually *was* a deep psychological underpinning for the lengths he was willing to go to in order to beat Bozeman in a tournament—but it was nothing Bozeman would ever guess. In fact, Bozeman reminded Mark of his father, who had mercilessly humiliated him until he died of a heart attack shortly before Mark's thirteenth birthday. Bozeman looked nothing like his father, but when Mark played chess with him, when Mark was around him, it was as if he were in his father's presence again. It was uncanny. Something about Bozeman and Mark's father was identical—and it made Mark despise Bozeman deeply. Mark's father would do things like introduce him to people as his switched-at-birth son. He'd say, "Doesn't look like me, does he?" and smack Mark playfully on the head. "Not nearly good-looking enough!" Then he'd laugh, and he had the kind of laugh that pulled others in, so that the strangers would wind up laughing too. Until his late teens, Mark was chubby, and his father was relentless in pointing this out to Mark and anyone else who happened by. In public places he loved to call Mark "Fatty" and "Tubby" and "Lard-butt," and a dozen other insulting names. Once, in sixth grade, his father had come to pick Mark up from school when Mark had hurt his ankle climbing the ropes in gym. His father had come into the gymnasium, and when Mark moved slowly, somewhat reluctantly toward him, the gym teacher said: "Looks like Mark's moving a little slow."

His father answered, with the gym class sitting quietly on the hardwood floor, listening: "He always moves slow, unless there's food around. Then he's Speedy Gonzales."

The class laughed uproariously at this. Mark was at his heaviest stage in sixth grade: a chubby kid with fat cheeks and big thighs. His father was tall, muscular, and handsome. Encouraged by the laughter, Mark's father pulled a foil-wrapped butterscotch out of his pocket. "Sometimes you can lure Mark with candy," he said, performing for the class. He held the butterscotch out as if it were a dog treat. "Come, Mark!" he called. "Come!"

The class screamed with laughter. Boys rolled on the floor. The teacher turned away.

At his father's funeral, Mark didn't cry. As an adult, he realized that his father couldn't have always been cruel, that his relationship to his father could not possibly have been so one-dimensional, that they must have in some way loved each other, in some way cared for each other—but if they did, Mark didn't remember. As an adult, his father was nothing to Mark but an ugly memory, a memory that was awakened by Bozeman.

Out on the deck, across from Mark at the breakfast table, Jeffrey's eyes remained fixed on the cover of *Egg Monsters from Mars*. Over a green field far below them, a trio of turkey vultures floated lazily, gliding through the wide circles of a rising thermal. Mark pulled the earrings from his bag and put them on. "Hey, Jeff," he said. "What do you think?"

Jeffrey finally looked up from his book. His eyes went for a moment to his father's face, and then to the earrings, which Mark was showing off by shaking his head slightly. Jeffrey said, "I've got a ball game today. You didn't forget, did you?"

"What ball game?" Mark yanked off the earrings and slapped them on the table. "Penny!" He hurried off the deck with Jeffrey behind him. Penny was eating breakfast with Louise in the kitchen.

"Mom!" Jeff said, before Mark got a chance to speak. "He forgot my game!"

Penny and Louise were sitting on stools with revolving seats. They spun around simultaneously to face Mark and Jeff. Louise was already taller than her mother: her feet rested firmly on a crossbar near the bottom of the stool, while Penny's feet dangled freely. Side by side, the contrast between Penny and her daughter was startling. Louise, with her unkempt, bright blue hair and orange T-shirt and tattered jeans, looked like a creature from another planet compared to Penny, with her auburn hair cut neatly in a bob, her khaki pants, and soft blue shirt with the cuffs rolled up precisely on her forearm.

Mark crossed his arms over his chest. He glared at Penny. "Why didn't you tell me he had a game today?"

"I did," Penny said. "I told you weeks ago."

Louise went back to eating her breakfast.

"Oh!" Mark shouted. "And when I told you what I was planning for the match this weekend, you just conveniently forgot to remind me about the ball game!"

Penny said, "I'm not your secretary." She turned her back to him. "But if this saves you from making a fool of yourself," she added, "that's fine with me."

"Oh," Mark said. "You think so?" He went around to the other side of the counter, intending to carry on the argument with Penny—but when he saw Louise resting her chin in her hands, looking him in the eyes with a smug, contemptuous grin, he smacked her. His hand shot out as if with a will of its own. The impact of the flat of his hand against her cheek made a clap loud enough to startle him.

Louise issued a high-pitched, shocked, squealing noise, and jumped off the stool holding her cheek.

Penny slammed the counter. "Mark!" she yelled. "For God's sake! What's wrong with you?"

Jeffrey stomped out onto the deck.

In Mark's head, there was a tumult of words. He wanted to tell Penny that he wouldn't stand for her manipulating him. He wanted to tell Louise that he wouldn't allow her to look at him like that, with a look that was an out-and-out challenge to his authority. She ever did it again, he'd slap the look off her face again. He wanted to tell Penny that Louise was testing them, with her hair and wanting to get her lips or her eyebrows or her belly button pierced, with all her smart-alecky back talk, and if they let her get away with it, there'd only be bigger trouble down the line. He had a dozen things he wanted to say at once, and as always when that happened, his face grew dark, his back stiffened, and he wound up walking away, because if he stayed he was liable to strangle someone.

Mark went out to the breakfast table to get his bag. Jeffrey was on the far end of the deck, leaning over the railing, looking down to the valley. His wiry, kid's body appeared limp, as if he were very tired. In the kitchen, Louise sobbed to her mother, "He'll wind up killing me!" and then went up to her bedroom. Mark listened as she climbed the steps lethargically. When he heard her bedroom door close, he slid the earrings into his bag and crossed quickly through the house.

He was in the driver's seat of the van, putting the keys in the ignition, when Penny appeared at the open window. She held the car door with both hands, as if it were a lectern. "You're just leaving?" she said. "Just like that?"

"Exactly." Mark stared straight ahead at the carefully maintained landscaping of his neighbor's house. "I'm playing Bozeman today."

"What about Jeff's game?"

"You take him."

"I promised to take Louise to the mall."

"Take her after the game."

Penny closed her eyes for an instant and took a deep breath. She leaned into the window. "You know," she said, "you're not the only one who can just leave."

Mark quit staring at his neighbor's yard and looked at his wife. "You knew I'd forget about Jeff's ball game unless you reminded me. You always remind me. You didn't want me to play in this tournament, because you determined I'd make a fool of myself, and then you determined you'd just put a stop to it."

"That's not the problem." She leaned close and spoke softly. "You want to make a fool of yourself, go ahead. Shoot me for trying to stop you."

"Then what's the problem?"

"You know what the problem is."

"I slapped Louise?"

"I told you last time I didn't want it to happen again."

Mark nodded, anger rising in his throat. "I'm a monster," he said. "I beat my kids . . ."

"You're not a monster," she said evenly. "You don't beat your kids. But you can be cruel. Lately you've been cruel a lot. To all of us."

Mark stared hard a long moment at his wife. He said, obviously having to control his anger, "That was more than two years ago the last time I slapped Louise—and she deserved it then, too. I love her just as much as you do, but she's a willful, rebellious teenager—and if we don't stop her, she'll walk all over both of us."

"This isn't about discipline; it's about you." She stepped back from the car. "Don't you notice Jeffrey hardly ever looks at you anymore?"

"That's bullshit."

"It's not bullshit. Open your eyes. At least Jeff is tough enough to tune you out."

"And Louise isn't . . ." he said, spelling out Penny's implication.

"Look at her, for God's sake! She's been looking ill. What does it take—" Her face was stiff as a corpse's, which only happened when she *really* angry. "Have fun at your tournament," she said. She walked away, back to the house.

———

At the tournament, Mark was beaten in the first round by one of the weakest players in the club. He didn't stick around to see Bozeman win. He got back in the van and drove to the park where Jeffrey was playing. After the argument with Penny, he hadn't even made it all the way out of the driveway before relenting. She was right. He had been mean to everyone lately. He knew it; he wasn't blind—but he didn't know why. Some mornings he'd wake up enraged, as if his whole body were smoldering—no reason he could pinpoint. Sometimes the feeling lasted throughout the day, and he couldn't keep himself from snapping and barking at people. This was not something new for Mark: he had always had periods of surliness like this. He told himself it was just who he was. He could be moody. He could be a bear in the morning. This was not so terribly unusual.

But Penny was right. It had gotten out of hand lately. And he shouldn't have slapped Louise. He should have sent her to her room, or made her spend the day in the house. When he thought about Louise, when he heard the high-pitched, shrieking noise she made, so surprised at being slapped, he was sorriest. Her words before trudging up the stairs—"He'll wind up killing me!"—played over and over in his mind. He knew she didn't mean it. He knew it was just teenage dramatics. But that she'd even think such a thing hurt deeply. He remembered seeing Louise born, the way the doctor's hand disappeared through the blue paper sheet that covered Penny's belly, like reaching down into a magician's hat—and out came Louise, a C-section baby, her head perfectly round, her beautiful blue eyes taking in the world for the first time. He felt something enter him then, love laced with commitment. He took up Penny's hand and kissed her fingers while the nurses poked around at Louise, jabbing her with a needle and making her cry before carrying her across the room to him and placing her in his arms. When it was over and they wheeled Penny away and brought Louise to the nursery, he went into a bathroom and closed the door and knelt down and touched his forehead to the tiled floor and thanked God, thanked God again and again, wiping the tears out his eyes brusquely with the back of his arm.

By the time Mark arrived at the park, he was resolved to redeem the morning. He could be funny when he wanted to; he could always make Penny and Louise laugh when he made the effort. Jeffrey was tougher. Sometimes he had to resort to jumping on the kid and tickling him. Jeffrey had always been a serious, intense kid with a need to be on top of things. He was almost precisely the opposite of Louise, who was an habitually dazed, dreamy girl, overwhelmed by every one of life's small details. On school mornings, Jeffrey was the first one out of bed. When the school bus pulled up, he was waiting at the curb. Louise had to be dragged out of bed every morning. To the best of Mark's memory, she had never once caught the school bus without having to run for it. Often, Penny had to drive her to school.

Mark wound up parking illegally, with two tires up on a bright yellow curb. The blacktop lot he walked through on his way to the game was filled with minivans and late-model cars. The weather was magnificent: a few high, thin clouds drifting through a blue sky, light breezes, sunshine. No wonder the parking lot was full. The weather had nudged out every parent in town. From the baseball diamond came the clichéd shouts of the ball game: a man's rough-loud voice yelling "Batter! Batter! Batter!" and "Stay awake out there!" Mark had grown up on the streets of Brooklyn, playing Kick the Can, and Ringalevio. He didn't know much about organized sports like Little League. Every time he heard someone shout "Batter! Batter! Batter!" he wondered what the hell it meant.

On his way to the bleachers, where he had already spotted Penny and Louise sitting side by side, both of them looking sad and distracted, he had to walk behind the batting gate, and he saw that he would pass directly behind Jeffrey, where he was sitting in line on a bench with several other uniformed boys, intently watching the game. He considered whether he should say anything to his son, decided not to, and then said, loudly "Hey, Jeff! How's the game going?" as soon as he got close to him. Jeff turned to him and smiled shyly, as if he weren't quite sure how to react. He said, "It's going good," hesitated a moment, and then added, "Thanks for coming," before turning his attention back to the game.

By the time he reached the bleachers, Penny and Louise had both noticed him. Penny squeezed over, making room for Mark beside her. The bleachers were packed, and Penny's squeeze caused a chain reaction down the line. Mark climbed up and sat beside her.

"What happened," Penny whispered. "Did you lose in the first round?"

"You got it," Mark said, forcing a small laugh. As resolved as he was to work his way back into his family's good graces, he still felt a slice of anger rise up in him at Penny's remark. He pushed it down. He leaned over Penny, toward Louise. "Hey, Honey," he said. "How about if I take you to the mall, after the game? We'll give your mom a break."

"I'd rather go with Mom," she said, without looking at him. "If you had given us a break this morning," she added, "I wouldn't have to be here now, at this stupid game, watching my little brother running around dressed up like an ice-cream man."

Between Mark and Louise, Penny sat rigidly, concentrating on the ball game, as if her husband and daughter weren't really there at all, as if she couldn't hear a word they were saying.

Again, Mark made himself laugh, but this time the laugh came out tinged with disdain. "You're laughing at the way your brother's dressed?" He wanted to make Louise laugh at herself, which, thank God, he knew she was capable of doing. "Honey," he said. "I hate to be the first to point this out to you, but . . . your hair is bright blue."

"Funny." Louise said, with a scowl.

"Jeffrey's pitching!" Penny said, to no one in particular. She shouted, "Go, Jeff! Batter! Batter! Batter!"

Mark looked at his wife. She didn't appear to see him. She was watching the game. Next to her, Louise leaned back slightly and undid three more buttons of the white denim shirt she was wearing over a black T-shirt. Before the last button was undone, Mark recognized the black band shirt. It was one he had expressly forbidden her to own, let alone wear; it was one she had told him she had thrown away. When he saw it, his face turned red. His inclination was to grab her by the neck and drag her out of the bleachers. He pushed it down. His heart beat hard. Louise leaned back on the bleacher, supporting herself on locked arms, looking up at the clouds, her neck exposed as if she were sunbathing—and, of course, in that pose her shirt fell open further, revealing a column of white words that stood out sharply against the black background of the T-shirt. Although he knew what they said, Mark read them anyway, as if to reassure himself that such a T-shirt really existed, that someone somewhere sold the damn thing, that his daughter had actually bought it, that she was really wearing it to her brother's Little League game. The white column of words read:

Need Me
Use Me
Fuck Me
Erase Me
Kill Me
Kill Me
Kill Me

Mark slid off the bleachers and walked away, back toward the van. He was so angry he hardly saw where he was going. He felt as if the whole world were pulsing, as if the ground were undulating and might turn liquid under his feet in the next second or two. At the van, he jumped up into the driver's seat and sat there a long time, holding the steering wheel tightly, staring out the window, not seeing a thing. Every once in a while he'd shake his head. He asked himself how she could wear such a shirt. What did it mean? He thought again about what she had said that morning, before walking away up the stairs to her room—"He'll wind up killing me!"—and he thought again about the words on the band shirt. He was genuinely confused. What the hell did it mean? What was Louise's problem? There were times, and this was one of them, when he felt as though he had been locked into a life-and-death struggle with Louise from about the time she turned twelve. When he thought about his battles with Louise in that manner—as a life-and-death struggle— he began to weaken again. Did Louise really feel threatened by him? Did she really, on some level, on *any* level, think he was trying to hurt her, to *kill* her.

He wasn't trying to kill her; he was trying to protect her. He didn't hate her; he loved her.

Mark leaned back in the driver's seat as a powerful swell of resignation tugged at him. He thought, the hell with it. Things went the way they went and there wasn't any use trying to resist. Then, on the floor by the passenger's seat, he noticed the canvas bag with his chess set and the monster makeup kit, and, spontaneously, he snatched up and broke open a tube of skin glue. He pulled down the sun visor, positioned the vanity mirror at eye-level, and squeezed out a thin line of clear glue from just below his eye to the bottom of his jaw. He pressed the skin together over the glue, and—voilà!—an instant, horrifying scar. He touched the scar, grinned, and then laughed. He liked it. There was something mysteriously appropriate about it. He pulled out the blue-black bruise paint and touched up the edges of the scar to make it even more ghastly, and then added a couple more scars for good measure, and darkened the area around his eyes. When he was done, he looked like he had just been in a nasty auto accident. Or else he looked like a ghoul.

When he was satisfied with his makeup job, he drove the van around behind the bleachers, parked it illegally again, and walked the short distance to Penny and Louise with his head down, looking at the tops of his shoes. As he was about to climb up next to Penny, a roar erupted from the crowd and everyone on the bleachers jumped up simultaneously. On the baseball diamond, the kids were screaming, and the third base coach was frantically waving three runners around the bases as way off in right field a boy ran after a ball that had been hit well over his head. A deep male voice yelled, "Grand slam! Grand slam!" When the last runner rounded the bases, the crowd sat down, and Mark pulled himself up next to Penny, who squeezed over slightly to make room before she actually looked at him. She was smiling broadly when she turned to Mark, her eyes full of pleasure and excitement. When she saw him, there was a second of hesitation, as if it took a moment for his face to register. Then she gasped and clutched her heart. At the far end of the bench another woman noticed him and fell off the bleachers when she jumped up to get a better look.

"Mark!" Penny hissed. She leaped over him and climbed down to see about the woman who had fallen.

Louise said, "Nice going, Dad." She looked at him with a mixture of pity and disgust.

Mark said, "It's a joke," and then climbed down from the bleachers to see about Penny. He found her talking to Mrs. Gess, one of Louise's old teachers from elementary school. Mrs. Gess was brushing away two grass stains from the knees of her jeans as Penny apologized, saying, "I'm so sorry. It was— My husband—"

"I'm fine," Mrs. Gess said. "Really." She looked at Mark for a instant, and then back to Penny. She patted her on the arm and climbed back up to her seat.

Under the bleachers, with Louise approaching, Penny stepped toward Mark, stood toe to toe with him. "What the hell is the matter with you?" she said. From the ball field there was the crack of a bat connecting with a ball, and the crowd stood up yelling.

"It's a joke," Mark said. He opened his hands, as if to say, "I can't believe you're upset." He added, "I thought I'd amuse you."

Penny was silent a long moment, staring hard at her husband, as if she suspected a more sinister motive but couldn't quite figure out what it might be. Finally, she said. "I'm not amused."

"Fine," Mark said. "I'll just go home."

"Good idea," Penny said. "And take Louise with you. She's not feeling well."

<hr />

In the car, on the way home, Mark found himself grinning. "Louise," he said. Louise was bunched up in her seat, holding herself as if she were cold, looking away from him, out the driver's window. "Louise," he repeated.

Louise grunted. Very softly. She had buttoned up her shirt, and she appeared to be a little sweaty. She seemed especially thin and fragile, curled up in the bucket seat.

Mark's grin turned into a smile. "Did you see Mrs. Gess go sailing off the bleachers?"

"Very funny," she said.

"You didn't think so?" he nudged her, pushing her knee playfully.

Louise shrugged and grunted.

He laid his hand on her knee. When he noticed that she was sweaty, he turned up the air-conditioning.

Louise turned it down. "I'm chilled," she said.

"You're sweating."

"I'm chilled and I'm sweating, that's right."

Mark pulled over the side of the road. "Are you okay?" he asked. "How sick are you feeling?"

She shrugged. Her eyes appeared watery, as if she were close to tears. "I want to change my name," she said.

Mark decided to endure the change of subject. "To what?" he asked.

"JesusChrist," she said. "One word. JesusChrist Fletcher."

Mark was quiet a long moment. On the road, a car drove by fast enough to rock the van with its gust of wind. "You want to be known as JesusChrist Fletcher?"

"For the shock value," she said. She was speaking with her eyes closed, as if she were overwhelmingly tired. "What do you think?"

"I think," Mark said, "that you're fourteen. I think you're trying to suggest that I'm crucifying you. Or something like that."

Louise made a bemused face, as if to say, "I hadn't thought of that, but . . ."

"Is that it?" Mark said. He was trying to sound sincere, but there was a touch of anger in his voice that he just couldn't seem to control.

"I don't know," Louise said. "I think you've lost me."

"Louise," Mark said. "I'm trying to talk to you, Honey. What was that about this morning? That, 'He'll wind up killing me' thing? I mean, Louise, you don't think—" He stopped when he heard the sloppy emotion entering his voice.

Louise spun around to face Mark, her expression furious. "You wouldn't let me get my lip pierced!" she shouted. Then, suddenly, she was sobbing uncontrollably and holding her arm to her eyes to blot the streams of tears.

"Jesus Christ!" Mark said.

"Yes?" Louise answered, between sobs. She seemed to be struggling for an attitude, a posture that would allow her to regain control of herself.

"What is it? What's wrong?" At the sight of her sobbing, all of the day's conflicts went out of Mark's mind. They were instantly replaced by fear. "Are you sick?" he asked. "What the hell does getting your lip pierced have to do with anything?"

Louise couldn't stop sobbing, though she was obviously trying. She kept angrily wiping away tears with her forearm and with the heels of her hands. "You wouldn't let me get anything pierced," she said. "My eyebrows? No. My lips? No. My nose? No. My belly button? No."

"What the hell are you talking about?" Mark didn't know what, but now he was sure that something was seriously wrong. He was all the more frustrated because he didn't have the remotest clue. He said, "Cut the crap, Louise. Tell me what's wrong."

"I can't," she said, her voice deflated; the anger and defiance suddenly gone.

"Louise . . ." Mark touched her forehead and his hand came away slick with her sweat. "Louise," he repeated, "you're scaring me." He brushed back her hair, which, blue or not, felt as silky and fine as ever. "Just tell me what's wrong. What does my not letting you get pierced have to do with anything?"

Louise's face scrunched up and her lips formed around a word, but no sound came out. Then she sighed, as if giving up. She said, emotionlessly, "I got pierced."

"Where? You got pierced?"

"Where you could never see it."

"Where I could never see it?" Mark felt as though he were working on a riddle. He had seen Louise only the day before modeling her new bathing suit, which hadn't left many places on her body he—or anyone else—couldn't see. "Your breasts?" he said. "You had a nipple pierced?"

She shook her head and backed away from him, making herself small.

If it wasn't her breasts, there was only one place left. Mark had heard that women could be pierced there, but—it didn't seem possible. "Not your breasts?" he said. "You're sure?"

She nodded and slid even farther from him, until her back was pressed against the door.

If someone had told Mark that his fourteen-year-old daughter might one day reveal to him that she had herself pierced . . . down there, and that he wouldn't give a damn, he would never have believed it. But he didn't give a damn. He saw her cowering in her seat, afraid of him, and there were only two thoughts in his mind: one, that the piercing must have gotten infected, and that he had to take her to a hospital; and two, that she was afraid of him. She was genuinely afraid of him. The second thought felt like it might kill him. It felt like a knife inserted low in the belly, ripping its way up toward his heart. "For God's sake, Louise," he said. "Stop looking like I'm going to hit you."

"You're not?" she said. "You're not mad?"

"Of course, I'm mad. What do you think?" He started the van.

"Wait," Louise said. "Where are we going?"

"To the hospital." He put the van in gear. "You've probably got an infection."

She nodded slowly, her eyes filling with tears. "I knew it was getting infected," she said. "I didn't know what to do." She started sobbing again. "I'm sorry."

Mark said, "I'm sorry, too," and started to pull out onto the road.

Louise grabbed his arm. "Dad," she said. "Don't you think you should . . ." She gestured toward his face.

"Oh . . ." he had forgotten about the makeup. He parked the van again, pulled a tube from his bag, and smeared a glob of Vaseline over the longest scar.

Louise said, watching Mark work on his face, "Are you sorry because you sort of forced me into it? I mean, not letting me get pierced anyplace else?"

Without looking away from his work, he said, "Don't push your luck, Louise." In the bottom of the vanity mirror, he saw her watching him.

She said, "I don't feel *really* bad, Dad. I think it's just a little infection."

"That's good," he said. He wasn't having any luck getting the makeup off. The only immediate result of his efforts was to smear the bruise paint. When he tried to tug the skin apart, his fingers slipped on the Vaseline and he got makeup all over his face and shirt. He sighed and fell back in his seat. Then he flipped the visor back up and pulled the van out onto the road.

"What are you doing?"

"Sorry. I can't get it off. I'll have to take you the way I am."

"Terrific," she said. "They'll get one look at us and call the tabloids. I can see the headline: Monster Dad Delivers Mutilated Daughter to Docs."

Mark grinned, amused. "Very funny," he said, and then, just as he was about to begin to lecture his daughter about why he didn't want her to get pierced, why he wouldn't let her get tattooed, why he didn't like her hair blue, he stopped himself. *Later*, he thought. She seemed to be relaxing a bit. And she seemed grateful that he hadn't exploded and screamed at her once she told him what she'd done. He touched his daughter's knee, and she put her hand over his, the way she used to when she was a little girl. From the time she was a toddler to only a few years ago, whenever they were driving someplace, just the two of them, he'd put his hand on her knee and she'd put her hand over his, and they'd drive that way a little while, a few minutes maybe, before he'd have to use both hands to change gears or to turn, but it was like a message had been sent, a connection made. It was a gesture he had almost forgotten. "Put the seat down," he said. "Try to rest till we get there."

"Okay," she answered. She put the seat down and stretched out and then pulled her knees to her chin and folded her hands between her ankles like a child getting ready to sleep. "Are you going to tell Mom?" she asked, her eyes closed. "Will Jeffrey find out?"

"We'll see what we can work out," he said. "We'll see how many promises I can extort from you for keeping my mouth shut."

Louise said, her eyes still closed. "I'm going to pay for this, I see."

"Absolutely," he said. "But try to relax for now."

Louise settled down deeper into her seat.

For the rest of the ride to the hospital, Mark wouldn't let himself think about Louise. If he let himself think about the piercing and the infection, he'd get too anxious. Given the way he looked, it seemed doubly important to be calm and in control when he reached the hospital. Louise was going to be fine; he knew that. She'd have a minor infection; they'd give her some drugs; it would all work out. That was the bottom line. And eventually these teenage years would pass, thank God. For the moment, he just needed to stay in control. Instead of thinking about Louise, he thought about Bozeman, about the match he had missed by screwing up the first game. He imagined himself casually putting on the earrings between moves, with Bozeman watching. He could see Bozeman's face, the way his eyes would widen, the way his fat cheeks would turn red. He loved it. He loved thinking about it. He found himself smiling, picturing himself making trips to the bathroom and returning each time with a new scar or some ghastly face paint as Bozeman got more and more flustered. The guys in the chess club would laugh, and maybe Bozeman would, too—but his concentration would be screwed up, his game would be weakened, and Mark saw himself concentrating all the harder, studying the board, searching and finding the right moves, until at last he beat him. "Checkmate," he'd say. He'd look Bozeman in the eyes and say, "Checkmate, you son of a bitch."

"Dad," Louise said. "What are you grinning at?"

"Nothing," he said. They were at the hospital. Mark was about to pull into the emergency-room lot. He said, "Ready for the docs, mutilated daughter?"

"Guess so," she said. She made a face, as if both perplexed and amused by his grin. She watched him carefully as he parked the car.

"Here we go," he said, and took one last regretful look at himself in the rearview mirror before getting out of the car. When Louise didn't move, he asked her again. "Sure you're ready?"

"Are you sure?" she asked. "Did you get a good look at yourself?"

Mark shrugged, as if to say, "What can I do?" and then went around to get her door.

The Revenant

—⟶⟩⟨⟵—

FIRST, A TEENAGE GIRL FLASHED ME AT A MARILYN Manson concert. I had only reluctantly agreed to take Vee, my fourteen-year-old daughter, because I didn't want to spring for a pair of twenty-five-dollar tickets and take her to the civic center way over in Roanoke for the concert. I didn't know much about her music, but I knew enough that there was no way I was going to let her go alone—and it was either let her go or tie her down. So I found myself at a Marilyn Manson concert, and while I was there among several hundred tough-guy teens waiting for the concert to begin, this girl flashed me.

She couldn't have been more than fifteen. She wore a bright red choker. I was standing several feet away from Vee, at the outer edge of a crowd that thickened into a knot of bodies near the front of the stage—which appeared to be about a mile and half away. I must have looked like a security guard or a bouncer, standing rigid with my arms crossed over my chest, watching the crowd intently, my eyes going back and forth from Vee to the intermittent spectacle of someone lifted up over the throng and passed along on waves of hands until he or she fell, usually headfirst, into a gap in the tight surface of bodies. I'm six-three, 280 pounds, built solid. I've always worked out, since I was a boy in Brooklyn and discovered I could avoid trouble if I looked like only a fool would mess with me. The kids in general were keeping their distance and looking elsewhere—except for this one girl. She stood about eight feet away, her back to the stage, and she looked right through me, the line of her vision crossing my body somewhere about neck level. The way her eyes were focused, it was like I wasn't there, though she couldn't help but see me. She was looking at me. She had short hair, a thin, attractive face, and a lanky body. No breasts to speak of. A black T-shirt with the word HOLE in plain white lettering enclosed in a white circle. Baggy pants she seemed to swim in. A dazed, I'm-not-here look in her eyes.

She stood there silently, her hands thrust deep in the pockets of her baggy pants, and I stood there silently, my arms crossed over my chest. We were two points of silence in a mass of squeals and shouts that coalesced to a hollow din. I had just looked away from her, back toward Vee. I was feeling an uncomfortably familiar anxiety, one I hadn't felt in a while, but had felt almost every waking moment in Vietnam: a pervasive sense of danger somewhere within what I was seeing but invisible to me, as if the source of danger were going to suddenly materialize and I had better be looking in the right place when it did. I couldn't quit staring, searching. When I turned my eyes back toward her, she pushed her baggy pants down to mid-thigh and pulled them up again quickly—and then just remained there staring through me with that lost look. It happened so fast, I wasn't sure it happened at all, but the image burned itself instantly into my permanent memory. She wore black panties that narrowed to strings across her hips and contrasted sharply with her fair skin. The triangle of black fabric was pulled to one side and ran in a dark line down the center of a sunny thatch of blond hair. My mind reacted to the sight like a strip of film. She was both the camera snapping the picture and the picture itself. I registered the image and it remains burned in place to this moment.

I wondered if she expected me to do something. I had turned fifty the week before. She was a child. I looked into her eyes. Her gaze remained blank as she backed into the crowd and disappeared.

Vee approached me. "Do you have to just stand here like this?" Her face was bunched tight with anger, her lips a thin line, her eyes squinting.

"Deal's a deal," I said. We had agreed on everything beforehand. She could come to the concert as long as I came with her. She could stand with the crowd rather than sit in the stands, as long as I was nearby and she stayed on the edge of the crowd. No going anywhere near the mosh pit. This was, after all, a band in which every performer was named after a serial killer. I said, "Just pretend I'm not here."

"Right," she spit out, and stomped away.

A moment later the lights went down, and an evening of almost unbearable sound commenced. I couldn't believe the volume of the music. Literally, it was shocking. The sound pummeled me, every thump of the bass a jab to the body. Relentless, overwhelming sound. After three hours of it, I was exhausted—and pissed off. When the lights finally went up and the general din resumed, I headed for the exits with Vee, who seemed to have forgotten momentarily how upset she was that I had insisted on taking her to the concert. She was pumped up with excitement, like all the other kids filing out of the civic center in a thick stream of dyed hair and pierced body parts. She floated along a few steps in front of me, and I could see her searching the crowd, hoping to find someone she knew, someone with whom she could share her excitement.

Then the next thing happened.

First, there was the girl who flashed me. Then this.

A group of three guys and one girl came along walking in the opposite direction from the exiting crowd, and the girl recognized Vee. She squealed and took Vee by the hand and pulled her out of the line. The boys apparently didn't know Vee. They scowled and stood back from the girls and waited. I stepped out of the crowd and one of the boys looked toward me and our eyes met. The girl was chattering about the concert and embracing Vee, who appeared slightly nervous and awkward. The boy said, "What are you looking at, Fuckhead?" and then he spit on me. He might have been sixteen, maybe seventeen. A high-school kid. He was scrawny, almost as tall as me, and like many of the boys that night, he was shirtless. He was built wiry and tight. I leaped toward him and the fool stepped into my punch. One instant he was standing, full of himself; the next he was out cold on his back, bleeding from the nose and mouth. I grabbed Vee roughly by the arm and pulled her away.

Vee never said a word to me that night. Nothing. In the car on the way home she sat in the back seat, silent for the hour-long drive. I didn't ask her who the girl was. I didn't ask her anything. Something was going on. First the girl flashed me; then I knocked out a kid, a boy; and by the time I was sitting in the dark front seat of the car, driving home on a narrow country road under a bright full moon, I knew something was happening.

When I first got back from Vietnam, I wasn't all together—though nothing much happened to me there. Compared to some other guys, to most other guys, I was lucky. I saw some things, yes. And there were images that seemed to hunt me, stalking me and coming vividly to life when I least wanted to see them: the wrecked, bloody face of my lieutenant; the body of a young woman draped over a tree limb like an article of clothing hung to dry. She was naked. Something happened when I saw her. I came upon her in a small clearing, slanted lines of sunlight filtering through a porous roof of leaves. I walked right up to her. Her breasts were small, barely developed, the nipples puffy. I couldn't help looking at her, noticing the shapeliness of her calves and thighs, my eyes focusing a long moment on her sex. Her throat had been cut in a fat red line from shoulder to shoulder and there was a circle on the ground where the dirt had soaked up her blood. And there were other things, other images. . . . But it was six months maybe, at the most, that I was messed up, before I got it together.

I dealt with it.

You can let things destroy you, you can let them eat you alive—or you can *master* them, you can *command* them. And you can get on with your life.

I was twenty-four when I got home. I had been to college; I had my degree. Useless, granted. In anthropology. A no-name college. But I had finished. I had done my turn in the service. Six months, maybe, I was a mess, before I met June, my first wife, and I put my life together. I got a decent job with the phone company, which turned into a decent career. With June's work, we made enough money to get a nice house. We did okay. I did okay. The marriage didn't last, but I'm not alone there. At least we never had kids to make it more complicated.

Those six months though. . . . It feels like I spent most of them driving. I couldn't get myself together. I just couldn't. Nights, I'd wake up at four A.M. Every night, weeks in a row. Most nights, my stomach would be aching, a deep, generalized pain, a cramp that wouldn't let go. I'd take a shower and let the hot water run over my chest and stomach. I can see myself in that narrow shower box, which was lined with white tiles and had a bright light that shined down into it so that my memory of it is this bright vision: my pink naked body, the wide bulk of it leaning back so that the top of my head touched the tiles and the pulsing stream of hot water hit my stomach. I'd writhe under the water. It helped, but not enough. Eventually I'd dry off and dress and get in the car and drive till the pain finally stopped, which usually took three or four hours. I drove thousands of miles that way. Thousands.

After I married June, I never had another four A.M. stomach ache. They just stopped. I had gotten my life going again. I was back on track. Things went well with my job. I got raises and promotions. If I ask myself now whether I was happy then, I can't answer. I think I was happy. I know I wasn't tortured anymore by Vietnam, which I came to think of as a place where my life had gotten derailed for a brief time. I got past it. Even when June left me, I handled it okay. She had gotten involved with a consciousness-raising group. They thought of themselves as feminists. I thought of them as a group of angry, unhappily married women, and I was upset and worried when June took up with them. Turned out I was right to be worried. Suddenly I was getting the whole anti-male litany, night after night: I was uncommunicative, unresponsive, an insensitive lover, and on and on. She lives in Washington state now. She's married again and has two boys. She sent me a picture once. Her husband wore a red ascot.

But a couple of months after she left, I met Marcy, and everything was back on track again.

—⁂—

The night of the concert, Vee fell asleep sobbing. Marcy and I could hear her from our bedroom, where we lay side by side in bed, rigid and awake, both of us looking up at the ceiling. Vee is our only child. Marcy couldn't believe I had knocked out a high-school kid. "You humiliated her," she had said when I told her.

My stomach hurt. It was a warm night, mid-May. The windows were open; the ceiling fan revolved lethargically. Marcy lay beside me with her eyes open. She's a big woman, almost as tall as me. She's vulnerable and acutely sensitive at times, which is precisely how she doesn't look. She appears to be stern and angry. A disciplinarian. The third-grade teacher everyone hated. It's worry that makes her look this way. She worries about everything.

When Vee finally stopped sobbing, Marcy said, "She just wants to be alive. She just wants to live her life."

"Really?" I turned on my side and leaned close to her. "The kid spit on me," I said. "He *spit* on me."

Marcy crossed her arms over her eyes. She turned away from me.

I leaned over her, and I realized my hand was clenched into a fist. I wanted to hit her. I had never struck a woman in my life, and yet I knew what I was feeling. I wanted to grab her by the throat. I wanted to hurt her and the desire to do so swelled within me like something wild that needed to be turned loose.

I slid away from her. I got out of bed. I put on some clothes and went out the sliding glass door to our bedroom deck. The air was still. It was a little after one in the morning, a Friday morning. Our deck looks out over a line of suburban backyards: maple trees, elms, basswoods, oaks, all surrounded by neatly mown grass, picket fences, red-brick patios and walkways. Our nearest neighbor had just put a stone bench under the oak in the center of his yard, with an in-ground light illuminating the area. All of the houses had sentry lights that stayed on all night, relegating the darkness to corners and the shadows of things. Most nights I would have thought the view from my deck was peaceful and quiet, ordered and lovely; but that night I found the stillness frightening. I was sweating, and I felt like I needed to run. I needed to get out of there. The stillness was suddenly somehow loud. The lack of movement felt like lack of air, felt like I was suffocating. I couldn't breathe right. I tried to laugh it off, but I found that my eyes were full of tears. I was crying. I was crying and I hadn't realized it.

I don't have the words to explain the intensity of what I felt out there on the deck that night. It was as if this feeling had come out of nowhere, risen up out of the stillness, this terrifying sense, like fear multiplied and squared. I absolutely did not know what was happening. I thought for a moment that I might have been drugged—but the only thing I drank at the concert was a Pepsi, and that out of a can. The feeling was huge; it altered the world. I had this sense that everything I saw was painted on a canvas: the world itself was a painting on a canvas, and I could see it wavering. I could see the corners beginning to curl. I laughed. I wiped tears out of my eyes with the back of my arm. From inside, Marcy called my name. "Jeff?" she said. "Jeffrey?"

I went into the bedroom and knelt beside her.

"You're crying," she said. She looked scared. "Why are you crying?" She wiped a tear off my cheek.

"Listen," I said. "I'm going for a drive."

"A drive?" She sat up. She looked startled. "It's one in the morning!"

I explained as best I could. I told her something was happening, I didn't know what. I needed to get in the car and drive. She tried to dissuade me. She tried to get me back into bed. She wouldn't let go of my arm until I yanked it away from her. Then I took my wallet from the night table, and the car keys from the hook by the kitchen window, and I drove away with Marcy standing in a pool of yellow light outside our front door, her hands clasped together as if in prayer.

Friday evening found me sleeping fitfully in an Atlanta hotel. I had driven through the night without much thought to where I was heading, and by the time the sun came up I was in Georgia, following the signs to Atlanta. In the car, in the dark, driving in the company of massive tractor-trailers, I had cried for a few hours before falling into the soothing, hypnotic trance of long-term driving. I didn't know why I was crying. I didn't know what I was doing. I was just driving, moving. When the sun came up, I thought about stopping to call home, but I didn't know yet what I would say. I thought I might have had an anxiety attack out on the bedroom deck. I thought that might explain it. Something about the concert—the overwhelming noise, the girl dropping her pants, my hitting that kid—had brought it on. I needed to ride it out. I'd be fine. And by the time I drove into Atlanta, I really was feeling a lot better, though still shaky. I got off on an exit that led to Spring Street, and Spring Street led to a parking garage, which led in turn to a high-rise hotel, where I checked in and took a room on the twenty-first floor.

The key to my hotel room was actually a card with a magnetic strip. When I slid it through a slot on the door handle, a green light came on, and the door unlocked. Inside I found a massive bed and a writing table, and a back wall that was all glass and led out to a narrow balcony overlooking the city. I stood out on the balcony a little while and gazed upon the cityscape: the intertwining strips of highway clogged with morning traffic, the array of tall buildings, including one structure that looked like a spaceship perched atop a column. It reminded me of something out of the Jetsons, a childhood cartoon show set in a futuristic city. I felt good out on the balcony, a dry morning breeze ruffling my hair. I was definitely feeling better. There was nothing of the panic from the night before. I went back inside and pulled the curtain over the window, darkening the room. I stripped out of my clothes and got into the bed. In a few moments, I was sleeping.

By the time I woke up, it was dark again; and when I pulled back the curtains, I found a nighttime panorama. The spaceship building was a soft blue circle surrounded by the glittering lights of the Atlanta skyline. Long lines of red and white tail- and head-lights moved along the highways. Twenty-one floors up, the noise of the traffic was the principal sound: a loud, windy rush. As I stood out on the balcony watching and listening, I felt as though I were waking up from a very long sleep. And I *was* just waking from several hours of restless sleep—but it felt like something more than that. It felt like Rip Van Winkle. I said aloud, "Sleepy Hollow." Then I thought about Marcy and Vee, and for a moment I was out-and-out shocked at myself, at what I'd done, getting in the car and driving away from them, abandoning them. What could they be thinking? I wondered if they might not have called the police by now. In seventeen years of marriage I had been a model of loyalty and faithfulness—and then I just up and disappear. What could they be thinking? What was *I* thinking?

I went back into my room, sliding the glass door closed behind me, shutting out the traffic noise and replacing it with the loud drone of a fan. I sat on the bed and picked up the phone, intending to call home, intending to apologize to Marcy, intending to explain that something had happened to me, something I didn't understand. I had panicked and fell back on an old habit of driving, and I had wound up here in Atlanta, in this hotel where I was calling from, and that everything would be okay, would be fine, I'd be home again in a few hours. I was sorry. I was very sorry. I picked up the phone, and carefully read the directions. I punched 8 for an outside line; and then I hit 1; and then I entered my area code; and by the time I actually got to my number, I knew it wasn't over, whatever it was that was happening, this wave that had picked me up and was carrying me along. I put the phone back in the cradle. I straightened myself out and left the room. Then I was back in my car and driving around downtown Atlanta.

The evening was just beginning. Men and woman strolled along Atlanta's city streets, looking like they weren't going anywhere in particular. I guessed because of the hour that most of them were heading to dinner somewhere, some restaurant. I drove around for a couple of hours, just looking. At one point, I found myself driving through a series of poorly lit, empty streets, a place in the center of the city, but hidden away somehow: useless reality, back streets, back entrances to buildings. I was driving slowly, I had been driving slowly all evening. I probably looked like I was cruising, looking for some action, because a man walked out of the shadows in front of the car and motioned for me to stop. He was dressed in beige pants with red shoes and a black shirt under a bright yellow jacket. He was an explosion of color walking out of the dark, and it wasn't hard to guess what he would offer if I stopped the car: drugs or sex, sex or drugs. I didn't stop. I drove past him and when I came to an entrance ramp, I took it.

The highway was thick with traffic. I imagined someone looking down at me from their hotel balcony: now I was one of the gliding lines of red and white lights. I drove for a half hour, forty-five minutes and then exited, meaning to turn around and head back to the city, maybe back to the hotel. I was thinking that I had to call Marcy. I had to at least let her know I was okay, even if I couldn't tell her what I was doing because I didn't know myself yet. I could at least call her. I could at least try to explain. When I got off the highway, I drove by a shopping plaza where two police cars were parked with blue lights flashing in front of a long, windowless building that looked like a factory or a bowling alley. The parking lot in front of the building was crowded. Along the curb was a line of motorcycles. While I watched, the police put two guys into the back of a car and drove away. A small group of young men dressed in tuxedos walked through a thick red door into the white building. Over the door, in red neon script, were the words: *The Gentleman's Club.* I pulled into the lot. One of the tuxedos came back out and stood alongside the door with his arms crossed over his chest.

I guessed it was a strip bar, a club with exotic dancers, girls who stood on your table and took off their clothes while you gawked. I wasn't sure, but I would have bet. Something about the atmosphere of the place. I could feel it. Why I pulled into the lot then, why I parked and got out of the car and started for the entrance, was a mystery to me. I wasn't especially interested in sex. I hadn't been in many years. In high school and college, I was interested enough. Those years, the late '60s, sex seemed all anyone was interested in: it was as if the whole nation entered adolescence simultaneously. Sex this and sex that, on television, in movies, in books and magazines. I slept with several women then, though I couldn't recall many of the particulars. It had been almost thirty years. A couple of years into my first marriage, desire just about disappeared. June and I had sex maybe once every couple of months, and then it was fast, and, as June loudly complained some years later, unsatisfying. With Marcy, the lack of much desire for sex was one of the things that made us compatible. Once Vee was born, we pretty much stopped. Ever since, it had been a once-in-a-blue-moon thing.

So why was I stopping at a sex club? I didn't know. Best I could make out, it was like a wave I was riding and that was where it took me. I walked past the guy in the tuxedo, who nodded pleasantly. I passed through the red door into a place that was like nothing I had ever seen before or have seen since. I felt as though I had walked through a crack in the culture's armor and I wound up in a place where all the rules were in suspension: the place was Dionysian, bacchanalian. Music screamed. Women stood on table tops, naked or on their way to being naked. More women strutted around the barroom. In a far corner of the bar, elevated a few feet above the crowd, a black mechanical bull bucked and swayed, impaled on a silvery, hydraulic tube, ridden by a woman dressed only in her skin and a mane of waist-length red hair that flew around her with the gyrations of the bull. When I first saw the bull and the woman, I stopped and gawked. I think my mouth might have actually been hanging open. While I watched, a boy climbed up on a platform and handed some bills to a guy in a tuxedo, and the bull stopped bucking for a moment while the boy climbed on and settled himself in the saddle. The dancer stood in front of him grasping the pole in both hands, her feet wedged under the saddle, her waist at the level of the boy's head. A large group of young men around the bull began to yowl and hoot, and then the bull began to buck, tossing the boy forward and back. With each forward toss, the dancer thrust her pelvis toward the boy who was pulled away from her by the motion of the bull, and with each backward toss, the boy would lunge for her sex, his mouth open, while she expertly kept herself inches away from him. The more the bull bucked, the louder the crowd yowled.

I watched for a while, until the pure shock of what I was seeing dissipated, and then I made my way toward the bar, which was actually a dance stage where a woman was swinging on a trapeze suspended from the ceiling, taking off her clothes one article at a time and tossing them down onto the bartender to the amusement of the drinkers. I stood for several minutes behind a guy with a Semper Fidelis tattoo on his bicep, until a waitress in a tuxedo jacket and a bikini bottom approached me and took my order for a drink. She explained that all the tables in the bar were currently occupied, but as soon as one was available, I could take a seat. A dancer would come and perform for me. Until then, I could stand and watch or I could sit and watch. She pointed to a line of cushioned benches that ran along the wall of the bar-room. When she walked away, I saw that she was wearing a thong. I watched her until she was out of sight, then carried my drink to the back of the room and took a seat on the bench.

I observed the scene—attractive young women walking around in various degrees of nakedness; mostly very young men, boys really, shouting and waving bills at the women, who came to them and let them place the bills under garters; naked women gyrating on table tops, swinging from trapezes, riding mechanical bulls—with an attitude somewhere between numbed shock and amusement. I didn't know what I was doing there, at The Gentleman's Club. I was watching. I was having a drink. In a minute, I thought, I'd get back in my car and drive to the hotel, and I'd call Marcy and tell her I was coming home. I took a sip of my drink, and was about to put it on the floor, slide it under the bench, and head out; then I noticed that, across from me, only maybe ten feet away, where a dozen guys were sitting in a line on the bench, there was a waitress. I assumed she was a waitress because she was wearing the same tuxedo outfit as the girl from whom I had ordered my drink. She had a cute, girlish face, with short, dark hair cut in a bob, and she sat on the bench with the line of men, chatting with the guy next to her. A girl dressed in jeans and a T-shirt sat on the floor at her feet, between her open legs. While the waitress chatted with the guy, the girl on the floor nuzzled between her legs. From the motion of the girl's head, she appeared to be licking the wait-ress. Every once in awhile she'd stop and she too would talk with the guy, as if she were taking a momentary break from what she was doing to throw in a few words of conversation. This was so strange, it shook me up. I began to feel frightened and anxious again—because I found it hard to believe that what I was watching was actually happening. Every once in a while the wait-ress would close her eyes and throw her head back against the wall and hold the girl's head in her hands, pulling her deeper between her legs. This was in a crowded barroom. This was with scores of people milling around. Part of me just couldn't believe it was happening, and that part of me wanted to cross the room and touch them, just to see if they were real. Instead, I put my drink on the floor and walked casually out of the bar.

Outside, I felt wildly disoriented. I stepped out into the spring air, out of the wailing music and into the parking lot of a place that looked like any suburban mall anywhere in the world, and for a moment I couldn't remember where I was; and before it came back to me—Atlanta, The Gentleman's Club, the hotel—I was pale and sweaty and nauseous. In the car, back on the highway, the feeling evolved into fear as intense as it was back at home the night before out on my bedroom deck. Driving the car along the highway my arms were stiff and my body was tight and cramped. I drove back to my room and got undressed and lay a long while naked under the covers. I was sweating. There was something physical going on inside me. I didn't know what it was. Outside, I could hear the sound of the traffic, like a reminder—*You're in Atlanta; you're not at home*—and I'd have to think to remember how I got where I was. I felt as though I were coming apart. I felt as though something inside me was unraveling, something that had once been wound tight and secure.

I lay in bed for hours, willing my mind blank, before the fear began to dissipate. It happened slowly. It ebbed out of me. It left me feeling opened up and vulnerable. I was wide awake. It was a little after one in the morning. I told myself that I was having an episode of craziness. That was the only way to explain it. An episode of weirdness. I wished it weren't happening, but it was. I'd figure it out. I'd handle it. I'd ride it out, and then I'd get it together again, the way I always had, the way I knew I could. I kicked off the blankets and turned on the lights, and I was startled by the sight of my naked body stretched out on the bed. It must have been a very long time since I had looked at myself naked. I felt as though I were confronting a stranger. My body was pale and doughy, an unhealthy hue of white. I touched the soft mound of my belly and pushed my fingers down into the thick mat of hair that surrounded my penis. The room was brightly lit. The sheets were white. I touched my eyes and my temples and my cheeks, as if I were a blind man trying to recognize someone. I touched my knees and my thighs and the place under my scrotum where my legs came together. I pushed one finger up between my buttocks, and then I held my scrotum in the palm of my hand, and my penis rose quickly, stiff and hard, and I looked at it swollen there against my stomach with something like a sense of wonder. I couldn't remember the last time I masturbated. Not in years, many years. I sat up on the edge of the bed and pondered the possibility of masturbating like a man considering the terms of a difficult equation, and while I thought about it, the erection disappeared.

I went out on the balcony. I stayed there a long time, naked, looking out over the city. It's awfully hard to explain this. I can't, really. It was like, out there, I was in a maze and I was trying to find the right turn. It's like there was a problem set before me and I was experimenting with solutions. Only, I didn't understand the problem. I couldn't see the maze. I knew I had to do something. I had no idea why or what. People out of their minds talk about wires implanted in their heads controlling them, making them do stuff. That's what it was like. I was not in control of myself. Things were moving me. I felt like a marionette—but in some way I knew that I myself was the hand pulling the strings, making myself move. I went into the room, and the way I remember what happened next is this: I sat on the bed, intending to call Marcy, to call home. I hesitated, trying to figure out what I would say, how I would explain myself to Marcy and Vee, and while I was hesitating I pulled out the night table drawer, where there was a thick phone book, a Yellow Pages. I took it out and opened it at random and found myself looking through several pages of advertisements for escort services. Now, this seems hard to believe, the way so much of what happened seems incredible to me now. But that's how I remember it. I opened the Yellow Pages and I was looking at ads for escort services.

The one I called wanted to know where I needed an escort at three in the morning. I said it was a private party. I said it was in my hotel room. When she asked what kind of an escort I wanted, I said young. When she asked how she should dress, I said casual. I said jeans and a T-shirt would do. I said thin is preferable. I said she doesn't have to have much in the way of breasts. She laughed. There's a switch, she said. Then we worked out the payment. I gave her my credit card number over the phone. When I hung up, I went back out on the balcony. I didn't bother to get dressed, and a half hour later my escort arrived. I opened the door in response to her knock. I was still naked. She took one look at me and a smirk crossed her face. She made a sound somewhere between a snort and a laugh, and sauntered past me into the room. She said, "Not much for formalities, are you?" She gestured toward the door, which I was holding open, and the look on her face said, *Well? Are you going to close it?* I closed the door and leaned back against it, and for a moment we both just looked each other over. I asked for young and they sent young: she looked to be a girl in her late twenties. She was small, maybe five-three, five-four at the most, with heavy, round breasts that pushed against the fabric of a black, official Disney World, Minnie Mouse T-shirt. Minnie was pictured in bright red and white, with her arms akimbo and look of reproach on her face. There was a caption. I forget what it said. At first I was upset about the size of her breasts—but it passed.

I cleared my throat. I didn't know what to say. I was standing there naked in front of a stranger and I remember that I didn't feel awkward at all. I looked into her eyes. She had a face that would have been beautiful if it weren't marred by toughness, by an orneriness that made her look as though she might turn her head and spit on the floor at any moment. She had short black hair that lay flat over her forehead and angled down toward the back of her neck, barely covering her ears. She had dark eyes and a round face. She stood with her arms crossed under her breasts and one knee bent, adding to her I'm-tough, I've-seen-everything look. All she needed was a toothpick between her teeth to complete the image. "Well," she said, her voice gentler than her appearance, "at least I know you're not a cop." She had a Southern accent. I couldn't tell if she were putting it on or not. She said, "Where are you from, Honey?" She sat on the bed and started to take off her shoes, which were sneakers, white, Nikes. When I didn't answer, she went on. "You know," she said, "what you want will be another two hundred fifty in cash. That's over what you've already paid." She paused then, watching me, one leg crossed over the other, holding a sneaker dangling from her finger by its heel.

I said, "What is it I want?" I thought she might actually know something I didn't.

She made that laugh-snort sound again. She said, "You have the money, Darling? It has to be cash."

I shook my head. I didn't. I didn't have anywhere near two hundred fifty in cash.

She put her sneaker back on. She said, "Well you better get dressed then. For what you paid, I'll go have a cup of coffee with you. That's all."

"That's okay," I said. "You can go. I don't know why I called."

She looked perplexed. "Honey," she said, "you're stark raving naked. Why do you *think* you called?"

"I don't know," I said. "You can just go ahead and go." I walked past her, toward the balcony. When I slid open the glass door, she said, "Wait," and she got up from the bed and touched my arm. I stopped. I stood in the open door to the balcony with a breeze blowing comfortably against my bare skin. "What?" I said. "You can go. I'm sorry I called. Honestly. I don't know why I did." I covered my eyes with my hands. I sighed. "I'm out of my mind," I said. "I'm having some kind of period of craziness or something." I rubbed my eyes. "You can go," I said. "Really. I'm sorry."

She stepped back and looked me over. She seemed partly annoyed and partly troubled. She said, "Do you— Is it that— I mean, do you like women to see you naked?"

I shook my head.

"I didn't think so." She looked down. "You don't appear especially excited."

"Go ahead and go," I said. "I'm sorry—" I looked down at myself. "I'm sorry I'm naked," I said. I gestured toward the door, and then I turned my back on her and went out on the balcony.

I stepped up to the railing. I grasped the wrought iron in my hands. I was looking down. At the moving lines of red and white lights. I looked down directly below me, at an empty side street, dark in the moonlight.

She came out on the balcony behind me. She took my arm in her hand and pulled me toward her, turning me around to face her. She lost the Southern accent. "Honey," she said, "you're not going to do anything crazy, are you?" She said, "You're not thinking about jumping or anything, are you?"

"No," I said. "I'm not thinking about jumping." My voice was shaky.

She took my arm. She touched me gently. "What is it with men?" she said. "What happens to you guys?" She touched my cheek. "Come here," she said. She stepped into me. She put one of my hands on her back and held it there. She put my other arm around her shoulder. "Dance with me awhile," she said. "It'll make you feel better." She pressed her cheek against my chest. She held me in her arms, and her body began to sway a little, moving gently side to side.

I only resisted for a moment. Then I leaned into her.

"I like dancing," she whispered. She touched the back of my neck with her fingertips. "Dancing always makes me feel better."

I tried to say something in response, but it took me a while before I could talk.

"That's okay," she said. "Just dance with me."

I did. I danced with her an hour or more, silent at first but then talking a bit back and forth. By the time she finally left, the Atlanta night was fading into paleness, the outlines of buildings were emerging out of the dark. She told me her name was Sally. She told me she had two children, the first when she was fourteen. She told me that she loved dancing—just standing someplace alone and swaying to whatever music she could conjure. Something about it, she said.

After she left, I got in bed and fell asleep soundly.

—⁕—

When I finally got home, no one was there. I had driven back to Virginia through downpours and thunder. Somewhere in North Carolina, with dusk coming on, I saw a lightning bolt hit a telephone pole, sending pieces of a transformer sailing in flames. By the time I pulled up in front of my house, it was late and there hadn't been a storm for a while, but the wind was still gusting the way it does in thunderstorms: quiet for a time, then building and building right to the edge of being frightening. It didn't take me a second to figure out no one was home. There were no lights on. The driveway was empty. I had taken off and disappeared for some thirty-six hours without so much as a phone call. I figured Marcy was in Alexandria with her sister. I could see her there sitting at the kitchen table with her sister and her sister's husband, and her parents, who lived nearby, and maybe even her sister's husband's parents, who lived two houses over. They were all close. *We* had all once been close. I imagined them sitting around the kitchen table, talking: a family conference, the proffering of support and love. Vee would be upstairs with her cousin. There'd be music on. She'd probably still be talking about the concert.

Once inside, I wandered through the house awhile, going from room to room, picking up things here and there—a knickknack, a picture, a book— and looking it over as if it held a secret I had forgotten. In the kitchen, I opened the fridge and rummaged through it, rearranging bottles and red and blue food containers. I found an unopened, plastic container of bottled water. I broke off the cap that sealed the top. I held the bottle over my lips and squeezed it, shooting a line of spring water into the back of my mouth. It tasted good. I took another long drink and carried the bottle with me up to my bedroom, where I sat on the bed and noticed for the first time the envelope lying on my pillow. It was beige, same color as the bedspread. It blended in. Had I turned on the lights, I would have seen it right away. But I hadn't. The house was mostly dark.

I didn't open the envelope right away. I knew there would be a letter inside. I figured I knew most of what it would say. As soon as I walked into the house, I knew that everything had changed. I could feel it. Like an emptiness. In one sense it was sudden. In another, it was a longtime coming. I went out on the balcony and stood in the gusting wind. I left the door open and the wind blew into the house. I could hear curtains rustling. In another room, a door slammed. I was just beginning to have the faintest glimmering then of what was happening to me. Now that I've gone back over things many times, I have some better ideas. But then, out on the balcony, I was struggling. I felt as if I were closing in on something, as if the first pieces of a puzzle were about to fall into place. I knew it started with the concert, with the girl, and I reviewed what happened, picturing her, and it occurred to me then that I might have imagined the whole incident. Not imagined it: hallucinated it. Saw it, saw her, vividly, though she wasn't there, not in the sense that others could see her. Think of it. Think of what I saw: a fifteen-year-old girl dropping her pants on a crowded concert floor. Would I have been the only one to see? Wouldn't there have been some comment? It occurred to me then that she might not exist at all, that I might have created her—though I can still see her image vividly. She was like a switch that turned on the whole episode. It occurred to me then that I might have taken down that girl from her tree in Vietnam, clothed and altered her and placed her among the concert crowd. She would have been the right age. I thought, maybe, twenty-five years earlier her naked body was like a switch that turned off something inside me. Maybe. I thought, twenty-five years later she returned. I'd believe she were a ghost, if I believed in ghosts, which I don't. But if I did, I'd be convinced of it. Picture her. Think of how silent she was. Her small breasts. The red necklace like the tattoo of a wound.

That night, out on the balcony, I thought back to Vietnam. I wanted to push the notion out of my mind, and, for a time, that night, I did. I got rid of it. It was a crazy idea. I had nothing to do with that girl's body winding up draped over a tree limb—or no more at least than anyone else who was alive at the time. As far as what happened to her was concerned, I might as well have not been there. I might as well have been protesting the war in front of the Pentagon. I had nothing to do with it. I wasn't there when it happened. I had no idea who did it or why. It was just something I saw. I was on patrol, and I saw it, and that was all. I had no more direct involvement than some hippie in San Francisco, some priest in New York, anyone who was alive in 1969, anyone who's ever paid taxes, or shopped in a supermarket, or laid down fifty bucks for a pair of jeans. I would have stopped it if I could. I wasn't there when it happened. It was just something I saw passing by.

But seeing it did something to me. That much, twenty-five years later, was clear. That much, out on the balcony that night, I accepted. It was like the first piece of the puzzle had fallen into place. I'm still working on it. It's a puzzle about the body—my body, that girl's. There's a connection. It's not about guilt or responsibility, though that's there, that's one of the pieces. But it's something different, its something more. My hand and hers. My throat and her throat. Our bodies. The music did something to me: the volume and the intensity. The violence did something, my punching that boy. I didn't understand then. I still don't entirely now.

But that night in my empty house, when I first realized I might have hallucinated the girl at the concert, it was electric, sparks were snapping inside me. The wind gusted, blew through the house. For a moment, I sensed the beginning of fear: it was like a fist closing around my heart. Instead of running, I let my body rock a little bit. I let it sway. That helped. That made things better. In Atlanta, out on the balcony, while I danced with Sally, the city blazed around us, the blue light on the skyline turning lazily, the red lights of the cars merging into a glistening line that looped and spun. When we turned, the stars and the moon whirled. At one point in our dancing, I pressed my lips to Sally's hair and whispered that I loved her. It was crazy, I knew it. Immediately, I said, "I'm sorry. I'm so sorry." She rubbed my back. She kept dancing. She said, "It's okay, really. It's okay." She kissed my chest. I held to her. I held her tightly and I blessed her. I blessed her and begged her forgiveness, holding her tightly as we danced.

Monsters

—◁▥◁▥▷—

I WAS SIXTEEN, A SKINNY KID WHO WALKED WITH
his hands in his pockets and his eyes on his feet, with dark, curly hair that
stuck up where I wanted it to lay flat and lay flat where I wanted it to stick
up. I wasn't very interesting. I had grown up in Brooklyn playing ringolevio
and Johnny on the pony, and I had been friendless from the time my parents
moved out to Long Island when I was thirteen. My personal hygiene was du-
bious. I rarely took showers, often forgot to brush my teeth, and wore the
same dingy, rat-holed underwear for weeks. Besides all that, I was sneaky,
willing to lie whenever, and a Peeping Tom. I must have had some good qual-
ities, but they don't occur to me at the moment.

Victor Trane, or Train, as everyone called him, was the only kid in Northwood High liked by all the various cliques, from the jocks to the skaters. He
was one-of-a-kind, Train. He'd wear creased pants and a dress shirt one day;
the next day, jeans and a T-shirt; and the day after that he might show up in
khaki pants and a knit polo shirt. Some days he'd wear a jacket and tie. He
didn't come to school in clothes so much as outfits.

Train was a part of our consciousness at Northwood. He was without competition the most popular kid in school, especially among girls. The fact that
he was a musician, a guitar player who had his own band, called the Worms,
had something to do with his attractiveness to the opposite sex, but mostly I

think it was because he was handsome, no matter what he wore. He was one of the taller kids in eleventh grade, he was muscular, and he had intense, ice-blue eyes and dark hair, and a face with all its features in proportion, unlike my own face, which was graced by large, stick-out ears. I was about average in height, but I had lanky arms that felt sometimes like they reached all the way down to my knee caps. I wasn't ugly so much as I was odd looking. Luckily, I was pretty much invisible to most of the kids at Northwood, though there were a couple who got on me, calling me Big Ears, and sometimes Dumbo, which was a dual insult, referring both to my ears and my intelligence.

I wasn't dumb, though. I was bright. I had always been bright. That's how Train noticed me. We were assigned to the same group in an English peer-review workshop. Northwood is a campus-style school comprised of several buildings linked by glass walkways. English and art shared a building separated by a grassy courtyard from the gym building. From English, you could look over a circular fountain surrounded by benches, into the gymnasium through a single, large window at the front of the building—which is what I spent most of my class time doing. The teacher was an old guy named Mr. Hanson, so bored by teaching he'd sometimes stop in the middle of a lecture and yawn and close his eyes, as if he needed to nap for just a second. I sat in the back of the room, by the window, where I could watch girls climbing the ropes in gym.

It was spring already, most of the school year gone by, when Mr. Hanson put me in a group with Train, Melissa, and Janet. For a few minutes, once the groups were assigned, the cinder-block room was noisy with the sound of chair legs scraping against the tile floor as the class arranged their desk-chairs in small circles of four and five students. Then the room erupted into loud talk and laughter as the formality of the straight rows disappeared and students loosened up with each other. Mr. Hanson let the talk and laughter go for a few minutes before he slapped his desk a few times and suggested we get to work. Janet and Melissa were all smiles, looking across their desks at Train, assuming he'd get things going, which he did. Janet and Melissa were two of the least attractive girls in the class, but Train was friendly to everyone, and both girls were beaming in his attention.

"All right, ladies," he said, "and gentleman . . ." He looked over to me and seemed perplexed for a moment. "What's your name?" he asked. "Have you always been in this class?"

Janet and Melissa laughed.

"All year," I said.

"Mike Swiggart," Melissa said.

Train seemed a little embarrassed at not knowing who I was. "Don't mind me," he said. It was a western day for Train: he was wearing jeans and snake-skin cowboy boots with pointy toes, and a red cowboy shirt with shiny buttons. He stuck his feet out into the middle of the circle. "It's these boots." He pointed at the toes, which looked like they were made for hole-punching. "They cut off the circulation to the brain or something." The girls laughed, both of them bringing their hands to their mouths. "Seriously . . ." Train said.

I said, "No problem."

"Mike, then." Train handed me two neatly printed sheets of paper, and took a crumpled page of loose leaf from my desk top. "Why don't I read yours and you read mine?"

A brief flash of disappointment showed in both girls' eyes before they exchanged papers and began reading, and then the class grew quiet with everyone involved in each others' essays.

We were midway through a unit on poetry, and we were supposed to be workshopping rough drafts of a poetry review. The assignment was to locate a book of contemporary poetry, read it, and write a review. Train chose *Lyrical Ballads*, by William Wordsworth and Samuel Taylor Coleridge. As soon as I realized what book he was reviewing, I looked up at him, but his eyes were focused intensely on my sheet of loose leaf. I went back to his essay. The first sentence read: "Mr. Wordsworth and Mr. Coleridge are important American poets." The thesis sentence, which came at the end of the introductory paragraph, exactly where it was supposed to be, read: "Wordsworth and Coleridge are important poets because they understand the modern world in which we live, use language precisely and in an interesting manner, and because their poems look to the future with a bold and exciting vision." The rest of the essay was a really pretty impressive manipulation of vagaries and generalities. In a little under five hundred words he created the impression that he had read and enjoyed a book he had obviously never opened.

I was no one to talk, however. I hadn't even made an attempt at starting the essay. Rather than come to class completely empty-handed for the rough-draft peer review, I had grabbed a poem out of my closet where thousands of them were stacked in two cardboard file-cabinet boxes. I had been writing poems from the age of five, three or four a week, usually. I was serious about poetry. I had already read most of the modern poets thoroughly—William Carlos Williams, Wallace Stevens, T. S. Eliot, Ezra Pound, W. B. Yeats—and I was working my way backward, through the symbolists to the romantics and Blake, and reading eclectically along the way. My favorite poet was Gerard Manley Hopkins. His poems excited me, and his poetics fascinated me, his sprung rhythms and curtal sonnets, the way he played with syllables and sounds. I may have been uncertain about everything else in my life, but I was sure that I was destined to be a great poet. I knew it was coming, it was only a matter of time.

Up until a few years earlier, my poems were mostly about my father, who lived in Chicago with another family. He moved away when I was three. I had already figured out that to my father I was an unfortunate mistake from his youth. Most of my early poems are addressed directly to him: they're full of *you*'s, where *you* is always him. Later, the subject range widened some, and the poem Train was reading was about the environment: it meant to suggest that the world was polluted because our hearts and souls were polluted. Something like that anyway.

By the time Train looked up from my poem, the girls were already talking about their essays. He said, "Whoa, Cowboy." His outfit appeared to affect the way he talked. "This is sterling. This is, like, heavy. You're a poet, man." He looked surprised. His mouth had fallen open slightly. He looked happy, as if he had just discovered something wonderful. "You're the real thing," he went on. "A real, live, walkin', talkin' poet."

The girls looked up from their essays and over to me. "You wrote a poem?" Melissa said, leaning over to look on Train's desk.

Janet said, "But this was supposed to be a book review."

"Screw that," Train said. "The guy's a poet."

I was embarrassed and pleased at the same time. I don't show my poems to many people. I used to show them only to my mother, whose response was always, "Very nice, Michael," followed by some comment about how special and sensitive I was. The last time I showed her a poem was when I was thirteen and we had just moved out to the Island after she married Jim. It was a suicide poem. It said that as soon as she was done reading it, I was going to kill myself. I had no intention of killing myself, of course. I was just trying to make her see that I was unhappy about the move to Long Island. I gave it to her at night and then waited up in bed for her to come running to my room. She didn't, and eventually I fell asleep. In the morning, when I asked her if she had read it, she said, "Yes. Very nice, Michael. You're a sensitive boy." She handed the poem back to me, picking it up off the kitchen table where I had left it for her the night before. She kissed me on the forehead.

Train was staring at me. I said, "I'm glad you like it," and then shrugged my shoulders and shook my head in an idiotic gesture that indicated I didn't know what else to say.

Melissa, either unaware or unconcerned that she was glowering, said, "Too bad you can't turn it in, since it's supposed to be a book review."

Train said, "It's only a peer review," being uncharacteristically abrupt with her. "What about mine?" he said to me. "What did you think?"

I faltered a moment and then said, "Did you, like, know that this was supposed to be a book of contemporary poetry?"

"It's not contemporary?" he said. He reached into his book bag and pulled out a thin black volume. When he opened it, the spine was stiff and the binding cracked, as if it were being opened for the first time. "It looked like a new book . . . ," he muttered as he read the title page. Then his expression changed rapidly from chagrin to amusement. He looked up from the book, smiling at me.

Janet said. "When was it published?"

Train said, making his smile imbecilic, "Uh . . . 1798?" Which made us all laugh, as he intended.

After class, he walked with me to civics, even though he had gym, which was in the opposite direction. The tiled corridors at Northwood seemed to have been designed to amplify sound: between classes, pushed along by thick knots of people, you had to talk loudly if you wanted to be heard. "Whoa, man," Train said. "You saved my ass, Mr. Mike. Hanson would've cooked me I turned in that shit."

"You think so?" I said. To my surprise, I was at ease talking to Train, even though about a million kids said hello to him as we walked along, and every single one of them looked at me, like, *Who the hell is that?* That was one of the secrets of Train's popularity: everybody felt at ease with him. It was like you felt safe with Train, like you didn't need to have your guard up. "*Lyrical Ballads*," I said, with a smirk. "Not a good choice."

"Looked like a new book . . ." He shook off the subject. "Listen," he said. "You know my band, the Worms?"

"Sure," I said. I was five-ten then, which was as tall as I was going to get, and Train was already a couple of inches taller. I had to look up when I faced him, which I found awkward, so I was walking with my hands in my pockets and my eyes on the ground, only looking up at him every now and then. I said, "I heard you play at a couple of the dances."

"We suck, man." Train was a quiet a long moment. His expression was pained. He looked down at me, and our eyes met. We were coming up on the boys' room, and when we reached the open door, he pulled me inside. "Listen," he said. "You know, I'm like major-league into my music." The boys' room was not empty. There were a couple of football-player types standing in front of a row of five porcelain sinks and mirrors, combing their hair. Behind them, the two stalls were in use, as were three of the five urinals. Train backed me against the white tile wall, leaned against it with one arm, forming a small, private room, and talked to me as if there were no one else around. "My brother," he said. "Man, my brother's a monster. He's like one of the three best keyboard players in L.A., and that's saying something, Mr. Mike. *L.A.*," he said, looking at me as if to say, *You must appreciate the significance of that.*

I said, "I'm impressed. Sincerely. " I repeated, as if awed. "*L.A.*"

"Thing is," Train said, dropping his voice a touch, "I'm not there yet, but I'm going to be that good, too. On guitar. I'm going to be a monster and my brother and I are going to play together. That's what I dream about. But first, man, first I've got to make it on my own. With my own band. And the Worms, Mr. Mike, the Worms are not cutting it." Then he looked at me intently and pointed a finger at my chest. "Michael," he said, "I can tell this about you. From that one poem. You got it, man. You've got talent to a serious degree. You, man," he said. "You've got to do the lyrics. You're the guy I need."

Train looked hard at me then, and the look in his eyes was almost pleading, as if what I said next was of crucial importance to him. "Sure," I said, listening to myself speak the words. "I can do lyrics," I said. "No problem."

"Cool," Train said. "Can you sing?"

I said, "Sure. I can sing." I *could* sing. I had been in chorus from sixth through eighth grade, where I had learned how to read music, and when I quit, Mrs. O'Reilly wrote me a personal letter, urging me to stay on. She said I was her best tenor. I quit anyway. I quit because Bill McDaid always tormented me in chorus, standing behind me on the bleachers and flicking my ears or spitting on my head. The two times I complained to Mrs. O'Reilly, I wound up in a fight with him after class, and both time I had to run away before he turned me into paste. So I quit. I said to Train, "I can read music, too."

"Terrific," Train said. His blue eyes were glittering, and his lips were pulled back in a smile revealing toothpaste-ad teeth. "I'll pick you up at eight tonight. I'll call you for directions. You're in the book, right? Swiggart?"

"Sure," I said. The bathroom had emptied out at that point. We were both going to be late for class. "Where're we going?" I asked.

"My place," he said. "We'll see what we can do together." He started out the door and then stopped and turned around, half out in the hall. "I'll invite some of the guys," he said. "You have a girlfriend?"

I shook my head.

"You got a girl you like?"

Without thinking, in a instant, I said, "Daphne Mueller."

"Cool," he said. "Talk to you later," and then he disappeared into the corridor.

That was how Train and I got together. Our first band, called the Wrath, was only a few months away from forming. Much was about to happen—but I wasn't thinking about it then. I was thinking about Daphne Mueller.

Daphne lived a few blocks away from me, and I had been spying on her for more than a year. I found her a few months earlier, on a winter night, during a snow storm. My mother and Jim, my stepfather, were in the middle of a screaming match. I bundled up in my black quilted jacket and hood, and walked right past them, out the kitchen door into the backyard in the middle of a near-blizzard, and neither of them asked where I was going. I knew they wouldn't. It was like I was invisible in that house. I went out back and crossed my yard through the snow and went out to the road. I was heading for a small park that had an actual red caboose as its centerpiece. I liked to go there alone at night sometimes and sit in this little compartment at the top of the caboose, where I could lie on my back and look out a small window. I pulled the drawstring on my hood until my face was completely covered except for a tiny hole over one eye. I was walking along the sidewalk, past a house dark except for the flickering blue light of a television, when I saw the bright yellow light of an uncurtained window shine out of the basement up on to the snow.

To me, at that time, that kind of light, that bright yellow light shining out into the dark, it was irresistible. I couldn't help myself. Even now, I see that light, I want to check it out. I walked past the house and then ducked down alongside a line of hedges. I waited a moment, crouched down there, and looked around to see if anyone might have noticed me. I watched and listened. No one was out that night because of the weather. The curving suburban street, surrounded by small lawns and brick houses or wood houses with aluminum siding, was dark except for an occasional house light through which particles of snow hurled themselves down into the grass. The only sound was the wind banging into houses or riffling through bushes.

I crept along the hedge line, keeping low, until I was directly across from the basement window. On the tips of my boots, I stole toward the house, keeping well back from the outline of light on snow, being careful not to leave tracks easily identifiable as footprints. Near the wall, there was a long icy trench where no snow had gathered because of the way the house blocked the wind. It was perfect for me. I could crawl along the ice without leaving a mark, hidden from sight by a mound of snow.

When I reached the window, the first thing I saw was a single bed against the front wall. The window curtain was already pulled, but I was able to look in over the top of it, where it hung off a curtain rod on brass rings. There was a second window above the bed, the window through which I had caught the first flash of light shining out toward the sidewalk. The bed was neatly made, with a sea-blue quilted comforter. The floor, instead of being concrete, was hardwood, shiny blond slats brightly polished, and my first thought was, *This is a hell of a basement.* I saw several books lying around and a violin case next to a music stand. Then I noticed a bra and panties on the seat of a chair next to a dresser and mirror. Hung over the back of the chair were a pair of stonewashed denims and a Northwood High School sweatshirt.

I would have waited there all night after seeing those clothes on the back of the chair, but I didn't have to. In a few minutes, Daphne came into the room, wrapped in a fat pink towel knotted at her breasts. I was breathing so loudly I was glad for the howling of the wind. She stood on her toes and pulled the curtain over the front window, and then sat on a cinnamon throw rug in front of her bed, with her back against the mattress and her legs stretched out, and she began to brush and then braid long auburn hair that reached halfway down her back. She was beautiful, and it wasn't an ordinary beauty. There was something about her eyes that was quick and darting, a kind of nervous, frightened beauty. It's hard to explain. She was thin and elegant and alert, as if listening for something. As she moved her arms and torso, brushing and braiding her hair, the slit where the towel edges didn't meet grew wider and wider, until she was naked from her feet to the place where the towel knotted at her breasts.

When Daphne finished brushing her hair, she discarded the towel and put on baggy, cotton pajamas. I guess if you can fall in love with an image, which I think you definitely can, I fell in love with her then. By the time I got back to my house, I was damn near frostbit. Sometimes I'd watch her when she was only reading a book or just lying on her back, looking up at the ceiling. She seemed lonely. I wondered what she dreamed about. For a while, I went back to her house every night, but then I cut back to once or twice a week, figuring I was sure to get caught, no matter how careful I was, if I went every night. By the time I met Train in English, I was still spying on Daphne occasionally, and no one had ever come close to catching me. I felt like I knew Daphne intimately, though I had at that point never spoken a word to her.

After Train walked out of the boys' room, I hung around several more minutes. I think I was dazed. I can still remember the musical, echoing sound of swirling water in one of the johns. I went into the stall and jiggled the handle to get the water to stop, and then I just stayed in the stall, looking right through the pen and pencil graffiti. When I finally headed to class, I was so late that I had go back to the office and get a pass. Later, at home, after school, in my empty house, I wandered from room to room, talking to myself, checking myself out in every mirror I passed. "Damn!" I kept saying. "Man!" Train wanted me to write song lyrics for his band. It appeared he was also thinking I might sing. This second notion had me in a semi-intoxicated, close-to-psychotic dream state. I didn't think twice about the lyrics. I was sure I could do it and it didn't seem like a big deal—but standing on stage and singing with Train's band . . . Wow. I saw myself leaning over a microphone in the crowded gymnasium as everyone swayed to the music, hanging on my every word. I saw girls pushing against the stage, reaching up to touch my feet. I saw myself looking over them all to Daphne Mueller, who was looking back at me, longingly, from a corner of the room.

At dinner, over chuck steak and potatoes, I announced that I was going to Victor Trane's later, because he wanted me to write lyrics for his band and maybe sing with them.

"Really," my mother said. She was in her robe already, and she pulled the wide collar up toward her neck. "You're going to play with a band?"

"How are you getting there?" Jim said. His tone of voice made it clear that he sure as hell wasn't taking me. He was drinking a scotch and ice with his dinner, and he lay both his beefy arms on the table, the thick fingers of one hand gently touching the tumbler of scotch. He was a big man, with curly hair and a round, pudgy face. He was muscular once, but all his muscles had long ago turned to flab that rolled over his shirt collar and pushed against the seams of his clothes.

"Train drives," I said. "He's got his own car."

"Is that so?" Jim said.

"Something wrong with the kid having a friend who drives?" My mother leaned over her plate, toward Jim; her robe brushed against her food.

Jim met her eyes for a moment and then went back to eating.

I let the subject drop. A little later, Train called for directions, and when he pulled up in front of the house, I was waiting for him at the curb. He drove a Dodge Viper. A late-model, candy-apple red Dodge Viper. He leaned across the passenger's seat and pushed open the door.

"Damn!" I said, sinking into a leather seat that was like a copilot's seat in a jet cockpit. "This is awesome!"

Train had ditched the cowboy outfit in favor of more upscale, casual attire: charcoal twills and a pressed, blue-striped shirt. "Bad home life?" he said.

"Why?"

"Waiting for me in front of the house instead of letting me come in and meet the folks."

"You don't want to meet my folks. Believe me."

Train looked over me, toward my house, as if checking for my parents. "Too bad," he said.

I touched the dashboard, running my hand over the slick black surface. "How fast is this thing?"

"How fast?" He leaned back in his seat, threw the car into gear, and left a black stretch of hot rubber from my front door to the corner of the block less than an eighth of a mile away, at which point we were already doing better than sixty.

"Hey," I said. "Train . . ." We were coming up on a dead end, going way too fast to make the necessary right-angle turn. I gripped the upholstery and looked frantically toward the door, trying to locate the seat belt.

Train hit the brakes and the car did a three-sixty, coming to a full stop in the middle of the intersection. "Fast enough?"

My face must have been white, because he broke up once he got a good look at me. He laughed so hard he bumped his head into the steering wheel.

"That was cool," I said. "That was awesome."

"All right," he said. "Mr. Michael! Poet extraordinaire!"

"Uh-oh." I pointed to a man coming out of his house and approaching the car. He looked seriously unhappy.

Train glanced at the man with a flat, unconcerned look. He hit the gas. A few seconds later the guy was a memory and we were out on the main drag, driving at a reasonable speed, heading toward his house.

Train's parents were both lawyers. His dad worked for the World Bank and his mother was with some private firm. I knew this because they had both given talks at school. "How about your folks?" I asked him. "You get along with them?" We were nearing his house, which I had never seen before, but I guessed would be a small mansion.

"My parents are all right," Train said, making a little gesture with his shoulders. "You'll meet my mother."

"Not your father?"

"His job keeps him on the road a lot. He's like in Kenya now or someplace."

When we pulled into Train's garage, I was a disappointed. The house wasn't the mansion I had been expecting. It was a big house, but nothing to make you stop and gawk. Once inside the garage—where we parked between a Volvo and a BMW—Train hit a button on a remote-control device and the garage door descended slowly behind us. I followed Train outside to a terra-cotta path that circled an in-ground pool surrounded by brickwork and flower boxes and covered with a thick green tarp. We were walking away from the main house toward a much smaller building that was separated from the pool by a garden and a couple of mimosa trees.

"That's my mother," Train said, without looking back toward the house, where a woman was sitting behind a bay window, talking to a guy in a blue business suit across a long, brightly polished dining-room table.

I looked back toward the house, as if I hadn't really noticed them until he said something. "Really?" I said. "That's your mother?" She had the same dark hair and dark eyes as Train—but she didn't look anywhere near old enough to be his mother.

Train put his hands in his pockets and turned back, almost reluctantly, toward the dining room.

I asked, "Who's the guy?"

"I don't know," he said. He had a glimmer in his eyes and a strange half-smile. "Like I said, my father's away a lot."

"Oh." I had no idea how to continue. I was grateful when he started back along the path without waiting for me to elaborate.

The building behind the pool turned out to be a recording studio. At the entrance, Train pulled a key from his pocket, unlocked the door, and with a flourish flung it open for me to see. The interior looked like something out of a movie. The walls and ceiling were covered with space-age looking white acoustic tiles, and the floor was made of some kind of hard, deep-red rubber material, almost like a tennis court. There were boom mikes hanging from the ceiling, and stand-up mikes next to music stands, and musical equipment everywhere: drum sets, guitars, saxophones, keyboards, horns, a double-bass, a violin, a banjo. . . . There was even a huge electric harp with foot pedals and an amplifier next to the soundbox. Against the far wall, a long, rectangular window looked into a dimly lit control room, where I could see an elaborate audio console and more microphones and computer gear.

Train said, "Pretty cool, huh?"

"This is unbelievable," I said. "Can you, like, cut your own albums here?"

"Cut an album?" Train said. "Where have you been living, Mike? What's an album?"

I blushed deeply at that and tried to laugh casually, as if amused at myself. Where *did* I come up with a phrase like "cut an album"? My mother was the only person I knew who still owned a turntable and albums to play on it. Before leaving my house, I had showered and put on clean clothes and brushed my teeth, and I had left, I thought, looking pretty good. With all my fantasies of singing with Train's band, and with Train coming and picking me up in his Viper, I was actually thinking of myself as a pretty cool guy. Then I went and said something like "cut an album."

"Come on," Train said. He touched my arm. The touch was like absolution.

I followed him into the control room, quietly. I was hesitant to talk, and that turned out to be just fine, since what Train had in mind was to put on a show for me. While I watched, sitting in one of the console chairs, he picked up an old Martin D12 guitar, slung its strap over his shoulder, and started to play. At first he just ran through a bunch of fast riffs and jazzy scales, interrupted by little bits of dialogue I hardly understood, explaining where the riffs came from, who developed them, who did what the best on which piece. Then he got serious and pulled up a stool next to a console and started popping in CDs of guitar greats from Django Rhienhart to Eric Clapton. He played bits and pieces of classic guitar stuff, and then repeated it perfectly, to my ear at least, on the D12.

When Train said he was serious about music, he was telling the truth. I listened to him for more than hour, and the last piece he played was something he had written himself. To say I was impressed would be a serious understatement. Before that night, I had never taken music seriously. Music, to me, was entertainment, like the movies or TV—something you did to relax. It wasn't art, Art with a capital A, like Poetry and Literature, like Painting and Sculpture. But that night in that dimly lit control room, with all the everyday, worldly noises blocked out and Train hunched over his guitar, I learned how much alike music and poetry could be. Train fingered the neck of that guitar and notes came out of the soundbox and fell together into riffs that reached inside me. I felt then, for the first time, how musical notes could work like the syllables of words in a poem, syllables that fell together into a series of sounds that somehow reached inside and opened up something through combinations of thought and recognition and sound. I got seriously excited about writing songs with Train. And I saw that there was obviously more to him than cool clothes and lots of self-confidence.

Before he quit, I was wanting to impress him back. I was wanting to run home and find my best poems and read them for him. I was waiting for him to stop, so I could talk, so I could tell him how good I thought he was, and explain that I was serious about poetry in the same way he was serious about music—but before he quit, his mother's voice came into the room through a speaker, making me jump almost straight up out of my chair and ruining the mood entirely. Her voice was liquid smooth, with a Southern accent. "Victor, honey," she said. "Your friends are here."

The sound was so clean, it was as if she were standing in the middle of the room, invisible. Train put the guitar down, pressed a button, and leaned toward an intercom mike. He said, "Be there in a second, Joyce."

He hustled me out of the studio, and when I tried to stammer my appreciation for his music, he cut me off. "I invited a bunch of the guys," he said. It was a beautiful spring evening, warm, with just a little dampness in the air. "So you could meet them."

I would have preferred to talk to him than meet his friends. I wasn't sure what it was I wanted so badly to say—it had to do with poetry and music, the connections I was feeling—but I nodded, as if to say "Fine."

Across the yard, all the lights were on in the house. Every room—and there were lots of rooms—was lit up bright. We walked along the brickwork of the pool and entered the house through French doors that opened into a plushly carpeted great room. Inside, we descended a small flight of stairs to a short hallway that led to a foyer and the front door. The walls of the house, from the great room to the foyer, were hung with oil paintings and art objects—strange things to my eyes, hangings that looked like concrete-covered machinery, sculpted dishware, all manner of oddness. If Train's mother was around, I didn't see her.

Train opened the front door and a dozen kids rolled in with loud greetings and hand slapping. Like Train, they exuded an air of confidence. The girls, without exception, were good looking. All but one had blond hair, though the shades were different. Train introduced me to them, and although some of them must have recognized me from classes we'd shared over the past couple of years, they all treated me as if I had just moved into the neighborhood. Only one of them, a guy named Jo Jo Arnold, mentioned having seen me around Northwood.

The group was evenly divided among the sexes, and it took me a second to figure out that they were all couples. It dawned on me as the girls began to fold themselves under the arms of their boyfriends. Vivian, a small girl with platinum-blond hair and extraordinarily large breasts, which she called attention to by wearing a flaming red blouse with a neckline that dove into deep cleavage, asked Train where Emily was. Train answered by pointing out the door as a white Pontiac Firebird pulled up under the driveway lights. It came to a stop beside a van in which, apparently, everyone else had arrived. "There," he said, pointing at a girl who exited the driver's side, waving and yelling hello in a high-pitched voice. She was gorgeous, of course, but unique in her looks, with carrot-orange hair that exploded off her head in a fiery nimbus. She wore boots and painted-on jeans and a blue suede jacket that contrasted vividly with her red hair. After taking a few quick steps toward the front door, she stopped and looked back to the Firebird, as if waiting for someone, and then the passenger door opened and Daphne Mueller hopped out, laughing, pulling up her pantyhose under a leather miniskirt. "I had to change, I had a run!" she squealed, a high-pitched mix of words and tittering laughter. She hurried up to Emily, who took her by the hand, and together they blew into the foyer to the squeals and hugs of the other girls, who acted like they hadn't seen either of them in many years. I shrank back against the wall. It was first time I had ever heard Daphne Mueller speak.

Daphne, it turned out, was a good friend of Vivian's and Lucille's, who were going out with Tommy and Gary and were good friends of Emily's, who, of course, was going out with Train. It was complicated. The important thing was that lots of girls wanted to go out with guys who were tight with Train, because of Train's band and because Train's house, as I was soon to learn, was a cool place to hang out. Daphne didn't know me from Adam, but she jumped at the chance to meet me because it meant she could hang out with Vivian and Lucille at Train's. Once the introductions were over, we all descended to the basement, which was a labyrinth of carpeted rooms surrounding a wide billiard room with a tournament-size pool table, a home theater system in a far corner, and a well-stocked bar against one wall.

Everyone headed straight for the bar, and a few minutes later there was music coming through wall-mounted speakers as guys with beer bottles dangling from their fingers stood around the pool table, getting ready to shoot a game, and girls were busy mixing exotic drinks, using a variety of ingredients pulled from a refrigerator under the bar. Train took me and Daphne with him and Emily to a dark room down a short hallway, where we sat on the floor in a circle around a bong—which was something I had never seen before, except in an illustration from *Alice in Wonderland*. I pretended to be comfortable, sitting alongside Daphne, who had her legs folded under her and was sitting on her heels with her skirt up around midthigh. I pretended to know what was going on, when actually I had only the slightest glimmering. I figured we were about to smoke some kind of drug, since Train had just flamed up a torch of a cigarette lighter, his face red and shimmering in the firelight. I wasn't nervous about it at all. I was excited. I was into it—but before we could get started, Vivian and Tommy found the room. "There you are!" Vivian said in a harsh whisper. They joined us in a circle around the bong. "Trying to hide out!"

"Sshhh," Emily said, laughing. "There's not enough for everybody."

"Well," Vivian said. "Hurry up then."

I was the last one to take a hit and I was able to figure out how to do it by watching everyone else. I choked like crazy, of course, and everyone laughed, but the laughter was good-natured—and after a while everyone was too stoned to pay any attention to what I was doing anyway. I couldn't hold the smoke in at all, and I don't think I got even a little bit high, really—but it was easy enough to act like it, laughing at whatever was said and telling everyone, man, how high you were. Then Train left and came back with a bottle of bourbon and a bunch of plastic cups, and in short order I was definitely tipsy and everyone else in the room was wrecked. Daphne was drinking bourbon like it was Pepsi.

"Man!" she said. "This is so cool!" She was referring to her surroundings. "My asshole units make me *live* in the fucking basement!"

"Whoa," Train said. "Major hardship." He cast an amused look in my direction.

"Really," Daphne said. "You're so fucking lucky, Train."

Emily looked at Daphne and said, "You're out of it, Daph."

While the rest of us were sitting cross-legged or with our legs stretched out, Daphne was kneeling: I figured because if she sat down her miniskirt would wind up around her neck. "Don't be ridiculous," she said. "I'm not even a little high!" Then she stuck her tongue out and made a wrecked face, which was intended, I guess, to be funny, but she overdid it and actually looked kind of frightening, as if she were suddenly having a fit. We all stared at her.

Train said, "I think it's time for me and Emily to find a little quiet space." He got up, pulling Emily with him. Then Vivian and Tommy got up and a second later it was just me and Daphne.

The room was small and windowless, with a cot against one wall and a dresser at the foot of the cot. The only light, the little of it there was, came from the dimly lit hallway. Daphne smiled across the room at me, seductively. I smiled back. I found it hard to believe this was the same girl I had been watching for so long. In her basement, alone, she seemed intelligent and vulnerable and lonely. Here, since she got out of the car she had been behaving brazenly. I didn't get it. I didn't understand how the girl in the basement and this girl could be one and the same.

When she figured out I wasn't going to respond to her smile, Daphne pointed to the bottle of bourbon alongside me. "Want to share a swig?" she said.

I said, "Sure," and took a drink and handed her the bottle.

She laughed. "No," she said. "This is what I mean." She crawled across the floor and sat beside me. As soon as her body touched mine, it was like somebody flipped on a heater switch, and the furnace came on with a roar. I was hot from the top of my head to my feet. "Here," Daphne said. She leaned back and took a long swig from the bottle. She was wearing a light blue, boatneck blouse that floated lightly over her breasts. The smell of her perfume was faintly musky, and it got mixed up somehow with thump of the bass coming from the music down the hall. When she tilted her head up, I could see the lines of her neck flowing down past her collar bone to the soft skin of her chest. I got flushed and breathless. She put the bottle down, but she didn't swallow and drop her head. Instead she turned to me and put her mouth against my mouth and her hand on the back of my neck and shared the whiskey with me, from her mouth to mine.

"Cool," I managed to cough out when we were done. I was breathing as though I had asthma, as though I were undergoing mild convulsions—but Daphne didn't notice. With her face so close to mine, I could see how drunk and high she was. You could have driven a Mack truck through her pupils.

"Mike," she whispered, "do you go to Northwood?" She kissed me on the neck and touched my chest with the flat of her hand.

I didn't bother to answer. I don't really think I could have spoken a full sentence anyway. I kissed her on the lips. She kissed me back hard, our teeth clanking into each other. I dropped my hand under her blouse and it slid under the top of her bra and then I was holding her bare breast in my hand. She responded by leaning her body into me, pushing me back against the floor and crawling on top of me. She pushed her body into mine while she was kissing me, grinding her hips into my hips, and before I realized it, I had an orgasm. I could feel the stain spreading out in a circle through my undershirt.

I pulled away from her.

"What?" she said. "What's wrong?"

I said, "I think I'm going to throw up."

"Bad news," she said. She stood up and then quickly sat down on the cot. "I'm a little dizzy myself," she said. "You okay?" She scooted back and patted the mattress, indicating I should join her.

"Not yet," I said. "I'll be right back." I started for the door.

"Wait!" She stretched out her arm. "Pass me the bottle." She was smiling seductively again. "To keep me company until you get back."

I handed her the bottle, kissed her, and went out into the hall where I checked myself out. The stain wasn't too bad. It was up high, near the waistband of my pants. I found a dark place, pulled my shirt and undershirt off, blotted myself dry as best I could and put my shirt back on without tucking it in, so it covered the stain. The undershirt I tossed into a corner. I considered going right back to Daphne, but I was sticky and it seemed like a good idea to wait a least a few minutes, to give myself time to dry off a bit as well as rejuvenate. I decided to find a bathroom, wash up, and then go back.

The billiard room, to my surprise, was completely empty. The music was blaring, but there was no one there. The couples, I figured, must have all retired to private rooms, having prepped themselves sufficiently with drinks and drugs. I followed the hall up the stairs toward the kitchen, where I had passed a bathroom earlier. Before I got to the kitchen, though, I saw Train sitting on a brick patio at a small table just beyond the great room's French doors. There was a bottle of bourbon on the floor at his feet and he was looking up at a night sky dazzlingly bright with stars as he picked out a jazzy riff of chords and notes, his left hand moving in staccato bursts of speed up and down the neck of the guitar.

I was anxious to get back to Daphne, and if he hadn't looked down at that moment and turned to find me watching him, I don't believe I would have stopped. I would have cleaned up a bit and hurried back down to the basement—but he did turn and look, and I went out to join him for a moment on the patio.

"Where's Emily?" I pulled up a seat at the table next to him.

Train drummed his fingers on the guitar's soundboard. "It's hard to make them understand. Do you have this problem?" He leaned over his guitar, as if I were someone from whom he expected commiseration.

"What problem?" I said.

He went about pouring us both drinks, taking up the bottle at his feet and removing two plastic glasses from a stack on the table. He did all this with the guitar in his lap. "Don't they bug you for time and things? Like they want all this shit from you? Jesus," he said. "The hell with it, man. Just fuck her." He pushed a drink toward me and took a quick swallow from his own. When he put his drink down, he sloshed a bit onto the table, and I could tell he was drunk, though he wasn't slurring his words or acting stupid.

"So she's not here?" I said. "She took off?"

Trains made a sweeping gesture with his hand and said, "Gone, man." He took another drink. "And I was really looking forward to fucking her. Jesus, man, she is something otherworldly in bed." He smiled at me. "How's Daphne?"

I froze a second and then laughed awkwardly, trying to cover the hesitation. "Man," I said. "Your mother. . . . Like, she has no problem with any of this?"

"What? You mean Train's Motel and Bar for the Underaged?" He smiled wryly. "Joyce and I have a deal. When she has a boyfriend here, I don't go upstairs, and when I have friends over, she doesn't come downstairs." He pushed his hair back, off his face. "Works out for both of us."

I didn't know what to say. I took another sip of whiskey.

Train picked a few notes as he looked across the table at me. "Are you shocked?" he asked. "About my mother?"

"She's young," I said. "You said your dad's gone all the time."

"I didn't think you'd be judgmental, man. That's cool." Train nodded his approval of my response. "But my mom's a bitch. She's a bitch's bitch. My father's an asshole and my mother's a whore. She's why my brother left. He couldn't hack it."

"Oh," I said. "That's—"

"Me and you, Mike—" Train put the guitar down, leaning the neck against the table. "We're simpatico. You know what I mean?"

I thought about it for a moment. "You mean," I said, "like, you with your music and me with poetry? Yes," I said.

Train smiled at me then, and the smile was like a handshake, as if we had just made a deal of some kind. "At first, man, I didn't see it—but then I read the one poem. Man, just the one poem and, like, zap!, there it was. I'm like this with my brother, too," he said. "In tune. He split without finishing high school. I'm going to finish though. I figure why not. It's cool."

"Sure," I said. "You need to—"

"Whoa!" Train said, loud. "It's a vision of beauty!" He looked past me, toward the French doors.

When I turned around I found Daphne standing in the light of the doorway, one hand on her hip. "You abandoned me!" she said, her tone of voice comically exaggerated—as if she were so shocked she was about to faint.

"No, no!" Train jumped up and went to her, putting an arm around her shoulder. "I waylaid him. I swear."

Daphne dropped her head onto his shoulder with a pout on her face. She looked good, not as drunk as I figured—though she seemed to appreciate Train's help walking.

"He found me out here brokenhearted," Train went on. "Emily walked out on me and Mike here kept me from drowning myself in the pool."

"Emily walked out on you?" Daphne pulled away from him and took his head in her hands. "You poor boy," she said. She wrapped her arms around his neck and kissed him on the lips.

"Whoa," Train said. He looked at me. "I'm feeling better already." He waved for me to join him and Daphne and when I hesitated he came over to the table, dragging Daphne along, and pulled me up by the arm. "Grab the bottle," he said. "Let's show Daphne the recording studio."

"You have a recording studio?" Daphne said. She slurred her words.

I was a little drunk at that point, but Daphne and Train were blasted. I wasn't sure how I felt about showing Daphne the studio, since what I had in mind was going back down to the basement with her, and I didn't know how to feel about the way she had kissed Train on the lips—but at that point the liquor was doing its work on me too, and I grabbed the bottle and took a long, burning swig. When I joined Daphne and Train, all three of us were laughing. We marched across the yard like the Three Musketeers, Daphne in the middle, my arm around her waist, Train's arm around her shoulder. Daphne kept saying, "Wait! Wait! Where are we going?" and Train and I would yell, "The studio!" and all three of us would laugh as if we were the funniest threesome on the planet.

Once we reached the studio and got inside, Train didn't even turn on the lights. He waltzed us all over to the stage in the semidarkness, where we tripped and crumpled in a bunch onto the carpet, laughing and giggling at first, before we all three got quiet. There was a dim light coming into the studio through the control-room window, not enough to see clearly, but I could make out Daphne's shadowy figure in front of me, and Train behind her—and I could see that Daphne's blouse was pushed up and her bra was pulled off and Train's hands were on her breasts. I remember feeling confused and excited at the same time. Daphne had one leg thrown over my legs and her eyes were closed. She was making a soft moaning noise and when I looked down, I saw that her miniskirt was up around her waist, and then her panty hose were being pulled down, revealing frilly, blue panties. I started to back away, confused about what was happening, but Daphne put her hand on my neck and pulled me toward her, and then I was kissing her breasts and I was out-of-control excited. Before that night, I had never so much as touched a girl. I had never been kissed. I was sixteen.

I forgot about Train. I buried my face in her breasts and kissed and licked as she held the back of my head in both hands. Then, suddenly, she threw one leg over me as she rose up to her knees with an unpleasant grunting sound and said "Hey! Hey!" I didn't understand what was going on. She was half-crawling on top of me, pushing me down as if I weren't there, as if she were trying to crawl away. Then she fell down on top of me and I could feel her weight and Train's, and she kept saying "Hey! Hey!" like she couldn't think of what she really wanted to say—but the alarm and fear in her voice were clear, and I tried to pull out from under her, but I was pinned by their weight, and I could feel her being pushed into me as she tried to scramble away. Then the weight lifted and she rolled off me and jumped up toward the center of the room and fell down as she tried to walk away, tripped up by the panty hose around her calves. I was lying on my side at the edge of the stage. Train's shadow laughed. I looked toward him as he stood up, and in the light from the control room I saw him peel off and toss away a sloppy condom—and then I figured out what had just happened.

When I looked for Daphne again, she was hurrying out the door, pushing through it with her shoulder as she pulled her skirt down. I was confused, but I knew that I wanted Daphne to understand that I didn't know, that I didn't know this was going to happen. I was frightened, concerned as much for myself as for her. I didn't want to get in trouble. I wanted to explain that I didn't know what was happening. I followed her out the door, chasing after her, and I caught sight of her just as she rounded the house, heading for the front drive. I ran to catch her, stumbled on a loose brick and plunged head first into a bush. As I got myself up and back together and saw that I was unhurt, I heard the door to the studio open and close. Train stood there, in front of the studio, looking relaxed, straightening out his clothes. I hurried away before he could see me.

I rounded the side of Train's house and walked in shadows toward the drive. Through the walls, I could hear music coming up faintly from the basement. In front of the house, Daphne was standing in the brightly lit driveway. She appeared stunned and confused as I watched her from the shadows. The white Firebird she had arrived in was gone, and she was standing where it had been parked. The driveway was so brightly lit, it was if she were onstage, under spotlights. She looked as though a magician had just made the Firebird disappear before her eyes and now she was standing where it had been, amazed. She held her face in her hands. Her mouth was open slightly. As I watched, I felt like I was spying on her again, the Daphne who was quiet at her mirror brushing her hair, who sometimes sang softly in her empty room, as if trying to cheer herself up as she went about some chore. I was about to walk out to her, to try to explain myself to her, to ask what I should do, when she bent over and threw up. A thick stream of yellow slime came out of her mouth and nose and splashed at her feet, dappling her shoes and legs. Then she stumbled out of the light, into the shadows, where I saw her kneel down and wretch violently, making horrible, guttural noises. I took a few steps in her direction, and she picked up her head and looked toward the sky. Thick globs of yellowish mucous were hanging from her nose. Chunks of vomit were matted in her hair and spit dribbled from her mouth.

I turned around and walked away from her. I'm not sure exactly what happened to me then. I've thought about it, about that moment, a thousand times. Something clicked off in me. Something just turned off at the sight of her. I remember thinking at the time that Train had probably only given her what she wanted all along, and then I spun around and walked away angrily, furious at her for a brief moment, and then simply not thinking about her at all. It was if nothing had happened, it was as if she weren't there anymore. I was drunk, but that's not the whole story. Something else happened. Something I've never fully understood. I was angry, and then I was just blank, and by the time I got back to the yard, Daphne was completely out of mind and I was feeling pretty good. My thoughts jostled around in an odd way that seemed natural to me then. I thought how ugly Daphne looked, I thought how she was something beautiful turned ugly, and then, by the time I returned to the backyard, I was thinking about the pure beauty of music and poetry, and I wanted to explain what I was thinking to Train.

I found him lying on his back on a small hill of neatly mown grass, his arms folded casually behind his neck as he looked up at the stars. I sat beside him and pushed him to get his attention. I wanted him to listen.

"What?" he said, after I pushed him. He turned on his side, rested his head on his hand and looked at me.

I was thinking to explain this dream I had about words, how I wanted one day to fashion a stream of words into a beauty as pure as sunlight. I wanted to write words like a river of light, words that flowed like music, like one perfect sustained note, something beautiful and enduringly perfect. I don't remember what I actually said, but I'm sure it was nothing like that. It was something like, "I love words. I love music."

Train smiled brightly. "We're going to be good together," he said, and he made a gesture with his hands, as if he were holding his guitar and his fingers were flying over the neck playing a quick musical riff. "Monsters," he said. "We're going to be monsters." Then he lay back again on the grass, folding his arms under his head, and I joined him, taking up the same position. We lay there together for a long time, looking up at a massive bright field of glittering stars, dreaming.

Sabbath Night in the
Church of the Piranha

—◁▯▯▯▯▷—

MATT AND CHRIS PENROSE LEANED AGAINST THE wall on either side of their living room's towering windows and peeked down the sunlit driveway, where Matt's mother struggled to get out of her car seat. His mother was heavy, always had been, all the long years of his childhood and adolescence, which he remembered as one unending moment of yearning for escape. His father was short and muscular from daily workouts at the YMCA gym. Anyone else watching a powerfully built little man straining to help a heavy woman out of her bucket seat—most anyone else would have found the sight amusing. Matt, however, didn't. Nor did his fifteen-year-old son, Chris.

"Penrose," Chris said. "You told them to quit popping in like this." He stepped back from the window and crossed his arms over his chest like a schoolmaster addressing an undisciplined child. "Now she's going to demand to see my room again; I'm going to say no again; she's going to look at me with disgust again, like how could I possibly have the audacity not to allow her to inspect my room like some kind of Marine sergeant; then she's going to look at you with contempt for not being tougher with me and I'm going to tell her off again; then she's going to—"

"Well, perhaps . . ." Matt interrupted. "Perhaps some of that can be avoided, Chris? Do you think?"

Chris paused pregnantly, his face a mask of indignation. *"Master,"* he said.

"I'm not calling you 'Master.' Forget it. 'M' is the best I can manage."

"I can live with M."

"Fine, M," Matt said. "While we're on the subject of names, perhaps you could manage to call me dad once in a while. You used to call me dad. Now I'm Penrose."

"When was the last time I called you dad?"

"You always used to."

"Since I moved in?"

"That's the point. Since you moved in I've been Penrose."

Chris stared at his father in silence, as if waiting for Matt to comprehend the absurdity of his argument. He was a tall, muscular kid with sandy blond hair that he wore longish, partly covering his ears. A silver Egyptian ankh dangled from his right ear lobe.

"Okay," Matt said. "So you weren't calling me anything last couple of years with your mother."

"I didn't talk to you for two years."

"Okay, but before that you called me dad."

Chris continued with the schoolmaster stare.

"Okay," Matt said. "How about this?" He touched the fingertips of his right hand to his right temple, paused, and then formally offered his request. "M," he said. "I'd appreciate it if you would call me dad, rather than Penrose."

"I'm not calling you dad," he said. "Forget it. Best I can do is . . . Penrose."

"Forever?" Matt said. "That's it? I'm *Penrose* forever?"

"Maybe if you'd refer to me as I've requested," Chris said, "I'd be more in-clined to refer to you—"

"You want me to call you Master! That's not fair."

"Why is it not fair? It's not Master like 'I'm your master.' It's a title, like 'professor' or 'doctor.' Besides," he added, "calling you dad puts me in exactly the kind of subordinate role—"

"Don't start with the lectures!"

"Exactly the kind of subordinate role that you're afraid calling me Master will put you in."

Matt counted to ten. "You *are* in a subordinate role," he said. "I'm the fa-ther. I'm the old guy with the wrinkles, you're the young guy with the mus-cles. I get the authority, you get the sexy girlfriends. That's the way it is."

Chris shrugged.

Matt went back to the window. His mother had gotten herself turned around so that her legs were out of the car and her weight was balanced on the outer edge of the seat. His father was crouched beside her with his arms around his knees.

Chris said, "What are they doing here anyway?"

"Another surprise visit, I'd guess." He stepped back from the window.

Chris slapped the curtain as if it were someone's face. "This is the Sabbath night, Penrose. I put in my request for the house weeks in advance. I told you."

"Did I know they were coming? Did I invite them?"

"Can't you tell them they can't stay the night?"

"No. I can't."

"So I'm supposed to just call everything off." He grabbed his hair, as if he were considering pulling it out, and then marched away and up the stairs toward his room.

Before following him, Matt waited a moment, contemplating the wood-grain pattern of the living room's brightly polished floorboards. Halfway up the stairs the expected report of Chris's door slamming bounced around the house like a hammer blow. He paused and drew a deep breath. Chris had been living with him for exactly six months. He had moved in at the beginning of the summer, after his mother decided she couldn't live with him any longer—which is what she had decided about Matt two years prior. She had ample justification in both cases. Matt was an inventor, and during the thirteen years of their marriage, as the income from various successful inventions grew to a substantial amount, allowing him to devote full time to the tinkering and thinking that led to more inventions, that's exactly what he did: he spent all his time working on inventions until he mostly forgot that he had a wife and kid who might like his company now and then. Living alone had jogged his memory, but after it was too late. Chris didn't handle the divorce well. Two years of drugs and promiscuity and multiple school expulsions had finally driven his mother to give up on him. She dropped off his stuff on Matt's doorstep. Chris showed up a couple of days later.

To Matt's amazement, the first six months had gone relatively smoothly. Given that the kid had refused to talk to him at all from the time he turned thirteen, given the many forced weekend outings of silence and hard stares, it felt to Matt like a small miracle when he showed up at the door and said,

"Mom says I should live with you." Behind him in the driveway a beautiful girl waited at the wheel of a red convertible. Matt said, "You can have the upstairs bedroom." Chris waved to the girl, she drove away, and Matt had been living with his son ever since. For the first month their talk was all cursory and formal. *May I. Yes, you may. Would you mind. No, I wouldn't.* But eventually the dialogue warmed up. This new church Chris had founded felt to Matt, in many ways, like the first real test of the relationship.

He called his new religion the Church of the Piranha. First he had called it the Church of the Mouth of the Piranha, until Matt had pointed out the awkwardness of the two prepositional phrases and that the acronym for Mouth of the Piranha was MOP, and if he dropped the "of the Mouth" part, the acronym would be COP which, while not ideal, was still preferable. Chris's title in the new church was Master of Fire and Air. Patty Walker, his girlfriend, was Master of Earth and Water. First Patty was Mistress of Earth and Water, but they had a vote and decided that Mistress sounded subordinate to Master. Now they were both Masters.

It was easy enough to laugh at them. It took Matt weeks before it occurred to him that not only were they serious, but what they were doing was admirable. They were inventing their own religion. They were exploring the sacred with fresh eyes. "Church of the Piranha" sounded ridiculous at first, but their point was, as Matt understood it, that living in the moment was the only remedy for the fact of death and violence—and what more apt symbol for violence and death than the Amazon's all-devouring piranha? Yes, *piranha* threw you off at first, but Chris was cunning as well as smart, and he loved the contrast between the voracious piranha and the peaceful fish symbol of Christianity—which you found everywhere in this part of the country, from bumper stickers to the town's official emblem.

Matt continued up the stairs to Chris's room. He knocked on the door, and almost instantly Chris slid out into the hallway, as if he had been waiting. Chris had installed a lock on the door soon after moving in. Matt hadn't seen the inside of the room since. Whenever he knocked and waited in the hall, Chris would open the door just wide enough to slide through the opening before pulling it closed behind him. The fact that Chris had a lock on his door and wouldn't allow anyone in his room infuriated Matt's mother and was the cause of a fight last time she visited. Matt wasn't bothered by it. He had no problem with Chris insisting on a space that was entirely and un-questionably his own.

"Well?" Chris asked. "You want something, Penrose?"

"How about this," Matt said. He put his hands on his hips and looked up slightly to meet Chris's eyes. At six-foot even, Chris was just slightly taller than him. "Change your get-together for another night, and I'll arrange to be out of the house the whole evening. I'll even buy you a couple of deli trays from Harris Teeter."

"*Deli trays* . . ." Chris's head dropped to his chest. "*Get-together* . . ." he said, looking at the floor.

"Okay," Matt said. "Whatever. You know what I mean."

"This is a *Sabbath ceremony*, not a *get-together*. We're not going to *snack off deli trays*, we're going to *drink the blood of life*."

"You're going to what?"

"Figuratively," Chris said. "Just like you Christians."

"I'm not a Christian."

Chris snorted.

"What does that mean?"

"Penrose," Chris said. "I can't cancel tonight's gathering. It's the Sabbath."

"Why does tonight have to be the Sabbath? It's your own religion. You founded it. Why not next Wednesday night, when I'll be at a conference in Dallas?"

"Because I declared tonight."

"Can't you undeclare it."

"No. It's declared. It's done."

"So that's it," Matt said. He clasped his hands on top of his head. "There's no compromise possible."

"I didn't say that."

"Give me a hint. What kind of compromise were you considering?"

"We'll do it with you all here. Just let us have the basement."

Matt was silent. He hoped his stunned disbelief showed on his face. "And what am I going to tell my parents about why a dozen kids are chanting by candlelight in the basement?"

"The truth," Chris said. "You ought to try that, Penrose. You don't always have to avoid a confrontation. You are an adult, you know."

To keep himself from strangling his son, Matt thrust his hands into his pockets. He closed his eyes and nodded. "Look," he said, evenly. "Try to understand. Yes, I'm a grown man. There's nothing I have to hide from my parents. It's just that they're getting old, and I'd rather not explain to them that you've started a new religion called the Church of the Piranha. That's all. I don't think that makes me a coward."

Chris shrugged. "Think what you will."

Downstairs, the front doorbell rang. "Okay," Matt said. "How about I get them out of the house by six for dinner and a movie, and keep them out till ten or so? Can you have your ceremony done with and everybody out of here by then?"

"Eleven."

"Fine. Eleven."

"And Patty's spending the night."

Matt massaged his temples. The doorbell rang again. "She sleeps on the downstairs sofa."

"If you insist," Chris said.

"I insist. And look, since I'm doing most of the compromising here, how about if you let me call you Chris just while—"

"No."

"Just while my parents are here."

"No. No way. Forget it."

"I cannot call you Master, let alone ask my parents to call you Master."

"Then just avoid calling me anything, the way you've been doing." He put his hand on the doorknob. The bell rang again.

"All right, how about this? Will you just agree not to ask my parents to call you Master when they call you Chris?"

Chris closed his eyes, as if struggling internally a moment. "I guess I can live with that," he said, and then quickly slid back into his room.

Matt knocked on the door. "Chris— I mean M. If you'd come down sometime soon to say hello to them, I'd appreciate it."

Again, the bell rang. Matt hustled down the stairs to the door, and then hesitated a second while he took a breath and gathered himself. His reflection looked back at him from the hall tree mirror and surprised him. Probably because he had been looking at Chris so much, his own appearance struck him as fusty. He had on brown penny loafers, khaki slacks, and a black knit shirt.

His graying hair was cut short and neat, and though his body was generally fit and trim, he definitely had a belly.

The chime rang again and this time continued ringing until he opened the door and tried to look surprised, as if he didn't know they'd been standing on his doorstep ringing the bell for the last five minutes. "Mom, Dad," he said. "What are you guys doing here?"

"Growing old on your doorstep," his mother said. "You mean to tell me you didn't know we were out here all this time?"

"Have you been here a long time?" Matt looked past his mother to his father as he stepped out of the house and held the screen door open against his back. "How you doing, Dad? You look good."

"A little winded," his father answered. "We're thinking about getting us one of those handicapped seats for your mom, the kind that swivel around."

"Over my dead body," his mother said to his father. "Like I'm some sort of invalid."

"It's not saying you're an invalid, Marilyn. It's just taking us forever every time getting out of that damn car."

Marilyn dismissed the argument by looking back to Matthew. "Where's Chris? Is he home?"

"In his room," Matt said. "Come on in." In order to make more space for his mother, he stepped back into the house, leaving his father to hold the door open. He offered Marilyn his hand to help her up the single step into the house.

"I'm not an invalid," she said, refusing his hand and grasping at the door frame for support. "I'm just having problems with my back," she added, and pushed on into the hall.

"Dad," Matt said, closing the door behind his father, "you should have told me you were coming."

"Hal," Marilyn called from the kitchen. "Get our suitcases."

Hal started for the door, but Matt took his arm and directed him toward the kitchen again. "We'll get them later."

"She's tired," Matt's father whispered to him, by way of an excuse for her crankiness. "She didn't sleep well last night."

In the kitchen, Matt went directly to the cupboard and took out the coffeemaker. "How long you plan on staying, Mom?"

Marilyn had settled herself into a seat at the head of the kitchen table. "The weekend," she said. "That is, of course, if we're welcome."

"If you'd have told me you were coming," he said, setting up the coffeemaker, "I'd have changed my plans for tonight."

"You have plans?" his mother said. "Since when do you have plans?"

Matt finished pouring coffee into a paper filter, then put the bag down on the counter and turned around to meet his mother's eyes. He was quiet long enough for the silence to be meaningful. "Mom," he said, "try to be nice." He added, "About tonight, though, you'll just have to join me and Sylvia for a dinner date."

"Sylvia?" Marilyn said. "Who's Sylvia?"

Hal took a seat at the table and looked toward Matt, as if he too were interested in his answer.

"She's a friend," Matt said. "We're having dinner and seeing a movie, and now that you're here, you'll have to join us."

"Oh, Matthew," Marilyn said. "You know I hate—"

"Sorry, Mom. But you'll like Sylvia. You'll enjoy chatting with her. Dinner's on me, of course." He looked up at the kitchen clock. It was three-thirty. "We'll need to leave in about two hours."

"*Sylvia,*" Marilyn said. "What kind of name is that? Is that a Jewish name?"

"I think so," Matt said. "I've never asked."

Marilyn was silent. She looked to her husband and then back to Matt. "Is she a divorcée?" she asked.

"Twice," Matt said.

"Twice divorced."

"It's not that uncommon these days."

Marilyn snorted. "Well, you can forget the coffee at this point," she said. She started struggling out of her chair. "I'd better just go right up and take a nap if you expect me to be civil to your new friend."

"Good idea," Matt said. "I could use a nap myself." Behind him, the coffeemaker gurgled and growled. The aroma of fresh coffee spread throughout the room. He pulled the plug on the machine and shoved it aside.

Halfway up the stairs to his bedroom, which is where he let his parents sleep when they visited since his mother couldn't abide the mattress in the guest bedroom, Marilyn stopped and fixed Matt with a reproachful stare. "You mean to tell me," she said, "that boy of yours is not even going to come out of his room to greet his own grandparents?"

Matt looked ahead to Chris's room. "He's probably sleeping," he said, and then continued pulling his mother up the stairs. "I just remembered. There's going to be a minor problem with my bed."

"That boy's been ruined by his mother," Marilyn continued, huffing up the last few steps. "He has the manners of a pig."

"I've been working on a new invention that kills bedbugs."

"I see," she said, looking at Chris's door, "that you're still allowing him to have a lock, ignoring my advice on that matter, as usual. Have you at least looked the room over?"

"I've given the room a look over," he said. "It's fine." At the top of the stairs, all three stopped for a brief rest. "I'm working on an idea that uses a small electrical current to eliminate bedbugs."

"Bedbugs?" Hal said.

"If there's no problem with the room, why was he so adamant that we couldn't see it?" Marilyn asked.

"Privacy issue," Matt said. "Bedbugs, actually, can be a serious problem in large institutions," he said to his father, looking past Marilyn. "Especially in developing nations."

"Whose got bedbugs?" Marilyn asked, startled.

"No one's got bedbugs, " Matt said, nudging his mother toward his room.

"What are you talking about? What about bedbugs?"

"He's working on a new invention," Hal said.

"I'm just tinkering."

"That's what you always say, and then you go invent something that makes you even richer."

"I'm hardly rich," Matt said.

Hal and Marilyn both snorted.

At the entrance to his room, Matt let go of his mother's arm and went about gathering together a tangle of wires and batteries and contact strips spread around the floor on one side of the bed.

"What is all that?" Marilyn put her hands on her hips. She sounded as though she were admonishing him for a messy room.

Matt dropped a clump of wires into a cardboard box. "What I was just explaining," he said, and continued straightening up. "It's a simple idea for using a couple of rechargeable batteries to produce a tiny electric current that either kills or startles bedbugs. Either way, it should get rid of them."

Hal had gotten down on his knees and was looking up under the bed, where the one remaining wire that Matt hadn't gathered led. "There's batteries under here," he said. "You've got batteries rigged up."

Marilyn looked utterly perplexed. "Why on earth would you fool with your own bed?" she asked. "You don't have bedbugs. You're not going to . . . infest your bed or—"

"Mom," Matt said, "I'm not infesting anything. I'm just—"

"Is this the ground?" Hal asked. He had slid entirely under the bed and was holding up a metal rod.

"Dad, please don't mess with that."

"Don't worry," Hal said. "I'll put it back where it was."

"I've been testing the batteries," Matt said to his mother. "My idea is to use rechargeables to keep the expense down."

Marilyn sat on the edge of the bed. "So you just plug it in when you go to bed at night?" She plugged in the cord, which was resting on the night table. "And you get rid of the bedbugs?"

Matt unplugged the cord. "You'd only plug it in when the batteries needed recharging."

"And you say there's a need for this?"

"In developing countries," Hal answered for Matt. He took a seat on the opposite side of the bed from his wife and began untying his shoe laces. "Probably in orphanages and jails and the like, right?"

"I'm just tinkering," Matt said. He lifted the box and started for the door.

"He'll probably make another million," Marilyn said, as if another million were a boil or a canker sore.

"I'll knock in about an hour." Matt stepped out of the room, and pulled the door closed behind him. When he turned around, he found Chris standing in front of his room, watching him. Matt made an exasperated face and leaned back against the wall.

Chris watched him a long moment, in his eyes an unappealing mix of disdain, contempt, and sympathy. He slipped back into his room without a word, locking the door behind him.

Matt carried the box of wires down to his basement workroom and stored them neatly in a labeled, plastic bin, before continuing on to his study, which was attached to the workroom. He fell back into a plush leather chair and put his feet up on a corner of his desk. In front of him on his computer screen, a mountain stream gurgled peacefully under a blue western sky. An assortment of calendars, maps, and diagrams was pinned above his desk. The remaining three walls were lined with floor-to-ceiling, custom-made bookshelves, where his library of brightly colored books, numbering in the thousands, were arranged by size for the order and the attractiveness of the look, which comforted him even though it made it harder to find a particular book when he needed it. He closed his eyes and settled down to rest awhile.

⸻◦◦◦⸻

The house was dark and quiet when he returned from dinner and a movie with his parents, the slight scent of incense that permeated the ground floor the only indication that Chris's Sabbath had gone on as planned. Marilyn's sourness at not getting to meet Sylvia had turned into sullenness midway through the dinner. Sylvia, of course, didn't exist. Matt had simply made her up. At the restaurant, he invented an excuse—after a fake phone call—for her not being able to join them. Now, after getting his parents settled in his bedroom and closing the door on them for the night, he walked through all the darkened rooms of the house, sniffing the air for smells more dangerous than incense, locking windows and doors, and going about the general tidying up and arranging he did every night before retiring.

In the basement, the incense was thick enough to gag on. Off to one side of the rec room, in a shimmering pond of watery moonlight coming down through a small, rectangular, ground-level window, a dozen red candles were arranged in a circle. Trails of wax dripped down the candle bodies, where they pooled and hardened against the tile floor. Matt had just knelt by the candles, and was considering whether to clean up the mess or wait and ask Chris to do it in the morning, when a pile of sheets on the couch across the room spoke to him. "Mr. Penrose?" they said. "Is that you?" Startled, he fell over backward onto his butt. "Hi, Patty," he said, when he remembered that Patty was spending the night on the couch. "I was just admiring the candle circle. How'd the ceremony go?"

Patty didn't answer immediately. He continued, "I didn't wake you up, did I? I mean, you didn't just wake up and find me . . ." he tried hard to sound amusing, "*lurking* in the shadow here or anything. I hope I didn't frighten—"

"No," Patty said. "I saw you come down."

"Good," Matt said. "I wouldn't want you to think—"

"That you're some kind of pervert? No. Chris told me how you always inspect the whole house before you go to bed."

"He did, did he?" Matt tried for a casual, fatherly laugh. His eyes, however, were only now adjusting to the darkness of the basement, and as the couch and the figure upon it gathered shape and definition, he saw that Patty was naked except for a flimsy sheet that she held clasped to her neck. He guessed she didn't realize that, given the way the sheet was clinging to her skin, there wasn't much point in even bothering with it. He looked down at the candles, perplexed for a moment.

He knew that Chris and Patty were sleeping together. Chris had told him. Patty's mother had even told him. She had called late one evening, sobbing as she explained having found birth control pills in Patty's room—but, she continued, they had talked and she guessed sixteen, Patty's age, was about average these days for becoming sexually active, and she was glad at least that Patty was acting responsibly and using the pill. She had sobbed through much of the phone call, her voice taking on the slightest hint of anger only when she recommended to Matt that he talk to Chris about the need for using condoms anyway, to prevent the spread of STDs. Matt had found the whole conversation damn near unbearable. He agreed to talk to Chris, which he did, in an equally unbearable conversation. He was sorry, he told Chris, that he had been sexually active for so long at such a young age—but he was glad, at least, that he was behaving responsibly about pregnancy and STDs, and then he said, "You are, aren't you? I mean, using condoms." The word condom got stuck someplace just above his Adam's apple and came out as a single syllable—*condns*. "Certainly," Chris said. "Of course." As if the question were absurd. And then that was that. They hadn't talked about it since, except indirectly when Matt insisted—regardless of the pretense in the gesture, which Chris pointed out disdainfully—that Patty sleep in the basement whenever she spent the night.

"Well," Matt said, confused and troubled by chatting in the dark with his son's unclothed girlfriend, but not having any idea how he should act. "Well," he repeated, "I'll probably go to bed now."

"Good night," Patty said. "Mr. Penrose."

In the guest bed, upstairs, across from Chris's room, Matt pulled the sheets to his chin and pondered the oddness of having a naked girl who called him Mr. Penrose sleeping in his basement. He checked the alarm setting on his wrist watch, which he was wearing to bed, to reassure himself that it was properly set. His plan was to rise at six in the morning, wake Chris, and have him take Patty out to breakfast somewhere. He was welcome to bring her back to the house after that, but under no conditions could she be eating breakfast in a sheet or pajamas or whatever when his parents came down. God knows what his mother would do if she suspected Chris's girlfriend was allowed to spend the night at the house. She'd probably try to have him and Patty's mother both arrested for corrupting the morals of minors.

Matt fell asleep thinking about the whole notion of minors having morals that might be corrupted, seeing images as he drifted toward dreaminess, of minors in little Puritan outfits with catechisms under their arms, and then the next thing he knew someone was screaming as if about to be murdered. The screaming went on for quite a while before he realized that someone some-where really was screaming; and then, in the following instant, that the screams were coming from the room next to him; and in the instant after that he was up and stumbling still half asleep through the hallway to his bedroom, where he saw the incredible sight of his mother screaming in the center of his flaming bed while Chris and his father slapped at myriad, candle-sized licks of fire with what appeared to be two of his neatly folded dress shirts. Chris was naked. His father was wearing black-and-white striped silk pajamas that made him look like a Mafia don.

By the time Matt was conscious enough to realize he should do some-thing, the flames were all out. He took his robe down from the hook on the back of the bedroom door and handed it to Chris, who looked down at him-self as if just suddenly aware of his situation, and then put the robe on quickly. Matt opened the bedroom windows. Chris opened and closed the door to fan the smoke out. Matt's father crossed his arms over his chest and looked at his wife, who was holding her clasped hands up over her mouth as if dumbstruck.

Matt said, "What the hell happened?" The battery recharger was plugged in and he yanked it from the outlet. "Did you plug this in?" he asked his mother, who appeared to be unhurt but still speechless, though Matt could see by the way her expression was shifting that words were only a little way off. She nodded.

"You shouldn't have done that," he said. "I don't know what you were thinking."

"You should have told me!" she yelled, finding her voice, and simultaneously hauling herself off the mattress. She backed out into the hall past Chris and away from the bed. "My God, Matthew," she said. "You could have killed us." And then she backed up more until she disappeared from sight.

Hal had gotten down on his knees to check under the bed. "It was just the dust ruffle caught fire," he said. "Looks like a battery exploded."

Matt slid under the bed on his back and joined his father. "Oh," he said. "I'll have to think about that."

"Is this really strange?" Chris said, watching his father and grandfather chatting under the bed. "Is it me or is this weird?" He was standing with his hands in the pockets of the robe, looking like Hugh Heffner.

Matt slid out from under the bed and sat up.

From out in the hall, a girl's squeaky voice yelled "Quit it!" and "Let go!" and then squealed franticly.

Hal said, "What the hell?" and bumped his head on the underside of the mattress.

Matt started for the hall, but before he had taken a full step his mother appeared in the doorway, dragging Patty behind her by the arm. Patty looked terrified. With her free arm, she held Chris's bed quilt to her breasts. Marilyn's face was dark red, the meaty fingers of her big hand wrapped around Patty's arm just below the shoulder. "This little slut," she yelled, "was lounging in his bed." She pointed to Chris like a witness identifying a criminal to the jury.

Patty started to cry. She looked to Matt imploringly. "She's hurting me."

"Let her go," Matt said, finding his voice.

Chris, who had looked to be in something like shock, came to life with his father's words and jumped to Patty's aid, yanking her out of his grandmother's grasp. "Look at her arm," he said to his father, holding Patty's arm up for him to see. Patty clung to his chest as he held the quilt up over her back. The white skin of her arm was dark where Marilyn had grasped it, four finger marks vivid in a blue-black outline.

"Matthew," Marilyn said, pointing again. "I want you to take these two—these two—"

Before she could complete her sentence, Matt said to Chris, "Take Patty down to the kitchen and get her a drink of water."

"Matthew!" Marilyn yelled.

Matt said, "Try to calm down, Mom." He followed Chris and Patty into the hall, and closed the door on his parents without looking back at them.

In the kitchen, Patty curled up in a chair and drank the glass of water Chris handed to her. Matt sat across from Patty at the table and rested his chin on his hands. The house was quiet again, except for the sounds of his parents moving around in the bedroom. It sounded like they were getting dressed and packing. Every once in a while Marilyn would bark a command to Hal.

Chris said, "What time is it, anyway?" He was leaning against the sink.

Matt looked at his wrist watch. "A little before five."

Patty placed the empty glass on the table and looked at Matt. Her eyes were watery, but she seemed composed. "I hope you won't tell my father about this, Mr. Penrose. He'll kill me. I swear."

"Patty," Chris said, sounding disappointed in her.

"He's not like your father," she snapped back at him. "I'm in serious trouble he finds out about this."

"I thought your parents understood," Matt said. "About you and Chris."

"My mother," Patty said. "My father'd kill me."

Matt covered his face with the palms of his hands. "Patty," he said, "you see the position this puts me in? This is why I told Chris you have to stay downstairs when—"

"But, Dad," Chris interrupted. "It's so hypocritical. Everyone knows—"

"Apparently her father doesn't."

"It's still hypocritical on your part," Chris answered, without hesitating. "You know we're sleeping together but we still have to pretend like—"

"Will you shut up, Chris?" Patty laid her hands flat on the table. "It's his house. He has a right."

Matt went to the kitchen sink and drew himself a glass of water. He hadn't been paying any attention to Chris's argument anyway. He was stuck back a few moments in time when Chris had called him "dad" for the first time in many years. He took a sip of water and then said, "Thank you, Patty."

Patty said, "I apologize for sneaking up here in the middle of the night."

Matt nodded. "How's your arm?"

She lifted her arm out from under the quilt to examine it. The darkness had faded some, but the finger marks were still clearly visible. "It'll be okay," she said. "I've always marked real easy. Will you tell my father?"

"I don't see that I need to," Matt said. "It's your mother I've always spoken with. I do think you should talk to her about tonight."

"Oh, that's no problem," Patty said, relief bubbling over. "I talk to my mom about everything." She jumped up, holding the quilt with both hands. "Jesus," she said. "I'm really tired." She asked, rhetorically, "Okay if I try to catch another couple hours' sleep?" and then started for the basement. "Thanks, Mr. Penrose." She trotted down the stairs trailing Chris's quilt behind her like a bridal train.

Chris started to followed her, and then stopped at the head of the stairway. "I'll be back up in a minute," he said. "I just want to talk to her a second."

"Fine," Matt said. "Just come on back up."

"In a minute," he answered.

Alone in the kitchen, Matt dimmed the lights and massaged the back of his neck with both hands, digging his fingers into the tight skin. All noise had ceased upstairs and down, and he imagined Patty and Chris whispering to each other in the basement while his mother and father whispered in the bedroom. Momentarily, he knew, he'd have to negotiate with his mother. She'd be furious and indignant and genuinely outraged—and God only knew what she'd do or threaten to do. Still, oddly, her imminent rage was not the foremost thing on his mind. In fact, it was only something half-hidden in his thoughts, something he knew he'd have to deal with shortly. He was thinking, instead, about Chris, about why he'd called him "dad" at this particular time, in this particular situation. He was pretty sure Chris had done so without realizing it, but still he had done it. He was thinking about that, and, even more oddly, he was remembering moments from his own childhood.

Mostly, he was remembering being switched by his mother. He hadn't thought about her switching him in years, the way she used to make him go out and cut a branch from a tree, and then get undressed and stand in the bathtub and wait for her. He had to take off his clothes so they wouldn't get ruined. He had to stand in the bathtub in case he bled, so he wouldn't make a mess. He had learned early to cut a big switch, because she'd always beat him harder if the switch was too small. He'd forgiven her for all that ages ago, but he guessed that the sight of Patty trying to cover her nakedness, and seeing the bruise on her arm—he guessed that had jarred his memories. Suddenly he was recalling being sent to bed without dinner for saying he didn't like mashed potatoes; being slapped in the face in front of his friends for some mild curse he issued without thinking; being made to stand in a corner facing the wall at a family Thanksgiving dinner because he didn't come to the table the first time he was called. He could forgive her, because she thought she was being a good parent; because she believed being a strict parent made for a good child; because she was a marred human being who carried too many of her own scars having to do with her own father, who was genuinely a beast; because he never doubted that she loved him.

He could forgive her, but apparently he hadn't forgotten a thing.

In the basement, the lights went out and then Chris started up the stairs. Matthew could see him out of the corner of his eye. Upstairs, the bedroom door opened and his parents marched out into the hall and started down the stairs. Matthew could hear them, and obviously Chris could too, because he stopped just outside the kitchen and sat down on one of the top steps, hidden from the living room where his grandparents would soon be descending. Matt three-quarters closed the kitchen door to the basement stairs, further hiding Chris from sight. He turned around in his seat as his parents neared the bottom of the steps, and he saw immediately by the way his mother was walking with her nose up in the air that she intended to make a dramatic gesture and leave without a word. He was relieved for a moment, before he realized she'd never make it past him without saying something.

In the living room, directly across from where he sat at the kitchen table, at the point where she clearly meant to turn and march out the door, she struggled a moment and then stopped and faced him. She said, "This behavior is criminal, Matthew. Criminal. I have half a mind to report you to the police. That boy's walking all over you, and you're too much of a coward to stand up to him." Then the sanctimonious mask plastered over her face cracked, and her eyes filled with tears. "And don't you expect to see us in this house again until you start acting like that boy's father. Because you won't." She turned and hurried away, throwing open the front door and stepping out in the darkness without waiting for her husband, who had lingered behind her on the stairs and was looking at Matt as if he wanted to say something but couldn't come up with anything for the life of him.

Matt winked at his father and said, "I'll talk to you soon."

His father nodded and then followed Marilyn outside.

As soon as the front door closed, Chris came into the kitchen. "You think she means it?" he said. "You think she'll stay away?"

"I wouldn't get my hopes up," Matt said. He gestured toward the chair opposite him. "Sit down a minute, please."

"Uh-oh," Chris said, sounding almost a touch excited. "Am I going to get a fatherly lecture?"

"I told you," he said, once Chris was seated and facing him, "Patty could stay here the night, but she had to sleep in the basement. You knew what that meant. It meant she could stay here, but you couldn't sleep together here. Not here. Not in the house."

Chris placed his hand on his heart. "Let me make sure I understand this," he said. "You know we're sleeping together, and you're not telling us not to, but you're insisting we do it, like, in the back seat of the car, or the bushes or something, as long as we don't—"

"I don't want to argue with you. If I could tell you not to have sex and you wouldn't I would but obviously I can't."

"Excuse me?" Chris said. He seemed amused.

"Look," Matt said, "I don't think it's too much to ask that you follow a few rules."

The amusement went out of Chris's face. He said, "I did. I followed your rules. I did exactly what I wanted to do and lied to you about it."

"Those are my rules?"

"Did you ask Grandma to quit the surprise visits?"

"No," he said. "I never got around to it."

"But you told me you did," he said. "Why do you do that? I mean, you've always been like that. It's one of the things I hated most about you. You just invented this Sylvia. I heard you lying to them up and down. You did it to me all the time growing up. You'd tell me we were going one place when we were really going someplace else; you'd tell me something would take ten minutes and it'd wind up taking an hour; you'd tell me you could take care of something and then you'd never even try. Why do you do that? I mean, what's wrong with you? Why can't you just be honest? Why do you always have to be such a liar? I mean, I don't know. . . . Do you know?"

Matt said, "Is this the price you pay to hear your kid call you 'dad'? Anything else wrong with me?"

"Who called you 'dad'?" Chris said. "Not me."

"Yes you did," Matt said, as if he had caught Chris red-handed at something. "Earlier," he said. "You called me 'dad.'"

Chris appeared to be frozen for a moment. He turned away from Matt and coughed, and when he turned back again he was spitting out words. "You're a liar," he said. "You're totally fucked up. You and your neat house, your everything-in-order, your fastidious picking-up-after. You're sick. Do you realize that except for conferences, you hardly ever leave the house? You spend whole days in your workroom. You grocery shop on Saturdays. That's your big day out. You're a mess. I feel sorry for you. You're totally pathetic."

"Really," Matt said. "Anything else you want to tell me?"

"Yes," Chris said. He stood and pushed his chair back. "I apologize for sneaking Patty up to my bedroom. I promise," he said, fiercely, "I will never do anything like that again." From midway up the stairs, without looking back, he said, "Good night, *Penrose*."

Long after Matt heard the door to Chris's room close and lock, he remained motionless in his seat at the kitchen table looking out the window above the sink. He was deeply tired. He slid the chair back and tilted it against the wall and put his legs up on the table. The house at last was quiet. Outside, the sky was beginning to lighten, the black of night edging toward the slate blue of morning clouds.

He closed his eyes and his breathing got slower and deeper. *Sabbath night,* he thought, *in the church of the piranha.* In his mind's eye, he saw the only images of piranha he'd ever seen—a cow ambling into a river and then being reduced to bones amid a watery frenzy of teeth and blood—from some hyperbolically dramatic television documentary. *They attack in swarms,* a voice-over was saying. *They eat you alive.* He saw himself as a young boy stepping into such a river—he was half-dreaming now—and coming out all grown up but as a skeleton, a collection of bones he had to tape and pin and cobble together to keep from falling apart. He saw himself as a skeleton man wearing a floppy felt hat, which he courteously tipped to a passing stranger. He laughed out loud at the image and then was jolted fully awake as his chair snapped back upright. He stood and stretched, still amused at the picture of himself as a skeleton man, at his odd little mini-dream. As he thought about it more, though, starting up the stairs, it became more disturbing—as did the memory, back again, of Chris saying good night. The kid had sounded like he despised him, like he knew him and had judged him a failed human being. Matt tried to think about it a moment longer and then shook it off and continued up the stairs to bed, toward what he much hoped would be a sleep of peaceful and uncomplicated dreams.

Acid

—⊶⊷—

THE LIVING WORD WAS JEROME'S BOOKSTORE. IT was a cubbyhole, a small room jammed with Bibles, inspirational books, and cards for religious occasions, and it was located in a Long Island shopping plaza, between a record store and a bridal boutique that had gone out of business months earlier and was about to reopen as one of a chain of restaurant-bars that catered to college students. On the street outside The Living Word, Jerome stared through the restaurant windows as a crew of workers prepared for opening night. From the ceiling, King Kong hung vertically suspended, one huge hairy arm swiping at a biplane dangling from a rafter just out of reach. His other arm was wrapped around a red supporting column, as if he were leaning out from it, holding on to keep from falling. A scantily clad Fay Wray, trapped in Kong's grip, pressed the back of her hand to her forehead, on the verge of fainting.

From behind him, Jerome heard the sound of knocking on glass, and he turned around to find Alice waving for him to come into the record shop. Alice was the sales clerk and manager. At twenty-two she was only a couple of years older than his youngest daughter, but that didn't keep her from flirting. With the tip of her finger, seductively, she pushed her black, buttonless, boat-top blouse down off one shoulder. Jerome put his hands on his hips and frowned at her. In response, she pouted elaborately, making her bottom lip quiver as if she were about to cry. Jerome laughed and went into the record shop.

"When are you going to stop playacting Jezebel?" he said, as soon as he pushed open the door.

"Don't start." Alice pulled her blouse back over her shoulder, and glanced up at a large concave mirror suspended above her head like a satellite dish. There were no customers in the store. "I have a favor to ask."

"What?"

"Take me out tonight."

Jerome laughed again.

"I'm serious. Just for a couple of hours. Your wife'll never find out."

Alice sat behind the counter on a barstool, her hands in her lap, her black jeans and black blouse contrasting sharply with fair skin and platinum blond hair cut short as a man's. Jerome stared at her for a long moment, waiting for something in her expression to give her away, but she returned his stare unflinchingly, and in the end he couldn't tell if she were kidding with him as usual or if she were serious. He said, as if trying to understand, "You want me to take you out tonight."

She nodded, expressing exaggerated amazement at his lack of comprehension.

"Where?"

"Next door. The new place. I want to drop acid."

Jerome laughed again, this time throwing his head back and folding his hands over his belly.

"Cut it out." Alice pursed her lips. Her slightly pointed nose in combination with short hair pushed back off her forehead gave her a birdlike look, her hair like a bird's cap.

"What?" Jerome said. "You're not serious?"

"You did it!" Alice's voice traveled up an octave. "You did drugs! You were wild!"

"That was twenty-five years ago, " Jerome said. "I told you like a warning, not like you should try it."

"Well, that's not the way I heard it. I'm serious. I want you to take me out tonight."

Jerome went behind the counter. He stood in front of Alice and took her hands in his. Their image was reflected in the concave mirror. Jerome was a tall, heavy man, bearlike in build, wearing a plain white shirt and blue jeans held up by bright red suspenders. His long graying hair was pulled back neatly in a ponytail, and he had a gold crucifix earring in his pierced right ear. Alice was skinny, dressed all in black, hunched forward on her counter stool. "Alice," Jerome said, "you don't want to drop acid. Believe me. Drugs will only make your life more of a mess."

"Bullshit," Alice said. "My life can't be any more of a mess."

Jerome knew what Alice was talking about. She was in love with a performance artist from Brooklyn who called himself St. John of the Five Boroughs. They had been going out for over a year when he abruptly dumped her. He said she was too bourgeois, too middle-class. This happened a few months ago, shortly after Alice mentioned the possibility of marriage. Jerome felt a twinge of guilt over this, since Alice had met St. John in The Living Word, where she had been visiting when he came in to buy a Bible and a crucifix for use in one of his performances. When he left he had Alice's phone number. "Look," Jerome said. "You're still pining over—"

"*Pining?*" Alice pulled her hands away. "Jesus."

"Forgive me," Jerome said. "I *am* fifty-two years old."

Alice said plaintively, "My father would be fifty-five if he weren't dead."

Jerome covered his eyes with one hand, and his chin dropped to his chest. "Alice," he said, "you're letting yourself get carried away."

"Am not." She jerked his hand away from his eyes. "All I want to do is drop some acid. I want to shake up my life."

"What do you need me for?"

"I trust you. You've got experience."

"Go with your mother." Jerome walked back around the counter. He glanced at the rows of CDs that filled the shop, at the brightly colored, rectangular packages. A mostly nude Prince reclined beside a rap CD that pictured four men totally naked except for the sawed-off shotguns and military attack rifles that covered their privates.

"My mom's in St. Thomas with her latest."

Jerome stepped between the two waist-high, black columns that would set off an alarm if he tried to leave without paying for a CD. "Alice," he said, "stop feeling sorry for yourself. And don't be stupid and take a chance on screwing up your life." He pulled the door open halfway and a soft, electronic chime sounded.

Alice leaned forward to the counter and propped her chin up in her hands. "I'll be there tonight around midnight," she said. "I'll feel better if you're there. I mean, I'll understand if you can't. But I'm dropping acid tonight no matter. I already decided."

"Mistake," Jerome said. "Big mistake." He left the shop.

The rest of the day, Jerome straightened out and dusted off stock in The Living Word. He moved a new edition of C. S. Lewis's Narnia chronicles into the display window, next to a T-shirt that had a black handprint with a red circle in the center of the palm. At five o'clock, from behind his counter, he watched Alice pull down the metal gate over her storefront and insert and turn the keys that activated the alarm system. When she turned around and saw him looking at her, she mouthed the word "midnight," winked, and crossed the parking lot to her car. As she walked away from him, Jerome's eyes fell to her legs. He noticed every crease in her jeans and the movement of her body within her clothes. His breathing slowed a little. He didn't turn away until Alice unlocked her car door and stepped out of sight. In front of him on the counter, a collection of art on religious themes was opened to a portrait of his namesake: da Vinci's "The Penitent Jerome." He stared for a moment at the saint's wasted body before snapping the thick book closed with a loud clap.

Jerome was annoyed at himself. Noticing Alice, noticing her physically, produced a kind of heat inside him, a kind of heat that could be released only by touch. He had been married now for a little over twenty years. He had two daughters in college. He thought he had grown past the real desire for other women. He would always notice other women, he knew that. He would always be aware of their bodies, of the way they moved—but there was a line between noticing and wanting, and it was a line he didn't intend to cross. When he was a young man, he had slept with every woman he could get into his bed. He had been a jazz musician, he played sax, and he lived for only two thing: women and music. When he wasn't doing one or the other, he was doing drugs: mostly marijuana and hashish, but coke too, and some horse. He could still see himself walking along Houston Street toward the Village. He walked with a swagger, his sax in its case. He had a place way over on Broome Street and he'd cut across on Essex and walk down Houston into the Village, like there was a spotlight on him all the way. When he got to whatever club he was working, when he played his sax, he fell into a deep place. He'd play with the group, whatever they were doing, a lot of Dizzy, "A

Night in Tunisia," "Groovin' High," a lot of Miles, and he'd be with them, one star in a cluster, one piece of light, and then something would happen, he'd break out flare up and the guys would back off and let him play. That's what jazz was like when it was good. That was why he did it. He'd be playing and then something just happened, he flew away, he'd be unconscious, flying, he'd get high soaring up to a place and then he'd level off and coast back in like gliding back down into his place in the cluster of lights, and the audience would applaud and the guys would throw him a nod a little gesture that said yes, he had been out there.

That was the good part. But the good part was tied up with the bad part in a way he could never understand. Anger was the bad part. Something that was anger and more than anger. At first it was only in the morning. He'd wake up with it. He'd get out of bed, his senses raw, like his nerves were all exposed, something heavy wrapped around him like a smoldering robe. He wasn't sure where it came from, he wasn't sure it mattered. There were his father and mother who hardly seemed to notice him. He was the youngest of six children, they didn't have time. There was his career as a musician, the next step just not coming, the recording contracts, the money and fame. That didn't matter, it was playing that mattered, still it weighed on him, seeing others move up while he stayed behind. But it was more than that. It was something inside him furious, something enraged. He couldn't rest, the anger pressed against his skin. It seeped into every part of his life. Then in 1972 he beat up a woman he had picked up after playing a club. He beat her up after having sex with her.

They had been lying together on his single bed. It was a summer night, the window next to the bed was open. There was a straight back chair beside the window, and it was covered with clothes: several shirts were draped over the back, and pants were hung over the shirts. The seat was piled high with dirty clothes. From his bed, where he lay on his side, knees pulled up to his chest, he stared at the chair and at the buildings beyond the window. There was no breeze. The air was heavy. The sheets under him were wet from the sweat of sex, thick knots of his shoulder-length hair stuck to his face and neck. It was near dawn: he hadn't quit playing till after two A.M. The moon must have been bright, because he could see the building out the window clearly. He was thin in those days, thin and wiry. The woman who lay behind him was tracing the outline of his ribs with her fingertip. She followed the hard bone from the side to the center of his chest and back and then down to the next one. She lay behind him, so she couldn't see that his teeth were pressed together, that the corded muscles down his neck and to his shoulders were tight and hard. He had been doing blackbirds, thick amphetamine capsules, he couldn't remember how many. He was crashing, he told himself he was crashing, to hold on. Who was he? Who was the woman behind him touching him? Why did he want to slap her hand away, a minute ago he had been driving himself into her? Her touch was gentle and his whole being seemed to shrink from it. He told himself he was crashing, he told himself to hold on: who was he, he was thirty-two years old, he was floating away he was sinking under, he was a musician, he was in bed with a woman he had met a few hours earlier, she was tracing the outline of his ribs with her fingertip. He was crashing. If he could hold on. He wanted to cry and he had no idea why he wanted to cry. He told himself it was the speed, but he felt lost, even though he knew exactly where he was: in the same apartment he had lived in then for five years, on Broome Street in Manhattan, in walking distance of the clubs where he played. He felt trapped, locked up, even though he knew he was free to do whatever he wanted, he had the money he needed, he had the access to drugs, there were women to spend the night. His body began to shudder, as if he were chilled. When she completed the outline of his ribs, her hand went down lower, to touch him. She bit him gently, taking the flesh in the small of his back between her teeth. He turned around. Her eyes were glistening, playful. He hit her the first time when she leaned forward to kiss him. He said, "Don't touch me." She was more surprised then hurt. He hadn't hit her hard. He had slapped her. She said, "You . . ." and faltered. She hit him back, a half-slap, half-push at his chest, and something huge inside him flared white and hot and he flailed at her, beating her, kneeling over her and striking until her body stopped resisting, the flesh went soft under his fists.

He spent a week in jail. There was no trial. His lawyer bargained with the city's lawyer and he got off with a suspended sentence. During his week in jail, he spent most of his time on his back, lying on his cot, looking out a barred window at the sky. The night of the beating he had crawled away from the bed on all fours. The nightmare image of himself crawling naked away from the bed was locked into Jerome's memory. It had never gone away, in all the twenty years since: the image of her startled eyes when he first slapped her, the feel of her body breaking under his fists, the animal explosion of grunts and screams from her and from him. Sometime long after she had stopped screaming, he crawled to the window. He had blood on his hands and face. He pulled himself up and looked out: the world was pulsing like the skin of a creature whose heart was beating hard. Color vibrated. The stars were white flames that flared like drum beats. In jail it was different: colors settled, stars cooled.

After they let him out, he began taking long walks at night, and on one of his walks, he wound up all the way downtown, by the river. It must have been about five A.M. He was cold, and he was coming up on Trinity Church. A thin, haggard man with long, windblown hair. The building was open. He entered through the central portal, and when he pushed open the inner doors and stepped into the interior, he was looking along the aisle toward the altar, where Christ looked down at him from the cross. He hadn't been in a church since he was a boy. He had been raised Roman Catholic. He had been baptized and had received communion, and that had been the end of it. Twenty, maybe twenty-two years since he'd been inside a church. He genuflected, crossed himself, and walked to the altar, where he knelt and lay his head on the chancel rail. He didn't know what he wanted. He was sobbing, and when he looked up again at the cross, he felt something warm and calming spread though him. He thought it might be the memory of himself as a boy in church with his family, kneeling in a pew between his brothers and sisters, watching the priest say mass, hold the gold chalice up to the light from a stained glass window, as if offering it to the light, offering the chalice up to the light as if the light were alive and might take the chalice from his hand. He had felt warm then and safe and that feeling returned to him there at the chancel rail in Trinity Church. But it felt like something more than memory, like his anger was being transformed: bile turned to honey. After that, everything changed. He started going to confession every week and receiving communion every morning. He quit playing the clubs. He quit taking drugs. He met Sylvia and got married. They opened a Christian bookstore on Sixth Avenue. When they had a child, they moved the bookstore to Long Island.

Jerome put the art book in the display window, next to the C. S. Lewis, and then closed up the shop and went home. He found Sylvia in the kitchen pounding a slice of beef with a wooden mallet. She was surrounded by food: a caldron of tomato sauce bubbled on the stove; in the half-opened oven, two apple pies cooled; on the counter beside her, bottles of spices were scattered among piles of raisins and pignoli. The tangy apple-pie smell overwhelmed the small kitchen. "What's this?" Jerome said. He put his hand on the counter and it slid over a slippery film of baking flour.

"This?" Sylvia pointed at the beef. "It's braciole."

"No. I mean all of this." Jerome clapped his hands and a little cloud of flour dust floated slowly to the floor.

Sylvia shrugged and made a gesture with her hands as if to say she didn't know why he would ask. "I'm cooking," she said. She rinsed her hands in the sink and dried them on a green dish towel that pictured a line of geese flying in formation. She hung the towel over the faucet, held Jerome by the shoulders, and kissed him on the lips. "Just because the kids are gone doesn't mean I can't cook anymore. I like cooking."

Jerome stepped around her and looked into the pot of sauce. "There's enough here for a month." He went to the kitchen window and looked out into the yard. In the reflection from the window, he could see Sylvia standing with her hands on her hips, looking at his back. Her expression wavered between anger and concern. In the twenty years they had been married, she had grown stout—not fat, but stout, almost matronly. She had turned fifty a week earlier, and last month, Beth, their youngest, had left for college: that, Jerome told himself, was why she was making a meal big enough for an army.

"Did you go to mass this morning?" she asked. "Did you receive communion?"

Jerome closed his eyes and leaned forward until his forehead touched the window. The glass was cool and wet.

"Did you?"

Sylvia claimed she could tell a difference in Jerome's behavior on the rare days when he missed mass and communion—probably not more than a dozen in the past twenty years. She said he got edgy and tense and hard to live with. He walked out of the kitchen without answering, and sat in the recliner in front of the living room's bay window. The house around him was orderly and neat, as always, and as always he found that calming. The polished hardwood floors gave off a kind of warmth, and Jerome leaned back and settled into the comfortable familiarity of his surroundings.

From the kitchen, Sylvia called: "Do you want a glass of wine?"

He didn't answer. She was right about church: he began his day with mass and communion the way other people started theirs with coffee and the newspaper. If he missed mass, he was off balance the rest of the day. When he received communion, when he knelt at the chancel rail and extended his tongue and tilted his head to the priest, and the priest placed the wafer of the host on his tongue—when he received the body and blood of Christ into his own body, he felt transformed. He felt himself change as the wafer dissolved on his tongue: a warming light seeped into the dark places in his body. But he hadn't missed morning mass. He had gone at six A.M., as always. He sat in his regular seat in the back of the church, under the stained glass window portraying Christ's heart surrounded by a fiery light, and he had received communion.

The bay window in front of the recliner was lined with shelves crowded with knickknacks. Jerome picked up a soapstone sculpture of a dolphin and held it in his open hand. He liked the soft, doughlike feel of the stone in his palm, the warmth it had absorbed from sitting under the window radiating into his hand. He touched the dolphin to his forehead and held it there a moment, his eyes closed. Then he put it back on the shelf and went into the kitchen. Sylvia was pouring sauce into jars. She had bright blue potholder mitts over both hands. "I'm sorry," he said. "I'm acting sullen."

"What's wrong?" Sylvia put the pot back on the stove.

He hugged Sylvia and kissed her on the cheek. "I think it's Beth . . . the kids being gone."

Sylvia nodded. Her eyes got teary.

"I think I'll go for one of my walks after dinner."

"It's getting cold out," she said. She returned to pouring sauce into jars.

Jerome leaned back against the sink. "Then maybe I'll go for a drive," he said, casually. "Later on."

After dinner, he watched television with Sylvia. When the eleven o'clock news ended, and Sylvia started upstairs for bed, he told her he wasn't sleepy, and that he thought he'd go out for that drive he had mentioned earlier. At first Sylvia continue up the stairs slowly, without replying. Then she joined him where he was sitting on the couch. "Are you sure you wouldn't rather talk?" She put her hand on his knee.

"It's not talk," he said. "You know how I get. A long walk or a drive soothes me."

"Okay. If you're sure." She leaned forward and kissed him on the cheek.

"But try not to wake me when you come back in. You know what happens if I wake up once I've gone to bed for the night."

"I'll be quiet." He watched Sylvia walk up the stairs, and he listened while she prepared for bed. From where he sat on the couch, he could hear the floor creaking over his head, and each sound told him where she was in the bedroom and what she was doing. The silence meant she was standing in front of the dresser mirror in her nightgown, brushing her hair. The floor creaking again meant she was walking to the bed and pulling back the quilt. He waited until she was in bed a few minutes before getting up from the couch and getting dressed to go out. When he left, he pulled the door closed with a loud click, and he rapidly turned the key in the lock so that the dead bolt would snap closed loudly. By the time he started the car, it was midnight.

<hr />

Jerome hadn't been inside the bar for more than a few seconds when he heard his name being called from someplace over his head. The place was jammed with kids who didn't look like they could possibly be twenty-one, though that was the drinking age in New York. Alongside him, two girls were holding each other at arms' length and squealing with delight as they looked each over and prepared to embrace. When he looked up, Jerome saw Alice leaning over a railing and waving to him. He smiled up at her just as a young ox shouldering his way through the crowd knocked him into a fortune teller in a glass case. Jerome would have grabbed the kid if the crush of bodies hadn't closed around him instantly. He leaned against the glass case as the fortune teller, apparently jolted into action by the collision, began mechanically dealing out a hand of tarot cards, accompanied by an eerie, high-pitched, violin music. He turned away from the black-clad, wizened features of the gypsy-dummy, and stood on his toes, trying to locate the stairway that led up to the second level. Before he could find it, Alice popped out of the crowd behind him and took his arm.

"I already dropped, I don't feel anything yet, I'm glad you came." She jumped up and kissed him on his forehead. "I thought you'd come," she said.

"Is there someplace to sit?"

Alice pulled Jerome through the crowd, toward the back of the bar. The decor of the place was overwhelming, a hysteria of clashing artifacts: a 1940s street sign next to a glass-encased statue of Elton John; Marilyn Monroe standing on a subway grating, her dress blowing up as she tries to hold it down; a portrait of Charles Barkley wearing a T-shirt that advertised Nike sneakers and read: "The meek shall inherit the earth . . . but they don't get the ball." The place was packed with stuff that ranged from an antique Amoco gas pump to a full-size, red-and-white '57 Chevy with an Elvis mannequin in the driver's seat, to an old-fashioned round clock on a lamp pole, the kind you might have found in a railroad terminal or even on some town's main street, before they were universally replaced with digital time–temperature displays. And overlooking it all was the massive King Kong, Fay Wray in hand.

As they made their way toward the back of the bar, the crowd thinned and the noise level decreased significantly. Jerome realized there was music coming through a PA system: Ella Fitzgerald was scatting her way toward the end of "Black Magic." By the time they found a place to sit, the Fitzgerald number was over and the Talking Heads were on. Jerome slid into a booth that was enclosed on three sides, like a small private room with a wall missing. Alice sat across from him. Over her head, light from an adjoining booth filtered through a round, multicolored, stained-glass window. A waiter appeared almost instantly. Alice ordered an Irish coffee and Jerome ordered bourbon.

"So how come you came?" Alice asked, smiling. Then, before he could answer, she leaned over the table and her smile turned into a grin. "But I knew you'd come. I could tell."

"I came to talk you out of the acid."

"Uh, uh," Alice said. "That's not it. Don't bum me out. I want this to be a good trip." She reached across the table and put her hand over his. "It's weird," she continued. "You look different in this place. We've known each other a couple of years now, right—but I've never seen you except in my shop or yours. You definitely look different."

"Who wouldn't look different here?" Jerome gestured toward a group of skeletons playing soccer.

"These are big tripping bars," Alice said. "That's what gave me the idea. I used to go to one of these in the city with John and everybody was always tripping."

"Not hard to understand."

"Well? Do you know why you came?"

The waiter showed up with their drinks before Jerome could answer. Alice put a twenty on his tray. "We're not staying long," she said. The waiter told her he'd be right back with the change.

"Alice . . ."

"What?"

"I don't know what you're thinking. I'm . . ."

Alice's Irish coffee came topped with a pyramid of whipped cream. She lowered her head and licked half of it away with one swipe of her tongue. "You wouldn't be here if you weren't interested. That's something John taught me. To cut through the pretense."

The waiter returned with the change. When he left, Jerome said to Alice, "I'm worried about you doing acid."

"I don't think so. I mean, maybe that's why you think you're here . . ." Alice appeared to weaken slightly, as if some of her confidence were slipping away. Then she crossed her arms on the table and leaned close to him. "Come on, Jerome. You've been staring at me for two years. I'm already tripping, so don't play mind games with me. I know you're interested. I can tell by your look. It doesn't matter what you say, you can act like my uncle all you want. Your eyes don't lie."

"But it does matter what I say."

"Bullshit. You can't hide your heart. You can't hide what's in your heart."

Jerome picked up his bourbon. "It's not my heart. I'm not trying to hide my heart."

"You're screwing around with me. You're playing with my mind." Her eyes got teary. "Now I'm getting scared. I'm getting bummed out."

Jerome reached across the table to touch her.

"Shit." She covered her face with her hands. "John does acid all the time. He says the world is like a mask that acid burns away. When he does acid he can see what's under the mask."

"What's he see?"

Alice shrugged. "I don't know. I'm getting scared." She took her hands away from her face. Her cheeks were wet and her mascara was smeared. Black lines ran down from her eyes like soiled tears. "I do acid once and I'm getting hysterical." She laughed and covered her face again.

Jerome touched her arm and found her muscles tense. He tried gently to pull her hands away from her face, but it was like pulling on the arms of a stone sculpture. He moved around the table to sit beside her. "Alice," he said. He put his arm around her. "Are you all right?"

She shook her head.

Jerome took her wrists in his hands and pulled her arms down. Her lips were opened slightly and her teeth were pressed together. She appeared to be staring at something that wasn't there. Jerome held her face in his hands. He tried to turn her head to look at him, but she resisted.

"I'm scared," she said through clenched teeth. "I'm really scared."

"Of what?" Jerome leaned back into the table, trying to get Alice to look at him.

"I don't know," she said, and then her eyes made contact with Jerome's, and some of the stiffness went out of her.

"Why don't we leave," Jerome said.

"Will you take me home?"

"Yes. I'll take you home." He put his hand under her arm and guided her out of the restaurant and to his car. It was a clear night, the sky bright with stars. Once Jerome was on the road, Alice lay down on the front seat and rested her head on his thigh. He stiffened at first. Then he saw beads of sweat on Alice's upper lip and her forehead, and he wiped them away with the palm of his hand. He asked, "Are you feeling any better?"

Alice nodded. "I don't know what happened," she said. "This feeling just came over me, like something terrible was all around me—like in nightmares when I was little and I knew something horrible was right behind me but I couldn't see it."

"Is it gone now?"

"Almost," she said. "It's melting away. I saw your eyes and it started. It's like melting away, it's almost all gone."

"You're high," Jerome said. "It's the drug."

"It's different." She nestled her head into his thigh and stomach as if he were a pillow. "I don't feel high. I don't feel all messed up. I feel clear. It's like something warm is spreading through me, melting away everything bad."

"You're high," Jerome repeated.

Alice pointed up, out the windshield. "Look at the stars," she said. "How bright."

Jerome had to lean down a bit so that he could look up out the window. "There's nothing there. The light we're seeing, whatever made it, it was billions of years ago. There's nothing really there."

Alice looked up at Jerome and then back out the window. "What makes you so religious, Jerome? What makes you a religious man?"

Jerome was quiet. He looked down at Alice and saw that she was examining her hand. She held her opened hand in front of her face and moved her fingers slowly, as if she were playing a piano in slow motion. Her eyes were full of wonder. "I'm thankful," Jerome said. "I feel like . . ." He didn't know how to continue.

"I know what you mean," Alice said, still examining the workings of her hand. "It's just like feeling thankful that makes you good." Then she pulled herself up suddenly, and knelt beside Jerome. She kissed him. "But we're going to be bad tonight," she said. "Just this once. We're going to be so bad we're good."

Jerome pulled the car into the entrance to Alice's apartment complex, and she directed him to her parking space. Once they were out of the car and on the concrete walk that led to her apartment, Jerome put his hand on the small of Alice's back. "Are you feeling any steadier?"

Alice reached behind her and took Jerome's hand and slid it down into the back pocket of her jeans. She held her hand over his. "I like it better there."

Under his palm Jerome could feel the liquid smoothness and warmth of Alice's body moving. Energy flowed into him: his heart beat faster, his thoughts scattered and bounced, like molecules of water heating up in a bowl. His breathing changed, became more rapid, so that he knew if he tried to speak a whole sentence the final words would be clipped or chopped off entirely. He didn't speak. He kept his hand in her back pocket as they walked up a flight of stairs. Alice leaned into him, her head against his chest. At the door, she produced a key and sighed as if the mundane detail of having to unlock the door wearied her. When she had trouble getting the key into the lock, she seemed surprised.

Jerome steadied Alice's hand with his own. He unlocked the door, pushed it open, and stepped into her apartment. The place was small, essentially one room divided into a living area and a kitchen. There were two open doors off a short hallway beyond the living room: one led to a bedroom, the double bed unmade, sheets and bedspread crumpled on the floor; and the other opened into a bathroom.

"Sit down." Alice gestured toward a frayed couch strewn with clothes. As she pointed, a brindled cat darted out of nowhere, between her legs, and jumped up onto the counter that separated the kitchen and living room. The cat startled her, and she lost her balance. She would have fallen if Jerome hadn't caught her. "Whoa," she said. "Maybe I am stoned." She looked around. "Colors seem different. More intense." She squinted and looked at a spot on the wall over the couch. "Does acid build? Like keep getting stronger?"

"I can't remember," Jerome said. He was standing behind her now, letting her lean back against him. "It's been more than twenty years."

Alice was staring at the same spot. She said, "I think the walls are breathing," and then she laughed. "No," she said. "I'm okay." She turned to face Jerome and put her arms around his waist. "I don't feel stoned." She stood on her toes and kissed him on the lips. "Wait here." She walked off, down the hallway. With her hand on a doorknob, she stopped and turned around, and looked back at Jerome. The hallway was dimly lit, and in it's shadows Alice's features seemed softer, almost flawless: her skin not dark in contrast to her white hair, but honey-colored, as if she were an exotic, a native of a tropical island. "I feel like . . . in harmony with things. I feel a . . . connection . . . Like . . ." She spoke slowly, each word taking its own good time. "Right now I'm feeling like everything is a kind of moving quilt, and I'm one piece of the quilt over here, and you're another piece over there." She smiled, her eyes catching Jerome's eyes, and then she disappeared into her bedroom, closing the door behind her.

Inside his head, a voice asked Jerome what he was doing. Jerome said he didn't know. He pushed a terry cloth robe aside and sat down heavily on the couch. His heart was still beating hard. His skin felt prickly. Across the room, the cat was perched on the counter watching him, its tail resting on what appeared to be a stick of butter. Again the voice inside his head asked him what he was doing, and Jerome answered again that he didn't know. It didn't seem possible that he would actually go to bed with Alice, and it didn't seem possible that he wouldn't. What's the truth, he asked himself, and he answered that he wanted to sleep with her, he wanted to touch her, he wanted to enter her and feel each movement of her body deep inside him, and he wanted her to feel him, he wanted her hands and lips to touch him. That's the truth, he told himself; then he told himself that he wasn't going to. When he asked why not, he had no good answer. He wasn't the same man who once put a woman in the hospital, who once crawled away from sex with blood on his hands and face. That man was long gone. That wasn't what would keep him out of her bed. And it wasn't his wife or his family or his religion, though those thoughts were there: Sylvia sleeping on her side, her hands folded to her breast; the priest in the dark confessional sliding open the window between the chambers and waiting for Jerome to speak; his daughters as children, as young women now off in college, away from home. Those thoughts were there but they felt powerless, weak as sunlight at dusk. If he didn't do it, it would be because he just didn't anymore. It wasn't the way he lived. When this answer came to Jerome, he laughed at himself, and not a pleasant laugh, but a laugh that carried a note of disdain.

Across the room, the cat leaped down from the counter, jumped onto a ledge and slithered out a barely open window. The apartment was still. Jerome realized that a long time had passed since Alice went into the bedroom. It occurred to him that something might have happened to her. He knocked on her bedroom door. When she didn't answer, he went hesitantly into the room. She was lying on a wide ledge under a long double window. She was on her back, covered by a single white sheet, looking up at the stars. In the flickering light from a red candle burning on top of a white plastic dresser, she looked like the woman in a magic act, the one the magician makes float up on thin air. When Jerome knelt alongside her, he saw that she was naked under the sheet, the thin fabric clinging to her body, taking on the texture of her skin. She was breathing very slowly, her chest hardly moving. Her eyes were fixed on the sky. Jerome touched her shoulder, and she whispered, barely audibly, "There's nothing there."

It took Jerome a moment before he realized she was talking about the stars, about the starlight, repeating what he had said in the car.

She turned to look at Jerome. "You can touch me. If you want to."

He touched the palm of his hand to her cheek.

Alice turned back to the window. "I'm someplace special," she said. "I'm someplace strange."

"I know," Jerome said. He kissed her on the forehead and left her staring out the window, her eyes moving from star to star. Half an hour later he was back in his own bed, lying quietly under a spread next to Sylvia. Her body was warm and he edged closer to her. His heart was beating slowly now, steady and calm. His thoughts felt clear and solid. Alice was young. She was alone and drugged, looking out her bedroom window at the stars. He was with his wife and sober, looking, now, out his own bedroom window, at the same stars. They were different and they were the same, the three of them, everyone, wrapped in urging bodies, under the dead light of the stars.

Small Blessings

—⟨⟩—

COUPLE OF YEARS AGO, CONNIE CAME HOME FROM
work to find Doug, her second husband, swaying in nine feet of water like an
aquatic Frankenstein, cement-filled milk jugs tied to his ankles, his extended
arms bobbing in front of him, the hands lifting and falling slowly, as if waving a lazy good-bye to all the things of this world. Soon as she saw him, she
swore off men forever, for eternity. She kicked off her pumps at the shallow
end of the pool, took a seat on the rubberized lip, and sat a long while with
her feet in the water just watching him sway, all that gorgeous long blond
hair floating around his head in a sunny nimbus. Not that it had been a surprise. Some two years earlier, when they had first met at the hospital, where
Connie was still employed as a nurse, he'd been on suicide watch, con-
strained in a straight-jacket—and there wasn't a week went by after when he
didn't mention at least once the possibility of taking his own life. She'd met
her first husband at the hospital too, in detox. He'd died in a drunken-driving
accident three weeks after the church ceremony, only a few days back from
the honeymoon. The other party in the fatal accident was a two-family brick
Colonial. His car had actually gone straight into the front of the garage, crashing through the wooden door in what probably would not have been a lethal
collision were it not for the brick wall at the other end. He went through that
too before winding up—this is ironic—in the deep end of an in-ground pool.

He technically drowned also, though the police said it was likely a good thing, given that his head injuries would have left him in a vegetative state. So. Small blessings. She still had the pictures somewhere.

For the last two years—she had only recently turned twenty-eight—Connie had dated women exclusively. Being gay had its problems, but, truth is, she never really decided if she was gay or just a woman understandably wary of men, who was dating other women because that was the only alternative to being alone—and she hated being alone. Living as a lesbian on Long Island gained her access into a large and lively social circle. She had a ton of women friends—straight, gay, and bi—with whom she could spend an enjoyable evening at a club in the city, or go out with to see a play or a movie or whatever. There was no lack of things to do and good people to do them with, though she had yet to date anyone with whom she could imagine actually settling down and making a life. First problem, she had to admit—and this is primarily why she had always really doubted she was a gay woman—was the sex. No matter how wild or kinky it got, no matter the strap-on or sex toy in use, it just was not the same thing as it had been with James and Doug, husbands number one and two. Or, for that matter, with Billy, Ahmad, Ralphie, or Brick—the other four men she'd slept with in her life. She'd been with Billy and Ahmad at Syracuse University, and Ralphie and Brick, two city boys, on Long Island, before James. She'd been raised on Long Island, in Huntington, in a house overlooking the bay, and it seemed only natural to return there after finishing her degree. Brick was dead, from a drug overdose. Ralphie had disappeared, simply up and left the city with no word. For all she knew he could be dead too.

For the past three weeks she'd been dating a woman named Kellen, a doctor who worked with the criminally insane at Bellevue. She was a gentle and compassionate woman, who was already beginning to drive Connie crazy—though Connie wasn't sure it was Kellen who was driving her crazy or just the fact that Kellen was a woman and somehow devoid of something she seemed to need and had been doing without for a couple of years. Not that Connie could have told you what the thing she needed was. She didn't know. Men were simple compared to women. A conversation with a woman was an act of social engagement that included the communication of feelings and ideas along with the sharing of information. Men on the other hand barely knew how to speak. Oh, they could talk if pushed, but after a little while it was almost as if they resented the intrusion of actually asking them if they could just please try to go a little beyond the succinct communication of pertinent facts. Men were infuriating. But. Still. Lately Connie had found herself thinking a lot about men.

On a sultry Friday night in late summer, after a long day at the hospital, two years plus after Doug's suicide, Connie looked at herself hard and long in her dresser mirror and admitted she wasn't gay. Maybe she was bi, but she doubted that too. Mostly she was just pretty open and free about sex, and she figured what she'd done here was give lesbianism a fair shot, and now it was time to admit that it just wasn't her. There was some kind of dynamic involved in the relationship between a woman and a man that wasn't there between a woman and woman and she missed it. She addressed herself in the mirror and admitted what she'd been thinking and not admitting for a long time. She said aloud, "I want a man." She had been hanging around gay women for so long and had spent so many hours talking the politics of heterosexuality that she felt a deep blush of shame in actually hearing herself speak those words. Needing a man, she knew, was a manifestation of self-loathing. She sat down on the edge of her bed, buried her face in her hands, and cried—which, as always, quickly made her feel better. Once the tears stopped, she pulled out her frilliest thong and tossed it on the bed to be joined by her sexiest jeans and white silk blouse. When she stripped out of her nurse's uniform on the way to the shower, it felt like shedding an old skin.

⊸αΩ𝄐Ⴜൔ⊸

Coyote Ugly Saloon, a downtown bar featuring sexily clad barmaids gyrating and flirting with mostly male patrons, was the last place in Manhattan any of Connie's crowd would ever spend a Friday night; so when she pushed through the door into much hooting and hollering over the background roar of Guns N' Roses, she didn't even bother to scan the crowd. No one she knew would be caught dead on the same block as the Coyote Ugly, let alone in the midst of this sweaty crowd of what looked to be hormone-addled frat boys, lonely middle-aged men, and horny tourists. The handful of women present who weren't standing on the bar and dancing or serving drinks all appeared to be Connie's age or younger. If there were a black or brown face among the masses, she didn't see it—which might have had something to do, she thought, with the big Confederate flag pinned to the ceiling, it's red, white, and blue bars and stars marking the place with a giant X. On the spur of the moment, crossing the floor on the way to the bar, she couldn't decide what was more offensive, that Confederate flag or the hundreds of frilly, multicolored bras hanging from the rafters like numberless tokens of male conquest. If she hadn't been out on the town in the hope of hooking up with someone for the night, she would have been offended enough to leave; instead, she found herself grinning at the outrageous political incorrectness of the place while she watched the legs and well-toned tummy of a twenty-something braless barmaid in painted-on, hip-hugging blue jeans and a skimpy, red halter top who stood on the bar with the palm of one hand pressed against the ceiling and the other wrapped around a beer bottle as she swayed lazily to lyrics about an insane bitch who looked pretty tied up, or something like that.

Between the dancer's legs, a chalk-board beer list was visible against the wall of the bar, above a sailor's cap flung over a couple of bottles of Bud—hats being another of the principal décor items in the bar: bill caps mostly, but cowboy hats too, of course, white ones, black ones, even a red one with a yellow feather. In the couple of seconds between considering a beer and deciding on bourbon instead, Connie's thoughts took one of those deep, quirky digressions as she heard some little person who seemed to reside somewhere in her chest, approximately in the heart area, suggest that her life was a joke. Two dead husbands at twenty-eight and a failed two-year stint as a lesbian. How the hell did this happen to an ordinary, good-looking, Long Island girl who'd grown up with a stay-at-home mom, a businessman father (till she was fifteen), followed by a nice-enough stepfather after her dad died of liver cancer—which was a memory, actually, she didn't like to revisit. She'd been close to her father. He was a cheerful man of delusory enthusiasms who believed utterly in the extraordinary capabilities of everyone he loved. Connie's mother was a saint, her uncle was a genius, his business partners were brilliant, and so on. He told Connie endlessly, repeated as if a litany, that the world was her oyster, that absolutely anything was possible, that whatever she wanted she had only to set her mind on it and it would be hers. Dad. Dad. He must have died in agony, though of course he forbid her to see him once he got too bad.

When a man's voice interrupted her sudden reverie, she was grateful, and when she turned to find a tall, handsome guy who looked to be approximately her age if not maybe a few years older, she flashed him her prettiest smile. He had just asked her what she was drinking. "Makers on the rocks," she shouted—as the screeching music necessitated—and then added, coyly if loudly, "And here I was thinking I might have to buy my own drink."

"A woman beautiful as you?" he said, showing off his own bright smile, rows of white, expensively cared-for teeth announcing at the very least a solid middle-class upbringing. "Not likely." He leaned over the bar, extending a fifty-dollar bill in the direction of a passing barmaid with a green laurel wreath tattooed around her bellybutton. She plucked it gently from his fingers with a seductive smirk, he shouted his order, and few minutes later he was holding a Red Hook by the neck as Connie stirred her bourbon and looked up at him playfully. She was enjoying this. It had been a long time. With a man, anyway.

"My name's Ira," he said. Very cool. Very confident. Just shy of cocky.

"Connie," she shouted back. "Thanks for the drink."

"You're welcome," he said. "Let me guess: you're in the arts. I'm thinking artist of some kind: actor, dancer, musician . . . I'll go with dancer. That's my final guess. You've got a dancer's body."

Okay, so maybe he was a little too slick. Still, she smiled as if enchanted. "Nurse," she said.

"No kidding?" His surprise seemed genuine and the little honest sparkle in his eyes emphasized the essentially theatrical introduction. "I'm a doctor," he said. "Pediatrics. I'm just completing my residency."

"Congratulations." She offered her hand, which he shook gently. "That's a hell of an accomplishment."

"Thanks," he said. "Where do you work?"

"Pilgrim State."

"Out on the Island?"

"Uh, huh," she said. "But no shop talk, okay?"

"Absolutely," he said, his free hand flying up palm forward as he took a small step back. "Believe me. I understand."

"So what's a doctor like you doing in a dive like this?" she said, and immediately upon hearing the squeaky lameness of the question, brushed her hair back off her forehead with both hands. Predictably, his eyes dropped to her breasts. Men were like computers in that way: they were all programmed to respond identically to certain key strokes.

"I'm here with my brother." He turned his back to the bar as he looked over the crowd toward the rear of the room. "He's been a little depressed," he said, apparently still trying to locate his brother. "This is a place it's hard to stay depressed in, don't you think?"

"Sure," she said. "If you say so," she added, pretty sure he couldn't hear her over the music.

"There he is." He nodded toward a far corner. "He's a great guy. He's a musician, he plays sax. He used to have a group that did pretty well for a while."

Connie looked to the back of the room, where Ira was pointing, and saw a long-haired guy with sunken cheeks and what looked to be multiple face piercings and tattoos. He was leaning against the wall and watching one of the Coyote Ugly girls up on the bar twirling a blue hoola hoop to the shouted encouragement of the crowd. He seemed almost frightened by what he was seeing, his eyes squinting slightly and his lips pressed together as if something bad might be about to happen. "That's your brother?"

"That's him," Ira said. "I know he looks kind of out there," he added, "but he's really an amazingly brilliant guy. He's a musical genius, really. And you know, musicians," he went on, "they've sort of got to look like that. It's part of the business."

"Really," Connie said. "You know what he looks like? He looks like, if there were like a magic mirror somewhere, and if you looked into it you saw your reverse, bizzaro image, your everything opposite? He looks like you looking into that mirror."

Ira laughed politely. "You're funny," he said. "But I'm telling you, he's brilliant. We've got that in common. And I only wish I had his talent."

"Really," Connie said. "So you're what? You're out here trying to get your brother laid?"

"That's a little crass, isn't it?" Ira crossed his arms over his chest. He watched Connie a moment, intently. "He's a good guy," he said, "having a terrible time. I was hoping he might meet somebody. Nothing simple as the way you put it."

"And he can't do that for himself? Meet someone, given he's a genius and all?"

"Not if he never leaves his room except to go out for a gig and then goes right back to it afterward."

"And that's the way it is?"

"I think he's developing agoraphobia," Ira said, nodding toward his brother. "That's why he looks scared shit over there."

Connie turned her back to the bar to get a better look at Ira's sad brother. She saw that his long black hair was streaked with gray, and that his face—if it weren't so sunken and marred by an eyebrow piercing and some kind of silvery gem pinned to his nose—might potentially be handsome. "You love him?" she asked Ira. "You love your brother?"

"Oh, yeah," Ira said, without hesitating. "I love the guy." He tilted his head back and half drained his beer while he looked at his brother, who was still leaning against the wall in the back of the room, appearing more and more frightened.

"Just out of curiosity," Connie said. "Did you think for a second, when you first saw me—" She waved her hand back and forth from Ira to herself. "Did you ever think, me and you?"

Ira showed her the back of his left hand and pointed to the ring finger, at a narrow circle of pale skin.

Connie laughed. "All right," she said, and when she picked up her drink and made her way through the crowd toward the back of the room, Ira didn't follow.

The music stopped for a moment as she was in the midst of a knot of boys uniformed in khaki slacks and knit shirts—college boys she'd have guessed, though they looked more like high-school kids to her. One of them, a short one, shorter than Connie, said, "Hey, Beautiful? Where you going?" which for reasons probably only known to such groups of young men, provoked general laughter. Connie pushed through them to Ira's brother and touched his arm familiarly, as if he were an old friend. In a mirror on the back wall, she saw the group of boys return to their shouted conversation as the music came on full blast, more Guns N' Roses.

Ira's brother looked down at her anxiously. Like Ira, he was tall, but up close it was clear that he was considerably older than his brother. She guessed early to mid-forties. "Hey," she said. "Ira said I should come over and say hello."

"He did," the brother said, and his voice was startlingly low and gravelly, so that he sounded like he was growling as well as talking. He looked back to the bar, where Ira had his back turned to them as he watched the dancer with the hoola hoop being helped to the floor by two huge, biker-looking guys wearing denim and do-rags. "Why'd he tell you to do that?" he asked, his eyes still skittish, and his posture, the way his whole body leaned back from her touch, defensive.

Connie let go of his arm to hold her drink with both hands. "He said I'd find you interesting. He thought I'd like you."

"He thought so?" the brother said. "I wonder what made him think I'd like you?"

Connie pushed her hair back off her forehead with both hands. "Wild guess, I suppose. Maybe he thought you'd find me attractive."

The brother nodded, as if her attractiveness was something they could all agree on. "So what did my brother tell you?" he asked. "He tell you I'm some sort of genius musician?"

"Something like that."

"It's bullshit," he said, and he looked down at himself, as if just to make sure he was still in the same body. "Looking for genius," he said, "you definitely in the wrong place."

"That's okay," Connie said. "I'm actually not really a genius either."

He smiled, exposing slightly yellowed teeth. "I'm a sideman," he said. "I've played with some greats: played with Miles Davis couple of years before he died."

"I've heard of him," Connie said.

The brother laughed. Something in her response seemed to loosen him up. "That's good," he said. "Ira get around to telling you my name?"

"Didn't get around to it," she answered. "Too busy telling me what a genius you are."

"Ash," he said.

"Jesus." Connie stepped back and looked over his slight frame and long, frizzy hair, the sallow skin and sunken cheeks and burned-out eyes. "Jesus," she repeated. "That's perfect. Ash."

Ash seemed confused for a moment; then he grinned and finally he laughed. "Want to get out of here?" he asked.

Connie said, "Why would I want to get out of here?"

"Why would you want to get out of here?" He looked around the bar room, his eyes finally coming to rest on the Confederate flag. "I wouldn't know where to begin," he said.

"Try the bras," she suggested, gesturing toward a rafter where a dozen pink and red bras dangled in a clump. "The bras might convince me."

"Okay," he said. "The bras."

"All right," she said. "Shall we say good night to Ira?"

Out on the street, under the red and silver Coyote Ugly Saloon sign, a misty rain gathered in the otherwise clear, summery air. Connie ran a finger along her arm and wiped away a streak of moisture. Above her, the sky was clear, and even squinting she couldn't see the mist that she felt on her skin. Ash joined her on the sidewalk, the music and shouting of the bar spilling onto the street with him for a moment before the door closed again. She said, "It's wild out here. It's misting"—she gestured toward the sky—"but I can't see it."

Ash looked up over the rooftops. He was wearing a plain black T-shirt that was frayed at the neck line, and he placed his open hand on it, over his heart. He inhaled deeply. "Smells like it though," he said, his voice, if anything, even deeper and more ragged out on the street, away from the screaming music. "Smells like rain, don't you think?"

Connie sniffed the air with what she hoped was comic intensity, and, yes, she did smell it: the faint tannic odor of wet leaves.

"My place is close to here," Ash said. "Do you want to walk? It's a nice night to walk in the rain, don't you think?"

"Are we going to your place?" Connie said as she looped her arm though his.

"Can't imagine where else," Ash said, and he started down the block, heading toward the East River.

"Is that—" Connie said, and then she hesitated a moment. She was about to ask if he had always sounded like he did, and then worried the question might somehow be hurtful. She found a gentler phrasing. "Have you always had such a deep voice?" she asked.

Ash looked up and touched his Adam's apple, indicating the source of the problem. "Growth on my larynx. Nothing serious, just can't afford to have it taken care of right now."

"But it's benign?"

"Oh, yeah," he said. "I'm a singer— Was a singer, anyway. It's an occupational thing. It happens."

"A singer?" Connie leaned back to look him over. "I can see that," she said. "You could be like an Axyl Rose or Steve Tyler type."

Ash looked half pained and half amused. "I'm a serious musician," he said. "Sorry if that sounds pompous, but I'm not an *act*, a entertainment commodity." He laughed. "Okay," he said. "So I am pompous."

"That's all right," Connie said. "I'm enchanted. I never hooked up with a serious musician before."

"Is that what we're doing?" Ash said. "Hooking up?"

Connie didn't answer immediately. She walked alongside him in silence that was awkward for a moment before easing into a comfortable quiet. A few blocks later, he asked her how old she was.

"Twenty-eight," she said. "And you?"

"Forty. Just turned forty a few days ago."

"Happy birthday."

Ash nodded and pointed up the block. "I'm just around that corner. It's a fifth-floor walk-up. Think you can handle it?"

"The stairs I can handle," she said. "No problem."

"And me?" Ash said. "Starting to wonder about me?"

"You know," Connie said, "we're actually getting kind of wet here." She stepped in front of Ash, stroked his hair with both hands, and then showed him the wet palms of her hands before leaning forward and kissing him lightly on the lips. "Just a couple of things we should get straight first," she said, gently. "I'm out looking for a wild night, you know what I mean? Nothing more than that. Things in my life, they've come to this point— It's like— I don't know. It's got nothing to do with you: you're just the one lucks out. I'm looking for one wild night. Long as you understand, that's it. And also, incidentally"—she reached into the inside pocket of her jacket and pulled out a foil-wrapped condom—"this is part of the deal. Okay?"

Ash kissed her on the forehead and gestured toward the lighted foyer of an anonymous gray building a few doors down the block. "Let's get out of the rain," he said, and he touched the small of her back as he started toward the lighted building.

On the steps, under the doorway arch, protected somewhat from the mist that had gathered now into a visible fog and was moving rapidly toward a drizzle, Ash unlocked the door, but instead of stepping into the foyer, he switched off the light and then sat down on the slate doorstep with his back against the closed door. "Long as we're being honest—" he said, looking up at Connie. "Want to sit a minute?" He interrupted himself, gesturing toward the dark, empty street with its nondescript line of buildings. "It's a lovely view, don't you think?"

"Thanks," Connie said. "But, isn't your ass getting wet?"

"Kind of."

"I'll lean," she said, and she crossed her legs and leaned back against the door frame. The city was quiet for a Friday night. She could hear Manhattan's constant background rumble of engines accelerating and decelerating, and, overhead, the low rumble of an airplane somewhere off in the distance—but no street shouts, no siren screams. "It's peaceful here," she said, looking down at Ash, where he had pulled his knees to his chin and wrapped his arms around them.

"You can hear the ships out on the East River," he said. "We'll hear fog horns tonight. I'm surprised we haven't heard one yet."

"I'll listen for it," Connie said.

Ash nodded. "It's a strange life, isn't it?"

Connie looked away from him, up to the rooftops, and an image opened in her mind of Doug floating in the deep end of the pool, the way his arms bobbed up and down, seeming to wave good-bye.

"Anyway," Ash said. "Things you should know: I'm an alcoholic. I've abused every drug known to mankind. I've wasted my life, wasted my talent. I've rotted my teeth—" He pulled out a dental appliance, removing his front teeth for a moment before snapping them back into place. "—destroyed a couple of organs, and in general fucked up totally and irredeemably." He paused a moment, as if pained at what he had to say next. "And the drug problems are ongoing," he said. "As is the alcoholism."

Connie said, "Do you have HIV?"

Ash shook his head. "That," he said, "thank God, I've avoided. I've got recent medical records upstairs, which you're more than welcome to peruse."

"Gosh," Connie gushed, hugging herself. "This is *so* romantic."

"Look," Ash said. He leaned his head on his knees and tilted his face up toward Connie. He seemed suddenly much more relaxed. "It's okay if you want me to walk you back to the bar. Honestly. It'll be all right."

"You know," Connie said. "You're not the only one with a life gone off course."

"I'm not?" he said, and then added a moment later: "I'm probably more like 'wrecked on the rocks' than 'off course,' don't you think?"

Connie didn't answer. She felt the story of her two dead husbands pushing up from someplace in her belly. The story wanted to push all the way out and be told—but instead her eyes teared up as it receded, sinking back down into her bones.

"What?" Ash said. "What do you want to say?"

"Past couple of years," she offered. "My partners of choice have not been men."

"A little sexual confusion? That's certainly unusual," he said. "Especially in this town."

"That's what I thought, too," Connie said. "So." She opened her arms and looked down at a rivulet of rain funneling between her breasts, and at the bottom of her blouse and the legs of her jeans, which were soaked through. "You know," she said. "We're both really wet."

Ash stood and unlocked the door. Like a gentleman, he held it open for her.

———

Once up the five flights of stairs and inside Ash's door, Connie had silently undressed him, and let him do the same for her. In the dim light from a open window that overlooked the black metal railing of a fire escape, they draped their wet clothes over the sink that was on one side of the room and then dried each other off with a stack of yellow Burger King napkins before getting into the bed on the other side of the room. After several minutes of kissing and touching, after the application of mouths to skin and fingers to soft and warm places, Ash rolled over on his side and turned his back to Connie.

"That's all right," she said. "Really. Don't go away."

"I'm right here," he said, his gravelly voice barely audible. "Just give me a second."

She stroked his back, running her hand over his arm and along the surprisingly youthful skin of his shoulder blade to the small of his back where there was a patch of downy hair. She kissed him on the neck. "Forget what I said before, about looking for a wild night. This is nice, really. This is fine."

"The mind is there," he whispered. "It's the body that's wrecked."

"I'm fine," she said. "I swear. This is good."

"Give me another second," he said. "Okay?"

She touched his shoulder and turned onto her back, clasping her hands under her neck and propping herself up on the pillow so that she could look around the room. The place was neat but small, even by city standards: one room with a sink, a hot plate, and a mini-fridge. She noticed the slight but recognizable odor of aftershave in the air. "Where's your bathroom?" she asked.

"Down the hall," he said. "Three tenants, one bathroom."

"Bummer."

"Truly."

"Are you going to turn over and talk to me?"

"One more minute."

"Okay," she said. "I'm counting." Across from her, in the far corner of the room next to the open window, a saxophone was propped up on a stand of some kind. She noticed it for the first time while she was gazing blankly at a light that had gone on in one of the buildings across the courtyard. It was almost as if the shiny brass instrument had magically appeared out of the shadows. It was half hidden by the room's single black, straight-back chair, which was positioned directly in front of the window, so that Connie couldn't help but imagine Ash sitting there alone in this tiny room watching the world go by. She leaned over and kissed his shoulder. "Kind of strange for Ira to take you out to a bar," she said. "Isn't it? Given . . ."

"I haven't had a drink in a long time." Ash lay his head on his bicep and talked into the wall. "Ira doesn't know about the drugs. Truth is, I've been pretty good with that, too. Still, not enough. I keep backsliding. Then, you know, I swear never again. Until I do again. Then . . . Etcetera. It's pathetic, really."

"But," Connie said, "are you getting better? Are things improving?"

"I guess so," he said. "You could say that. Until they get worse."

"You're a pessimist," she said, "aren't you? You're a cynic."

"No, I'm not. I'm just, what is." He turned around, propped his head up on his hand, and peeled the sheet down off Connie's body, giving it a yank when it got stuck on her feet, pulling it away to leave her entirely exposed. "My God," he said, after a moment of gazing at her. "My God," he repeated. "It hurts to look at you."

"Why?" she asked, and she sat up slightly to better peer down at herself. She looked pretty much the same as she did in high school, probably better, since she had taken up running as an adult and so was likely in better physical condition. Her body had always acted pretty much oblivious to all the traumas of her life. Fathers and husbands could die in her arms, but her body just went on glowing. "Is there a problem?" she asked, raising her eyebrows.

"No problem," he said, turning his gaze away from her body and to her eyes. "Except I don't really know anything about you, and you already know a good bit about me."

"What do you want to know?"

"Tell me one thing deep," he said. "One thing that reveals a little of you."

"I'm pretty revealed," she said, gesturing toward her body.

"No, you're not," he said.

"Oh. Okay." She squinted dramatically, miming deep thought. "Let me see," she said. "One thing . . ." She considered once again telling him about James and Doug, and once again the words wouldn't come. "Okay," she said. "My father died when I was young." She paused, meaning to stop there, but almost instantly she found herself speaking again. "Last good memory I have of my father," she said, "I'm about fourteen and he's carrying me up the stairs on his back." She laughed. "I mean, I'm not a baby here, either. I'm fourteen and I'm literally on his back and he's climbing up the stairs like a horse. He was like that. He used to say 'Who's the pretty girl?' and tickle my chin, to make me laugh. I'd be like it made me furious, but it was just so dumb, so incredibly dopey—You had to be there. We could make each other laugh, like, unbelievably hard, just, like, hysterical laughter, dumbest things. He, you know— He played with me. We literally played with each other, like a couple of kids."

"He sounds like a good man."

"He was." Connie paused momentarily and then she was off again, talking. It felt almost as if she were remembering stuff she actually meant to tell Ash, as if they were an old couple and she had meant to tell him these things and had just somehow forgotten. "I used to have this dream," she said. "It was kind of a mix of a dream and daydream, where I'd be in his hospital room when he was sick—he died of liver cancer—and I'd just, in this dream, I'd just touch him." She was surprised at how fast the thoughts were coming. "I'd touch him and then he'd— The whole cancer thing, it would all be over. Just like that. I'd touch him, and it would be over, and he'd be back, just like that." She supposed she shouldn't have been surprised when tears started coming, but she was. "I don't know why I'm crying," she said. "It's actually a sweet dream. I have this power in the dream: I just touch him and everything is okay again, everything is fixed. I touch him and he's back, everything's back good again. It sounds weird, I know, but it's a sweet, sweet dream. It is. Really." She was annoyed when she saw how solemn Ash looked. He appeared stricken gazing down at her. "Look," she said. "It's nothing bad, really." She noticed that she sounded frightened, and that annoyed her even more. "Fuck you for looking at me like that," she said, and the words came out loud, much louder than she intended. "You can just go fuck yourself, all right?" She could feel the redness in her face, the anger rising up off her like heat.

Ash climbed over her and went to the chair by the window where he sat quietly, looking out at the rain.

Alone in the bed, Connie turned her back to him, petulantly, like out-of-sorts child, and then, an instant later, she realized with great clarity just how crazy she was acting. "Jesus," she said. "I think I just freaked. Did I just freak out?" she asked.

"It's not a problem," Ash said.

"No. I did," she said. She got out of bed and knelt alongside him. "I mean—I don't know what just happened. I just—"

"Honestly," he said. "Not a problem." He put his hand on her shoulder and she threw her arms over his legs and lay her head on his thigh. She was trying to think of another thing to say, something that might undo the strangeness of her behavior. From somewhere out on the unseen East River, the fog horn Ash promised sounded, its low groan rumbling through the air. They both turned their heads when they heard it, and Ash's hand closed slightly on her shoulder as Connie's arms tightened around him, pulling him closer. Then a long time passed in silence as they stared out the window, watching the blank backsides of the street's mute buildings, watching a soft rain pour down over the city.

Eventually, Ash reached over her for the saxophone. He put the reed in his mouth and touched it with his tongue as if he were tasting it, as if he were feeling for something crucial in its texture. Then he leaned over the instrument and began to play a series of plaintive notes that coalesced into a melody Connie thought she might have heard before, but wasn't sure. She was amazed that so soft a sound could come out of so imposing an instrument. Soft as it was, someone across the courtyard apparently heard, because a young man wearing only boxer shorts stepped out onto a fire escape with a beer bottle in hand and gave Ash a perfunctory wave before settling onto a bench set up next to the window. The fire escape above him was lined with a green tarp protecting him from the rain. Ash nodded back and played a little louder. Connie kissed him on the thigh, meaning to encourage his playing, realizing she was hearing him for the first time. She could feel the music within her, as if it were coming from her as well as from Ash, and she thought the sound was extraordinary: moving and painful and peaceful all at once. On the fire escape across the courtyard, a young woman holding an infant joined the man in boxers. They were both handsome, with deep brown skin and lithe bodies, and they looked very young, barely in their twenties. Rain dripping off the green tarp surrounded them like a mesh curtain. The woman sat next to the man and leaned her head on his shoulder. She was wearing a summery, flowered robe, and after a moment she opened it and put the baby to her breast. Connie was impressed with their lack of modesty—the man in boxers, the woman with a baby at her breast. Then she remembered that she was naked in the shadows, as was Ash, and she laughed and said to Ash, "I like your neighborhood." Ash nodded, acknowledging he had heard her, and kept playing, the notes of his melody floating out across the courtyard, sailing over the rooftops and up into the still darkening sky.

Silver Dollars

—⟨⟨⟨⟨⟩⟩⟩⟩—

ALICE GAVE COON TWO SUBWAY TOKENS AND TOLD
him to go ride the trains for a few hours. Coon, angry, snatched the tokens
from her hand and started for the door. "Coon," Alice said, "we'll play a game
of checkers tonight, after supper." He turned in the doorway. They lived in the
basement apartment of a three-story house in Brooklyn. It was four o'clock
and the late afternoon sun came in through the window at his shoulder, a window dressed with bare, white Venetian blinds, and it fell in strips across the
room. He looked as though he were standing behind bars. "You promise?" he
asked. He looked a little worried. "A whole game?"

"After supper," Alice said, "I promise."

Coon hesitated in the doorway. Alice was sixteen, five years older than
Coon, but he felt that she needed him to look after her. She was stupid about
people. Last year, one of the college guys she was always picking up got her
pregnant. When she told Coon, she put her head in his lap and cried. At first
he was angry and pulled away from her. Then he paced around the room
looking, at ten years old, exactly like a little man, like a miniature father.
"Why'd you let him get you pregnant?" he asked. "How could you?"

Alice wiped the tears away. "What do you know about it?"

"More than you, it looks like."

Tears welled up in Alice's eyes again. "He said he was using something!" she shouted. "How was I supposed to know? He said!"

Coon shook his head. "How were you supposed to know," he repeated.

Later he stole some money to help her get it taken care of. He was a good thief. He could find a way into most any apartment in Brooklyn when he wanted to, most any apartment in the city, he guessed. But before he gave her the money he made her promise one thing: "You never call me your pet brother again. You never call me that to anybody."

Alice looked sad when he said that. "Where'd you hear me call you that, Coon?" she asked. Before he could answer she said, "I'm sorry, Coon. I'm real sorry," and she held him in her arms and cried.

For a while they just sat there in the dimly lit living room of their parents' apartment, alone, with Alice crying. Coon had a dark purple birthmark that came down from his temples in a band that covered his eyes like a mask, which is why he was called Coon. It was because of that birthmark, he thought, that no one in the world ever treated him right. "You just never call me that again," Coon said, and Alice nodded and hugged him tighter. Since then Coon had never heard her call him her pet brother, but she still called him Coon. Everyone did, even though, except for the birthmark, he was a strikingly handsome kid: a thin, small boy with straight, dusty brown hair and light skin. In the summer he had to be careful to stay out of the sun, because he burned so easily, and in the winter it seemed he could never get warm enough. His facial features were delicate, almost feminine: he was a pretty child, or at least he would have been a pretty child, if not for the birthmark.

Coon stepped back into the apartment. "You've got one of those jerks from college coming over again, don't you?"

Alice said, "Stop acting like you're my father!" She put all her weight on one leg and her hands on her hips, and she rocked in a way Coon couldn't bear to look at.

He left, slamming the door behind him. Once outside he opened the window, stuck his arm through the blinds, and tossed the two tokens Alice had given him into the kitchen at her feet.

Alice turned away from the mirror that hung alongside the kitchen stove, where she had been fixing her hair. "I forgot," she said. "My little brother's a hot shot. He doesn't need tokens to ride the trains."

Coon made a face. "Don't forget to get him out of here by six-thirty and get supper going for Mom and Dad."

"I know, I know," she said.

He added, "And you look like a jerk." Then he slammed the window and started down the block.

One day last week Alice had shown up for supper with her hair cut short, slicked back on one side, and dyed orange and platinum. "It's punk," she said. "It's the latest." Their father's face turned about the same colors as Alice's hair, but for all his screaming and slamming things around, and threatening, Alice wouldn't budge. It was the style and she liked it. Finally he cursed her and his whole family and went out to get drunk, which was something he did a couple of times a month anyway. Later that night, their mother tried to talk to her, but when Alice told her to mind her own business and leave her alone, she quietly retreated to the living room where she took a seat in front of the TV and turned on one of her shows. So, for a week now Alice had looked this way. She had always worn tight-fitting clothes, but now the skirts were shorter and even tighter, and she had stopped wearing a bra and started wearing flimsy, ragged shirts, so that, as far as Coon could see, she might as well be naked from the waist up. It bothered Coon. He wanted her to be ladylike, but instead she was . . . Her word was the best. She was punk.

Coon stepped onto a subway train heading for uptown Manhattan. He took a seat and watched the graffiti-covered doors slide closed. In a minute the train lurched and then was off rattling and rocking through the long, dark tunnels. He sat back in the harsh yellow light of the car and looked at his reflection in the window across from him. He stared at his eyes peering back from behind their black mask. When he grew up, he thought, he wanted to be a big-time thief, maybe a murderer. He wanted people to be scared of him and do whatever he told them. "If I say jump," he said aloud to his reflection, "they'd better jump!" He was alone in his car—all the traffic this time of day was going the other way—and he felt comfortable among the familiar shrieks and howls of the subway. He laid his head back against the glass and looked up at the roof of the car. Someone had spray painted there, in orange Day-Glow colors, a huge portrait of an erect penis rising from two monstrous testicles. Coon barely noticed it. He liked to daydream while riding the train, and already he was imagining himself being driven around in a Cadillac half a block long, giving orders over a phone in the back seat. He wanted a big apartment for his family uptown, and to have it furnished with the best. When Coon tried to imagine what "the best" was, though, he blanked, and eventually resolved to hire someone to furnish the apartment for him. "That's how they do it uptown," he said aloud.

Coon liked uptown New York, and he swore that's where he'd live when he grew up. Now he settled for walking the sidewalks in front of the fanciest buildings, daydreaming. There were even a few buildings where, by climbing the fire escapes or getting up on a roof, he could peek into the window and get a glimpse of the people who lived there. The train continued to rush over the tracks as he thought about his best find, a rooftop uptown with a skylight that looked down on an indoor swimming pool. Getting to this rooftop wasn't easy: it involved a few leaps and jumps that made even as accomplished a city athlete as Coon nervous. But once he got there he was glad he did it. Most of the time the pool was empty and there was no one to use the fancy lounge chairs spread around the tiled deck, or the three diving boards at one end of the pool, each a different height. Then Coon would just stare down at the blue water and daydream while he waited for the woman he had twice seen using the pool, hoping she would show up again.

She must have been, he thought, a model or an actress or something like that, because he had never seen a woman on the street who was so attractive. She had light blond hair, almost white, and tanned skin. The first time he saw her she was wearing a one-piece white bathing suit, and she swam slowly and steadily back and forth across the length of the pool, lap after lap for almost an hour; then she got out, took a towel off the deck, and left. The second time, she had two children with her. One was a boy about the same age and build as Coon; the other was a girl a few years older. That time she was wearing a robe as she lay in a lounge chair and watched the children swim. It never occurred to Coon that she might be their mother until he heard the boy call to her in a frail, squeaky voice, and he heard the word "mother" float up to him dreamily, as if across a great distance, and still the relationship didn't sink in until much later. It didn't seem possible that she could be anyone's mother.

Coon was thinking hard about this when he felt a hand on his shoulder. At first he didn't respond. He thought he was on the roof, looking down at the pool, at the woman lying on a lounge chair. Then he felt himself being shaken.

He opened his eyes and saw a well-dressed man sitting alongside him.

"Are you all right?" the man asked. He was sitting sideways on the bench, looking at Coon. His right hand was on Coon's knee.

Coon sat up straight and edged away from him. "I'm okay," he said. "I didn't see you get on the train."

"I guess not," the man said. "You were sleeping."

Something about being asleep on the subway bothered Coon, and he resented it. "I wasn't sleeping."

"Oh," the man said. "Okay."

Coon backed away another inch and looked hard at the stranger. He was wearing a three-piece, gray, pin-striped suit, without a wrinkle in it that Coon could notice. He had on a white shirt and a dark tie. His face was thin and clean-shaven, and he had big, brown eyes, with dark circles under them. The circles under his eyes made him look a little ragged, regardless of how well and neatly he was dressed.

"Why are you staring like that?" the man asked.

Coon said, "I'm not staring."

"Oh," he said, and turned away from Coon and sat back, stretching his arms out along the seat so that his forearm was behind Coon's neck.

Coon turned sideways in the seat. "You rich?" he asked.

The man smiled. "Why do you ask that?" he said. Then after a minute he added, "I'm certainly not poor."

"You're not rich!" Coon said. "Else you wouldn't be on the subway."

The man smiled again and looked as though he were impressed with Coon's observation. "What's your name?" he asked.

"Clay," Coon answered. "What's yours?"

"Talbot," the man said. "Everybody calls me Tal."

Coon nodded and Tal smiled again and ruffled Coon's hair in a friendly, fatherly way.

Coon resisted his first impulse to jump away from the stranger's hand. He wasn't sure whether this man was rich, but if he was rich, maybe there was something he could get from him. He let him ruffle his hair, and he didn't pull away when the stranger's hand rested for a moment on his head. "You really rich?"

Tal looked around the still empty car, and then moved closer to Coon. "Here," he said. He reached into the inside pocket of his jacket and came out with a crisp hundred-dollar bill. He offered it to Coon.

Coon didn't move.

"Go ahead," Tal said. "Take it."

Coon scowled. "What do I have to do for it?"

"Nothing," Tal said. "Nothing at all."

Coon stared at him, trying to figure out what this man wanted. Tal's eyes were sunk deep beneath the ridge of his eyebrows. Surrounded by dark sleep-circles, his eyes looked black. Coon started to reach for the bill, making only the slightest move with his hand. He looked at Tal's black eyes and saw the yellow light of the subway caught there, glittering. He took the bill and held it a moment, as if to give the man a chance to change his mind; then he pushed it deep in his pants pocket. Weakly he said, "Thank you."

"Good," Tal said. "That's a lot of money, you know."

"I know!" Coon said, still nervous, but with some wonder in his voice.

"Good." Tal stood up in front of Coon. He was wearing black shoes polished to a bright shine. On one of them there was a smudge of something crusted and yellowish. Carefully, he took a handkerchief out of his pocket and rubbed at his shoe until the spot was gone. He folded the handkerchief and started to put it back in his pocket but then apparently thought better of it and dropped it on the floor. He kicked it under the seat. "I'm tired of riding this train," he said. He sounded sleepy.

"You sound tired," Coon said.

Tal nodded. "I can't get a good night's sleep anymore."

Coon stared up at Tal, and Tal looked back down at Coon. For a while they stayed like that, staring at each other like the strangers they were, trying to read each other's faces. Then the train slowed down for another station stop. "I'm going to get out here and take a cab," Tal said. "Do you want to come with me?"

"Where?" Coon asked.

"To where I live," Tal answered.

Coon shook his head, but it was only half-hearted. He didn't want to lose track of a man who gave away hundred-dollar bills.

Tal yawned and rubbed his eyes. He seemed to pick up a little as the train came to a stop. "Come on," he said. "I've got a milk-shake machine in my apartment, and there might be some more of what you already got waiting for you there."

"Money?" Coon said.

Tal gestured with his eyebrows, as if to say, "sure thing!" Then the car door slid open, and Tal waited.

"Are you sure you're rich?" Coon said.

Tal nodded. "Come on," he said. "Let's go."

"Sure," Coon said. "I could use the money."

From the outside, Coon had been disappointed with Tal's building. It was uptown, but it wasn't the fanciest part of uptown. Once inside, though, he wasn't disappointed at all. It was the biggest apartment he had ever seen, and it was carpeted from wall to wall with a rug that looked too white to walk on. In a corner of the apartment was a grand piano, and all along the walls were books and paintings and sculptures.

Coon had waited in the doorway as Tal entered the apartment.

"Come on," Tal said, and he gestured for Coon to join him on the couch.

On the way over, in the cab, Tal had said something about Coon's clothes, about having to get him a new wardrobe, and Coon had looked down and noticed how scruffy and dirty his sneakers were. Now he hesitated to walk on the white rug.

"Don't be nervous," Tal said. He joined Coon at the door and put his arm around Coon's shoulder, leading him into the living room.

"This is a nice place," Coon said.

"Thank you," Tal said. Then he stopped and yawned so loudly that it frightened Coon. "Excuse me." He took his closed fist away from his mouth, shook himself, and continued to show Coon into the apartment. "You know, you're not the first little friend I've had," he said. "Come here. I want to show you something."

Coon let himself be led into the bedroom, which, like the rest of the apartment, was carpeted in white. He sat down where he was told, on the edge of an oversized bed, on a white quilt, and waited while Tal took a box out of a dresser drawer.

Tal sat alongside Coon and held the box in his lap. "You know what's in here?"

Coon shook his head. It made him nervous to be in such a fancy apartment, but he was truly curious now about Tal, about a man who could live in such a place. Coon had thought, from first meeting Tal on the subway, that he had some idea what the man wanted. But now, in the midst of such a luxurious place, he wasn't sure.

Tal took the cover off the box. Inside there was a Polaroid camera and pictures of several boys, all around Coon's age.

"Who're they?" Coon asked.

Tal nodded once or twice, as if answering someone's question. Then he jerked back a little, as if a shiver had run through him. "What was that, Clay? What did you say?"

"I asked who they were," Coon said.

"Oh! They're my friends. Whenever I make a new friend, I take his picture." He took out the Polaroid, leaned back and snapped a shot of Coon.

Coon smiled.

"That means you're one of my friends now," Tal said.

"Okay," Coon answered.

Then Tal leaned over and kissed him on the cheek.

Coon jerked away and fell back awkwardly on the bed, his head resting on a pillow. Tal leaned over him, holding the box in his lap. His eyes seemed to grow darker as Coon looked up at him.

Tal's breathing grew heavier and slower. "Don't be afraid of me," he said, and he smiled.

"I'm not afraid."

"Good. Good," Tal continued. "My father, you know, used to kiss me like that, just when I was your age. Every night, when he put me to bed."

As Coon watched, Tal smiled again, but this time his head jerked as he smiled and his black eyes blinked wildly.

"Let me show you something else." Tal picked himself up off the bed, sighing as he did so, as if it were a great effort. He replaced the box in the top drawer, and then he pulled the whole second drawer out of the dresser and placed it on the bed alongside Coon. It was filled with boys' clothing: there were several sets of socks, pants, briefs, T-shirts, shirts—everything but shoes. The clothes were all crumpled and stuffed into the drawer.

"These are some outfits that I bought for my friends." He took out a shirt and showed Coon the label. "See that," he said. "Only the best."

Coon nodded, though the label meant nothing to him.

"And here," Tal continued. He reached into the bottom of the drawer and felt around until he pulled out a couple of bright gold rings and shiny silver dollars.

Coon perked up at the sight of the rings and money. "What are they?" he asked.

"That's what my best friends get," he said. "Here," he added. "Look," and he handed Coon one of the rings so he could take a better look.

Coon saw that one side of the ring had diamonds embedded in it. "Gee," he said. "I bet this cost a lot of money."

"That ring," he said, "cost several thousand dollars," and he gently took the ring out of Coon's hand.

"Several thousand dollars," Coon repeated. "Really?"

Tal put the drawer back in place.

"Hey," Coon said. "How come your friends aren't wearing those rings and stuff?"

Tal blinked a few times. He took a handkerchief out of his pants pocket and wiped his eyes. "Oh," he said, "they have lots of other rings and clothes. These are just what they've left behind. They're not using them just now."

"Oh," Coon said.

Tal sat close to Coon on the bed. "You see, I'm very good to my friends, Clay."

Coon nodded, and he didn't resist when Tal lifted him and then pressed him down on his stomach against the bed. Now he knew what Tal wanted—it was what he had guessed all along—and he felt almost glad that Tal was doing it, though it wasn't something he liked. This had happened to him before, when Virac, the drunk who lived next door, had caught Coon trying to steal a radio out of his apartment. He, too, had done this to Coon, and said it was punishment for being a thief. Then over the next three months, till he moved away, he did it to Coon four more times, each time paying him twenty dollars and saying that he'd have him arrested for trying to steal his radio if he told. Coon never told. Now he remembered the hundred-dollar bill in his pants pocket. He wanted to reach down and hold the money, but he'd have to wait till Tal was finished before he could get to it. Still, he knew the bill was there, and now he knew it was really his.

When Tal stopped he was breathing loudly, and he pulled away from Coon and sat on the edge of the bed. While Tal fixed himself up, Coon pulled his pants back on and straightened out his hair. Then he smiled at Tal, glad the worst part was over, and hoping that now Tal would give him something more.

"See," Tal said. He was almost whispering, and his head bobbed while he spoke. He seemed to be having a hard time keeping himself awake. "See," he said, barely audible, "now you're one of my best friends."

"Good," Coon said. He was eager for what would come next, but while he waited, Tal's eyes closed and his head fell to his chest. He made a snoring sound.

Coon shook Tal's arm. "Hey, Tal," he said. "You said you might have something more for me." Tal didn't wake. Coon shook him again. "Hey, Tal," he said.

When Coon saw that Tal wasn't going to wake up, he stood and quietly pulled out the drawer with the box and looked inside. Alongside the box there were stacks of coins, mostly silver dollars, but lots of other coins too, half dollars, quarters, foreign coins, subway tokens. Coon touched a few, looking furtively back at Tal as he did. Then he looked at the photos inside the box. There were six of them, each of a boy about his age, each taken in Tal's apartment. In the next drawer, Coon noticed there were six of everything: six pairs of pants, six silver dollars, six rings, and something Tal hadn't shown him—six heavy gold necklaces. Coon started to open the next drawer, but Tal stopped snoring and pushed it closed before Coon could get a look inside. When he turned around Tal was looking at him. He looked like his father when he came home drunk. His mouth hung open and his eyes were dazed. "Are you okay?" Coon asked.

"You didn't take anything out of those drawers, did you Clay?" Tal asked in a whisper.

"No," Coon said. "I didn't."

Tal blinked several times and then he nodded. "Good, Clay. You don't want me to be severe with you. I can be very severe."

"I didn't take anything," Coon said.

"Good." Tal patted the bed alongside him. "Come sit by me."

"I have to get going," Coon said. "What about what you said before? You said you'd have something for me."

"Do you have to go?" Tal asked.

"I have to be home for supper."

"Oh." Tal looked hard at Coon. "Well," he said, "you'll be back again, won't you Clay?"

Coon shrugged.

"Would you like one of those rings? One with the diamonds?"

"Sure!" Coon said. "Sure I would!"

"Then you come back tomorrow," Tal said. "Come back and I'll have a ring for you, and maybe we'll buy you a new wardrobe. And . . . And . . ." Once again Tal's head started bobbing and dropping to his chest. His eyes closed. He was having a difficult time finishing his sentence. "And . . . there will be . . . surprises . . . surprise . . . ."

"But what about now?" Coon asked.

"Oh," Tal said. His arm moved as if it were something dead and heavy. He reached into his jacket pocket and pulled out a new silver dollar. "Here," he managed to say. "Here."

Coon put the coin in his pocket, next to the hundred-dollar bill, and when he looked up Tal appeared to be sleeping again. "Tal?" Coon said. When Tal didn't answer, he reached for the bottom drawer, the drawer he hadn't yet seen, and started to pull it open slowly.

Tal's arm shot out and slammed the drawer closed. "Don't make me angry!" he said. "I can be very severe, Clay. Do you hear me?"

Coon moved away. "I'm sorry Tal," he said. "I was just looking."

"I know," Tal said. He sighed and his voice turned sleepy again. "I know. Come back tomorrow and you'll get your reward." Then he laughed an odd, low laugh, and added in a whisper: "And don't show anyone the money, Clay. They'll take it away from you."

Coon didn't need to be told. "I know," he said. "I won't."

Tal smiled weakly. "I just can't keep myself awake," he said, and in a moment his head had dropped to his chest and he was snoring again.

Coon's eyes moved back and forth from the drawer to the figure on the bed. Tal appeared to be sleeping soundly: he was sitting up and his chin was pressed flat against his chest. With every breath he took his head rose; then he'd exhale with a snort, and his head would drop and bob before rising again.

"Tal," Coon whispered.

Tal's head, eyes still closed, rose slowly and turned even more slowly to face Coon.

Coon backed out of the door. The man on the bed before him was still neatly dressed in a fine three-piece suit, but now his hair was messed up, and his face looked like a ghost's or a vampire's, the skin white and rubbery, the eyes so deep they looked like skull holes. The man looked dead: it was as if a corpse had sat up in its coffin, dressed in its best suit, and was looking at Coon.

Coon forgot about the rings, and the money and the gold necklaces. He backed out of the bedroom and ran out of the apartment.

Coon was late for supper. As he walked into the kitchen, his family was quiet. They were sitting around the table with dishes of soup in front of them. They had stopped eating.

"You'd better sit your ass down before this gets any colder," Alice said.

Coon sat at the table, in front of his spot.

"Go ahead," his mother said. She pointed to his plate.

Coon picked up his spoon and began eating. The room was small, and from where he sat Coon could feel the heat of the stove against his arm. The thick smell of tomato soup drifted from a pot on one of the burners. Coon ate his soup slowly. His father wanted supper and his family waiting for him when he came home from work. That was a rule, and Coon was waiting to be yelled at.

"Where have you been?" his mother asked.

"Out," Coon answered.

"Out," his father said.

"I'm sorry," Coon said.

His father breathed heavily as he looked about the table: at his wife, who had her hair in curlers and in a pink and blue checked kerchief wrapped around her hair and tied in a big bow on top; at the dark birthmark that masked his son's eyes; at his daughter, with her platinum and orange hair; at her blouse, which was ripped down the middle so that the insides of both breasts were exposed. He stared longest and hardest at Alice, and it was clear that he was too angry at her to have much left over for Coon.

"Look at this," he said at last. "Look at this," he repeated, gesturing with his hand. "My own private, goddamned freak show." Then he pushed his chair back and left the table.

Coon watched him through the window as he walked out of the apartment and up to the street.

"Fuck him," Alice said, once he was gone.

"Don't you talk that way," her mother said.

"Fuck you, too," Alice said, and she got up and stomped away to her room.

"See what you did," his mother said to Coon. She was resting her head in the palms of both hands and rocking it from side to side as she looked down at her soup.

Coon turned away from the table and found himself looking at his reflection in the mirror by the stove. Behind him he saw his mother. With her fingertips, she was pulling the skin back from her eyes and so distorting her face she looked monstrous. He tried to imagine in his mother's place the beautiful woman from uptown, the woman from the swimming pool who was some other boy's mother. He couldn't. So he squinted until she disappeared. Then he looked at himself looking at himself, and he squinted harder, trying to make his mask disappear. Soon his eyes closed, and then he thought of Tal, and he reached into his pocket to feel the silver dollar and the hundred-dollar bill.

"Well," his mother said softly, "are you going to tell me where you were?"

Coon didn't answer. He was busy dreaming of the diamond studded rings in Tal's drawer, of the grand piano in the huge, white-carpeted apartment, and of all the fine clothes and all the money he could get from Tal. He didn't even hear his mother's question. It was as if he had already gone to see Tal. It was as if he were already long gone.

Drunks

———⟨⟨⟨⟩⟩⟩———

I HAD AGREED TO MEET A DRUNK NAMED BARNEY at the Fourth Down as soon as I finished up, and Guy was looking at me as if I had just invited serious trouble into my life. We were setting up an electronics convention at Grossingers, and I was on my knees in front of a folding table, inside a booth constructed of corporation-brown partitions, a fat roll of red crepe paper in one hand and a shiny, silver staple gun in the other. As far as I knew, Guy had no name—I had just taken to calling him Guy—and he was mostly out of his mind. He had spent the previous several hours leaning on a broom and watching me work. He seemed to like me—or at least appreciate that I was doing most of the work and not complaining. He understood directions and he'd do whatever he was asked, but when he talked it came out gibberish—until I told him I was meeting Barney for a drink. Then he looked at me with terrific concern. I was twenty-eight, pink-skinned, wiry, and in good physical condition. He may not have been much older, but he was so beat-up his actual age was hard to guess. My hair was cut close to the scalp, and I wore a plain, gold ring high on my right ear. He had long, dirty-blond hair, flat and stringy and lusterless. I said, "Is there a problem?" and he answered, lucidly, "Barney's a bad character." When I pressed him for details, he went back to talking gibberish. I laughed it off.

I thought he was a drunk. Everyone I worked with was a drunk. Others might call them alcoholics, winos, street scum, etc.—but they called themselves drunks and as far as I could see they didn't have any particular problem with it. Of course, whenever I saw them they were up in the mountains, the Catskills, on what was a kind of drunk's vacation. Ordinarily they lived on the streets in Manhattan, which I have no doubt was a considerably tougher world. Periodically, though, Uncle Mike would drive the company van down to the Bowery and cruise the piss-and-trash byways looking for as many of the boys as he could find to make up a work crew. Uncle Mike owned the Monticello Employment Agency. The boys were a bunch of drunks who would work twenty-four to seventy-two hours straight setting up conventions, which involved mostly unloading trucks and hauling gear to booths. When they were done, they took their money back to the city and drank it up.

I was one of the boys, though I didn't live in the city. I lived in a small cabin on a hillside, not a long walk from Grossingers. My most expensive possessions were an old Apple II computer and a dot-matrix printer. I drove a dilapidated Volkswagen Beetle, in major disrepair, which I had bought for fifty dollars a few years earlier, when I first showed up in Monticello, responding to one of Uncle Mike's perpetual workers-wanted ads in a city paper. I did some drugs, mostly grass and hash and whiskey—but not a lot and I certainly wasn't a drunk. I was a poet. When I wasn't working a convention, which was most of the time, I wrote poetry a few hours a day, every day. A couple more hours, I read poetry. After that, my time was free. I hung out at Monticello Raceway or with friends who worked at the remaining Borsch-belt hotels. I was seeing two girls: Marlee, who went to school over the mountain in New Paltz and whom I saw on occasional weekends, and Viola, who was local and worked in the laundry room at the Concord.

It was a decent life. I had an undergraduate English degree from SUNY–Buffalo and a master's in creative writing from City College—education courtesy of my parents, who lived comfortably on Long Island, a kind of home-base for me, a place to return to whenever the money and jobs ran out. I figured that if I failed utterly as a poet I could either kill myself or go on and get a doctorate and teach literature in a university. One way or the other, I knew setting up conventions in Monticello was temporary.

I pulled myself up off the floor and set the staple gun and crepe paper down on the table. Guy leaned on his broom and gazed at me. For all his battered features—the pitted and creased skin of his face, the fatty growths around his eyes, his split bottom lip—there was still a puppylike quality in his demeanor, like he might amble over in a moment and try to nuzzle. The way he watched me, he seemed almost amused. I stretched and rolled my shoulders and did a variety of little calisthenics, trying to work out the kinks from several hours straight of stapling crepe paper to tables, turning them into display areas. I winked at Guy and said, "I'm meeting Barney for that drink now."

Guy replied, "Aballoonda du babba."

Which was pretty much what he had been saying all along. There were variations, like "Babba du aballoonda," and occasional extended riffs that brought in a wild variety of sounds—but he always came back to the basic aballoonda thing. Before, though, I didn't know he was capable of speech. I wondered if Uncle Mike had mistakenly picked up a mental out-patient off his medicine, figuring he was a drunk looking for a few days' work. I said, "What's your story, Guy? What's this 'aballoonda' about?"

He leaned a little closer to me and tilted his head, and I thought I saw a hint of recognition in his eyes, as if he saw something familiar in me and now he was going to let me in on his secret. He hesitated a moment longer, and then he said, with a musical lilt, "Balloo balloo balloonda."

I patted him on the arm and went off to meet Barney.

Outside the booth, workers were hustling around on the convention floor, which was actually a dining room divided into rows of booths by multicolored partitions. The convention was scheduled to open in the morning, and most of the basic setup was completed: the booths were constructed, the tables were draped, the signs and displays were in place. Through a pair of open doors at the back of the dining room, I could see a dozen trailers parked on an expanse of grass behind the loading dock. It was an early summer night, warm, with gusty winds that made it feel like it might thunder, though there were only a few clouds drifting under bright fields of stars, bright like they only get in the mountains. The trailers were full of electronic gear: computers, fax machines, copiers—mostly computers and peripherals and a ton of software. Company employees and Uncle Mike's crew were busy unloading the trailers and hauling the contents to the booths, which was the final stage in setting up a convention. After that, the salespeople showed up to arrange the stuff. On the loading dock, amid the squealing wheels of hand trucks and the rumbling of loaded dollies, Uncle Mike observed the work with his hands pushed into the pockets of baggy polyester pants, a scowl on his face. Uncle Mike always looked sullen. He didn't trust his workers. He felt he had to watch them every minute. Except me. Me he knew he could trust.

I whistled in Uncle Mike's direction and when he looked my way I yelled that I was taking a break and he just looked back toward the trucks. I had expected him to ask about Guy's whereabouts, since he had become my responsibility once Uncle Mike realized the problem. I figured great, he's not going to ask, and then I turned around and bumped into Guy. He backed away from me looking frightened and holding his face in both hands. "Excuse me," I said. "I didn't know you were behind me."

He nodded.

I knew all I'd hear in response was gibberish, so I didn't ask him why he was following me—but I didn't invite him to join me and Barney for a drink, either. Still, I left the convention area with Guy on my heels. I negotiated a maze of corridors to the main entrance of Grossingers, where Barney was waiting for me beyond the glass doors on a concrete bench. He was smoking a nub of a cigarette and sitting astride the bench as if it were a motorcycle. Barney was tall—six-one, six-two, a good three or four inches taller than me—and brawny. He was as thick and bulky through the arms and legs and chest as I was thin and wiry. I had worked a few hours with him setting up tables, and he had been funny and outgoing, telling me outrageous stories about the other drunks on the crew, like the one about a drunk who supposedly used to be a surgeon at a Los Angeles hospital before several bottles of whiskey were discovered hidden in the operating rooms. He didn't actually lose his license, Barney claimed, until he slipped during cataract surgery and accidentally removed part of a patient's nose. I didn't believe a word of it and I don't think he expected to be believed. He was entertaining me. When Uncle Mike pulled me away to start draping tables, and sent Barney back to unloading trailers, Barney said meet him for a drink at nine o'clock, and I said sure, we'd could go to the Fourth Down.

I walked out the main doors, Guy a few steps behind me.

Barney jumped up. "Aballoonda!" he said. "You're coming with us? Terrific!" He moved quickly toward Guy, as if about to put an arm around his shoulder.

Guy ran away, stiff-legged, back into the hotel. He stood behind the glass doors looking out, his expression a strange combination of offense and fear.

Barney grinned at me. "You think it was it something I said?"

"Is that his name? Aballoonda?"

"That's what I call him."

Guy remained behind the doors, holding the handles tightly in his fists. The night was dark, no moon that I could see, only bright stars and a few clouds—and the darkness outside made Guy seem illuminated all the brighter in the light from the lobby, as if he were center stage or on screen. I asked, "Is he a mental patient?"

"Who isn't?" Barney said. "Oh," he added. "I forgot," his tone of voice making it clear he hadn't forgotten at all. "You're the college grad. Mr. Harvard." His grin had turned into something a lot closer to a smirk.

"City College is not Harvard," I said.

Barney's hair was damp and freshly combed: straight back on the sides and down over his forehead. With the loose-fitting white denim jacket he wore, which was frayed at the collar and turned up against the breeze, the hair style gave him a '50s, street-corner hoodlum look. All he needed to complete the image was a shiny switchblade dangling from his fingertips. Then, as if he saw me trying to nail down his look and wanted to help out, he pulled a comb from his back pocket and ran it through his hair, sneering slightly and shifting his weight from one leg to the other as the comb moved from one side of his head to the other. It wasn't a joke. It wasn't a parody. I asked him how old he was and he asked me what the fuck did I care? And then I looked at his face closely, really, for the first time, and I saw that he could be as old as fifty and I wouldn't be shocked. His face was youthful, but age showed in his eyes, which were creased and lined as if he'd seen a few things.

Barney put his hands on his hips. "Well, hell, Harvard," he said. "Where's your wheels?"

I pointed to the parking lot. "Right this way," I said, and started for the car. Behind us, I heard the glass doors open. Guy followed us, but when Barney and I looked back at him, he stopped. "What's your story, Guy?" I said. "You're welcomed to come with us if you want."

Guy didn't respond.

Barney put his hand on my arm and directed me back toward the lot. "He's coming," he said. "Just don't pay any attention to him."

"You don't mind?"

"Mind? Ab's a pisser. I can't wait to hear him talk with a few drinks in him."

When we reached the car, Guy was right behind us. We got in the front and he got in the back. Barney seemed excessively disappointed with my VW. "Jesus Christ," he said. "This is it? This is your car?"

"Were you expecting a Mercedes?"

"No, Wise Guy," he said. He slapped me on the head.

I froze in the driver's seat, a weird smile on my face. I couldn't quite decide how to react. The slap had not been hard, but I was surprised by it. It hadn't been a baby tap either. I looked over at Barney while I started the car, hoping my expression would let him know I was perplexed and not particularly happy about being smacked on the top of the head.

Barney didn't appear to notice my expression. He twisted around to face Guy. "Aballoonda, my man," he said. He smacked him on the knee—hard. The slap resounded through the car. "You got a new buddy, here? A new pal?"

Guy shrieked more gibberish and pulled back, pressing himself against the door.

Barney said, "No kidding?" Then he leaned toward me, laying one of his beefy arms over my shoulder. "He says you're all right, Harvard. He says you're a stand-up guy." He touched the gold ring on my ear with a fingertip. "You a stand-up guy?"

I jerked away from his hand. "My name's Rick," I said, and then I added, with a good-humored laugh, "And would you mind keeping your fucking hands off me?" I turned a lavish smile toward him. Our faces were only inches apart.

He snorted and sat back in his seat. "Keep my fucking hands off you . . ." he said, as if amused.

"If it's not asking too much," I said. I slowed down at the guard booth and nodded to a security guy I knew would recognize me, and then rolled on down a hill and out the main gates toward the town of Liberty and the Fourth Down, which was a sports bar—beer and big-screen TVs.

"Where we going?" Barney said.

"Fourth Down, like I said."

"Nah. You don't want to go there, Harvard. It's for pussies."

I didn't say anything. I glanced in the rearview at Guy, who was still pressed against the door. I thought back to what he said about Barney being a bad character and wondered what he knew that I didn't.

Barney pointed out the window. "Go about another mile and a half, and there's a gravel road off on your left. Take that."

"A gravel road?" I said. "Where we going?"

"Trust me."

"I don't know you," I said. "Why would I trust you?" I said this with a little laugh that came out sounding fake. At that point I was keenly aware of Barney's size. I had been aware of it since he had laid his arm over my shoulder.

"Jesus," he said. "You paranoid or something, Rick?" He sounded offended.

"How do you know the area?" I asked. "Have you worked here before?"

"I was raised here."

"Here?" I said. "In Liberty?"

"The hell with me," he said. "What about you? What's your story? What did you study in college? Table draping?" He laughed loudly at his joke, and then settled back in his seat, as if expecting an answer.

"Poetry," I said.

"You're shitting me. What kind of poetry?"

For a moment, I actually thought about the question. I had studied incoherent poetry, which was the only kind of poetry my professors really admired when I was in school. Unfortunately, I insisted on writing poems that made sense, which located me squarely in the midst of masses of unpromising students. I remember I once asked a professor about this, a professor who was a well-known poet. She had just returned one of my poems with a look of mild disgust, as if I had forced her to eat something rancid. "What's wrong with a poem that makes a point?" I asked. "What's wrong with a poem that adds up to something?" I was pissed off and it was obvious. It was also obvious that I was criticizing her poetry, which seemed to me incomprehensible.

"Poetry's about music, about sound," she said. "When you make things add up," she told me, "it's a lie. Coherence is a lie. At least, the way you do it, it is."

I didn't get it. For the final essay, I wrote an incoherent paper titled "The Failure of Coherence."

She gave me an F.

By the time I left school, I was disgusted with academics. I went off to write poetry my own way, which is what I had been doing ever since. A day or two before the start of the electronics convention, I had finished a sequence of poems that reinterpreted well-known Greek myths.

I decided not to tell any of this to Barney. "Poetry poetry," I said. "What do you mean, what kind?"

Barney didn't answer. He appeared to be watching the road. The dashboard lights in my VW hadn't worked in years. We were on an empty stretch of highway. Without roadside lights, it was especially dark inside the car. I could see that Barney was leaning close to the windshield, but he was covered in shadows and I couldn't make out his expression or see what his arms were doing. When he spoke, his words floated lazily in the tinny space of the car. He said, "I never knew a guy went to college who wasn't at heart a pussy. And I been around."

"And I never knew a drunk," I said, "who wasn't at heart a lazy son of a bitch."

Barney laughed. "You can talk some smack," he said. "I'll give you that." He pointed up the road. "This is the turn coming up."

"I'm not turning on any gravel road, Barney. Forget it."

"Yeah?" Barney said.

We were on Route 52, just beyond the hotel grounds. There was nothing on either side of the road but dark woods. I didn't even see the gravel road until we were almost on top of it and Barney slid over into the driver's seat. He held my neck in the crook of his left arm like a vice. I couldn't breathe. He lifted me slightly and worked the brake pedal with his foot as he took the wheel with his free hand and guided the car into the turn and off the road. The right fender scraped a tree before we came to a stop. He turned off the lights, let me go, and moved back into his seat, watching me quietly while I wheezed and coughed getting my breath back.

"What the fuck's wrong with you?" I said, as soon as I could talk. I was surprised by the sound of my own voice—which was whining almost, close to tearful. I had one hand on the door handle.

Barney took a butcher's knife out of the inside pocket of his jacket. It had a black handle and a wide, serrated blade, and it was a least a foot long. He laid the knife on his leg. From another pocket, he removed a pair of leather gloves and slipped them on. I looked into the back seat—just to make sure Guy was still there, since I didn't hear the merest rustling coming from that direction—and saw Guy sitting up rigidly, leaning forward, his hands closed into fists.

"Barney," I said. "What the hell are you doing?" My voice was a little better, a little less whinny.

"I'm getting set up to slice you open from your dick to your neck and feed your heart to the animals."

"Oh," I said. I looked down at the knife. I thought about bolting, but I knew there was no way. "Why bother with the gloves? I told a half dozen people I was meeting you; the front desk saw us leave, plus the security guy. You might as well write your name in blood on the windshield when your done."

Barney leaned back against the door and smiled. He picked up the knife. "The gloves are just to keep the blood off my hands."

"Do you mind telling me why," I said. I was talking fast. "Are you going to kill Aballoonda too?"

Barney pointed up the gravel road with the knife. "I may not kill either one of you, and I may kill you both. It's all according. Drive up the road."

When I went to turn on the lights, he stabbed my wrist. I made a loud, high-pitched noise and pulled my hand back to my chest.

"Don't be a pussy," he said. "Leave the lights off and drive slow."

The road was lined with trees and I had to drive slow—a few miles per hour—in order to see where I was going. It was dark, the only light coming from the stars. Blood dripped from my wrist onto my jeans. I tried to figure out where the road might lead by picturing a map in my mind. As far as I could see, it didn't go anywhere. It occurred to me that he might be driving us to a secluded spot so that he could kill us and dump our bodies and be on his way—but I couldn't imagine why. Why would he want to do that? What would be gained? I said, "Does this road go anyplace?"

"Sure it does . . ." He looked into the back of the car, as if he had just remembered Guy, and he put the butcher knife back in his pocket. "It goes right back where we came from. If you were observant, Mr. College," he said, "you would have noticed the gate at the back of the field where the trailers are parked."

I had noticed the gate. It was rust red, it opened on metal hinges, and it was latched with a length of heavy chain. "This is that road? We're going back to the hotel?"

Barney looked into the rear seat again. "He talks a lot," he said. "Don't he, Aballoonda?"

Guy didn't answer. The car remained silent until we came up on the gate. I stopped well back from it.

"Aballoonda," Barney said. "Go open it. Be quiet."

Guy got out of the car, quietly, and went to the gate. He had no trouble undoing the chain, and as he opened the gate, I noticed that he lifted it, keeping it from squealing. He got back in the car and closed the door almost soundlessly.

Barney said, "Just do what I say. Just don't fuck around with me." He pushed me into the door and showed me the knife in his pocket, the tip of the blade pushing through the fabric. "I'll kill you if you piss me off."

"I get it," I said. "Whatever you say."

"That's the attitude. Keep that attitude, you'll see the sun rise tomorrow."

"No problem." I took hold of the wheel, my hands at ten and two o'clock. My wrist had stopped bleeding, and with my hand up in front of me, I could see that the cut wasn't anything much—but it still throbbed, shooting out a dull, pulsing pain.

Barney leaned into the windshield, so that his forehead was touching the glass. "Drive up, slow, behind that line of trailers." He pointed to a dozen trailers parked in a straight line, side by side.

Once I was through the gate, I could see the loading dock in the distance. Uncle Mike was standing outside, talking loudly into the back of a trailer. His voice and the voices that answered him wavered across the field like the muted, incomprehensible lyrics of a song. I drove slowly over the grass to the line of trailers, which was close enough to the loading dock that I thought someone might hear the car.

When we reached the right trailer, Barney touched my shoulder. "Let's do this fast," he said. He knocked the plastic cover off the overhead light and pulled out the bulb. Then he opened his door.

"What are we doing?" I asked.

Guy got out of the car and opened my door. Barney went to the back of the trailer, removed a lock and chain, and slid the door up. We were close enough to the dock now that I could make out what Uncle Mike was shouting. He was directing the crew, telling them which cartons to unload and where to take them. I guessed the distance separating us was only a little more than the length of a football field. I thought about yelling. I thought about running. Barney was looking into the back of the trailer and Guy was standing by my side. The stars overhead seemed to be blinking frantically. The temperature had dropped: I could feel a slight chill on the back of my neck and on my face and hands. I looked back at Uncle Mike, and I leaned toward the loading dock, just slightly. Guy put his hand on my shoulder and shoved me gently toward the trailer.

Barney jumped down and motioned for me to help him pull out the ramp. When it was more than halfway out, the rollers screeched and we both froze and looked back to the dining room, then continued when no one seemed to be looking our way. Inside the trailer, stacked against the back wall and hidden under green packing quilts, were more than a dozen computers, all brand new, unopened, still in their boxes. I said, "You're lucky if you fit two of those boxes in my VW."

Barney sneered. "Just get them out of here," he said. "Drop them next to the car."

It didn't take five minutes to unload the trailer, and then the boxes were spread around on the grass. Stacked right, they'd have been bigger than the car itself. Barney was behind me when I put the last box down. He pulled the butcher knife out of his jacket and sliced open the carton. "Empty it," he said. "Toss all the packing, put the computers in the car, don't lose anything."

While Barney sliced the cartons open, Guy and I unpacked them and loaded the car. It didn't take long before the cartons were empty and the Volkswagen was full. Barney covered the computers with quilts and closed the car doors. I waited quietly alongside Guy, surrounded by a junk heap of Styrofoam and cardboard. Barney was in front of the car. He looked toward the open gate and then back to the hotel, and then back toward us. For the first time, he appeared to be nervous. He started toward the trailer and gestured for us to follow. I whispered to Guy, "Maybe we should run. How dangerous is this asshole?"

Guy put a hand on the small of my back, nudging me toward the trailer and Barney.

"What is this?" I said. "Are you two partners or something? Do you work for him?"

Guy made a face. "Ab, ab, ab, ab, ab," he whispered.

Barney stopped at the trailer ramp. He watched us, his hands in his jacket pockets. He seemed to be waiting to see what we'd do.

Guy walked toward the trailer. I followed. Barney climbed the ramp and disappeared into the dark interior.

At the ramp, I hesitated. Guy climbed up and walked into the blackness—but something was telling me not to, something was telling me to run.

Barney stepped out of the shadows. "Don't be a jerk," he said. "I'm not going to do anything. Just come on up here."

I looked toward the hotel one more time. I had a bad feeling about getting into that truck: something way down deep was holding me back.

"Rick . . ." Barney's tone suggested he was losing patience.

I didn't like it that he called me Rick. I put one foot up on the ramp, and then I bolted. I'm not sure why. Something inside me just wouldn't let me climb the ramp into that trailer. It was like a black hole. It was like an open mouth. When I put my foot on the ramp, I wasn't thinking I'm going to run—but I did. I used the ramp the way a runner uses blocks. I pushed off it. I exploded off it.

Didn't matter. Barney leaped from the trailer, caught me by the legs, and before I could make a sound he had his hand over my mouth. He picked me up and carried me back into the trailer. I didn't struggle. I was too afraid. He pushed me up against a stack of boxes, his hand tight over my mouth. His eyes were so alive with hate they seemed luminous, like an animal's eyes in the dark. He didn't say anything. He stared at me and it was as if his look had substance, as if I could feel it entering me. Then his free hand moved toward his jacket pocket, toward the butcher knife. He was wearing the leather gloves again, and I knew that he was going to kill me. I was sure. I saw it in his eyes. Barney was maybe two seconds away from gutting me—and I did nothing. I didn't even struggle. It was as if his hand over my mouth were immobilizing me. I watched the knife appear slowly from his jacket pocket, his fingers white over the black handle. I was frozen. It was a stiff feeling, like the stiffness after waking up from a nightmare. I don't think I was able to move. The wide blade of the knife cleared the white fabric of the jacket. He leaned into me, putting more pressure on my mouth—and then his head jerked violently to one side and blood splattered onto my face. He went down flat and hard, bouncing once before he settled to the floor.

"Aballoonda," Guy said, looking only a moment at Barney, who was motionless, blood flowing from his lips and from his eyebrow and forehead. Guy glanced at me, as if quickly summing up the significance of my presence. He held a tire iron loosely in his hand. He tossed it onto Barney's stomach and scurried out of the truck.

I remained frozen against the boxes. From far away I could hear Uncle Mike's voice and the voice of a worker who sounded young, like a little boy. Uncle Mike sounded angry. The boy sounded happy. Together their voices made a kind of music, their voices and the gusting wind: a music wrapped up in darkness. The inside of the truck was black and the outside was a lighter shade of black. The opening at the back of the truck was like a frame on a contemporary painting, something that might have been titled "Black on Black, IV." Barney lay motionless at my feet, but it was as though his hand were still clasped over my mouth, holding me pressed against the wall. I stared at him and saw that his chest was moving regularly, rising and falling. The bloody side of his face had swollen up grotesquely, closing his eye, stretching the skin over his lips so taut it looked like it would burst. A foul smell started to fill the trailer: an ugly, acrid smell so thick I could taste it on my tongue, and I realized that it was the smell of shit and that it was coming from Barney. Still, I didn't move. I watched him, thinking nothing but smelling that terrible odor and listening to the wind and the voices and feeling the night air on my face and hands. I watched him until I heard my car start, and then the ability to move returned all at once.

I jumped from the trailer to the grass, and I saw that Guy was in the driver's seat of my car, looking out the window, as if he were waiting for me. I was startled for a moment by the stars, which seemed impossibly bright— as if someone had turned up the wattage while I was in the trailer. I knelt by the driver's door. I said, "What are you doing, Guy?"

Guy said, "Aballoonda du babba, du babba, du babba," which wasn't strange at that point, but what *was* strange was that I thought I might almost understand him. There was something in the tone of his gibberish, in the way he was saying it that I almost comprehended. The meaning was something like: "I'm fine. Aren't we both lucky? Let's get the hell out of here." Of course, I might have been making it all up. I couldn't tell. I knelt there by the car feeling as if the world were suddenly a very strange place.

Guy put the car in gear.

"Guy," I said. "You can't just take off." I pointed into the back seat. "That stuff doesn't belong to you." I moved back from the car and opened my hands. "It's my car," I said.

Guy tried to release the hand brake, but something apparently was in his way. He reached down and came up with a unopened bottle of Jim Beam. He held it up, scowled at it, and tossed it out the window where it landed on the grass with a dull thump.

He released the hand brake.

"Guy," I said, trying to sound patient. "You can't just steal all this stuff. It's not right."

He started to let up the clutch, and I could see that he was looking for the gas pedal with his right foot. Only, there was no gas pedal. There was only a piece of metal that the gas pedal had at one time been attached to, and which would operate the car just fine once he found it. Guy scrunched over to look under the dash. When he located the right piece of metal, he drove away, out across the field and through the gate and off into the darkness.

For a while I just stood there in the field, surrounded by a small mountain of cardboard and Styrofoam, under an insanely bright welter of stars, with Barney unconscious in a trailer at my back. I considered my options. I could walk into the hotel and explain everything to Uncle Mike, in which case he'd have the cops on Guy in a heartbeat. Given that there were really only two roads out of the mountains, Guy wouldn't get far before the cops found him and did whatever they do to someone who talks gibberish and just committed manslaughter and grand larceny.

I didn't like that option. Guy had just saved my life. I picked up a sliver of Styrofoam and tossed it in the air and watched it float to the ground, as if I were tossing the bones and waiting to see what they augured. The Styrofoam settled lightly on the grass, and I turned around and walked away through the field toward my cabin. I looked back once to the hotel, which was only a hundred twenty-five, a hundred fifty feet away—but it looked like another world, another galaxy existing in another dimension. I wasn't going back there and getting Guy busted. He could have my car. It was a piece of shit.

I walked slowly. It took about twenty minutes to get to the one-room cabin I rented, and when I got there, I still didn't know what I was doing. I ambled around my single room, running my fingers over my handful of possessions. From under my cot, I removed an airport carry bag, and I packed all my poems and notebooks. I zipped it closed and just stood there looking at it. I guess I was thinking about leaving and taking only my poems and few books. I unzipped the bag and took out a poem. It was about Dionysus, who, in the poem, I had portrayed as an Amway salesman. I had a hard time following the plot. It was difficult to believe this was my poem, that I had written it. Dionysus was pursuing Aphrodite, whom I had portrayed as an Avon sales representative. Somehow or other, I had gotten Ann Landers into this poem. She was giving Dionysus advice. Apparently when I wrote this poem, I was serious.

I put the poem back in the bag. I put the bag under the cot. I left the cabin and went out to Route 52 empty-handed. I started walking over the mountain toward New Paltz. The night was chilly, the way it always gets in the mountains. It was dark and the woods at the side of the road were loud with the rustlings of the wind. For a while I was afraid, as if it were dangerous to be out on the road at night, alone—but after a time the feeling began to fade. The road I was on went all the way over the mountain toward New Paltz. It wasn't like I was going to get lost. It wasn't like the road was hard to follow or anything: I put one foot in front of the other and if it hit blacktop I was on the road. I had no idea how long it would take to get to New Paltz, but I knew it wasn't close. I figured I'd have to hitch a ride somewhere along the line, but eventually I'd make it there. I'd come down out of the mountains and cross a green truss bridge over the Wallkill River and I'd be in a small college town where I had a girlfriend and I knew a few people—and I'd be far away from Uncle Mike and the boys, and from Barney.

Still, it was awfully dark. It was dark and I was jumpy. There were sounds all around me: the wind in the leaves, animals scurrying away from my approach, birds flapping out of trees. I had just come within a second of two of being murdered. It was a piece of luck that I was alive. Luck and Guy: Mr. Aballoonda, Mr. Gibberish. A few poems were going in and out of my head, but mostly I was just listening to the noises around me, and then eventually I relaxed and the sounds began to turn into something soothing, like the sound of water over rocks. I didn't want to think about what had just happened. I resisted trying to make sense of it. I resisted trying to understand. I didn't know what to make of Guy. How could I? His life was so far removed from my own. When I first saw him, I thought he was one of the most wretched and sad and pathetic human beings ever to cross my path—and now, here I was, alive only because he was alive.

It was too much to think about, so I didn't. There was the road and I followed it; there was the night and I walked toward it; and there was a wealth of sound that coalesced, from time to time, into a companionable music. As I walked, the desire to make sense out of things slipped away, and then it was like a layer of clothes came off. It got colder, but I felt lighter. I kept walking. I felt good. For the longest time there was only in my mind the night sounds and the one thought, that it was a piece of luck that I was alive, and the thought bounced around to the rhythm of my steps as I walked toward morning and town.

The Artist

he could see into the back seat, where Alice, his two-year-old daughter, appeared and disappeared and reappeared out of darkness as the car passed under streetlight after streetlight. He had been driving for more than an hour, trying to get her to sleep, and her eyes were still open. He located the dimmer control for the dashboard lights and increased the brightness just slightly so that he could read the time. "Daddy," Alice said dreamily. "Is it the fairy place?" "Not yet," Jim answered. It was almost nine. He dimmed the lights. "If you close your eyes, we'll get there faster." Alice closed her eyes, which surprised him. She was usually harder to fool than that.

A moment later, she was sleeping. Each time the light swept over her, she seemed to sink deeper and deeper into the car seat, her shoulder-length brown hair blending with the seat's brown, padded leather. Jim straightened out the mirror and turned the car around. When he drove Alice to sleep, he rarely traveled more than a few minutes distance from his home, so he wouldn't have to waste time driving back once she was out. He was efficient. At forty-six he was father to three children, all under ten; husband to a doctor; owner of an advertising firm; and, finally, an artist, a video artist: he created pieces that were thought of by some as "experimental" films. He didn't

Jim had the rearview mirror tilted so that

think of them as films and he didn't think of them as experiments—but he used the term himself sometimes.

A set of spotlights came on automatically as he pulled into his driveway. He parked the car, lifted Alice from her seat, and carried her up a sloping walk surrounded by flower boxes thick with blossoming azaleas. The polished mahogany doors at the front of the house were open to let in the early summer, evening breezes. Jim opened the screen door and stepped into a house so quiet that it surprised him. Jake, his four-month-old, would be asleep by now, but Melissa, the nine-year-old, should have been up and around, and he didn't hear his wife, Laura, on the phone or running the dishwasher or doing something somewhere, as he would have expected. The house was just plain quiet, which almost never happened. He carried Alice up a short flight of stairs into the great room and noticed Melissa's sneakers and socks on the rug next to the baby grand. If he hadn't been afraid of waking Alice, he'd have called out for Laura or Melissa. Instead, he continued on silently toward the back of the house. He found his wife and daughter in the kitchen sitting at the table with a man who looked to be in his fifties. He had hair down to the middle of his back pulled into a braid. He wore multiple earrings and a gold nose ring. Where the top two buttons of his shirt were open, Jim could see the bright colors of a tattoo. From the way the three of them sat staring up at him from the table with grins on their faces, Jim guessed that he was supposed to recognize the stranger. At first he didn't. Then, little by little, he saw the boyish face of Tony Diehl compose itself within the weathered face of the stranger. "Tony?"

Tony touched his chest with his fingertips. "Who else, man?" He stood and opened his arms, offering Jim an embrace.

Laura said, "He came just a few minutes after you took off with Alice." Before dinner, she had gone jogging while Jim watched the kids, and she was still wearing her skin-tight Spandex outfit. She looked good. She was five years younger than Jim—and she looked younger than that.

Melissa said, "He's been telling us stories about you, Dad, when you were young."

Laura got up to take Alice from Jim. "Your father's *still* a young man."

"Oh, please," Melissa said. "Forty-six is *hardly* young."

Jim handed Alice off to Laura. He asked Tony, "How'd you find me?"

Tony grabbed Jim's hand, shook it once, and then pulled him close and wrapped his arms around him. He stepped back and looked him over. "Christ, man," he said. "Twenty? Twenty-five years?"

Jim looked at Melissa and made a little motion with his head that told her it was time for bed.

"I want to stay up," Melissa said. "I want to hear about all the trouble you used to get into."

Jim said, "What have you been telling her?"

Tony answered, "None of the juicy stuff. Don't worry."

"Pleaaassse," Melissa said.

Laura, who had been standing quietly in the doorway with Alice, told Melissa to go get her nightgown on. "I'll get them off to bed," she said. "Why don't you guys make yourselves drinks downstairs and I'll join you when I'm done?"

Tony said, "Sounds good to me."

"I'm going to take Tony out to a bar." Jim put his arm around Laura and kissed her on the forehead. Then he directed Tony toward the living room. On the way to the front door, he said, to Laura, speaking loudly and without looking back at her, "We have a lot to catch up on." When he looked up, he saw Laura still standing by the kitchen with Alice on her shoulder, her mouth open a little. He called, "I'll be back late. Don't wait up."

Tony waved to her. "Hey. It was nice."

Jim reached around Tony and opened the door, his body leaning into Tony's, nudging him out.

"Hey, man," Tony said, as Jim pulled the door closed tight behind him. "Are you hustling me out of your house?"

Jim had on his standard summer outfit: loafers without socks, light-weight khaki pants, and a solid T-shirt. He said, "It's getting cool," and went to the back of his car, where a linen jacket was hanging from a hook above the side window. He put on the jacket, and took out Alice's car seat while Tony watched.

"What?" Tony said. He opened his hands, as if surprised. "Are you pissed off at me? I should have called, right?"

Jim put the car seat in the trunk and pointed to the passenger door, indicating that Tony should get in.

"Jesus Christ." Tony got in the car. When Jim got in and started the engine, he said again: "Jesus Christ. Some welcome."

"What is it, Tony?" Jim started for the expressway. "Am I not being friendly enough?"

"Hey," Tony said. "We did hang out a lot of years." He flipped the sun visor down and looked at himself in the mirror. "Have I changed that much?" He pointed at the gold ring in his nose. "It's the nose ring, right? The nose ring's got you freaked?"

"You're a funny guy, Tony."

"What's funny? You want to see something funny? Here, I'll show you my tattoo." He started to unbutton his shirt.

Jim grabbed his arm. "Stop it. Tell me why you're here."

Tony leaned back in his seat, as if he were suddenly tired.

Jim turned and looked at him. The boyishness he remembered was gone entirely. His skin had hardened and thickened: it looked as though it would feel ragged to the touch. His eyes seemed to have sunken into their sockets, and he had small, fatty growths around each eyelid. He was forty-two, four years younger than Jim, and he looked like a man in his late fifties or early sixties, a man who had led a rough life. "So where am I taking you?"

"I thought we were going for a drink?"

"You want a drink?"

"Sounds good to me."

"Fine, I know a bar. You want to tell me what's up?"

"I'm insulted," Tony said. He was lying back in his seat, as if too exhausted to move. "After all the years we hung out, I can't stop in to say hello? A social visit?"

"What's the gun for?"

"The gun?" He reached around and touched the middle of his back. "I didn't think you'd see. I mean, I *know* your old lady didn't see nothing." He took a nine-millimeter Beretta out from under the back of his shirt. He placed it on the console between them. "Let me tell you what's happening. You'll understand."

Jim said, "Isn't this a social visit?"

"You haven't changed, Bro." Tony sat up straight. "Actually, man. I can't believe you. Look at you! You look like Don Johnson, 'Miami Vice.' Slick." He slapped Jim's stomach. "How come you don't have a gut, like me?" He held his belly with both hands. "And what kind of car is this, Jimmy." He looked around the interior. "I never seen a car like this."

"It's a Rover."

"A what?"

"A Rover."

"What the fuck's a Rover. Sounds like a dog."

Jim said, "Tell me what's going on."

"I've got a problem. Fuck the drink. You have to take me into the city."
Tony stopped and seemed to think about how to continue. Then his thought
process apparently shifted. "But, Jimmy, man," he said. "Look at you. Stony
Brook, Long Island. This is like where the rich people live, right? You're like
rich now. You got a doctor wife. You got your own business. You live in a
fucking mansion. You look great, your wife's a piece of ass: I mean, what the
fuck is this? You're unbelievable man. Fucking Jimmy." Tony reached over
and slapped him on the stomach again. "I'm proud of you, man. I'm still a
small-time, drug-dealing fuck-up, and look at you. I'm proud of you, Jimmy.
I mean it."

Jim checked the side-view mirror as he picked up speed on the entrance
ramp to the Long Island Expressway. He pulled the car over to the extreme
left-hand lane and accelerated to seventy. "What kind of trouble are you in?
What do you need?"

"Don't you want to know how I know all this stuff about you?"

"I haven't kept a low profile."

"That's the truth. *The Village Voice!* Not that I would have recognized you
from the picture. Where's the curly hair down to your ass?"

"It was never down to my ass. Since when do you read *The Village Voice?*"

"I don't," Tony said. "Ellis showed me."

Jim seemed surprised. "I thought Ellis would have moved on a long
time ago."

"Oh," Tony said. "Like me, you're not surprised I'm still small-time—but
Ellis? Man, you don't know Ellis. Don't even think you know Ellis. The guy
you knew, those years? He's like completely gone. Totally. He don't even exist anymore."

"What happened to him?"

"Drugs. Twisted stuff. He's a sick puppy, man. If he's alive another month,
I'll be surprised."

"Why? What's he got?"

"Not like that," Tony said. He pointed to his temple. "He's sick this way.

He's out of his mind. He's not even human anymore, Jimmy. You won't believe the shit he's into. I tell you some of the stuff he's done, you'll puke right here, man. Right in the car."

Jim pulled into the slow lane, behind a tractor-trailer. He pointed to the gun on the seat beside him. "Put that on the floor or something. I want to pass this truck." Tony put the gun on the floor in the back seat, and Jim pulled back into the passing lane. They were both quiet for a long time then, driving in silence, in the dark. When they left Nassau County and entered the city, streetlights suddenly appeared above the road.

"Remember those two guys?" Tony said, as if the lights had suddenly wakened him.

Jim didn't answer. He knew what Tony was referring to without having to think about it. "We're in the city," he said. "You want to tell me where we're going? You want to tell me what the hell I'm doing here?" Tony had slumped down in his seat and put his knees up on the dash. Jim knew that he was staring up at him out the dark, checking out his reaction.

Tony reached down into his pocket and came up with a fat manila envelope. He opened the top. "Ten thousand dollars," he said. "I need you to give this to Ellis for me."

Jim took the money and held it up in front of the steering wheel. The bills stuffed into the envelope were held tight with a thick rubber band. He dropped the envelope onto the console. "What's this?"

"It's Ellis's. Jimmy, my man. Ellis has got millions in his place. All in envelopes just like this. He's out of his fucking mind."

"Millions?"

"You don't believe me?" Tony put his right hand over his forehead, closed his eyes, and pointed to Jim with his left hand. He looked like a magician about to identify a card. "Look at the back of the envelope. What's the number?"

Jim looked at the back of the envelope. The number was written large with a black marker. "One hundred and sixty-two."

"You do the math."

"Ellis has got one hundred sixty-two envelopes stashed in his place, each with ten thousand dollars?"

"More. And he counts them. Two, three times a day. Religious."

"Somebody would have killed him for it by now."

"Jimmy. Ellis is— Everybody's scared of him. Everybody."

"This is the Ellis I used to play chess with? This is the Ellis was our supplier?"

"No, man. I told you. That Ellis is long dead. This is some other guy." Tony reached over his head and turned on the interior light. He said, "Look at me, man," and he leaned close to Jim.

Jim squinted and reached to turn off the light.

Tony smacked his hand away. "I'm serious," he said. "Look at me."

Jim turned to look at him and then turned back to the road. "I looked at you," he said. "Will you turn off the light?"

"Just listen a minute." He put his hand on Jim's shoulder. "I need you to do me this favor, but you have to understand about Ellis. You can't tell just to look at him." He paused for a moment, then turned off the light. "We're almost there," he said. "I'll tell you a few things."

"Thank you."

"Ellis owns this building; he lives on the top floor—the whole floor. He's got a freezer set up in his living room. He'll show it to you. He shows it to everybody. When he opens it, you're going to see a cop." He pointed out of the car, to his right. "Take this exit," he said.

Jim pulled the car to the right, slowed down, and exited onto a cobblestone avenue strewn with garbage. "Where the hell are we?"

"South Bronx. Just stay on this a couple of miles."

Jim slowed down to twenty miles an hour, and even then the cobblestones tested the suspension. The streets on either side of him were empty. Whole blocks had been gutted by fire. "A cop," he said. "He's got a cop in a freezer."

"A dead cop."

"Is this a joke, Tony?"

"I wish."

"You want me to believe this shit? Ellis has a dead cop in a freezer in his living room, a couple of million dollars scattered around in envelopes . . . It's a joke. What else? Anything else you want to tell me about him?"

"Could I make this shit up, Jimmy? Really? Ask yourself, if I were lying, would I tell you shit this wild?" Tony clasped his hands behind his neck and tapped his foot. "I'm getting nervous just coming up here." He jerked around and retrieved the gun from the back seat. "I haven't told you half of it." He leaned forward and put the Beretta into its holster behind his back. "He sleeps with little girls from the neighborhood. He pays their junky mothers with shit and they come over in the morning and bathe him—these three little girls. They carry water to his bath. I'm talking eight, nine years old. Same thing at night. It's like some sort of ceremony, some sort of ritual. They fill the tub and then—" Tony stopped, disgust apparently overcoming him. "He wants me dead, Jimmy, and the guy's a stone-cold, pure-fucking-insane murderer. He's got this machete—" Again Tony stopped. He pointed out the window. "Turn right here."

Jim turned right onto a wide, well-lit boulevard. The area seemed to improve some: the streets were paved, the buildings weren't bombed out, here and there people were sitting on stoops. Alongside him, Jimmy could feel Tony's nervousness. "Let me ask you something, Tony. If Ellis is so bad, why are you still hanging with him?"

"Let me ask you something first," Tony said. "How come its different for you? You know what I mean? You tell me."

"What do you think? You think the gods picked me up and put me someplace else?"

"So tell me," Tony said. "All I know now is: one day no Jimmy. Twenty years later, they're writing about you in the paper. You're a big deal."

Jim looked at his wrist, as if checking a watch. "How long have I got, five minutes?"

"Give me the short version."

"The short version . . . At twenty-five I split to the West Coast, hung out, met this crowd of people who were into art. They got me into school, I busted my ass, got my degrees, met my wife in graduate school, got married, had kids, moved back East—" He stopped and looked at Tony. "Then you showed up."

"You know what I think?" Tony said. "I think the gods picked you up and put you someplace else."

Jim was quiet for a moment. "Okay," he said. "I'm not arguing."

"Amen."

"And you?"

"I don't know," Tony said. "Me. I got married once. It lasted a couple of years, I hated working. I lifted shit all day, I loaded trucks. Never had any money." He grimaced at the memory. "I don't know," he said again. "We couldn't have any kids, she wanted kids. I screwed around a lot . . ." He stopped and seemed to drift off.

Jim said, "So now you're working for Ellis again, and? What happened?" He picked up the money envelope. "You ripped him off?"

"Right," Tony said, mocking. "I ripped off envelope number one hundred and sixty-two, hoping he wouldn't miss it. Pull over here." He pointed to an empty parking space in front of an apartment building that looked seven or eight stories high. "We're here."

Jim parked the car. He turned off the engine and slipped the keys into his pocket. He turned to look at Tony, who was looking back at him intently. Tony picked up the envelope and handed it to Jim. "He gave it to me, Jimmy. He handed it to me, just like I'm handing it to you. Then he gets that fucking look that scares the shit out of me, and he goes 'You stole my money, Tony. You know what I got to do, don't you?' I go, 'What money? This money?' I try to give him back the envelope. He turns around, goes into the other room, I hear him taking the machete down off the wall—and I split. This is last week. Now I hear from everybody on the street that I'm a dead man. Kill me, you get an envelope. Ten thousand dollars."

Jim leaned back against his door. "And you didn't do nothing, Tony. Nothing at all."

"What do you mean, am I an innocent? Neither one of us is innocent, Jimmy. But I didn't snake Ellis, that's what we're talking about."

"You want me to go up there and see this maniac and tell him what? For old time's sake, he should stop being a lunatic?"

"Listen—"

"If this guy's so crazy, why do I want to deal with him?"

"Jimmy, listen to what I'm trying to tell you." Tony stopped and looked up at the car's ceiling, as if pausing to find the right words. "Ellis is about to be dead—soon. He's like a guy who's reached the end of some kind of twisted road. It's hard to explain this, but I know. I'm sure. He's trying to wrap things up. It's all gotten too warped, even for Ellis. The guy wants to die."

"This is just something you know. Intuitively."

"Yeah, intuitively. But other shit too. Like, in the last month, he's been showing everybody his money. And he shows everybody the dead cop. Everybody. And he's been ripping people off, ripping them off big time. He hurts people, every chance he gets." Tony hesitated for a moment, then shrugged.

"And he's wasted a couple of guys. Not street scum. These were guys with connections. With his own hands, with that fucking machete. I mean, Jimmy, he knows what he's doing. Somebody's going to kill him. He won't live out the month."

Jim picked up the envelope and held it in front of him. "So let's say you're right. Why's he going to take this back from me? If what you say's the case, he wants you dead. Like wrapping up loose strings. Maybe he'll want me dead too."

"He doesn't want you dead. He wants you to make a movie about him."

"He wants what?"

"He wants you to make a movie about him. That's all he's talked about since he saw the article."

"He wants me to make a movie about him?"

"It fits, man. It's like the end of his life, like his memoirs. He's been writing it all down, like a script. When he gets it done, he plans on coming out to see you."

Jim turned away from Tony. At the entrance to the apartment building, in front of the thick glass doors, someone had left a MacDonald's bag with a cup and a fries container next to it. Jim said, "Tony, I don't make movies."

"You want my advice, don't tell Ellis that."

"And what am I supposed to tell him?"

Tony picked up the envelope and tossed it into Jim's lap. "Listen, Jimmy. I wouldn't ask for this favor if I thought it would screw you. You're an old friend. We were tight once. All you have to do is go up there, tell him Tony told you he wants you to make this movie about him, tell him you'll make it if he'll take the money back and let it be known he's not looking for Tony's head anymore. That's all you got to do. He'll go for it. I know he'll go for it. He asks you why, tell him old-times' sake. Tell him you been through some shit with me: he knows that anyway."

"But I don't make movies. The stuff I do, it's nothing like a movie."

"It don't matter," Tony said. "You're not listening to me. Tell him you're going to get Steven Spielberg to direct the thing. Tell him Clint Eastwood's going to play him, and it'll open in a million theaters all over the world. Tell him anything. It doesn't matter. In a month, he'll be dead." Tony touched Jim's knee. "This isn't going to cost you, Jimmy. You keep me alive, and it doesn't cost you anything."

"Except," Jim said, "what happens if in a month he's not dead?" He looked through the dark car to Tony. Their eyes met. He said, "I'm sorry, Tony. I can't do this."

"Yeah, you can," Tony said, without hesitating. "Remember those two guys in Soho? Their friends' got a long memory, Jimmy."

"You'd blackmail me?"

Tony took the Beretta out of its holster and laid it on the console. "Take this if it makes you feel safer. This is my life we're talking about. If you won't do it because it's decent, because you owe me at least something—then you force me to push a little."

Jim looked out the window, at the litter in front of the building. Then he got out of the car, holding the envelope. When he reached the glass doors, he found that they were locked. Beyond them was a small, empty space and then another set of glass doors leading into a carpeted lobby where a young man wearing a crisp white shirt, a thin yellow tie, and a lightweight navy-blue jacket sat at a desk. He was watching a portable television. Jim knocked on the glass and when the man didn't look up, he grabbed the handles and rattled the door. The man at the desk jumped, startled. When he focused on Jim, he looked him up and down a moment. Then he hit a button. Jim heard a click and he pulled open the glass doors. When he reached the second set of doors, they were locked. The young man grinned, and pointed to a telephone hanging on the wall next to the doors. Jim picked up the phone. The man put a handset to his ear. Jim said, "Ellis Tyler. Top floor."

The man stared at him through the door as he spoke into the handset. "Who are you?"

"James Renkowski."

"James Renkowski don't tell me a thing, Ace." The grin had disappeared. "What do you want?"

"I'm looking for Ellis. I'm an old friend."

"An old friend," he repeated. The grin reappeared—more a sneer than a grin. He put the handset down on the desk, and then pulled another phone in front of him by yanking at a gray wire. He punched a few numbers and spoke to someone. Then he hung up and stared at Jim unblinking until an elevator door at the back of the lobby opened and two more young men stepped out. Like the kid at the desk, they were dressed neatly, wearing white shirts and narrow ties under summer jackets. When they reached the first set of doors, there was a loud click and they pulled the doors open. They both nodded casually toward him in the way of a greeting. Jim nodded back.

The ride up was quick. His two escorts stood one on either side of him. They were relaxed and quiet, and he didn't feel any pressure to speak. When they reached the top floor, the elevator opened onto a small, carpeted area where two chairs bracketed a door that looked as though it were made of solid steel. One of the young men sat down heavily, as if tired, and the other opened the metal door.

Jim hesitated a moment and then stepped into a room that was dark and smelled of incense. His shoes partly disappeared into a plush, black rug. The room contained a black leather couch and, positioned in front of the couch, a teak coffee table. Jim was about to take a seat on the couch when Ellis wandered into the room. He entered casually, his eyes on the floor, hands in his pockets, absorbed in his thoughts. When he looked up he appeared almost surprised to see Jim. "This is a shock," he said, his voice soft, barely a whisper. "You're one person I thought I'd never see again." While he spoke, he kept his hands in his pockets. He was dressed immaculately. His clothes—the dark blue suit and silk shirt buttoned to the collar—were tailored to a body thin and lanky as a marathon runner's. He was tall, six-foot something, and—just as Jim remembered—he stooped slightly, habitually, from the shoulders down, in the manner of a tall man used to dealing constantly with shorter people. His long hair was slicked back on his head and he wore glasses with thin lenses in a sleek frame. He said, "You've caught me at an awkward time, Jimmy. I have a business meeting coming up."

It took Jim a moment to respond. When he spoke, he was surprised at the ease in his voice and manner. "Ellis," he said, "you look different."

"You think so?" Ellis spread his arms and looked down at himself. Then he seemed to remember. "That's right," he said. He pointed at Jim and his eyes brightened a little. "You knew me in my fat days." Then he put his hands back in his pockets. "A long time ago, Jimmy."

"You look good."

"I'd invite you in . . ."

"No," Jim said. "That's okay. I'm here because of Tony." He reached into his jacket pocket and took out the manila envelope.

Ellis touched his hands to his temples. "I should have guessed," he said. Then he added, as if surprised at himself. "It didn't occur to me."

Jim said, "It wasn't a meeting I was prepared for either." He extended the money toward Ellis.

Ellis took the envelope, fanned through the bills, and tossed it onto the coffee table. He said, "Come in for a minute."

Jim followed Ellis through a series of dark rooms into a large, open area that appeared to serve as a combination living room-bedroom-dining room-bath. One wall was a line of open windows with a view of the Manhattan skyline. A line of crepe curtains fluttered in a breeze. The other walls were solid and barren: no art, no ornamentation of any kind. In one part of the room a teak dining table was surrounded by straight back chairs. In another part of the room, a queen-sized bed in a teak frame. Next to the bed, a free-standing, marble bathtub with brass claw legs. Next to the bathtub were three brass buckets the size of small garbage cans. As he walked past the open windows, his knees went loose and watery from the height. He glanced down at the street and noticed a newspaper kiosk next to a public telephone.

Ellis said, "I'm sorry I can't be more sociable, Jimmy." He took a seat on the couch and motioned Jim to sit across from him.

Jim took a seat, and Ellis made a gesture with his hands indicating Jim should talk.

"He wants you to take the money back."

"What does he think, because we all used to be friends?"

"Something like that," Jim said. "He asked me to cut a deal with you."

"A deal?"

"He thought you might be interested in having me do a movie. About you. About your life. He thought—"

"A movie?" Ellis said. "You don't make movies, Jimmy." He opened his hands, as if to ask Jim what he was talking about. "I've read about you. I saw your show. What you do, it's a kind of poetry with visual images."

"That's true," Jim said. "But I thought—"

Ellis put his hand up. "Stop, Jimmy. Don't embarrass both of us. Tony's not worth it." He turned around on the couch and leaned toward the windows, drawing in a deep breath of air, as if he needed the fresh air from the open windows to help him breathe. He filled his lungs and exhaled slowly. Then he turned back to Jim. "The fool tried to steal from me. He took an envelope with ten thousand dollars and replaced it with one with a few hundred. He thought I wouldn't notice. If I ever see him again, I'm going to kill him. If anybody who works for me ever sees him, they'll kill him." Ellis leaned forward. "There's nothing you can do for him."

Jim said, "Ellis . . ."

"Jimmy." Ellis's face tightened, a hard note came into his voice. "Come here," he said. "Let me show you something." Ellis put his hands on his knees and lifted himself from the couch as if it were an effort, and Jim followed him into an adjacent room with an eight-foot-long and three-foot-deep rectangular structure situated at its center like an altar or a cenotaph. The structure was covered with red drapery. At the back of the room was a worktable with a huge metal vise at one end. On the worktable, a chain saw rested next to a power drill and a set of pliers. A machete at least three feet long hung on the wall above the table. The blade was blood-stained, and there were lines of blood on the wall.

Jim said, "How long you been into woodwork, Ellis?"

Ellis looked at the worktable and then back to Jim. He didn't laugh. He pulled the red drapery off the structure, revealing it as a freezer with a thick black wire that trailed off into the black carpet. He said, "This is something I learned from you," and lifted the heavy white door of the freezer. Inside was a young man in a blue New York City police uniform. He looked like he wasn't yet twenty years old. His skin was an ugly, deep hue of purple. His eyes were open under bushy black eyebrows. Half his body was encased in ice, as if he were floating in it—his chest and face and the tops of his legs protruding above the cloudy surface.

Jim said, "You didn't learn this from me, Ellis."

"When you were just coming up, you cracked a guy's head open with a blackjack. Big public place, some bar. Everybody knew who you were."

"You've got the wrong guy. Never happened."

"No I don't, Jimmy." Ellis grasped the edge of the freezer with both hands and leaned over it, looking down at the frozen body. "I'll tell you something nobody else knows." He looked back at Jim, still leaning over the freezer. "I didn't kill him. He's like roadkill. I found him. That's why the cops have no idea. There's nothing to connect me. I just found him on the street, threw him in my trunk, took off. But I tell all the pieces of shit I have to deal with, all the small-time dealers—like you used to be—that I wasted him. They come in here, see a dead New York cop in a freezer, they'd put an ice pick through their mother's heart before they'd screw me."

Jim turned his back to the freezer. Through the room's open door, he could see the living room windows and the lights of Manhattan.

Ellis said, "So now we don't have to talk anymore about Tony."

Jim didn't respond, and then Ellis was quiet for a time. When he turned around, he saw that Ellis was still leaning over the freezer, staring down at the frozen body, but his eyes seemed vacant. Jim said, "I'd better go then."

Ellis nodded. He reached into the freezer and rubbed away frost covering the metal badge pinned to the cop's uniform. "Shield 3266," he said, and he closed the lid. Then he put a hand on Jim's back and led him out of the apartment, to the elevator, motioning the young men stationed outside the apartment to stay where they were. When the elevator doors opened, he put a hand on Jim's shoulder. "You got lucky," he said. "Don't let it get screwed up on you." Then he pushed him into the elevator and turned away before the doors closed. Jim watched him walk back to his apartment as the two young men stood on either side of the door, stiff as palace guards.

<hr />

Tony was waiting for him on the street, leaning back into the shadows of a small alley between apartment buildings. Jim had already walked past him when he stepped out of the darkness. "Jimmy," he said.

Jim laughed. He said, "You don't have to hide, Tony. It's straightened out."

"He went for it?"

"You're surprised?"

"No, I'm not surprised." He slapped Jim on the shoulder, a kind of congratulations or thanks. "I know Ellis, man. I know him like I know myself. What'd he say?"

"He's like a little kid. He's talking about who's going to play who, where we're going to shoot it, that kind of shit."

"And me? What'd he say about me?" He took Jim by the arm and pulled him back into the shadows.

Jim held Tony by the shoulders. "Look," he said. "I can't tell you he's happy with you. You have to go up and deal with him. You have to explain yourself to him."

"Shit. He's going to fuck me over, man. I know it."

"No," Jim said. "We have a deal. I make the movie, he doesn't hurt you."

"He doesn't *hurt* me, or he doesn't *kill* me?"

"He doesn't do anything to you."

"Are you sure, Jimmy? Because that fucking guy can hurt people so bad it's better to be dead."

Jim said, "No, Tony. This is a formality. This is for show. You got to go humble yourself up there. You know what it is. He'll make you grovel. He'll make sure the others see. You have to do it, Tony. Its for business."

Tony looked down at the ground, as if thinking things over. When he looked up, he said, "You sure about this, Jimmy?"

"Absolutely, Tony." Jim took Tony's hand and held it between his two hands. "It's cool," he said. "He wants Tom Cruise to play you in the movie."

Tony shouted, "Tom Cruise!" Then he laughed.

"All right, listen, can I go home now?" Jim reached into his jacket pocket for his car keys. "My wife'll be asking me questions for the next six months."

Tony stepped back for a moment, as if to look Jim over, and then embraced him tightly. "You saved my life, man. I got to thank you."

Jim whispered. "I just hope you're right, Tony. About Ellis not being around another month."

Tony stepped back. "Was I right about the movie?"

Jim smiled. Then he shook hands with Tony, and Tony hugged him one more time before walking away, out of the shadows and into the lights from the apartment building.

Jim watched from the driver's seat of his car as Tony waited for a short while on the street, and then disappeared behind the glass doors. Within a minute or two, he heard the muted sound of shouting voices, one of the voices clearly Tony's. Then silence. He drove to the newspaper kiosk he had seen from Ellis's apartment and parked in front of the pay phone. When he stepped out of his car, he heard a scream, distinctly, but he couldn't tell for certain where it came from. He looked up and found Ellis's window. He kept his eyes on the window as he picked up the phone and dialed 911. He could see Ellis's apartment. The crepe curtains had been sucked out by the breeze. They fluttered over the street. He gave the operator Ellis's name, the location of the apartment building, and the apartment number. He told her about the dead cop. The operator didn't sound interested. She wanted his name. He told her the dead cop's badge number and hung up.

He drove a block or two away and found another place to park where he could still see Ellis's window. A second or two after he turned off the lights and ignition, two police cars sped past him. Then there were police cars and paddy wagons and unmarked cars speeding down every street and through every intersection in sight, sirens screaming. Ellis came to the window and looked out. His hair was a wild. He was no longer wearing his jacket and his shirt was open to the waist, as if the buttons had all been ripped off. The three young men came and one pulled him away while another closed the window. They disappeared and a minute later the sound of gun shots crackled over the street. It lasted only a minute or two, but it sounded like a thousand shots were fired in that time. Then Ellis appeared again at the window, this time in the arms of a burly cop. Other uniforms seemed to be wrestling with the cop who had Ellis. It was like a brawl going on. The burly cop broke away from the others and the window shattered and half of Ellis's body hung out the window for a second—and then he was flying toward the ground, his arms extended along his side as if he were diving. Jim got out of the car and walked to the entrance of the apartment building, where a crowd was gathering behind police lines. He waited until the ambulances came and men and women in blue coats began carrying away bodies in black zippered bags. After he counted five bodies, he left.

On the way back to Stony Brook, he practiced not thinking. He tried to concentrate on his home and family, on his life with his wife and children, on projects that engaged him. When a disturbing thought or image came to mind—Ellis flying through the window, the shattered glass around him like the surface of the water breaking, or Tony embracing him on the street, thanking him for saving his life—when such an image or thought came to mind, he'd stop thinking and make himself go numb until it dissolved. Then he returned to thinking about his everyday life. But for most of the ride home he was numb and empty of thought, and at one point he felt himself getting shaky with the fear that something terrible had happened, that his life would change, that he wouldn't be able to go on living the life he had built with Laura, for Melissa and Alice, for the new baby, and for himself. He shook his whole body, like a dog shaking water from its coat, and he told himself that he'd do what he had to do, like always.

At home, he found everyone asleep. In their bedroom, Laura lay on her back, with the baby alongside her in a cradle. Alice had crawled into bed with her. She lay on her stomach with her head snug against her mother's breast and one leg flung on top of her mother's knee. Jim quietly removed a pair of pajamas from his dresser, went to the basement to shower, and returned to join Laura and the children in bed. He checked the alarm clock on the headboard. It was only a little after midnight. In an hour or two, Melissa would wake up and try to get into bed with everyone else. At nine years old, she was in the stage of regular bad dreams, and most nights Jim would have to hold her and comfort her, and convince her to go back to her own bed. She'd tell him, usually, that she knew it wasn't right, but she was afraid of her bed, she was afraid that there was something under it. He'd take her back to her room and show her there was nothing under the bed, and then he'd lay with her for a while as she huddled close to him, careful that no part of her body extended over the mattress. This night, he thought, he'd let her sleep with them.

Alongside him, Alice moved slightly and he lay the palm of his hand on her small shoulder, her soft skin warm and comforting. He tried to close his eyes, but they kept opening, as if with a will of their own. He imagined he was lying on a raft, a cedar raft of strapped-together logs, and got to the point where he could feel the bed rocking, as if it were floating, and in his mind's eyes he saw the stripped white logs of the raft as they drifted over a sea of murky water—but still, he couldn't fall asleep. It wasn't until hours later, when the quality of the light began to soften and the first few birds began to chirp and squawk, when he started working out in his mind the structure for one of his video pieces, when he began thinking about images and the way he might put them together, the image of Ellis flying from the window, the image of the young cop in the freezer, the bodyguards, Tony—when he began shaping and structuring the project in his mind, when he knew for sure that one day he would begin to work on it, then the tension in his muscles eased up some, and he closed his eyes, and when the sun came up, he was sleeping.

Stories in *Sabbath Night in the Church of the Piranha* were originally published as follows:

"The Instruments of Peace" in *Playboy;* "Sweet," in *TriQuarterly;* "Smugglers" in *Ploughshares;* "Sabbath Night in the Church of the Piranha," "Tulsa Snow," and "Gifts" in *The Missouri Review;* "Radon" in *The Virginia Quarterly Review;* "The Professor's Son" in *Night Train;* "The Match" in *spelunker flophouse;* "The Revenant," in *The Southern Review;* "Monsters," in *Glimmer Train;* "Acid" in *TriQuarterly;* "Small Blessings" in *The Notre Dame Review;* "The Artist," in *The Atlantic Monthly;* "Drunks," in *The Antioch Review;* and "Silver Dollars," in *The Greensboro Review*

"Acid," "Radon," "The Artist," and "Smugglers" were included in *Acid*, originally published by The University of Notre Dame Press, 1996, and winner of the Richard Sullivan Prize for Short Fiction.

"Gifts" and "Silver Dollars" were included in *Plato at Scratch Daniel's and Other Stories,* originally published by The University of Arkansas Press, 1990.

"The Revenant" was reprinted in *The Pushcart Prize XXIII.*

"The Instruments of Peace" was reprinted in *The Best American Mystery Stories 2000.*

"The Artist" was reprinted in *The Best American Short Stories 1995.*